RANGER'S KISS

"Relax, Anna, I'm not going to attack you."

"I know," she said without relaxing.

"How do you know?"

"You had to do that to plan our escape. I shouldn't have taken offense." She leaned into him just a little. "I'm surprised it worked. I'm not the kind of woman men lose their heads over. You'd think one of those three would have noticed."

It took his tired brain awhile to figure out what she was saying. She didn't think of herself as attractive.

He wanted to argue, but he had a feeling she wouldn't believe him. Slowly she warmed in his arms, and he felt the moment she relaxed into sleep. Her body seemed to melt against him.

"Sleep, Anna," he said against her hair. "I'll watch over you." He tightened his arms and she cuddled closer.

After holding her for a long while, he tilted her head up. It was time they moved on.

McCord looked down, wondering how to wake a woman who'd spent the night resting next to him.

He didn't even think of resisting the urge to taste her. He pulled her against him and nibbled her bottom lip.

One taste was not enough . . .

Collections by Jodi Thomas, Linda Broday,
Phyliss Miranda, and DeWanna Pace

GIVE ME A TEXAN

GIVE ME A COWBOY

GIVE ME A TEXAS RANGER

Published by Kensington Publishing Corporation

Give Me
A Texas Ranger

JODI THOMAS
LINDA BRODAY
PHYLISS MIRANDA
DEWANNA PACE

ZEBRA BOOKS
KENSINGTON PUBLISHING CORP.
http://www.kensingtonbooks.com

ZEBRA BOOKS are published by

Kensington Publishing Corp.
119 West 40th Street
New York, NY 10018

ISBN-13: 978-1-4201-1174-3
ISBN-10: 1-4201-1174-4

First Printing: July 2010
10 9 8 7 6 5 4 3 2 1

Printed in the United States of America

CONTENTS

The Ranger's Angel

JODI THOMAS

Chapter 1

Texas
April 1870

Annalane Barkley pulled her knees to her chin and lowered her head. Her ruined navy blue hat flopped forward like a gaudy curtain hiding her from the world.

She would give anything if she could go backward in time three weeks to the moment she decided to make the trip to Texas. She should have ripped her brother's letter into tiny pieces and stomped on it. Since the day Devin realized he'd never be as tall as his sister, he'd hated her. Why had Annalane thought two years apart would have changed anything? If he wanted her with him at Camp Supply it was for his benefit, not hers.

She vowed that if she lived through tonight, she'd demand he send her back to Washington, D.C. If she had to, she'd live with their great aunt Fretta, who dripped snuff from the left side of her mouth and had eleven cats, but she'd never come west again.

However, from the looks of things her brother, Devin, wouldn't have to pay for the ticket back. Her chances of surviving the night were growing slimmer by the hour.

Rain pounded on the roof of the one-room hut these Texans called a stagecoach station. Normally she loved the rain, but not this hard, fast downpour that thundered in rage. It shook the dust from the rafters, causing tiny bits of dirt to filter down through the damp air and turn into almost invisible mud balls on her skin.

Annalane raised her head enough to watch the four men trapped inside like her.

The driver of the coach was a little old man with nervous movements and a half-empty bottle sitting next to him for comfort. His bloodshot gaze darted around now and then like a rat waiting for a secret tunnel of escape to open up.

The station manager moved around in the corner that served as a kitchen. He was a beefy German who appeared to be multilingual only when he swore, which had been a constant rumble since their stage pulled in at full speed with outlaws in close pursuit. He'd had a meal of mud-colored stew waiting for them, but no one had ordered food.

The third man—a gambler she guessed—had a dull kind of politeness that was born more of habit than purpose. His dreary brown eyes reflected the look of a man who didn't much care if he lived or died. His collar and cuffs were stained with sweat and dirt, but a polished gold watch-chain hung from his vest. She'd never seen him check his watch, not once since he'd joined the stage at dawn.

What kind of man wears a watch and never looks at it? She smiled to herself, figuring out the riddle. The kind of man who owns only the chain.

Annalane moved slightly so she could study the fourth guest, a Texas Ranger, who'd got them to this shelter alive when the shooting started. He was long and lean, with a thin scar along his left cheek that had ended what once must have been a handsome face. His clothes were worn but well made, and his boots, though mud-covered, looked hand tooled. He had twin Colts strapped to powerful legs. The sun had baked his face until she couldn't tell if he was in his twenties or forties. Not that it mattered; she'd seen more talkative hitching posts.

Annalane sensed things in the way men moved that most people didn't notice. All those in the room knew of hard times, but this one, this Ranger, was battle worn. From the way he folded his muddy gloves into his belt, to the way he watched the window for trouble, hinted to her about his past. He'd fought, and killed, and survived many times.

Now, the Ranger was on guard. The others, including her, were just observers, or maybe future victims. The driver's hands weren't steady enough to fire a weapon. The station manager's apron was still wrapped around his waist, proving he wanted no part of any fight. Neither man could move fast enough to be of any help if trouble barreled through the door. The gambler didn't look like he cared enough even to defend his own life. Only the Ranger seemed ready.

Annalane cut her eyes back to the gambler. A coward, she thought, as she watched him flip cards onto the table. He'd run, or bargain his way through life, but never fight.

She looked back at the Ranger, who'd introduced himself as Wynn McCord when he'd climbed into the coach in Dodge. Like her, he carried a paper allowing him into the Indian Territory. Her letter said "visiting relative at Camp Supply." She had no idea what his said, but she guessed he hadn't come for a visit.

To her surprise, he glanced up and stared at her from across the room, with stormy blue eyes so piercing she had the feeling she'd been touched. His unnerving stare seemed to tell him all he needed to know in seconds. He shifted his attention back to the night beyond the window.

She stood, straightened the pleats of her traveling dress, and walked toward the Ranger.

As she stepped into the square of watery moonlight glowing on the dirt floor, the Ranger's arm shot out toward her. His fingers dug into her waist. He tugged her almost violently toward him and away from the light.

Before she could make a sound, her back hit the solid wall that framed the left side of the window and the Ranger's body held her in place.

"Thinking about suicide, lady?"

Annalane fought for breath.

"You stand in the light for long, a bullet's bound to find you." His voice was so low she doubted the others heard him.

Annalane pushed at his chest. She wasn't used to anyone being so close to her and this man towered over her as few could.

He moved back an inch. She could still feel the heat of his body and the dusty smell of leather and gunpowder that seemed to linger around him.

She straightened, deciding not to yell at him. She needed this Ranger if she planned to stay alive long enough to reach her brother at Camp Supply.

"I'd like to ask you a few questions." There was no need to do more than whisper. The man still stood so close she wouldn't have been surprised if he could read her thoughts.

As if she weren't there, he went back on watch. "I'm all out of answers. Ask someone else."

"I'm asking you." She knew she didn't have to voice the questions. He knew what she wanted to know. "And I want the truth," she added in her head-nurse tone, just to let him know he wasn't dealing with a frightened girl.

He looked at her then and smiled. "All right. The truth. Proper ladies like yourself should stay back East, where it's safe and your husband can take care of you just by locking the door at night."

He glanced at the broken parasol by the door, which

she'd thought would protect her from the rain, then at her very proper shoes now muddy and ruined.

She jerked off her worthless hat before he had time to glare at it and thought of telling him that she'd used most of her savings to buy this outfit. She wanted to make a good impression when she arrived at the camp that would soon become a fort.

When she'd dressed this morning she'd thought she would be meeting her brother by nightfall. He'd written that they would have dinner with the fort's officers. She had hoped to look more than just presentable. She wanted to look, if not pretty, at least able to fit the definition of "a fine woman." But obviously, even in this Ranger's eyes, she hadn't measured up.

This morning she'd thought she was still in a civilized world. Tonight she knew different. If anyone in this territory had an ounce of brains, they'd give the horrible place to the Indians and leave. If they did need a camp to keep some kind of order, they should have crossed the Red River and set it up in Texas.

She told herself she didn't care what Ranger Wynn McCord thought of her or her clothes; he'd been nothing but rude to her all day. When the firing started he'd shoved her to the muddy floor of the coach and demanded she stay there. When they'd pulled up at the station, he'd almost ripped her arm off, jerking her from the stage and telling her to run. When she'd turned to grab her small carpetbag, she swore she had heard him growl at her.

As Annalane opened her mouth to finally point out a few of his faults, she froze, seeing only cold steel across the depth of his winter blue eyes, and she knew he wouldn't care. For one second, she wished he'd let down his guard and she could see what was inside this hard shell of a man. Surely something lay beneath.

Had he ever wanted to belong somewhere, just for one

moment in time? Wanted it so badly he would believe a lie to think he was needed? Wanted it so desperately that he tried to mold himself into something he wasn't?

For one blink, she thought she recognized a loneliness that matched her own, but she doubted he had the hunger to belong somewhere as she'd had for ten years. The need to belong to someone ached in her sometimes like an open wound, but need and dreams had no place in her life.

She'd held to a dream once, then it had been shattered by one bullet. Annalane guessed this Ranger had never known love, not even for one minute. McCord had probably been born to this land and hard times. She'd not reach him with sentiment and crying.

Honesty was her only weapon and she prayed it would work.

"I have no husband to lock the door at night. I was married once for an hour before he left for the war. When he returned, his body was nailed into a box. I joined the army of nurses needed, and for four years moved between hospitals and battlegrounds." She knew she was rattling on, but she had to reach McCord. "I was baptized into battle medicine at First Bull Run, Virginia, in '61 and was there at the last in Bentonville, North Carolina in '65. There were dozens of other places where blood soaked the earth. Until last month, I worked at the Armory Square Hospital."

Something changed in the Ranger. He shifted. "I was at First Bull Run with Terry's Rangers. Hell of a battle."

She almost commented that a few of the bullets she dug out of Northern soldiers were probably his, but she remained silent. The war was over, had been for five years, even if the nightmares still remained.

"What do you want to know?" His voice was as low as the rumble of thunder outside.

"What are our chances? What options?"

The corner of his mouth lifted slightly and she had the feeling he hadn't smiled in a long time. "Spoken like a soldier."

She accepted the compliment. "One thing, remember." She held his stare. "The truth."

"I'm not in the habit of lying, Mrs. Barkley."

"No sugarcoating. Nothing left out." She'd been lied to enough to last two lifetimes. Even as she'd packed, she'd known her brother wanted her help for something other than to set up his medical practice. The silver lining in her predicament was that she'd spoiled whatever plan he had for her tonight by being late.

"Fair enough." She felt the Ranger's words against her cheek more than heard them. "I guess for what you did during the war and afterward, you deserve my respect. I saw nurses handling chaos that would bring most men to their knees. One angel in blue stopped by me in the shadows of a battle once. She wrapped my leg tight and whispered for me to hold on." The side of his mouth twitched in almost a smile. "I'm not sure I would have made it if that woman hadn't been so determined I would."

He looked at her and raised one eyebrow, as if wondering if she could have been that angel.

Annalane didn't answer. She'd done such a thing many times, as had all the other nurses. When they moved among the blood of battle they didn't think of sides, only of helping.

McCord shrugged. "I don't guess it matters now. You wore blue and I wore gray, but I figure we were in the same hell. You'll have your whole truth and my help if you want it."

She nodded, accepting his offer.

The German station manager passed around cups and offered coffee. The stage driver doctored his with whiskey. The gambler stared into the empty cup as if inspecting it for bugs before he allowed the station manager to pour coffee.

"Our chances?" Annalane whispered.

"The men waiting out there for this rain to let up before

they attack are a mixture of the worst men in Texas, led by a devil who calls himself Randolph Thorn. I've been chasing them for four months. I got a tip that they planned to rob the stage for the mailbag. They think there's something in it worth crossing into Indian Territory and risking their lives for."

"Is there?"

He hesitated, then, as if remembering his promise, answered, "Yes, but I wouldn't be worried about that if I were you. The problem you face is that Thorn and his men tend not to leave witnesses."

She saw his jaw tighten, but he forced out the truth. "If you got a gun with you and they get past me, you might want to use it. I've seen the way this gang treats women. If they find you here, you'll be wishing you were dead long before they kill you. Someone told me once that he heard Thorn brag that he kept a woman alive for four days just to hear her scream. When she was finally too weak to react no matter what he did, he left her bleeding and helpless for the coyotes."

She swayed.

The Ranger's hand brushed her waist to steady her.

"Options?" she whispered, forcing her back to stiffen.

"If we could put a gunman at each window, the firing would keep them away, maybe even kill enough that they'd leave."

She looked across the room. Not one of the others looked like he could protect himself, much less her.

He read her mind. "Can you handle a gun?"

"A rifle fairly well, but I've dedicated my life to saving others, not killing them."

He set his cup down and gripped her shoulder hard. "I need to know, Mrs. Barkley. Can you handle a rifle and fire to kill if you have to? Not to protect some mailbag, but to protect yourself."

All the hundreds of men she'd bandaged and held while they cried for their mothers or wives before they died filled her mind. All the men left broken and amputated who'd stared at her with hollow eyes, as if wishing she'd left them to die in battle.

She wasn't a coward. She faced the Ranger directly when she whispered, "I'm not sure."

She'd expected to see disappointment in his eyes, but instead she saw understanding.

As Annalane had all her life, she made up her mind and acted. "Whatever you plan, I'm going with you."

"It won't be safe. I could travel faster alone, maybe bring back help."

"It isn't safe here." She glanced at the other men. None of the three looked like they would hesitate to use her as a shield. "I won't slow you down. I promise."

The Ranger nodded once. "One condition. You follow orders."

"Agreed." She saw something in his gaze. "What else? What have you not told me?"

He bit the corner of his mouth, hesitating, then leaned so close his chin brushed her hair. With his breath against her ear, he whispered, "I think one of the men in this room usually rides with the outlaws. Problem is, I don't know which one."

Annalane would have fallen if his lean body hadn't shifted slightly to hold her up.

Chapter 2

Ranger Wynn McCord tried to tell himself he was just helping the lady out—being polite, that was all—but he knew the truth. From the moment he'd seen her in the coach, all prim and proper, he'd thought about what she'd feel like to touch. He didn't want to just help her; he wanted to hold her close. It had been a long time since he'd felt that way about any woman. He'd probably lost the ability to even talk to a woman like this one, but that didn't stop him from thinking about what they might do besides talk.

Now she was pressed against him from knee to chin and he didn't want to step back. She had that never-been-touched look about her and he wondered if, beneath all those pleats and buttons, a man had ever thrown a rope around her. She said she'd been married for an hour before her husband left. It would take a great deal longer than that to convince her she was desired.

He'd watched her all day while the others thought he slept. There was a grace about her that fascinated him. She'd talked to the gambler a few times after Frank Sanders told her he'd lived in Washington, D.C., but mostly she read from a little book she kept in her purse.

Since she was careful not to turn it where anyone could see the cover, McCord guessed it was one of those adventure/romance dime novels he'd seen around, written for people who wanted to experience the Wild West secondhand.

"Mr. McCord." Annalane Barkley's hand pushed against his chest, making him very much aware of just how close they were. "I'll have to ask you to . . .:"

"If you're going with me, we need a reason to step outside, Mrs. Barkley. Time's running out," he whispered without giving an inch. "So, shall we give them that reason, that we might need a little privacy?"

He moved his hand against the back of her head and pulled her to him. "Make it look like you can't keep your hands off me." Grinning, he had no doubt the proper Mrs. Barkley wouldn't have a clue about what to do. "We need to make it to the barn before the moon's free of clouds again."

She let out a tiny cry of surprise as his mouth lowered to hers. A moment later, her hand stopped trying to shove him away. She was frozen stiff in his arms, but she didn't break the kiss.

McCord had meant only to brush her lips. They were in far too much danger to take time for a real kiss, but he couldn't pull away. Her bottom lip quivered slightly as he parted her lips and deepened the kiss. She tasted far better than he'd let himself imagine in the hours he'd spent daydreaming about her.

"Hey!" the drunk driver yelled. "What's going on?"

McCord broke the kiss with an oath, but his hand still held her head in place. "Shut up, old man. Nothing that's any business of yours is happening. The lady and I have just found a way to pass the time."

He slowly turned toward the three men, staring at each one in turn. Daring them to say more.

When they were silent, he added, "Come on, Anna, let's find someplace without an audience."

"And where would that be?" The gambler shrugged, seeming to be enjoying the show they'd put on.

McCord wrapped his arm around the tall woman's waist and pulled her toward the door. "With this rain, no one is going to storm the place. We'll be in the barn." He glared at the men. "And don't come looking for us unless you're ready to die."

He grabbed his leather coat from the peg by the door and tossed it over Anna's head, then lifted her in his arms and headed out. She kicked and yelled and screamed, but the rain and the coat muffled all sound.

When he made it to the dry silence of the barn, he checked to make sure no one lurked in the shadows before pulling the coat off Annalane and laughing. This very proper lady looked madder than hell. Maybe he should have taken a little more time to explain his plan.

"How dare you!" She poked her finger into his chest as if it were a knife. "Do you know what they all think we are doing right now?"

"I don't care, lady. I just wanted out of there, and you said you wanted to come with me." He frowned at her. "If you want to go back just tell me, because where we're headed isn't going to be easy, and I can make better time without you. I left the mailbag inside. They can bargain for their lives with it, but I don't think any one of them would worry about you."

The woman proved she was not a fool. She said simply, "I want to stay with you."

He tugged his coat around her shoulders. "We got an hour, maybe more if this rain doesn't let up. We need to get as far away from here as possible before they notice we're gone."

She nodded.

"Any way you can shed a few of those skirts? They're going to get heavy once they get wet."

He'd expected her to argue, but she said, "Turn around."

The petticoats rustled as they fell to the floor. He fought the urge to glance back.

"I've practical shoes in my carpetbag," she said, pointing at the stage, halfway between the barn and the station.

He thought of telling her they didn't have time, but a minute probably wouldn't matter. Their chances of making it away were so slight, the odds wouldn't change much just because she switched shoes. He trudged out to the coach and grabbed her bag along with the extra Winchester the driver must have forgotten. He thought of taking a horse, but the animals were exhausted and someone from the station might notice a horse being unhitched and led away.

When he got back, she had pulled her wild hair down out of a ridiculous nest of curls and was braiding it in one long, midnight braid. The woman was practical.

"Ready, Anna?"

As she shoved her feet into lace-up leather boots, she said, "My name is Annalane."

"All right." He watched her, thinking he liked looking at her more than listening to her. The quick Northern accent grated on him. "If you can't keep up . . ."

"I'll keep up," she said. She didn't seem one inch shorter. The woman reminded him of a willow. He smiled, remembering how he didn't have to lean down to kiss her; he only had to turn his head to cover her mouth with his.

McCord tossed her worthless hat in the hay. "I won't leave you, Anna, don't worry. But tell me if you need to slow down."

"I'll keep up," she repeated without commenting on how he'd just thrown away the only hat she'd ever thought looked good on her. She packed up her carpetbag and moved it behind her as if she thought he might toss it as well.

He smiled. The woman wasn't far from wrong. He might have tried if he'd had the chance.

They walked out the back of the little barn and headed into a stand of trees that wound along a stream now busting its banks. Anyone watching the station would have had to be within three feet of them to notice them passing.

He'd expected her to slow him down, but she matched his steps. They moved for two hours, with her never more than a few steps behind him. When he climbed, he'd turn and offer his hand. She'd accept the help only as long as needed, then let go. She never complained.

The rain now became their ally, blanketing the sounds, erasing footprints.

He left the stream reluctantly and moved into the rocky hills. If he remembered correctly, they could cross over on foot and save a few miles. The boulders also offered some protection. The outlaws would have to leave their horses if they decided to follow on the uneven ground.

She bumped into him from behind. "Sorry," she said, sounding out of breath.

McCord turned. "How about we stop for a few minutes." It had been almost twenty-four hours since either of them had slept.

"I'm fine." She lifted her chin.

He grinned. "I know, but I'm a little tired. Ten minutes' rest and then we'll climb some more."

They moved between two huge stones and found enough shelter to avoid the rain. It was so dark he could barely make out her outline, huddled on a rock a few feet off the ground, but he could hear her teeth rattling. Pulling his flask from his pocket, he offered her a drink and was surprised when she took it.

When she handed the flask back, he told her to turn around and lift her feet out of the tiny trickle of water that streamed between the boulders. When she followed orders without speaking, he straddled the rock she sat on and pulled her back against his chest. "I'll rest on the rock, you rest on me. We won't be very comfortable, but we won't be as cold."

She hesitated, then leaned back against him. He propped the rifle at his side and circled her with his arms. She felt as stiff as stone.

"Relax, Anna, I'm not going to attack you."

"I know," she said without relaxing.

"How do you know?" He smiled at her in the dark. "I've already done it once tonight."

"You had to do that to plan our escape. I shouldn't have taken offense." She leaned into him just a little. "I'm surprised it worked. I'm not the kind of woman men lose their heads over. You'd think one of those three would have noticed."

It took his tired brain awhile to figure out what she was saying. She didn't think of herself as attractive.

He wanted to argue, but he had a feeling she wouldn't believe him. Slowly she warmed in his arms, and he felt the moment she relaxed into sleep. Her body seemed to melt against him. He shifted so that her head rested on his shoulder, then ran his hand down her leg from hip to calf. He told himself he was just seeing how wet her clothes were, but he knew something else drove him. He liked the nearness of this woman more than he'd ever liked any of the saloon girls who'd wiggled up to him wearing only their underwear.

"Sleep, Anna," he said against her hair. "I'll watch over you." He tightened his arms and she cuddled closer.

After holding her for a long while, he tilted her head up. It was time they moved on. The rain had stopped and it would be light before long. They needed to be on the other side of the hill before then.

McCord looked down, wondering how to wake a

woman who'd spent the night resting next to him. Her mouth was slightly open. Her warm breath fanned across his face.

He didn't even think of resisting the urge to taste her. He pulled her close and nibbled her bottom lip.

One taste was not enough.

Chapter 3

Annalane came awake one sense at a time—the warmth of someone close, the smell of rain, the feel of someone kissing her the way she'd always longed to be kissed.

Her body jerked as reality shot through her. The taste of whiskey blended in with the kiss that demanded she respond. His hands were beneath her arms, as if he'd pulled her up over his body, and his palms pushed against the sides of her breasts when she tried to breathe. He shifted his mouth and she felt the stubble of the beginnings of a beard as his tongue parted her lips, demanding entry.

Opening her eyes, she saw nothing but midnight shadows and the dark outline of the Ranger. She lifted her hand to shove him away, but he circled his arm and caught it, tucking it behind her back as he pulled her closer still.

"Not yet," he whispered against her tender lips. "I can't let you go yet." His arms were iron around her. "I haven't had near enough."

She knew she should pull away and demand he stop, but no one had ever kissed her with such desire, with such need, with such passion. Relaxing, she let the fire of it sweep over her.

He felt her surrender and slowed. The kiss went from

demanding to teaching, as he silently showed her what he wanted and rewarded her with bold strokes of his hands along her body as she learned each lesson.

For the first time in her life, she was mindless, floating in gentle waves of pleasure. The way he tugged at her bottom lip with his teeth, the way he held her so close and kissed her throat when he gave her time to catch her breath, then pulled her mouth back to his as if starving once more.

When his hand finally passed over the fabric covering her breast, she arched and cried out. He laughed against her mouth, then kissed her deep and long, not giving her time to react or even think.

"You taste so good," he whispered with his mouth still on hers. "It'll take me a long time to get enough of you, Anna."

Before she could answer he was kissing her again and she was welcoming his touch. Somehow in the nowhere of this land she could let down her guard and just react.

The sound of a horse, ridden fast, drifted into their world.

McCord groaned and pulled away. "Stay here," he ordered as he shoved her farther into the shadows and disappeared.

Annalane sat perfectly still, listening to her own heart pound. What had she just done? She could still taste him on her lips, still feel his warmth against her body. The grip of his fingers over her breast now burned through the layers of cloth. What had she done?

The fear of being killed by a band of outlaws no longer frightened her near as dearly as the fear of facing the Ranger when daylight came. She'd behaved like a wanton woman and he'd . . . he'd patted her on the bottom as he'd left her. No man had ever done that! All her life she'd never allowed anything so wild to happen. He had no right to . . .

"Are you all right?" His words drifted in the night. He sounded almost angry, as if in a hurry for an answer.

She nodded, then realized he probably couldn't see her. "I'm fine," she lied, wishing she could crawl back under the rock for a few minutes, or days, or maybe years.

His hand brushed her arm, then found her fingers and gripped tightly. "We have to move fast, Anna. We need to be over the ridge by dawn. I couldn't tell who was on that horse riding by below, but I don't think it will be long before more follow."

He didn't give her time to answer; he just tugged her out of the shadow of the boulder and began climbing. The rain had turned to a mist making her feel like she was moving in a dream.

She kept moving, trying not to think. Maybe she'd get lucky and they wouldn't make the ridge, and the outlaws would shoot them down. At least then she wouldn't have to face him. Never, never, never had she allowed a man to touch her the way he had. The only other kiss she'd truly received had been at her wedding. There had been no time or privacy for more.

She thought of how hard the Ranger's face had looked, even when he'd slept in the stagecoach, chiseled like weathered granite. How cold his eyes were.

How demanding his kiss. How bold his hands. She mentally slapped herself for letting her mind wander.

He'd advanced so fast she hadn't been able to think about how to reject him. This was all his fault. She should have nothing to be ashamed of.

If the man would slow down now, Annalane swore she would kill him. What right did he think he had to kiss her like that? To touch her. To wake her up to something she told herself she had been perfectly happy not knowing about.

Her anger stewed as she climbed. She barely noticed the eastern sky lighten. They were at the ridge by the time dawn washed over the rocks.

McCord jumped down off a rock and turned, lifting his arms to catch her. He swung her around. "We made it."

A smile lit his face, making him look younger—closer to thirty, not forty as she'd first guessed. Despite her anger and exhaustion, she smiled. They were safe, at least for now.

He set her on her feet, took her hand as if he'd done so a thousand times, and started down the shadowy side of the hill.

Halfway down, he stopped to allow her to catch her breath. While she rested against a cold rock, he searched the valley below.

"The driver told me you were going to meet your brother at Camp Supply."

She nodded as she fought exhaustion.

"He'll know the stage didn't make it in last night, and I'm guessing troops will be headed this way. If I'd been waiting for you, I'd be an hour in the saddle by now, maybe more."

If Devin hadn't planned to introduce her at dinner last night, she doubted he'd even notice she was missing. He was more likely to wait and blame her for being late than come after her, but Annalane didn't want to admit that to McCord.

The Ranger kept watching. "On horseback they could cut some time off the stage trail and be here in an hour, two at the most."

Annalane closed her eyes, wishing the driver hadn't been so nosy, but a woman traveling alone was a rare sight in these parts, and she thought it would help if he knew she had someone waiting to meet her. It might make her sound not quite so like an old maid. At least she hadn't told the driver more. She never told anyone the truth. What would people say, or believe, if she told them that her brother never contacted her unless he needed something from her? She swore that ever since he could talk he'd manipulated everyone around him. Life was some kind of game and people just cards to play to him.

She sniffed, thinking she was really pathetic. Even knowing what he was like, she'd traveled half a continent hoping that this time he'd act like a real brother. Maybe for once he was thinking of her, alone in Washington, and not just himself.

I will not cry, she silently vowed. *I will not cry.*

McCord startled her when he stomped back to where she stood. All she could manage was to glare at him when he cleared his throat.

"About last night . . ." he started, forcing out the words as if he were reading his own obituary.

"I don't want to talk about last night," she hissed through her teeth to keep from screaming.

"Good." He slapped his gloves against his hand. "'Cause I don't want to hear you talk about it. Never could tolerate the Northern accent. How about we just agree to talk as little as possible."

She didn't need a weapon, she decided. She'd kill him with her bare hands. She'd just grab his throat and bite him, then she'd watch the blood pump out of his long, hard body and say sweetly, in her most proper Northern accent, that she was wrong about not having the killer instinct. It appeared she did.

Before she could pounce, he plopped his hat on her head and dropped his gloves in her hand. "Put these on, Anna. There's brush the rest of the way down that'll cut you if you grab for a handhold, and the sun's going to turn hot enough to put that blush permanently on those cheeks."

He'd never know how close he came to dying, she thought. She'd let him live awhile longer. Not because he'd said something nice to her. A nice word would probably choke the man. But he had shown a degree of thoughtfulness. The dirty hat and the worn gloves couldn't make her look worse.

She sniffed again, deciding that on top of everything else, she'd caught a cold. The only silver lining to it lay in the hope that she'd passed it along to the Ranger while he'd kissed her.

"You getting sick?" he asked, already ten feet ahead of her.

"No." She picked up her bag and followed.

"Well, then hurry up. We want to be off this hill by the time they ride by here."

She almost laughed. Her brother was probably having his second cup of coffee and telling everyone about how his sister couldn't manage to do anything right, including get to him.

Two hours later, when they were almost to the trail that served as the stage road, she collapsed. Her legs simply folded. Three days with nothing to eat and little to drink. More hours than she could count without sleep. Like a clock running down, she stopped.

As she lay in the dirt, she heard the Ranger backtracking to her. She half expected him to yell at her to get up, but he simply leaned down, picked up his hat and her bag, then lifted her into his arms.

Without a word, he began walking, carrying her like she was a child and not a woman almost his height.

Annalane closed her eyes. She'd have to kill him later. Right now all she wanted to do was sleep.

Chapter 4

McCord walked half a mile before he found an old cotton-wood tree with branches almost touching the ground. He pulled Anna into the cool shade where roots bowed from the earth, making a natural cradle for her.

Anna's eyes fluttered open. She watched him, a mixture of fear and panic in her exhausted gaze, but she didn't say a word.

"You all right?" he asked, feeling her face to see if she had a fever. "We about froze last night in the rain, and now it's hot. I swear, Texas is the only place I know of where you can experience all four seasons within twenty-four hours."

She didn't act like she could hear him. McCord pulled his leather coat off her shoulders and spread it out on the ground, saying, "You'll be safe in no time, Anna. I promise." He tugged her arm, leaning her down atop his coat, with her head on her bag for her pillow. She didn't fight him, but the stiffness in her movements told him she didn't believe him.

"That's better." He patted her hip, liking the roundness of it on her slender frame. "Rest." There was no telling how long it had been since she'd eaten. He'd seen her shoving food around on the tin plates when they stopped yesterday, but he hadn't seen her lift a bite to her mouth.

He laid the back of his hand against her cheek. She was warm, but not burning with fever. When he began unbuttoning her traveling jacket, she moaned and shook her head.

"Easy now," he said, thinking that was probably more something he should say to a horse rather than a woman. "I'm just going to make you comfortable, then I'll watch the road for your brother."

Her fitted jacket was tight across her ribs and he wondered how she'd stood it all night when they'd been climbing in the rocks. When he finished undoing the last button, she let out a sigh and closed her eyes. He couldn't resist sliding his finger beneath the wool and feeling the warmth of her covered only by a layer of wrinkled cotton.

He brushed a few stray strands of hair away from her face. "You're quite a woman, Anna. You collapsed before you complained once." He pressed his lips against her cheek. "Sleep now, but remember that we're not finished, me and you. Not by a long shot."

She moaned something in her sleep and McCord brushed his fingers over her ribs. He liked the feel of her, the look of her; but most of all, he liked her spirit.

When he was sure she was sound asleep, he moved to where he could see down the road in both directions. If the army didn't come soon, looking for the coach, the outlaws would be finished with the men at the station and realize what they were looking for was not in the mailbag. Thorn, the leader of the worthless gang, would be madder than hell and heading toward them.

McCord tugged the envelope from a slit in the lining of his boot. The letter Thorn was fighting so hard to get wasn't in the mailbag. It never had been. The governor had trusted it to one Ranger. McCord had orders to burn it before letting it fall into the wrong hands. There'd been no need to ask—he knew he was expected to protect it with his life and deliver it to a Quaker who served as an Indian agent in this part of the world. This one document could change history, maybe end the Indian fighting years early and allow settlers and Indians to live in peace.

McCord knew without any doubt that he'd die before he'd fail. For the first time in longer than he could remember, his actions might save lives. He smiled, thinking he would do just that, even if he had to kill Thorn and all his gang to do it.

He moved away from Anna, fighting the need to lie down beside her, fearing that if he did, he'd frighten her even more than he had. He wanted her, but not tired and half-asleep, at least not the first time. He wanted her awake and willing in his arms, and to reach that goal he knew he'd have to go slow, very slow.

Problem was, he had no idea how.

McCord frowned and turned his back to her, hoping his need for her would ease. For a man who'd counted his life in days and never looked too far in the future, going slow toward anything was not his nature. He'd been seventeen when he'd ridden with a posse that tracked raiders who'd burned a farm near his parents' place. He'd killed his first man that night, seeing the bodies of the family they'd pulled from the fire and not the outlaw he'd killed. From that night on, McCord had always felt he'd been playing cards with the Grim Reaper, and one of these times he'd draw the short hand.

He glanced back at Anna curled in among the cottonwood roots. "Slow and easy," he promised, proud of himself for taking the time to talk to her a little and not just leave her among the branches. It had been a long time since he'd comforted a woman.

An hour later, he heard riders coming and watched until he recognized the blue uniforms of the cavalry.

McCord stepped in the trail, his hand up, his gun pointed down.

One rider stood out among the soldiers. A young officer on the short side who sat a horse like a greenhorn. He had to be Anna's brother, same black hair and dark eyes. Wynn remembered her telling the gambler on the stage that her brother was a new doctor who'd just been transferred to Texas before being sent to Camp Supply.

The Ranger decided he disliked the man on sight.

The short doctor, in a uniform that didn't quite fit, half climbed, half tumbled from his mount and hurried to catch up to a sergeant heading toward McCord.

"Ranger McCord." Sergeant Dirk Cunningham smiled and offered a friendly salute. "When we heard the stage was late and you might be on it, I headed out just in case you needed help." He laughed. "You know, burying the bodies or hanging the outlaws. I've known you long enough to know if there's trouble you'll be the last one standing."

McCord touched his hat in a two-finger return salute to a man he'd crossed paths with so many times over the years they'd become friends. "I thought you might be worried about me, Cunningham."

The sergeant shook his head. "Not you. I followed you when we was dodging Sherman in the war. You'd fight a twenty-gun man-of-war with a tug boat and still come out ahead."

The doctor finally reached them. Anna's brother pushed his way forward. "If you were on the stage, where are the others? My sister should have been with the stage, unless she missed her connection. I swear, if there was a dog in the road, she'd stop to help it even if it meant missing the stage." When both men just stared at him, the doctor added, "Was there trouble? Is anyone hurt?"

Cunningham took the lead. "Ranger Wynn McCord, this is Doctor Devin Woodward. You'll have to excuse his manners—he's worried about his sister."

Wynn faced Dr. Woodward. "Your sister is all right, sir." He turned back to his friend. "We were attacked by what looked like Thorn and about a dozen men, but we managed to make it to the station just as the rain hit." Wynn met the sergeant's gaze and they both knew they'd talk details later when they were alone.

"Oh, my God," Dr. Woodward yelled. "Was my sister hurt? If she's back at the station in pain, I'll hold someone accountable. We have to hurry!"

"No." Wynn turned back to the doc. "She's asleep right now. I brought her with me when I escaped in the rain. I figured her chances would be better than at the station once the rain stopped. We followed the stream behind the station for a few miles, then climbed over those hills."

Devin Woodward didn't look like he believed the Ranger.

McCord added, "She's quite a little soldier."

"You let her leave with you!" Dr. Woodward turned his anger on the Ranger. "You dragged a woman out in a storm and across those hills? Good God, man, you could have killed her."

McCord's jaw tightened. "I didn't drag her anywhere. Your sister is a strong woman who knows her own mind."

"My sister is an idiot. If she'd had any brains, she would have married and not taken on nursing as her cause. She's wasted her youth running from battle to battle during the war, and now will probably be my burden to bear for the rest of her life."

McCord thought of hitting the doc. One good punch should put him out for a while. Anna looked to be almost in her thirties and Woodward appeared to be just past twenty. He'd been too young to fight. He couldn't know how many men lived because of nurses who worked round the clock in roofless field hospitals and old barns turned into surgery stations. The doctors might have done the cutting and the patching, but it had been the nurses who bandaged and fought fevers and held men as they faced death.

Wynn looked toward the cottonwood and silently swore.

Anna, her back straight and his coat folded over her arm, walked slowly toward the men. The face that had shown such fire when she'd been mad at him, which was most of the time he'd known her, now looked stone cold, as if no emotion would ever reflect in her features. Only her eyes looked tired and sad, very sad.

"There you are!" Woodward shouted. "You had us all worried to death." He didn't move toward her but waited for her to join them. "I'd hoped to start setting up the infirmary today, but from the looks of you, we'll have to put it off until tomorrow."

McCord balled his fists. Just two punches. One to the doc's face, leaving him unwilling to talk around a busted lip and a few missing teeth, and one to his gut to knock some of the wind out of him. Couldn't he see that his sister had just walked through hell to get to him? Couldn't he imagine how frightened she must have been, and how brave?

The sergeant stepped past McCord and moved to Anna. "Are you all right, ma'am? Ranger McCord told me what an ordeal you had last night and I'm surprised you're still standing. May I be of some service to you?"

McCord saw her glance at the stripes on Dirk's sleeve before answering, "Thank you, Sergeant. You are kind."

Dirk Cunningham might be an old fighter, but there was enough Southern gentleman in him to know how to treat a lady. They left the doc standing in the trail as they moved to the troops still in their saddles.

"I need three good men to go with me back to the station and check on things." McCord fell into step on the other side of Anna. He could hear the doc following, asking questions and demanding answers, but no one listened.

The sergeant nodded. "I got two good boys you'll know, and a Yank who can shoot a flea off a rabbit's ear at a hundred yards. He's just a kid, so keep him out of any close scraps if you can, but he'd be good at lying low and covering your back."

McCord understood what Dirk wasn't saying as much as what he was. The "good boys" were Texans, probably ex-rebs, who could take care of themselves. The kid, a Private Clark, was green, but his skill could come in handy.

Cunningham helped Anna onto one of the extra horses the men had brought along. There was no time to say anything to her as McCord closed his hand over hers when he handed her the reins. He'd have to do his talking to the sergeant. "Take care of her, Dirk. She's a real trooper."

The sergeant nodded, understanding the Ranger's compliment. He turned to the doctor. "Awaiting your order to ride, sir."

Dr. Woodward straightened as if just remembering that he was the one in charge. "Go ahead, Sergeant. Start back. I'll have a word with the Ranger first and join you." When he faced McCord, the Ranger was already moving toward an extra horse and the three men waiting for him.

"I have a few questions," Woodward demanded.

McCord swung up on his mount. "Well, I'm all out of answers." He did wonder why so many folks seemed to be starting conversations with him lately with that statement. "Why don't you ride back to the stage station with us and maybe you'll find your answers?"

"I think I'll just do that." Dr. Woodward climbed on his horse. "I plan to ask the other passengers if you forced my sister to go with you, and if you did, sir, I'll have you know, I plan . . ."

McCord didn't listen to more. He and the three soldiers were a hundred yards ahead of the doctor before he could get his horse moving. The soldiers stayed right with Wynn, enjoying the entertainment of watching the little doctor try to keep up with them.

When they reached the station, McCord could read all the answers in the tracks, but he said nothing. He waved Clark, the sharpshooter, in from where he'd been hiding in case they'd been riding into a trap, and they all waited for the doctor.

The soldiers stayed on guard while McCord let Dr. Woodward storm into the stage station first. Two minutes later, he ran out and threw up at the side of the porch. "They're both dead!" the doctor said.

One of the soldiers swung from his horse and read the ground as easily as he might a headline in the paper. "Looks like there were ten or more of them. I'm guessing they came in fast." He scratched his head. "No shells in the mud, so they didn't come in firing."

McCord stood at the door and looked in. "The driver and station manager were already dead by the time Thorn and his men rode in."

"How do you know that?"

"There's half a dozen spent shells scattered among the cards by the table. One man who was here last night is missing. A gambler who called himself Frank Sanders. My guess is he shot the others, waited for a while to make sure I didn't come running from the barn, then lit out with the mailbag. I heard a horse traveling fast sometime before dawn."

Dr. Woodward wiped his mouth. "If this gambler killed those two, why did the gang ride in?"

McCord shrugged. "Maybe they thought the gambler left something behind. Maybe he took something they wanted. If so, they're after him and not us."

"So if we go after the gambler, we might just find this Thorn bandit everyone talks about."

McCord nodded.

Dr. Woodward straightened and tried to pull himself together. "The flaw in your plan, Ranger, seems to be we have no idea where this gambler went."

"I don't have to go after him," McCord answered. "I know where he's headed."

Woodward frowned. "And where might that be, Ranger McCord?"

"Camp Supply. Two people saw him and now know he's part of Thorn's gang. He'll be heading to try to permanently silence me and your sister."

Chapter 5

Annalane fought to keep awake enough to stay in the saddle as she rode, surrounded by soldiers, toward Camp Supply. The land rolled over low hills covered in the green of early spring, and she wondered how such beauty could ever hold danger.

Sergeant Cunningham fussed over her. When they reached the camp, he showed her to her brother's quarters, ordered men to bring a bath and a hot meal, then stood guard outside her door so she'd have privacy.

Devin's quarters were minimal. The room had been set up for four officers to sleep in a room, but the sergeant said all the officers had not arrived yet, so her brother had the room to himself. She managed to find everything she needed in either his supplies or her dusty bag. Soap, a brush, towels, clean underclothes.

She soaked in the tub until the water turned cold, then washed her hair. Pulling her undergarments from her bag, she put them on before wrapping herself in one of Devin's extra bedsheets. The food was simple: milk, cheese, biscuits with jelly inside, and creamy chicken soup. It all tasted wonderful. When she finished, she curled up on one of the bunks and slept soundly.

The late afternoon sun shone through high west windows when someone tapped on her door.

"Begging your pardon, ma'am," the sergeant yelled, "but one of the men who went to the stage station just delivered your trunk. He says to tell you that if you're able your brother would like you to dress and join the officers for dinner in an hour."

Annalane pulled the sheet tightly around her and opened the door.

The sergeant kept his eyes low as he set the luggage inside. He didn't look up until she asked if McCord had made it in with her brother.

Cunningham smiled. "Yes, ma'am. He checked to see if I was on guard, then went over to the barracks to clean up. The Ranger always eats with the officers the first night when he's in camp, just to pay his respects, but he'll be having breakfast with us come morning."

She understood. "He's more comfortable. I see."

Cunningham shook his head. "I don't think McCord is comfortable anywhere. It wouldn't surprise me if he sleeps wearing them twin Colts fully loaded and strapped on. But maybe he feels a little less uncomfortable around his own kind. I've heard that his family all died while he was off fighting. Haven't seen him care about anyone or anything in years, until this morning."

Before she could ask, he added, "The look he gave me when he told me to take care of you left no doubt about how he feels about you, ma'am."

She thought the sergeant must have read something more into McCord's order than was there. Maybe the sergeant was just hoping his friend had changed. All she had to do was listen to know that Cunningham and McCord had the same accent. Not Southern exactly, but uniquely Texas.

She thanked the sergeant as she closed the door, and

dressed in one of her plain navy suits she'd worn as a nurse. There had been only enough time and money to buy one good traveling dress. All the rest of her clothes were uniforms or housedresses. Years ago she'd had a few evening dresses and two Sunday dresses, but they'd long been packed away. There never seemed time for such things, and she always worked on Sundays when the nurses with families liked to take off.

Annalane hoped her brother would come to walk her over to dinner, but when she opened the door only Cunningham waited for her outside. He offered his arm and she accepted the gesture kindly. He filled her in on what her brother and the Ranger had found at the station. She knew there would have been one more body on the dirt floor of the shack if she hadn't left with McCord. The thought chilled her.

Four officers and one Ranger stood as she stepped into the small dining room. Her brother introduced her to each officer. They were all polite, but as usual none gave her more than a passing glance. She was not the kind of woman who drew a man's attention.

To her surprise, McCord didn't meet her eyes when he took her hand in greeting.

Devin hadn't introduced her to him, but the Ranger stepped forward and paid his respects just like the others. He'd cleaned up and had on clothes that looked free of dirt. If he hadn't been frowning, she would have almost thought him handsome. How could this man of granite, with his cold winter eyes that missed nothing, be the same man who'd kissed her so wildly in the darkness?

She didn't waste time with nothing words. "Thank you for saving my life."

"You are welcome." He finally looked up, staring at her as if he saw no one else in the room. "As I remember, you insisted on going."

"You could have left anytime after the rain started. Why did you wait?"

He lowered his voice. "I wouldn't have left without you. If you hadn't wanted to go with me, I would have remained and fought."

Annalane stared, knowing he meant every word.

Her brother tugged at her arm, insisting she sit between the captain and a tired-looking man with thinning hair named Lieutenant Dodson.

As Devin tucked in her chair, he said, "I asked one of the men to move your things out of my room and into the new infirmary. You can stay there. It wouldn't be proper for you to stay in the officers' quarters. I'm an officer so I belong there, and even though you're my sister, you are still only a nurse."

When she raised an eyebrow, he added, as if she'd asked, "The three-room infirmary is finished, at least on the outside. One wide front room that will serve as an office and examining room, one smaller storage room, and a large room to be set up as a small sick ward. Once we get everything out of crates, I'm sure you'll find plenty of room for a bed in the storage room."

"Nothing is set up?" She knew her brother had been at the camp over a month—surely he'd done something. It occurred to her that he might not know how. Surely any graduate from a medical school would know how to set up at least an office and examining room.

"I've been busy," he answered. "It's not my top priority right now. I'm not just the camp doctor, I'm also an officer."

She nodded, telling herself he was lazy, just waiting for her to do the work. He'd been that way as a child, and no uniform had changed his habits. Pushing aside a nagging worry that he might not have spent all his time away in medical school, she resigned herself to sleeping among crates tonight.

She glanced around at the proper table service and wished McCord were not a table away. He was the only one she felt safe with. He was the only one she wanted to talk to. She smiled. In truth neither of them probably had enough skills to keep a conversation going throughout an entire meal.

It made little sense—the man had barely talked to her—but in a deep, primal way she needed to be near McCord.

The captain was formal and polite, but not interested in talking to a woman. Her brother never spoke to her, except to tell her to answer the questions. Lieutenant Dodson, on her left, was a few years older than she was, thin and pale among the other men tanned by the sun. He told her he was the paymaster. The man reminded her of a hawk, and had the habit of blurting out questions in random order. Her answers quickly shortened to simply yes or no, since she had the strong suspicion he wasn't listening but trying to think of what to ask next.

By the time the meal was served, she'd formed a shell around herself. The men talked around her as if she were invisible. Her brother related his trip to the stagecoach station, including how the bodies looked on the floor and how many times each had been shot.

When one of the young officers suggested that such talk might not be proper in front of a lady, Dr. Woodward announced that his sister loved blood and gore. She'd been at half the battles during the Civil War and came home to work in a hospital for dying veterans when the war was over, as if she hadn't had enough after over four years.

When dessert was brought in, Annalane excused herself, saying she knew the men would want to enjoy their cigars with coffee and she was still very tired. They all stood and bid her goodnight, but she had the feeling that only Ranger McCord's gaze followed her out.

Sergeant Cunningham waited on the steps to see her to

the infirmary. "The boys have been scrambling while you were at dinner, ma'am, trying to clean up at least one of the rooms for you. I'm not sure where your brother thought you'd be sleeping when he ordered your things sent to a half-finished building with boxes everywhere."

Annalane thought of saying she doubted Devin cared, but she tried to smile as she said, "I'm sure it will be fine."

When she entered the building, she was met by the three men who had gone with McCord to the station. One looked barely old enough to shave and the other two were like Cunningham—they'd fought for the South. They were all smiling at her.

As the men stepped aside, she glanced into the larger room that would become the hospital bay and she laughed. They'd put a tent in the middle of a room lined with boxes. One of the privates stepped forward. "We figured we didn't have time to clean the place so we put up a new tent for you, ma'am, with supplies we found in some of these boxes."

Another added, "You got a lock on the door to the room, so you'll be safe, but you'll have your own apartment once you're in the building." He lifted the flap. "We put some coals on the grate so you'll be snug as a bug in here tonight."

Annalane laughed and clapped her hands. "Thank you, gentlemen. I've never had something so grand." They'd even put a little white tea set by the grate and a rug made from blankets on the floor.

They all smiled and would have watched her move in if Cunningham hadn't shoved them along. "Lock the door behind us, ma'am. We'll take turns tonight guarding outside, so all you have to do is yell if you need anything."

Annalane thanked them each again, locked the door, and stepped inside her very own playhouse tent. She had the feeling a few of the items had been stolen from her brother's room, but tonight she didn't care. She was in heaven.

First, as she'd done for years traveling with the supply wagons and medical tents, she unpacked her few belongings and laid them out so they'd be in easy reach when she was called to work. Then she dressed in her white nightgown and warm robe that tied empire style. The hem might be frayed and the lace threadbare in a few places along the collar, but she always felt elegant in her robe.

She sat in front of a little mirror and brushed her hair, then braided it in a long braid. Smiling, she remembered how her mother used to tell her that she might never be a beauty, but she had pretty hair.

Her parents had both died two years ago when a flu hit the city hard that winter. Devin had been in his first year of medical school and couldn't come home. She'd tried to keep working and deal with the debts. One by one she'd sold off everything they'd had, to pay bills and keep Devin in school. He resented having to join the army because there was no money to help set up his practice, but deep down Annalane had thought it would be good for him.

A knock sounded at the door just beyond the folds of her tent.

She checked her robe, slipped from her warm tent and opened the door.

McCord stepped inside, frowning. "Don't unlock the door unless you know who is on the other side."

"All right. Go out and knock. I'll pretend I don't know you." He'd been nothing but cold to her all evening. If she didn't know better she'd swear someone else had been in the shadows with her last night. Someone else had kissed her. Not this man who hadn't looked at her once during dinner.

He ignored her suggestion and raised an eyebrow at the tent.

She was thankful for the distraction. "The boys put it up for me. Isn't it great?"

He didn't smile, but at least he stopped frowning. "Yeah, it is."

"What did you need, Ranger McCord? It's a little late for a social call and I do have a guard outside."

McCord reached behind her and shoved the bolt. "I told that Clark kid, who's guarding this place like it's the national bank, to go eat some supper. I need to talk to you."

"About what?" He'd had an hour to talk to her at dinner and never said a word.

"About this." He leaned closer, backing her against the door, and hesitated a few inches from her mouth. "I'm going to kiss you again, Anna. If you have objections, you'd better voice them now. All you have to say is stop. Just say the word and I back away." The words were snapped like orders he'd rehearsed. "But if you don't . . ."

She could feel her breathing quicken but she faced him squarely. This was probably his idea of having a conversation with a lady. The man had the social skills of a turtle. "Well, first of all, my name is Annalane, not Anna, and I'll not tolerate being manhandled or talked to like I'm . . ."

He closed the distance between them and covered her mouth with his. She pushed on his chest and tried to turn her head away, but he held her with his body pressed hard against hers and his hand cupped around the back of her head. Evidently the conversation part of his visit was over.

This was no gentle kiss of hello, but a demanding, searching advance based on need and longing. He slid his hand to her jaw and urged her mouth open so he could taste and smother her complaint.

As she knew he would, he gentled when she kissed him back. He moaned low and twisted his fingers through her hair as he took her through the lessons he'd taught her the night before in the blackness.

Finally, when he moved his mouth to her throat, she breathed in deeply as he whispered, "That's the way, Anna.

I knew you'd feel this good, taste this good. I couldn't have imagined last night when you were lying against me."

He brushed the tips of his fingers along her chin. "I think I might have died if I'd had to sit across the room much longer without touching you." He held her cheek as he kissed her again and again while he mumbled something about going slow.

The thought of saying stop never occurred to her. She wanted a man who was gentle and caring, maybe even hesitant as a lover, but she'd not tell McCord to stop. She felt her body melting against his, needing his nearness, his touch, his kiss, as deeply as he seemed to need her.

Finally, he leaned away and studied her, drinking her in with his stormy gaze.

She knew he'd kiss her again if she tried to talk to him, so she lifted her arms to his shoulders and let her breasts rise and fall against his chest with each breath.

He raised his head and smiled at her as if he could read her mind. His hand circled round her braid and he tugged until she leaned her head back, offering him her throat.

He unbuttoned the first few buttons of her high-collared gown and began nibbling along her throat. He stopped where her heart pounded just below the surface of her skin and kissed just there. Then, as if in thanks for her offering, he returned to her mouth and kissed her lightly, playing with her tongue. He didn't have to say he missed her—he was showing her. There'd been no need to tell her he had to touch her—she knew.

When she pulled him closer, she felt his low moan more than heard it. "I know, Anna," he whispered against her ear. "I know."

Slowly, the kiss grew deeper. Her whole body felt like it was on fire. He stepped back and tugged at the ribbons holding her robe. When she protested, he pushed her hands away. When she tried again to hold her robe closed, he placed both of her hands behind her with one strong grip he opened the robe with his free hand.

She wiggled, trying to get free. He was going too fast, being too bold. She wanted a gentle lover, a slow lover, a hesitant . . . the feel of his hands tugging her robe free made her forget her list of wants.

She wouldn't stop him and he smiled down at her, knowing what they were doing was new and frightening to her.

"Easy now, Anna. Just relax against me. I wish there was time to go slower," he whispered as he kissed his way from her ear to her lips. "You know I'm not going to hurt you, don't you?"

She nodded and moved her hands to his shoulders, barely aware of when he'd released her.

"I'm going to touch you, if you've no objection. This will be no light brush over your clothes, like before. When I'm finished there will be no doubt you've been handled a bit." He kissed the corner of her mouth. "And, darling, you're going to love every minute."

When she opened her mouth to question this, his kiss stopped the words and his hand moved over the cotton of her gown to grip her breast boldly while his strong arm circled her. She jerked and twisted, but he didn't let go. Her breast filled his hand. His grip was strong, almost hurting her, but he didn't turn loose or let her free.

When she pulled her mouth from his, he let her turn and gulp air. His fingers spread out, pressing her breast against her pounding heart. She saw fire in his eyes, but she felt no fear of him, only of herself and what he might awaken in her.

She tried to turn away, but he didn't move. They both knew she could stop him with a word. She was fighting years of closing herself off from any tenderness, any loving touch, any passion. This cold, hard man seemed to understand her when no one else had even tried.

"Kiss me, Anna," he whispered, almost angry. "Kiss me."

She turned toward him, seeing the need in his eyes, and then the surprise as she raised her chin and moved her mouth to his. After a moment of hesitation, he took her offering fully.

When she finally calmed and stilled in his arms, he kissed a tear from her cheek and loosened his grip around her. "There now, that wasn't so bad, was it, darlin'. You're more afraid of something new than of me."

It crossed her mind that he was mad. She was with a madman. Who bossed her around. Who saved her life. Who kissed her with a passion that would probably set them both on fire any minute. He thought he could kiss her and handle her just because he wanted to. He treated her like a treasure. Like a woman. Like a passion too deep for either of them to understand.

His hand gently brushed over the thin layer of material covering her shoulder.

When he leaned down to take a first taste of her throat, she pushed away and moved into her tent.

He followed, knowing that he'd be welcomed as he moved up behind her, circling her waist and pulling her back against him. He wasn't imprisoning her now—she could have stepped away, but she leaned into him and sighed at the whirlwind of feelings circling through her body.

He kissed her ear and she heard his breathing, fast and heavy like her own. "Unbutton your gown." He spread his hands out wide at her sides.

"No," she whispered.

"Unbutton your gown." His order was muffled as his mouth moved down her throat.

"Only a few," she whispered back in compromise.

Her fingers fumbled, opening the buttons as he kissed his way to the hollow of her throat. There was something raw and hungry in his touch, as though he'd waited a lifetime to hold her.

She was beyond thought and full into pleasure. Slowly, hesitantly, she began unbuttoning more tiny buttons. He rewarded her with kisses along her neck and his fingers moving over her body.

When she reached the buttons between her breasts, he whispered again, "Now, pull the gown down off your shoulders."

He watched her slow progress. First one shoulder, then the other. The robe dropped to the floor but the soft gown hung at the tips of her breasts.

"You're so beautiful," he whispered.

She wondered if he was aware that he said the words aloud.

His hands moved to her shoulders and began to slowly slide down. He played with the material hiding her from him. He hadn't pushed her in this, he hadn't forced her. He'd simply asked and she'd done what he wanted. He could not possibly be as surprised as she was.

She closed her eyes, expecting him to shove the cotton down and stare at her, but he didn't. He turned her slowly in his arms and drew her against him and held her for a while. She'd never felt so treasured.

Anna cried softly against his shoulder without knowing why. All her life she'd discouraged men with a turn of her head or a frown. She'd been in mourning, or too busy, or thought herself too old. But there was nothing hesitant in this man's advance. Nothing shy.

She shook, aware of just how close he stood and how unbelievably natural it felt to press her body so close to his she could feel his heart pounding.

When his mouth found hers once more, he was giving, not taking. The kiss was long and pure. Her bruised lips took the pleasure of it like cool water.

Finally, he broke the kiss and pressed his forehead against hers. "We have to talk. I haven't got much time even for this heaven."

"I thought you didn't like to talk."

He grinned. "Believe me, there are a million things I'd rather do with you than talk, but this time it's important that you follow orders."

"Your orders?"

"Yes, my orders. That gambler back at the stage station, Frank Sanders, is part of a gang led by a man named Thorn. We've both seen Sanders and therefore can identify him. Which means Sanders, and maybe Thorn, will want us dead as soon as possible. I want you to promise to stay in the camp until I get back. Trust no one that Sergeant Cunningham doesn't trust."

He squeezed her shoulders. "Do I make myself clear?"

"I'm not in the habit of being bossed around, McCord."

"Well, I'm not in the habit of caring about anyone." He swore and added, "There is nothing I'd like more than to bed you right now and we both know I could, without you stopping me."

"Would you have stopped if I'd said the word?"

"I would. I will." He set his jaw as if testifying in court. "I said the words and I meant them. I had to let you know you had control. I know I came on a little fast and strong, but on my honor I would have stepped away if you'd ordered me to."

"A *little* fast," she mumbled, knowing her lips were bruised from his kisses and her throat probably black and blue from where he'd taken the time to nibble on her flesh.

He kissed her forehead. "I've a mission to finish and if I bed you tonight, I might end up leaving you alone with child. I'll not do that, Anna." While hugging her, he let his honest words flow over her. "I have a hunger for you, like I've never felt before. I don't know if it's that I want to believe you could belong to me, or if part of me already belongs to you. This doesn't feel like something we can cure in one night."

She was shocked by his caring. She had no doubt that he wanted her, but now she knew he cared. "You might get killed on this mission? Is that what you're telling me?"

"The odds aren't with me this time. I feel it so strong I'd already decided before I climbed on that stage that this would be my last ride as a Ranger." He lowered his head and kissed her bare shoulder. "If I make it through the next few days, will you be waiting for me? I'm not asking for any promises, I'm just asking that when I knock on that door again you'll throw the bolt and let me in."

She stepped away, shaking. He hadn't asked her to let him *stay.* This wasn't a marriage proposal or even a promise of one, but it was as close as she'd ever come to one again. She had always been a proper lady. What he was asking was that she'd welcome him in. Not just to her house, or room, but to her bed.

She fought back a sob, longing for him to whisper "forever" between them, but knowing she'd not ask for so much. She might never have him stay. Without a single doubt she knew it would take all the strength she had to take only what this Ranger could offer and then watch him leave when their time was over.

"Anna," he snapped. "Stop breathing so fast. You're driving me crazy."

She looked at him and then down at the gown almost falling off her breasts with each breath. Crossing her arms over her, she began to pull up her gown.

His hands shot out to grip her wrists.

She met his eyes, no longer cold, but stormy with anger and need.

"Don't," he said, gritting his teeth.

He hesitated as if refusing to explain why.

"Let go of me," she said. "Stop." She felt like she was bending him to the breaking point. She guessed there were very few things in his life he wanted or needed. Apparently she was one of them, but if he didn't let go right here, right now, they would never be equals, and for her there could be no other way.

"Stop," she said again, almost calmly. "Turn loose of me."

She saw the blink of his eye and knew she'd stood down a fighter who'd never backed away.

His grip loosened and gave. He stepped away and raised his hands in silent surrender.

She'd broken him, but passion still fired in his gaze like a fever out of control. "Sit down." She pointed to her traveling trunk.

He raised an eyebrow, but did as he was told. The trunk was too high to be a chair, but made a good bench and put her a head above him.

She walked over to stand directly in front of him. "You'll never take anything from me, Wynn McCord. Not one thing," she said. "Get that clear. You'll never take me. I think you'll have to learn to come toward me some other way than at full charge. If there is to be anything between us, there will be no orders." She'd give him everything, if he asked, but nothing if he demanded.

She sensed he was in uncharted territory, but he was a strong man and his face showed nothing of how he felt. His glare was so strong she swore she could feel it on her skin.

Slowly, she lowered her crossed arms and her gown slipped back to where it had been, barely covering the peaks of her breasts.

He glanced from her chest to her face, trying to read what she was offering. "I know no words, Anna. I'll never come a'courting. I'll never know what to say or how to tell you the things women want to hear."

"I don't expect such things," she said. "But I do expect honesty."

"You've told me that before, Anna."

She smiled. "And next time taking it a little slower wouldn't hurt."

Carefully, he raised his hands to her waist and tugged her toward him. Then he lowered his mouth and planted a feather kiss on the top of each breast before he looked directly into her eyes and said, "I'll work on it if you're willing to put up with me." He lowered his head and she felt his smile against her skin.

Anna began to shiver as he moved over her flesh. Her hands rested on his shoulders as he drew her to him and nuzzled between her breasts, then turned slowly from one to the other, breathing her in as if she were a flower.

When he straightened, he grinned at her as his hand moved up her ribs and tugged her gown down.

For a while he just looked and moved the tips of his fingers over her gift to him. "You are so beautiful," he said again as he lifted the weight of one breast and brushed his finger over her skin.

She would have fallen with pleasure if his arm hadn't held her up.

He stood and carried her to her cot. When he lay her atop the quilt, he knelt beside her. "Don't worry," he whispered. "I don't want to frighten you."

"I know," she whispered.

Part of her wanted to fight, to break away and run, not from him, but from herself. From feelings so long denied she'd forgotten how to live.

His big hand stroked over her bare body, pushing the gown lower until it barely covered her hips. She closed her eyes and moaned softly as he kissed her. Again and again, he moved up to her lips, his kiss deep with need as his hands branded her.

She relaxed, giving over to the pleasure of his touch. When he stopped, she opened her eyes, wondering how this man could have gotten so close, not with tender words and soft touches, but with honesty in his longing for her.

His hand spread out across her abdomen. "I have to go." He said the words slowly, as if forcing them out. "But I'll have your word you'll stay in camp before I go. Nowhere is totally safe, but you'll be surrounded here."

She didn't trust her voice. She simply nodded. He'd just shown her how much he wanted her. With his words he was telling her how much he cared for her.

She'd thought he would continue touching her, but he stepped away and picked up her robe. Silently she stood, barely aware of the gown falling away as she stepped into the robe he offered.

He tied it above her waist and took one of her hands, kissed it, and then pulled her to the door.

"Hell's fires won't keep me from coming back," he whispered as he pulled her to him one last time.

They held each other tightly for a minute, then he patted her on the bottom and pushed away from her.

A moment later, he was gone. Anna shoved the bolt closed and went back to the cot where she cried herself to sleep, knowing when he came back she would let him in . . . whether he stayed a night, or forever.

Chapter 6

McCord rode for half the night before he stopped to water his horse. The hardest thing he'd ever done was leave Anna, but deep down he knew leaving her was the only way he'd keep her alive.

The gambler was hunting them both, and McCord knew men like Frank Sanders would come after him first. He'd consider the woman easy pickings, not near the challenge a Ranger would be to kill. He'd want McCord out of the way so he could take his time with the woman. McCord doubted Sanders or Thorn had put the pieces together and figured out that the letter they wanted so desperately to stop from being delivered had been with a Ranger, and not in the mailbag on the stage.

McCord had to draw Frank Sanders away from Anna, and he had a mission he had to finish. If he had a choice, he'd meet the outlaws out in the open so Anna wouldn't be in danger. Then, when they were dead or in jail, he'd ride back and linger for a week in that funny little tent inside a building.

It was almost dawn, but he could still feel her against him. The woman had climbed into his blood and was pumping through every part of his body. He didn't want to marry her and have kids and settle down. He wanted to make love to her until they both died of hunger. He wanted to touch her all night long and wake her again and again with passion. He wanted to be so deep inside her he stepped out of this world.

McCord was so lost in his thoughts he almost missed the glint of sunlight off a rifle. The bullet came within a foot of his head as he dove off his horse.

He rolled into the brush, both guns ready and waiting. Nothing.

An hour passed. Not a sound. Frank Sanders was playing with him. The idea that McCord had escaped and taken another witness with him must have infuriated the gambler. Thorn and Sanders planned to pay him back by making him sweat awhile before they killed him. McCord wondered if the horse he'd heard riding past while he and Anna hid in the rocks that first night had been ridden by Frank. After he killed the others at the station, the gambler might have raced after them, knowing he'd be in real trouble if he failed Thorn by not finding the letter *and* by letting witnesses live.

McCord burrowed in and waited out the day, determined not to give the gambler any chance to fire again.

At dusk, he climbed on his horse and rode out before even the stars offered light. He'd have to be more careful, but when his job was done, he would track the gambler down.

By sunup McCord and his horse were safely away, miles to the north of where he'd been shot at. The Ranger needed a few hours' sleep and then he had to think. The letter in his boot was due by the end of the week to an Indian agent deep in the territory. He could make the ride in two days on a good horse. The question was, did he deliver it first, then find Frank, or try to find the gambler first, then burn leather to make it to the agent in time?

Only one answer came to mind. The outlaw could wait

a few days to be arrested; the letter had to be delivered. Hundreds of lives might be saved if the agent could put the governor's plan into action.

Splashing across the Cimarron River, he entered the rolling hills of Indian Territory. The outlaws wouldn't follow him this far. Once he was out of Thorn and his mens' rifle range, he could ride hard toward Medicine Lodge on the Salt Fork, where the agent was reportedly staying.

Anna was safe at the camp, surrounded by a hundred armed men, and with luck he'd be back in time to catch Thorn's whole gang before they caused any more harm.

Chapter 7

Annalane spent her first few days in camp setting up the long, narrow room at the front of the infirmary to serve as a doctor's office and operating room. She wasn't sure if it was curiosity, or the long absence of an infirmary in camp, but people dropped by to help and to complain about small ailments. Two of the three women in camp were pregnant and happy to see someone they could talk to.

Her brother walked in on the third day to nod his approval at the job she was doing. Shelves filled with organized and labeled supplies lined the wall. He talked of his excitement at being posted at his first fort, but said little about medicine. When she asked a few questions about where to put tools, he seemed unsure. She knew medical school was mostly two terms of lectures and some work on cadavers if students could afford them, but she was shocked at his lack of knowledge. A nurse, a week into training knew the names of medical supplies.

Before she could begin to ask more questions or suggest he might help set up his own office, Devin announced, "I'll be riding back along the stage line to inform the owners of their loss of employees. Not that it's the army's fault—we warned them not to try a run this far north. Teamster wagon trains a hundred long were safe enough to move from fort to fort, but it is far too early to even think about establishing a stage line." He pointed at her. "You were a fool to take a stage. You should have waited at Dodge until supply wagons with guards could have delivered you."

She hated the way he talked down to her, never thinking to ask if she'd had enough money to wait in Dodge. Before she could fire back, he stormed toward the door.

Glancing back, he added, "I'm assuming you can handle everything here while I'm gone."

"How long will that be?" Annalane asked, thinking one, maybe two days there and the same back should do it. What if the camp needed a doctor while he was gone? She wondered if her little brother had yet had his hands covered in warm blood. She doubted it. Being a doctor to him was more theory and grandeur than reality.

"I'll be gone a week," he said without meeting her gaze. "Maybe more. I have army business to take care of that doesn't concern you."

She straightened. "Devin, I'm here to help you, not do all the work. Don't you dare treat me like your servant."

He frowned. "Or what? Or you'll pack up and leave? Go ahead. You've never been much good at staying around. I doubt if it ever occurred to you that all those years during the war your family might have needed you around. Times were hard then, you know." For a moment he looked like the boy she remembered and not the man before her.

Annalane fought down words she knew she'd regret saying. She didn't have the funds to go anywhere and he was well aware of the fact. She might be able to make it back to Fort Worth, or even Austin, but then she'd be penniless, looking for a job. She wanted to also point out that if he thought it was hard at home, he should have tried being at the battles.

But she wouldn't tell him. That was the past. Hopefully he'd never know war, and in time her memories would fade.

When she didn't snap back, he softened slightly. "Look, sis, I know it's hard on you, but you're used to hard times. I want to help you, I really do. My plan is simple. Help me set up this place and get it started, then maybe one of the single officers will see how useful you are to have around. Lieutenant Dodson is a widower with three kids and having a hell of a time. If you play your cards right, you could be married to him by Christmas and have a man to take care of you."

"You're delusional." Who would take care of Dodson . . . and the three children . . . and the house . . . and . . . She frowned, knowing her brother would never understand that marriage is *not* a ticket out of work.

Devin laughed. "Come on, Annalane, you need a husband and Dodson can't afford to be too picky. It might not be a marriage of love like you and your first love thought you had nine years ago, but it would be practical. He's been in the army for over ten years, so he's made of sturdier stuff than the kid you called husband for an hour."

Annalane fought the urge to slap her only kin. If Sergeant Cunningham hadn't walked through the door, she might have. Devin had always been spoiled as a child and he hadn't changed much.

Cunningham saluted Devin, then addressed her. "I'm sorry to bother you this early, but I've been sent to tell you or the doctor that Private Price's wife is going into labor and everyone in camp knows Victoria is a screamer when she's not happy."

Devin headed for the door. "Take care of it, Annalane. I've got men waiting for me. Surely even you can handle a birthing." He was gone before she could answer.

Annalane grabbed a basket she'd put supplies in and shoved it toward the sergeant. "Let's go. Babies don't wait."

Cunningham led the way. "Did your brother ever deliver a baby?"

"Not that I know of," she answered, aware that most of Devin's experience had probably been on corpses.

"That's what I figured. He looked a might pale. How about you?"

"I've delivered a dozen or more near battlefields. Wives wanting to see their men one more time before the baby came." They moved through the tents and corrals along the outside of a wooden stockade that held supplies, as she added, "The hospital where I worked only treated veterans, but some women didn't know that until they arrived, already in hard labor. We kept a room ready for emergencies like that. Over the four years I was there, I welcomed many a life into this world and helped the mother mourn the passing of a few wee ones who didn't make the crossing."

The sergeant smiled. "Mrs. Price will be real happy you're here. She didn't much like the idea of having the doc come. She tried to talk to your brother last week about how to prepare, her being still two years from twenty and all. He told her she had no business following her man into unsettled territory and should try to make it home before she went into labor."

Annalane thought that sounded exactly like what Devin would say. She stepped into one of the new two-room cabins built for married men. The smell of fresh-cut wood greeted her, along with the sound of a woman crying for help. She sounded far more frightened than in pain.

"Set the supplies down, please, Sergeant. I'll need a stack of towels and a large washtub, cleaned and scrubbed with soap and hot water." She passed a man standing at the bedroom door, looking like he might pass out at any moment. "And, Sergeant, take Private Price with you."

Sergeant Cunningham followed orders.

Annalane moved to the bed already stained with blood. "I'm here to help, Victoria, so don't you worry. Together we're going to deliver this baby."

A girl not out of her teens looked up, wide-eyed and near panic. "I don't know what to do," she shouted, as if Annalane might be deaf.

"I do," Annalane answered. "You can call me Anna. I'll help you through each step. We're going to climb this mountain one step at a time." She pulled a small pair of scissors from her apron pocket. "First, I'm going to place these under the bed right below you. My grandmother used to tell me they will cut the pain in half for the rest of your labor." Annalane smiled, realizing the girl believed her. "And when the baby comes, I'll know right where the scissors are when it's time to cut the cord. Now, Victoria, the first thing I want you to do is lean back and relax. When the next contraction comes take deep, slow breaths and let the tightness roll over you, knowing that it's not pain, but just your body practicing for the job it's got to do."

The girl followed orders and Annalane did her job. Nine hours later, she carried a newborn son to the private, who still looked like he might pass out. He kissed the top of his son's head, then walked into the bedroom.

"You did a fine job, Anna." Sergeant Cunningham smiled.

She collected the stained towels and sheets. "She did all the work. I only helped."

When Anna got back to the infirmary, a meal was waiting for her. She hadn't expected her first duty to be delivering a baby, but she was glad. It reminded her of why she loved nursing. Not the dying and hurting, but the healing and helping.

She was almost asleep in her chair when someone stepped into the little clinic.

"I beg your pardon. Is it too late to call?"

Anna stood. "Lieutenant Dodson?" He was not a big man, in size or manner. She would have had to slump to be eye to eye with him, and Anna refused to slump. Despite what her brother thought, she wasn't interested in a man who planned to consider her because he "couldn't afford to be picky." "Is there something I can do for you, sir?"

His gaze darted over her as if taking her measure. She saw intelligence, but not kindness.

"I heard what you did today and I commend you," he began formally, then rolled his shoulders, forcing himself to relax. "I lost my wife to childbirth last year, so I know what a trial it is. My children are in Kansas City with her folks while I finish this tour, then I hope to have them back with me."

"You must miss them," Anna said, watching him closely, wondering why he'd come so late.

"It's not that, ma'am. It's the fact that they belong with me. I'm their father." He frowned. "I know I'm a military man, but I've always believed a wife belongs with her husband, and the children should be raised and disciplined by their parents. There is an order to things, in and out of the army."

"I see," she said, then waited for him to explain why he'd dropped by.

He glanced around the office, frowning at the piles of supplies still remaining to be organized, then continued. "I planned to ask you to dine with the officers tonight, but I see you've already eaten."

"Thank you, Lieutenant, but you needn't worry about me. I'll be fine here." She'd found the officers' dinner boring. "I prefer to eat my evening meal in silence. It's become my habit over the years."

"You are a woman too long alone." He said the words

slowly, as if he thought they might frighten her. "And this is not a country for women alone. It's the nature of things that men and women should be married. If not for love, then for convenience."

"I've been on my own since I was nineteen." She met his stare. If he expected her to be helpless and needy, he was about to be disappointed. "Now if you'll excuse me, I think I'll turn in."

He puffed up slightly, as if not used to anyone dismissing him. Then he nodded once and mumbled good night.

Anna stood in the doorway watching him walk away, but her thoughts were on Ranger McCord, not the lieutenant. If Wynn had stepped into her quarters, he would not have left without touching her, and one touch would have made all her exhaustion vanish. He'd told her that what was between them was not finished, and she agreed. He might bruise her lips with his kisses and hold her so close to him she couldn't breathe, but she knew he was attracted to her, he wanted her, needed her. There was no "convenience" in his passionate touch.

Dodson seemed about to propose a business arrangement. He hadn't even taken the time to get to know her. Anna had the feeling that, in his mind, any woman would do.

Anna would never settle for so little. She'd rather have one honest day with Wynn McCord than a lifetime of convenience.

"Miss Anna?" Private Clark's voice sounded from the other side of the porch. "Just wanted you to know that I'm on guard tonight. I'll put my bedroll in front of your door once you're inside so you won't have to worry about anyone else coming along just to visit."

She smiled. Clark was a good kid. He would have to be, for all the Texans to accept him. "Thanks," she answered. "I'm going to turn in soon, but thought I might circle the camp once to get some air." The smell of blood still lingered in her lungs. "Would you mind walking with me?"

"I'd be honored," he answered as he set his rifle just inside her door threshold before offering his elbow. He didn't seem to notice that her hair was a mess and she still wore the stained apron she'd had on all day.

She tucked her hand on his arm and they walked, talking quietly as the sun set. The camp was like an ant bed of activity with movement tonight. Someday, if the camp grew into a fort, the place would be surrounded by walls, but now most of the buildings and tents circled the stockade of supplies. Teamsters had brought in a line of wagons and everyone seemed to be helping with the unloading.

She watched the movements but spoke low to Clark. "You were listening to what the lieutenant said to me." It was a statement, not a question.

"It was hard not to. The door was open," Clark said, defending himself.

Anna smiled. "I got the feeling he'd come to ask me something."

Clark laughed. "I swore I heard the trap door about to fall, but you played it smart."

"Maybe we're just guessing what he wanted. Maybe he just came to thank me for helping with the birthing."

"Maybe," Clark answered. "My guess is he didn't know about McCord or he wouldn't have even been hinting."

She stopped walking and looked at the kid. "What about McCord?"

"He's your man. All the enlisted men know it. I'm surprised the officers don't."

Anna had to ask. "How do they know it?" She couldn't imagine McCord talking about their time together.

"McCord told us before he left. He said every one of

us better keep an eye on his Anna or there'd be hell to pay when he got back."

Anna started walking again, pulling the private along beside her. "I'm not his Anna and he's not my man."

"Yes, ma'am," Clark said as he fell into step beside her. "He also said not to argue with you no matter what crazy thing you said."

"Oh, he did," Anna said, more to herself than the kid. She wanted to get home and think about what Clark had told her, then decide whether to kill McCord when he came back. A few kisses and touches did not define ownership, even if those kisses still filled her dreams at night and the memory of his touch still warmed her each time she thought of it.

When they stepped back into the infirmary, she noticed Clark's rifle was missing beside the door, a moment before she saw two men standing in the shadows. Clark's muscles beneath her hand tightened, and she prayed the kid wouldn't go for his Colt. Maybe they should have locked the door before leaving, but they'd both felt safe inside the circle of the military.

"Evening," one stranger said as he stepped forward, a rifle pointed at Clark's chest. "We've come to ask you, lady, if you'd like to take a ride with us." He smiled, showing rotting teeth in a face weeks past needing washing. "There's a gambler who says he has a little game to finish with you. He says you ran out on him before all the cards were on the table."

The stranger laughed as if pleased with his politeness, then glared at Clark. "I guess you're coming too. If we kill you it'll draw attention, and I'd like to ride out of here the same way I rode in. Unnoticed. A soldier riding along with us will make us look all the more legal."

Anna panicked. "No. Tie him up and I'll go with you without a sound." She guessed they'd kill Clark when they were far enough away from the camp that no one would hear the shot.

"No," Clark answered calmly, his eyes staring at the man without any fear showing. "I go with her. I'm her guard. If I'm not outside someone will come check on her, but if we're both missing they'll think we're somewhere in camp."

Anna closed her eyes, wishing he wouldn't be so logical. He was signing his own death warrant.

The second stranger, a bookend of the first outlaw, moved out from the shadows. He had the same wide-rimmed hat that his partner wore, but his clothes were buckskin, not wool. If possible, he looked even meaner than the first, with a touch of insanity flickering in his whiskey-colored eyes. Both were men who would not be welcome in anyone's home. Something about them seemed more animal than human.

Clark raised his hands as the men took the Colt at his side and tied his hands.

"That's the way, boy," the first outlaw whispered. "Come with us nice and easy and we'll make the end quick for you."

The mad twin tied her, spitting out a giggle when his hand kept slipping to brush against her. He was having so much fun, he didn't notice when she twisted her wrist wide as he pulled the knot.

"Where are you taking us?" Anna demanded.

"Luther and me ain't got no orders to kill you, if that's what you're asking. We're just planning on delivering you."

Anna decided the smart one was dumb as a cow patty and his partner, Luther, smelled worse than one. When she opened her mouth to ask more, Luther wrapped a dirty bandana across it.

"Make a sound," the leader added, "and we kill your bodyguard. We weren't told to bring him along anyway, so if one of our knives happens to slip between his ribs we know it won't matter one way or the other to the boss."

Anna had no doubt he meant what he said. Luther pulled a long knife and began poking them with it.

While the leader waited and watched for full dark, Luther pressed the point of the knife against her throat and giggled when he drew a drop of blood.

Anna stood perfectly still, refusing to move or cry out. She knew she couldn't get away if he wanted to kill her, but she wouldn't play his game.

Each cut drew one bubble of blood. Two, three, four pricks. Luther watched each drop slide down her throat and melt into the lace of her collar.

"It's dark enough," the leader whispered as he shoved Clark and her out of the infirmary and around to the back where they'd left horses tied. A small wagon train of settlers had been picking up supplies before dark and the outlaws had no problem blending in among the other visitors.

Anna forced her mind to notice every detail as she dug her heel hard into the ground before they lifted her onto the horse. The outlaws had brought two extra horses. She knew they hadn't planned on Clark, so the other mount would have been for McCord.

She smiled. It had been three days since McCord left. If they expected to pick him up here, then they hadn't caught, or killed him. He was alive and she had no doubt he'd be coming after her.

All she had to do was stay alive until he reached her.

Chapter 8

Ranger McCord delivered the letter to the Quaker in charge of the territory. He stood, forgotten, as the man read suggestions from the governor of Texas. McCord could tell by the way he folded the letter away that the Indian agent didn't plan to put any new policies into action. The Indian Wars, which had been raging for thirty years in Texas, Kansas, and New Mexico, would continue. He'd ridden all this way and risked his life for nothing.

Thorn and his men wanted the trouble to continue, so they could play off both sides. Now they had won, not by interfering, but by the indifference of one man.

The Quaker looked up as if just remembering Wynn was in the room. "Thank you for delivering this," he said in a tired voice. "I have no reply."

Wynn backed out of the office and walked to his horse. He'd planned to find a meal and a bed for the night, but all he wanted to do was get back to Anna. She'd never left his thoughts. The possibility of asking her to marry him crossed his mind more often than he wanted to admit. He had a good-sized spread from a land grant his father bought fifty years ago. They could settle down in south Texas where things were calm and be hundreds of miles away from the fort line where trouble blew in with every new wind. Behind the line of forts a man could raise his family and worry about crops but here life was never easy.

He didn't want her to just let him in when he came back. He felt a hunger for something that might fill a hole in his heart that he'd been ignoring since the war. For the first time in more years than he could remember, Wynn wanted to stay.

Smiling, he wondered if she wouldn't mind wearing a ring and a gag. He'd never get used to that accent of hers. If he could just keep the woman quiet, she'd be darn near perfect. He didn't even care if she could cook. Hell, he'd been eating his own grub for so long, any food that didn't crawl off the plate looked good to him.

McCord swung into the saddle. He'd trade mounts at the edge of camp and make a few hours of hard riding before he slept. With luck he'd be back to Anna in two days.

As he always did, his mind focused on his goal and he rode hard with little food or sleep. Only this time he didn't feel like he was running away from something. This time he was riding toward her.

He was three hours out of Camp Supply when he saw soldiers riding fast. Wynn knew who they were by the way they sat their saddles. Seasoned soldiers, Cunningham and the two other Texans.

The men pulled their mounts up when they reached McCord, but only Sergeant Cunningham stepped down.

McCord slowly swung from the saddle, knowing something was wrong when his friend didn't smile. "What is it, Dirk?"

Cunningham didn't waste words. "From the markings, two men, probably part of Thorn's gang, took Anna and Private Clark at gunpoint two nights ago. We've been trailing them since dawn yesterday."

McCord didn't move, but inside he felt his entire body take the news like a blow.

"Captain's had every man out on patrol looking. We got lucky and picked up fresh sign this morning. Spotted a woman's footprint out back behind the infirmary yesterday as we left. About the time we figured we'd lost them for good, we spotted her print again near a creek bank. From there it was easy to follow the trail of four horses. Every time they stop, your Anna must be stomping around leaving footprints everywhere." He stared at his friend as he told the whole truth. "Along with fresh blood. They're heading due south."

"No body?" McCord said as he checked the cinch on his horse. "Clark's still alive."

Cunningham nodded. "That's my guess."

"Then we'd better get to them fast. Clark's not the one they want, so they'll kill him as soon as possible. I'm surprised he's lasted two days."

"I figure the men who kidnapped them don't do much without orders. So we've got till they get to camp, where the boss is." Cunningham reached for his saddle horn. "Looks like they're heading toward Red Rock Canyon. Once they're there, we'll never find them."

Both men mounted and rode without another word.

It had been a long time since McCord had felt anything, including hate, but he felt it now. He'd kill every one of the outlaws if even one touched Anna. He might have given up on ever being able to love anyone or anything in this lifetime, but he could still hate.

They rode until almost dark before they spotted movement ahead of them. Then, without a word, Cunningham signaled and the four men spread out, leaving no trail of dust big enough to notice if one of the outlaws glanced back.

McCord took the center, riding in the open, daring them to look back. He rode fast, but not full-out; he had to give the others time to move into place. As he climbed, he closed in on four riders, one in what looked like a blue dress. Anna, he thought. His Anna.

One outlaw led the line, pulling the two captives behind him. The other outlaw rode drag, but he wasn't on guard like he should have been. Not once did he look back, and from what McCord could see he held no weapon at the ready.

The captive next to Anna slumped in his saddle. It had to be Clark, but he was either asleep or hurt.

When they crossed over a ridge, McCord saw that the outlaws were moving toward two men camped out near a stream in the bottom of a shallow canyon. Both men were waiting, watching the riders approach. If they'd looked beyond the riders, they might have seen McCord in the long shadows, following.

He waited as the day aged and the outlaws slowly wound their way around rocks and streams toward the camp.

In the campfire light McCord swore one of the men had to be the gambler. He even noticed the flicker of gold from the watch chain on the gambler's vest. The other man in camp was tall and dressed in black. If this was an outlaw camp there would be one, maybe two men in the shadows on guard, but the Ranger had no time to worry about them now. Anna's and Clark's lives might be measured in minutes.

McCord knew his part. He could go no closer without the men in camp seeing him, and when they did he needed to be ready. He drew both his Colts, not bothering with the rifle, circled the reins around his saddle horn, and kicked the tired horse into a full run. With Anna and Clark halfway between him and the camp, Wynn knew he'd reach her long before the outlaws could make it to the others watching from the shadows.

The minute the outlaws, with their captives in tow,

spotted him, McCord opened fire. He hit the man leading the two prisoners with his first shot. The other outlaw grabbed at the rope on Anna's horse. Clark shouted something as he tumbled off his horse, hands still tied behind his back. A second later, Anna also tumbled and rolled from a horse gone wild from the noise.

The outlaw with Anna was so busy fighting to control the horses he didn't notice that he'd lost his captives. Both men at the camp grabbed their weapons and shouted orders.

Suddenly, shots exploded from every direction. The men standing at the camp jerked in a fatal dance with bullets. The outlaw on horseback tried to ride away.

A dozen more shots rattled across the sky and then the night fell silent. Both men at the campsite lay dead. The mounted outlaw screamed as his horse bolted, and tumbled. One of his feet remained in the stirrup dragging him behind his horse. One shot from somewhere left of McCord silenced the screams, but the outlaw's body still bounced over rocks as the horse ran.

The screams and the last shot echoed into the canyon until they were only whispers on the wind. McCord took a deep breath. He'd felt the peace after a battle many times. One more time he'd survived, but tonight his thoughts were for another.

McCord holstered his guns and headed toward Anna. He found her sitting beside Clark, wrapping what was left of her apron around the kid's arm. Both of them smiled as he neared.

"She said you'd come," Clark groaned. "Drove the two fellows crazy with her threats of what you'd do to them when you came."

McCord didn't look at her; he couldn't, not yet, not till he knew it was over. "You all right, kid?"

"I'm fine. They shot me in the right arm this morning

because I told them I was a crack shot. But Anna made them let her bandage it. She says I'm lucky the bullet went right through."

McCord saw Cunningham and his men moving into the campsite, making sure the others were dead.

Clark's voice shook a little. "They told us they were going to hang us tonight, then gut us like we was fresh game. They knew you'd be coming and they figured when you found our bodies, you'd be foolish enough to do something stupid."

Anna stood. "Which you did." Fists on her hips, she faced him. "You rode straight in here like a madman. It's a wonder you don't have four bullets in your chest." Her voice was fired with anger. "When I saw you barreling straight toward us, Wynn McCord, I almost had a heart attack."

McCord finally looked at her. "Startled men don't take the time to aim. I knew I could kill one, maybe two before they'd get a shot close to me. I was giving the sergeant and his men time to step out and open fire from other directions." He hesitated, fighting down a smile over her finally using his first name. Damn, if she wasn't adorable all covered in dirt and twigs. "Glad to see you, Anna."

When she straightened up as if planning to give him a lecture on being careful, he raised his hands in surrender and closed the distance between them. He couldn't very well grab her and kiss her in front of the other men, but he could at least get close.

The click of a rifle cocking sounded from somewhere in the night. It had to be the lookout the outlaws posted. The outlaw McCord had forgotten might be hidden in the night.

He dove at Anna, knocking her down a second before the bullet meant for her blasted into his back. He felt her beneath him, then pain exploded all other thought. The last thing he heard was another round being fired. He waited for the second bullet to hit, but before he realized it hadn't been meant for him, blackness washed over him, carrying him under like a huge wave.

In the silence of dying, he drifted back to the battlefield years ago when he'd fallen. The arms of the nurse who'd stopped to help him circled him and whispered, "You're going to be all right, soldier. You're not going to die."

Only this time McCord knew she was wrong. He'd finally drawn the short card.

Chapter 9

Anna frantically bandaged the Ranger, trying to slow the bleeding as the others built a travois to pull him home.

"Don't you die on me, Wynn. Don't you dare die on me."

He didn't respond.

Angry, she continued. "I don't care if my voice irritates you. You're not going to die. Do you hear me? You're not going to die."

Blood soaked the strips of cotton that had once been her underskirt. She pulled the bandage tighter, hoping to keep the blood from flowing out the hole in his back. When the men came to lift him onto the travois, she followed a step behind, giving unneeded orders for them to be careful.

Once they were moving, Sergeant Cunningham ordered one of his men to ride ahead with her and Clark. With luck they could be back in camp by dawn.

She didn't want to leave her Ranger, but Anna saw the logic. She hadn't sat a horse since her days as an army nurse, but she hadn't forgotten how to ride hard, and Clark, despite his wound, rode as easy as he walked. McCord's wound was too deep to risk traveling fast, and Clark's arm still needed proper care or the infection could kill him. The practical side of her she'd always depended on overruled her heart.

Clark signaled that he was ready and they were off. They rode fast across flat land, with only the moon for light, and reached the camp at first light. Anna swore half the garrison turned out to help.

While she cleaned up, three men washed a few layers of dirt off Clark. Another lit a fire in the examining room and spread out a buffalo hide on the table for the Ranger.

Anna doctored and bandaged Clark's arm with the room-ful of men watching. They groaned with the kid, like mid-wives at their first birthing. Anna grinned at Clark, guessing he was complaining more than necessary just to hear the echo.

As she wrapped the wound, one of the men who'd ridden with Cunningham asked Clark, "How'd you shoot that one hiding in the shadows without your firing arm?"

Clark thought for a moment, then started slowly into a story he knew he'd tell more than once. "When I heard the shot coming out of the night, I grabbed a rifle lying in the dust. The bandit, who'd been riding behind us all day yelling obscenities, must have dropped it when he was knocked out of the saddle. I raised it toward where I'd seen the flash of fire. It was so black I couldn't see anything but his eyes. I just shot between them."

"With your left hand?"

"My father always said, 'You got two, might as well learn to shoot with them both.'" Clark smiled. "I didn't want to mention that to the outlaws earlier. Thought they might decide to blast away at my left arm as well."

Anna smiled, doubting any of the men would call Clark a boy again. He had a wound he'd heal from and a story he might live to tell his grandchildren. He'd not only killed an outlaw, he'd saved other lives. If he hadn't fired when he did, the outlaw would have picked them off one by one.

Everyone fell silent as Sergeant Cunningham and one of his men arrived with the Ranger. There would be no laughter, no telling of stories now. A Texas Ranger was down.

They placed him on the buffalo hide, face down. He didn't make a sound. Then the men stepped back and watched as Anna cut off his shirt with shaking hands. Blood seemed to be everywhere.

Cunningham and one of the others she didn't know stepped up to help. Both took orders from her as if she were a general. They could make him comfortable, clean him up a little, but then it would be up to her.

When the Ranger's star hit the floor, everyone froze.

Anna took a step and picked it up. She shoved it into her apron pocket. "I'll keep this safe for McCord until he needs it again."

No one believed he ever would, but they all nodded as if agreeing that she should be the one to keep it safe.

When Anna had the wound cleaned, Cunningham seemed to think it was time for the audience to leave. He ordered everyone out except Clark, who'd fallen asleep in the corner.

Anna set to work, doing what she knew best. Years of working under all kinds of conditions kept her hands steady. She'd done her job when cannon fire still filled the air, when it was so cold that bloody bandages froze on the wounds, when sleep was a luxury she couldn't afford. She could do what had to be done now.

"Listen to me," she whispered to McCord as she worked. "You're going to live. You're going to come back. I don't care if you like my accent or not, you've got to hear me. You've got to come back to me."

Sergeant Cunningham returned with whiskey he claimed was for McCord when he woke up. Anna hardly noticed the sergeant moving around the room trying to find a comfortable spot. She talked only to Wynn as she worked, telling him everything she was doing and what kind of scar he'd have when she was finished. Over and over, she said, "You're going to make it through this. Hang in there. You're going to be good as new once you heal."

Finally, when she leaned back to rest her back a moment, the sergeant placed his hand on her shoulder. "He'll come back to you, Anna." He barked out a laugh. "Hell, if a fine woman like you ordered me to, I'd come back from hell itself, and I reckon McCord feels the same way."

An hour passed. Cunningham began sampling the whiskey. Clark slept on a cot in the corner, snoring away. Anna worked, with memories of a hundred hospital camps after a hundred battles floating in her mind. All of the horror she'd worked through, all the exhaustion, all of the skills she'd learned, all boiled down to this day, this time, this man.

If she could save him, all the years would be worth it.

"I'm never giving up on you, Wynn, so you might as well decide to live because I'm not letting you die," she whispered. "I hear Rangers are made of iron. Well, you'd better be. You're going to come out of this. Hear me good."

Finally she finished and wrapped the wound where a bullet had dug its way across Wynn's back. He'd lost so much blood she was surprised he was still breathing, but she could feel the slow rise and fall of his chest and the warmth of his skin against her touch.

Exhausted, she pulled a stool beside the table and leaned her face near his. "You're going to be all right, soldier. Hang on. I'm not going to let you die." Her fingers dug into his hair and made a fist. "I'm expecting you to come knocking on my door one day, and when you do you might as well plan on staying because I don't think I can let you go."

She fell asleep in the middle of a sentence, with McCord's shallow breath brushing her cheek.

In what seemed like minutes, someone woke her to tell her breakfast was ready. It took her a minute to realize that twenty-four hours had passed since they'd brought McCord in.

Anna left her meal untouched as she walked around Wynn, checking the wound, feeling his skin for fever. Wishing he'd open his eyes.

Finally, at Cunningham's insistence, she ate a few bites and drank a cup of tea. Clark ate everything in sight. Men took over the sergeant's watch by the door so he could get some sleep, and the day passed in silence.

Lieutenant Dodson tapped on the open door to the office just before dark. He waited until she nodded for him to enter, then removed his hat. She had no doubt he'd heard about what had happened, probably including small details like how she'd stabbed one of the outlaws with her scissors when he'd tried to tie her hands after she'd pulled free. Hopefully Clark had left out the ways the outlaw called Luther had threatened to rape her before they killed her. The words he'd used still made her cheeks burn.

Pushing aside the memory, she stared at the pale officer her brother had said couldn't afford to be too picky in finding a wife. That dinner her first night in camp seemed more like a hundred years ago rather than just a week.

Lieutenant Dodson began talking as if giving a speech. Anna barely followed along. The man liked to hear his own voice.

Anna didn't say much. Dodson had been politely cold to her both times they'd met and had obviously seen her only as a possible solution to *his* problem. Now he seemed to look at her quite differently. He even told her he had always admired tall women who could carry themselves well. It appeared, since she'd survived a kidnapping, her value had gone up in his eyes.

The change in the lieutenant bothered Anna far more than his flattery did. She was glad when the sergeant showed up for his nightly guard duty before Dodson lied and said that she was pretty. Anna had always known she was simply plain.

She didn't want to hear words she knew weren't sincere; she wanted to see the way a man felt in his face, and read the truth of his compliments in a touch.

All in all, she'd been lucky: two men in her life had been blind enough to see her as beautiful. One had been young and in love with love. The other lay on the table before her. She had no doubt, despite their shortsightedness, that both men had believed every word they said.

The lieutenant invited her to dine with him and Anna declined. She didn't even give a reason. She just said, "No, thank you."

The moment he'd gone, Cunningham closed the door. "Anna," he began in his slow, polite way that hinted they'd been friends for years and not days. "You need to get some sleep. I'll stay awake tonight and if McCord so much as twitches, I'll yell out for you. With the tent so close you'll probably hear him anyway."

Anna shook her head. "I'd like to have a proper bath and a clean change of clothes, but after that, I'll be back."

Cunningham looked like he thought it would be a waste of time to argue.

Chapter 10

McCord felt his body moving through layers of muddy water, floating slowly to the surface. He forced himself to take a deep breath and swore he smelled buffalo. He hated buffalo. Orneriest creatures God ever made. The only thing worse than having them roam over the plains, eating every blade of grass for miles, was seeing the thousands of carcasses rotting after the hunters shot them.

He tried to swallow, but couldn't. His mouth felt like it was packed with sand.

Opening one eye, he noticed he was lying on what looked like a buffalo hide, and just beyond that was a mass of midnight hair. "Anna," he whispered.

She raised her head and looked at him with eyes heavy with sleep. Her mouth opened slightly in surprise. "Wynn," she whispered, as if she'd just been dreaming of him.

She looked delicious. He moved to kiss her and felt the stab of a dozen knives in his back.

"Don't move," she ordered, her hand on his shoulder.

Memories came back with the pain. The feel of her beneath him a moment before fire crossed his back. Floating in darkness, unable to open his eyes. The sound of her voice constantly talking to him, pulling him closer to shore, not letting him sink away from the pain . . . away from life.

He closed his eyes and tried to think. Maybe he had died. It would be just his luck that hell would be full of Yankees and they'd all be talking.

He opened one eye again. No. He was alive and Anna was sitting beside him. He caught her fingers when she touched his hand, gripping tight, needing to know that she was real. Almost losing her had tortured his mind for days, and when he'd watched her fall off the horse he swore his heart stopped until he saw her rolling on the ground.

The fingers of her free hand brushed through his hair. "You're going to be all right, Wynn. Just rest. You've lost a lot of blood. Sleep now."

He smiled and closed his eyes, thinking of how he liked the way she said his first name. He hadn't heard a woman say his name in years.

When he woke again, morning shone through the windows, but the face in front of him was Dirk Cunningham's. The sergeant looked tired, but a smile spread from ear to ear.

"'Morning," the sergeant said. "You look terrible."

McCord groaned. "Where's Anna?"

Cunningham laughed. "She'll be back. I'm not surprised that my face wasn't the one you wanted to wake up to, but you could at least act like you're glad to see me. Anna said if you wake I'm to roll you over like you was a newborn and prop you up."

McCord swore as Dirk lifted his shoulders off the buffalo hide.

"Stop your complaining. I ain't never said I was a nurse."

"That's an understatement," McCord managed as soon as the pain subsided enough for him to breathe. "Where is Anna?" Somewhere in his dreams he'd thought he heard someone ask her to dinner.

"She went to tell the cook how to make broth for you.

He sent some over that Clark and me thought was fine, but she said it wasn't near thick enough." Cunningham shook his head. "That woman's been giving more orders than the captain and, unlike the orders we usually get from him, every man on the place does what she asks."

McCord wasn't surprised. She'd ordered him to come back from the dead, and he'd done so for fear she'd follow him down and spend eternity complaining that he didn't listen.

"I swear," Cunningham mumbled. "I have a hard time believing that woman don't fight for slavery. She's a natural master."

They both laughed. They'd never had slaves or believed in owning slaves. Like most Texans, they'd fought for Texas rights and it had cost both dearly. If either had anyone close to them they wouldn't be doing such a dangerous job. McCord had been alone so long he barely remembered how it felt to have family. The war had left him with nothing but land that had gone wild in the years he'd been gone, and no one who cared.

McCord forced down the pain in his back and his heart. "How long have I been out?"

"Three days, and she's barely left your side."

"I know," he answered. Every time he'd come close to waking, he'd known she was beside him.

Cunningham offered him whiskey, but he declined. "Water," he said.

The sergeant frowned. "I don't know about that. With all the holes in you, you're liable to spring a leak." He poured a cup of water and held it while McCord drank.

When he finished he asked, "What happened after . . ."

Cunningham knew what he wanted to know. "A dozen of the boys went back for the bodies. Both the men who kidnapped Clark and Anna were dead. The gambler's body and the man on watch, who Clark shot, were easy to recognize, but the man in black is a mystery. We brought the bodies back to the camp, but no one seems to be able to identify him. He could have been Thorn, who headed up the gang. From what I've heard about the man, he might have come alone, thinking he'd have time to torture Anna before the gambler killed her."

Anna entered, ending the conversation. She smiled when she saw McCord propped up.

The sergeant stood away from the table and showed the patient off. "I did what you said. I turned him over. He may look like trampled death, but he's well enough to complain about my nursing skills."

"She can see that," McCord grumbled. "Mind getting me a shirt from my pack in the barracks?"

Cunningham frowned. He didn't seem to like the idea of leaving. "Oh, all right, but she's been looking at that hairy chest of yours for days."

"And take your time," McCord said to Cunningham's back.

The sergeant nodded as he moved to the door. "I should have known you'd wake up meaner than a wet snake. You got no gratitude in your bones, McCord. If it weren't for knowing you'd do the same for me, I'd have left your bloody body out there in the middle of nowhere." He closed the door, still complaining.

Anna's eyebrows pushed together. "Aren't you going to thank him?" She set the soup beside his bed.

"He knows I'm grateful and he's right—I would do the same for him."

"It never hurts to say the words, Wynn." She pulled a chair beside his bed and picked up the spoon as if she thought he'd let her feed him.

McCord watched her, thinking how proper she looked. "Is that why you kept talking to me when I was near death, Anna? You thought there were words that needed saying?"

"I guess." She didn't look up at him.

"I don't know if I heard everything, but I remember you telling me over and over to stay." He took a drink of water and waited for her to say something. When she didn't, he added, "You commanded me to come back, not just from death, but to you."

She set the spoon down and laced her fingers, but still did not look up.

He saw the red burning across her cheeks, but he didn't stop. "You said when I came back to you it would be to stay. You told me I belonged with you." He grinned. "I think I even remember you yelling at me one night about how I was your man and I couldn't die unless you said it was all right." He laughed.

His Anna was a strong woman who'd never hesitated to tell him what she thought, but she remained silent now. Maybe she'd never said those words before. Maybe she had thought he was too far gone to have heard. He didn't care. She'd said them and that was all that mattered to him.

"Give me your hand, Anna."

"Why?" She finally met his gaze.

"I want to touch you." When she laid her hand in his, he tugged her toward him.

"You're still very near death." She tried to pull away.

He grinned. "I'm also very near heaven. If touching you kills me, I can think of no better way to die. Unbutton a few buttons on that very proper dress of yours, darlin'. I've been thinking of how soft you feel and how it might taste to kiss my way down your throat again."

"I will not, Wynn McCord!" She twisted free and opened the pot of broth. "I can't believe you'd even ask such a thing."

"I'm thinking more of doing than of asking," he said, still smiling, "and I'm thinking you'll let me too."

She stared at him and he had his answer in the need shining bright in her eyes. Her fingers trembled as she lifted the bowl of soup. "Now, eat your broth or I'll call the sergeant back and he'll pour it down you."

He didn't push touching her. He knew what lay beneath that plain blue dress and he'd wait. He couldn't stop smiling though. She'd been shy with him when she hadn't known where she stood, but the minute he had pulled her close, she knew how he felt. Nothing had changed between them. They both knew he needed her, but she'd come to him on her own terms, and he'd let her take her time.

He didn't move as she sat on the side of the table and began feeding him. Halfway through the meal he watched as the blush came back to her cheeks. She talked of the broth and how good it would be for him, but they were both very much aware that his hand rested on her dress, just above her knee.

He needed her near and she needed his touch, even if they couldn't seem to find the words.

That night when she checked his bandages and made sure he didn't have a fever, his hand slipped beneath her gown and gripped the warm flesh above her knee.

Her breathing quickened as he tugged her knee so he could brush her skin.

"We going to talk about this, Anna?"

She closed her eyes. "No," she whispered.

His grip tightened. "Am I making you feel uncomfortable, or am I hurting you in any way?" His hand moved a few inches higher.

"No."

"I love the feel of you." His touch turned to a caress. "I might not know how to be gentle, but I'll never hurt you."

She looked at him and smiled. "I know."

Then, without him even asking her to, she leaned forward and kissed him.

Chapter 11

That night set a pattern to their lives. She was all the proper nurse in the morning when breakfast was brought in and several of the men came to visit, but after lunch she'd shoo them all away, saying McCord needed his rest. Then, in the silence of the office, she'd sit on the table that was his bed and face him.

Without a word, he'd unbutton her blouse and brush the tips of his fingers over her warm flesh until she finally sighed, leaned forward, and kissed him fully. Anna had no idea if this was the way couples should act. She was far too old to worry about it. All she knew was that McCord loved touching her and she loved being touched.

His injury prevented them from going further, even though Wynn sometimes told her of what he'd like to do with her while she buttoned up her dress and unlocked the door to the late afternoon sun.

He grew stronger every day, and every night he held her a little longer before she moved away to her tent.

Logic told her he was a man without roots or home. The odds were he'd leave her, no matter what she said or how she cried, but when he did, he'd take her heart. She forced herself not to dwell on the future but only to treasure each hour they had.

On their fifth day together, McCord stood and dressed himself. His back was healing. He'd be whole again soon.

She watched as he reached for his Colts, then thought better of putting them on, but she knew a part of this Ranger would never feel completely dressed without the guns strapped around his waist.

"Anna, there's something I need to tell you," he said the first chance they had alone together. "I'm moving to the enlisted men's quarters tonight. Cunningham said he'd help me with my things."

"No," she said, feeling her back stiffen. Just like that, he was leaving her.

He reached for her, but she stepped away and they both knew he couldn't move fast enough to catch her.

He took two steps to the door and pulled the bolt closed. "This may be the last time we have alone for a few days. I'm not sure I'll have the opportunity or the energy to walk all the way across camp tonight."

She moved in front of him. "You're not well. You need to be here. You still need care."

"No, Anna, all I need now is a little time and you. Cunningham is rounding up an old buggy brought in for a wife who'd already left by the time it arrived. I could tie my horse to it and make it out of here. By the end of the week I'll be able to . . ."

A pounding on the door drowned out his words.

"Annalane! Are you all right?" There was no mistaking her brother's rant. "Why in the hell is this door locked? Annalane?"

McCord backed away to sit on the bed, his strength fading.

Anna opened the door. "Welcome back, Devin. Did you get all your business taken care of?"

"Never mind that—what are you doing here locked in my office with a man?"

Anna couldn't help it—she smiled. "Learning about love and all kinds of forbidden things."

Devin didn't buy the answer for one minute. "Stop being ridiculous. I know you weren't doing anything, but you must think of appearances. You might have just been doctoring a dying man, but someone . . ." Devin paused long enough to stare at McCord. "You don't look that sick."

"I'm not sick. I was shot."

Anna could see the dislike in McCord's eyes. If her brother knew how deadly the Ranger could be, Devin would walk more softly. She half expected even an injured McCord to stomp on her brother like he was a bug.

"He saved my life," she said simply.

Devin threw up his hands as he paced like a windup toy. "So what does that mean? Do you think you belong to him for life now?"

McCord smiled at Anna and she forgot all about her brother.

Wynn held out his hand and she walked into his arms. Without looking at her brother, she whispered to the Ranger, "Something like that."

He kissed her lightly. "You're mine, Anna. You have been since I first saw you, and like it or not, I'm yours."

She laughed. "I like it just fine."

"What's been going on here?" Devin yelled, but no one was listening.

Wynn kissed her, spread his hand over her hip and pulled her against him.

"This is outrageous," Devin shouted, then added, "This is unbelievable."

When McCord let her up for air, he said, "I'll go get the buggy. There's no use waiting a few days. Can you be ready in half an hour? I want you leaving with me."

"But you're. . ."

"We'll take it slow and the captain will give us an escort to Texas." He collected his hat and Colts, then turned back to her for one more kiss. As his lips moved away, he whispered, "Come with me, Anna."

Devin was five feet away. Her brother seemed to be gagging on the words he'd just heard.

McCord walked out the door without even looking at Devin.

Anna started to pack. She'd need bandages and blankets for Wynn. No matter what he said, the trip would be hard on him, but she didn't argue. She'd had enough of her brother and nothing sounded better than leaving.

Devin was still yelling and complaining about her deserting him when Cunningham helped her into the buggy. Wynn looked as strong as steel, but McCord noticed his side of the buggy had been padded with blankets.

They pulled out of the camp and headed southwest toward Texas. Everything had happened so fast, Anna just sat and tried to think. Change had always struck like lightning, but this time she'd stepped into the bolt.

Wynn didn't say a word until the guard following them waved and turned back. All at once the world seemed wild and empty and they were alone.

She was alone, she corrected, with a man she barely knew. A man who probably hadn't said a hundred words to her since they'd met.

All panic left when his hand closed gently over hers.

They traveled in silence until almost dark, then he stopped and led the horses to a small clearing where they had a stream for water and grass to graze. She insisted he rest while she made camp and offered him bread and dried meat from a basket one of the men said Clark insisted on putting in the back of the buggy.

Wynn looked tired as he lowered himself onto the blankets,

and by the time she'd packed the food away he was sound asleep.

Anna curled up beside him and slept. At dawn she awoke to his gentle kiss.

He didn't say a word when she mumbled something about being a mess and crossed to the other side of the buggy to straighten her clothing and wash her face with water from the canteen. After she'd combed her hair without a mirror, she faced him.

Wynn had hitched the horse and was waiting for her. He nodded a greeting as if they were little more than strangers. Neither seemed to know what to say. They climbed in the buggy and began following the ribbon of road made by wagons.

As the cloudy day cooled, he touched her leg. "We're going to hit rain," he said, then patted her skirts as if he thought rain might frighten her. "We'll need to make as many miles as we can before it starts."

They raced the weather, but by mid-afternoon the rain caught up to them. Wynn pulled the buggy beneath a stand of old cottonwood trees. They climbed out and he watched the clouds as she retrieved apples from their stash of food. When she handed him an apple, Wynn walked away from her and for one panicked moment she thought he might keep walking. He'd asked her to come with him in a hurried moment, with her brother watching. He'd been right about growing stronger, but had he changed his mind about her?

At the edge of the natural shelter, he turned around and walked back, his head down.

He didn't say a word, but took her hand and pulled her toward a cottonwood, where the air hung still and damp and branches almost touched their heads.

Anna waited. If she had any sense, she'd probably tell him to take her back to the camp. But she didn't want to go back. She wanted to stay with him. He was the first man in years who saw her. Not a woman alone, to be pitied. Not a battle-weary nurse. Not a sister to be passed along to someone else just because he "couldn't afford to be picky."

Wynn McCord *saw* her.

She glared at him now, praying he didn't suggest they turn back.

He put his hands on her shoulders and gently pushed her back against the tree. "I need to say the words, Anna. I need to make it plain between us."

She could barely hear him for rain and the wind and her heart pounding.

"I want you in my life." He stopped, but didn't let her move. "Hell!" he added. "That's not right."

She decided he looked like a man fighting the death penalty, but she guessed anything she said right now would not be welcomed, so she waited.

"That's not right," he repeated.

Tears threatened as she whispered more to herself than to him, "You don't want me in your life?"

"No. I mean yes." He swore. "Facing down outlaws is easier than this." He straightened and stared at her. "You might not guess, but I don't usually talk to a woman, any woman. So let me finish and keep your suggestions to yourself."

Anger flared, but she held her tongue. If he told her to drop her accent, she'd clobber him right here, right now, even if he was injured.

"I don't just want you in my life, Anna." He started again with no softness in his tone. "You are my life. I want you with me here in Texas. In my life and in my bed until we both die of old age. I think I was a walking dead man before you came along. The war took all the caring I had in me. I don't even know if I have enough to give you now. But I'd like to give it a try. I want to fight with you all day and make love to you all night. I want to build a house around you and have a dozen kids and stay in one place for the rest of my days. I want to stay beside you."

Anna understood. "What about what I want?"

He raised an eyebrow.

"Let go of me, McCord."

He pushed away, looking very much like he wanted to fight for her, but the only one to fight stood before him. His eyes narrowed, as if he thought she planned to ask for more than he had to give.

"I want you." She poked him in the chest. "Broken down, hurt, hard as nails, you're still the best man I've ever known. I want you."

A slow grin spread across his face.

She held up her hand. "But I have terms. You have to tell me you love me."

"All right, Anna. I love you." He circled her waist and pulled her closer. "I love every inch of you."

"And."

He didn't let go of her. "I had a feeling there'd be an 'and.'"

"You have to tell me you love me every day."

"I'll tell you and show you. How would that be?" He leaned down to brush his lips along her throat. "Marry me, Anna."

She felt his hands moving over her as if there were no clothes between them.

"Marry me, Anna," he whispered again as he cupped her breast. "I'm not alive without you."

She never said yes. She was too lost in the kiss. When they were both out of breath, he walked her back to the buggy and they continued without a word. He'd said the words she'd needed to hear.

Epilogue

Wynn and Anna McCord built one of the finest cattle ranches in Texas. When she died at the age of seventy-four, her husband and four sons placed her in a grave on the ranch. The stone at her head read, *To my angel, Anna McCord. One more time, "I love you."*

Wynn McCord joined his wife less than a year later. Everyone agreed that once she'd gone he was never really alive.

The great-great-grandchildren of Anna and Wynn still work the ranch today. If you ask any of them why they always settle on the McCord land when they marry, they all say the same thing. McCords stay.

Undertaking Texas

LINDA BRODAY

Chapter 1

South Texas
1883

Slender pink fingers of dawn drifted through a crack in the livery's loft and stabbed Stoney Burke in the eye. He shifted on the bed of hay and blinked, trying to recall where he was.

He'd been in so many towns they'd blended together into a patchwork of faces and problems.

Oh yes, he recalled this unsavory one. Devils Creek.

He had a dozen reasons to avoid this place. A friend he couldn't say good-bye to. A woman he couldn't forgive. A memory he couldn't erase. If he could avoid Texanna Wilder, all the better.

But fate had a cruel sense of humor in most cases.

Sooner or later he'd run into her, no doubt about it.

A heavy sigh came from deep within him. Stoney ignored his complaining bones and stood, settling his hat on his head. Then lifting the saddlebags that had served as a pillow, he slung them over his shoulder and made his way to the ladder.

Halfway down, all hell broke loose outside.

Had he run smack into a range war? Or maybe a jail-break?

Clearing the last steps in a giant leap, he flung his saddlebags aside and ran for the door of the livery.

Chickens running loose in the street squawked angrily, flapping their wings. Dogs aired their lungs, their barking fit to raise the dead, as though they were trying to rise above the loud voices of humans. And in the midst of all the clamor and carryings-on came the pounding of hooves as the morning stage thundered into town, adding another level of chaos.

Stoney knew of the lawless ways of Devils Creek, although the town had appeared as peaceable as a widow woman's rocking chair when he'd ridden in late last night.

Now he could've sworn he'd stepped into a full-scale war of some sort. A crowd formed a circle in the middle of Main Street, blocking Stoney's view.

For a second the mob parted and shock jolted through him. A hoarse oath sprang free before he could swallow it.

Someone had trussed up a woman like a turkey on Christmas morning. She lay in a heap in the swirling dust of the street.

His gaze hardened. The squawking chickens scattered this way and that when he stalked into their midst.

Pushing through the swarm of people, he saw that not only was a woman at the center of the attention, but a youngster clung desperately to the woman's skirts as well. The boy's lip quivered as he bravely tried not to cry. He lost that battle when a tear spilled and trickled down the patch of freckles on his cheek, followed by a sob.

Suddenly the boy launched himself, kicking and clawing, on the man who was attempting to drag the woman. "Leave my mama alone."

"What in the Sam Hill!" Stoney bellowed, wrenching the man's grip loose from the length of rope that remained after tying it around the woman's waist. Clearly intending to flog the woman, the scoundrel didn't see him coming. Stoney delivered a hard right hook to the middle of the well-dressed stranger's face. The man's narrow-brimmed bowler went flying as bones cracked under Stoney's fist.

"You broke my nose!" The jackass grabbed his bloody face, dancing in a circle as if trying to find a safe place to light.

"That's all I broke . . . for now. You'll get more of the same if you don't untie this woman and be quick about it."

The man's eyes lit on Stoney's Texas Ranger badge and widened a bit. He seemed to have trouble swallowing, although he hadn't totally lost his bluster. "This ain't none of your affair, Ranger."

Stoney set his jaw, his glare scanning the crowd. "I'm making it my business. You folks go on home." He swung around to the scoundrel. "I said, untie the woman. Now."

Anger reddened the fool's cheeks. He obeyed the order even though it clearly irked him to do so.

Stoney offered the woman a hand, lifting her to her feet. "Are you all right, ma'am?"

She wrapped her arms around the young boy. "None the worse for wear, I reckon. Thanks for rescuing Josh and me."

When she glanced up, Stoney got his second jolt of the morning and it wasn't even high noon yet. "Texanna? Texanna Wilder?"

He groaned inwardly. Yep, fate hadn't wasted any time.

"Stoney? Lord, I don't know what I'd have done if you hadn't come along! But I know one thing—this sorry excuse for a man would've had to kill me to get me to the altar." Texanna straightened her spine. Then before Stoney could stop her, she whaled off and kicked her assailant with her high-topped boot.

"I ain't done with you, woman." Mr. Jackass glared, holding his leg while blood streamed from his nose.

Splotches of red stained the fancy brocaded vest and white shirt. "You either, Ranger."

The man's hand sought the bulge in his vest pocket. If Stoney could hazard a guess the lump was a hidden derringer.

"I wouldn't," Stoney warned. "I'll drop you like a sack of manure before you can get that peashooter out and aimed."

The man reconsidered, letting his hand sag limply at his side.

"I determine when you're finished," Stoney continued. "And I say that's now. Stay away from Mrs. Wilder and her son or you'll regret that you didn't." Stoney slung the rope at the varmint before turning his attention to Texanna and her son. "You're shaking. Let's find you a place to sit down."

Taking her arm, he led her and Josh, whom he hadn't seen since the boy was a tiny babe, to one of the velvet couches inside the nearby Madison Hotel. Stoney removed his hat and propped it on his knee.

Tears clouded Texanna's pale blue gaze that was like melting snow on a mountaintop. "You're a sight for sore eyes."

Yep, fickle fate was having a hell of a laugh.

Stoney squirmed when she rested her hand lightly on his arm. He gently removed it and put distance between them. This meeting might've been unavoidable, but it needn't get cozy. He considered saving her to be nothing but a job, nothing more than helping a frightened kitten out of a tree. He'd rescued her from Mr. Jackass. This wouldn't turn into anything else.

He could promise that.

"I suppose you know about Sam." Her voice quivered with emotion as she mentioned her husband.

A curt nod was his only reply.

"Did you hear how he got killed?"

"Never heard the particulars." He felt in his vest pocket for a handkerchief and pressed it into her palm.

Texanna dabbed her tears. "Sam was gunned down in the barbershop . . . minding his own business."

Stoney didn't miss the subtle jab aimed at the Texas Rangers—and him specifically.

"Got caught in the crossfire between the customer he was shaving and a rival," she continued. "Never stood a chance. Sam stopped wearing his pistol right after we married. Said he didn't need it anymore."

Likely story. Cold anger swept through Stoney. He imagined Texanna badgering Sam about the Colt the same way she kept at him until he quit the Texas Rangers. His friend might still be alive if not for that fact. But she'd thought the job, and the Colt, too dangerous for a husband of hers. And look where it got her—where it got them all.

"Heard they strung up the murderer," he said when he trusted himself to speak civilly. "That's some justice."

"Doesn't bring Sam back."

It definitely couldn't do that. Thickness clogged Stoney's throat. "I meant to come and check on you. It's just . . ."

"Your work keeps you busy. I know." Texanna's voice dropped to an anguished whisper. "I'm still trying to get used to him not being here. Six months has passed and·it seems like yesterday."

Stoney clenched his jaw, unable to picture the world without Sam in it. "What sort of trouble have you gotten yourself into?" His voice suddenly sounded like he'd swallowed a handful of gravel.

"The rotten sort."

Stoney focused a hard stare out the hotel door. "I'm guessing it concerns that fellow in the street?"

"Marcus LaRoach. He and Sam were half brothers. He's trying to force me to marry him. He's already attempted to lay claim to my undertaking and barbering businesses. Says he has Sam's will, leaving him everything . . . including me. He's lying. If Marcus has one, it's forged. Sam wouldn't have left a mangy dog in Marcus's care. I've looked everywhere for the genuine document and can't find it."

"Meanwhile, you're still trying to run the businesses?"

"Doing a fair job of it. And I'll keep on until the law makes me give it up."

Some Texas laws weren't worth the paper they were written on, especially the ones concerning widows. She seemed determined though. Texanna always had a lot of gumption—he'd give her that.

"What did this LaRoach think to gain by binding you up like that?" Remembering the sight made him mad as hell. "And why did he suddenly get it in his head to make you marry him today?"

Texanna pushed tendrils of hair the color of ripe wheat away from her face. "He finally got tired of my sass, I reckon. Got all riled up. And when I kicked and tried to claw his eyes out, he tied me up and dragged me." A wobbly smile tilted the corners of her mouth. "If I'd had Sam's Colt handy, I'd have shot the no-good skunk."

"Where was the sheriff while all this was going on?"

Exasperation rattled from Texanna's mouth like the lid on a boiling pot. "That old bag of wind? He can't handle Marcus. Whatever Marcus wants, he gets."

"Not this time." The brittle clip in his tone was one he reserved for hard cases and scalawags of every description.

Still clinging to his mother's skirts, Josh sniffled and tugged at Stoney's sleeve. "Is Uncle Marcus gonna be my daddy?"

"Nope, he's sure not. I promise." Not as long as he had breath in his body. No one was going to hurt Sam's widow—despite how he felt about her—or his boy. "Your father set great store by you. He loved you more than his own life."

"I don't know why he had to die," Josh said, crying.

Before Stoney knew what was happening, the boy released his mother's skirts and crawled onto his lap. Stoney stiffened, unsure what to do. He'd never been much good with children. Didn't know what to say to them. He tried not to notice that Josh was the spitting image of Sam. Truth was, Josh had inherited his father's intense gaze, the quirk of his mouth, and the same stubborn tilt of his chin. Stoney's heart clenched tight around memories. He struggled to unglue his tongue from the roof of his mouth while his arm encircled the small, proud back.

"I don't know why Sam had to die either. Your father was a real good friend of mine and I'm going to look out for you and your mother. No one will make you do anything you don't want to. All right?"

Josh gave a solemn nod, swiping his sleeve across his nose.

"Bet you take care of your mama real good."

"I'm six and I have a real gun."

"But you're not allowed to use it yet, young man." Texanna gently ruffled the top of her son's head. "I said you could have your pa's pistol to remember him by when you grow up. What brings you to Devils Creek, Stoney?"

"Picking up a prisoner from the jail and taking him to Menardville for trial. Got in late last night so I bedded down in the livery. Haven't introduced myself to the sheriff yet."

Like most women with an eye for comfort, she probably preferred him to stay in the hotel, but that wasn't his style. He liked being able to see trouble coming.

"Don't expect much from him. Why don't you come and let me fix you breakfast? It's the least I can do for an old friend. We live above the undertaker's shop. At least for now."

"I appreciate the invite but I don't think that's wise."

"I'm not offering anything more than food," she replied stiffly.

"Please," begged Josh. "Eat breakfast with us."

Stoney found he hadn't the heart to dash the hopes of a little boy who stared at him with puppy-dog eyes. A short while later, over a plate of ham, eggs, and mouthwatering biscuits, he watched the small replica of Sam. Earlier the boy had hauled up water for his mother from the cistern in back of the undertaker shop and brought in wood for the stove. Then, for no particular reason, Josh had thrown his arms around Texanna's waist and hugged her.

Stoney's chest tightened. Sam would be proud of the young man Josh was growing into. If only he'd lived to see it.

Damn! There was that lump trying to block his windpipe.

Traces of Sam were everywhere in the small living quarters. Sam's hat still hung beside the door, his boots stood near an overstuffed chair, and a pipe rested in the ashtray. It was as though Sam had just stepped out for a minute and would return.

"I haven't had the energy to get rid of them yet," Texanna murmured.

"What?"

Texanna pointed to Sam's boots. "I know it doesn't make a nickel's worth of sense to hold on to a pair of worn-out old boots, but I can't just pitch them out, pretend he never existed."

"You don't have to apologize. Do what you think best, whatever helps you cope. The devil take everyone else."

"Mama's looking for some important papers," Josh piped up. "She says they'll solve all of our troubles."

Stoney cocked an eyebrow toward Texanna.

"The will," she answered to his unspoken question.

"She'll find it," Stoney assured the boy.

Josh's chest puffed out proudly. "I'm helping."

Stoney stared into Texanna's blue eyes. "I'm sure your mama appreciates it. She's blessed to have such a fine son."

Josh fidgeted in his chair. "Can I be excused, Mama?"

"May I," she corrected. "Where are you off to, young man?"

The boy pulled out a bag from his pocket. "Gonna shoot marbles with Matthew an' tell him we're friends with an honest-to-gosh Texas Ranger like Pa was."

"You watch out for Mr. LaRoach." Affording the man any smattering of respect by adding "mister" to his name severely irked her, Stoney could tell, but she obviously wanted Josh to treat everyone with regard, whether deserving it or not. "Stay clear of him. He's mad as a frog on a hot skillet."

"I will, Mama. I ain't 'feared a him though, with Ranger Stoney around." Josh took his plate to the washtub and sprinted out the door, hurriedly closing it behind him.

"Do you think you oughta let Josh out of your sights?"

"Marcus won't hurt him. He wants me, not my son. But a friendly warning, Stoney . . . Marcus LaRoach isn't anyone to cross. He'll itch to get even." A smile replaced the serious frown. "You sure knocked the living daylights out of him today and ruined his plans."

He returned Texanna's grin. It'd felt downright good to wallop the beady-eyed weasel. "I've dealt with far worse than LaRoach. It's you who needs to be careful."

Stoney meant to pay the man a visit and impress upon him what'd happen if he kept messing with Sam's family. Hopefully that'd make a believer out of LaRoach.

And if not?

Stoney didn't want to think about that part. He couldn't stick around forever. He had a job to do—a prisoner to collect and plenty more lawbreakers to arrest.

But his pledge to Sam Wilder on his wedding day came back to haunt him.

"Promise that you'll see to Texanna if anything happens to me," Sam had pleaded following the short ceremony.

If only Stoney had known she'd make Sam quit the Rangers and everything he'd loved. He had a real hard time feeling charitable toward her. To his way of thinking, she was as much responsible for Sam's death as the man who'd pulled the trigger.

Still, a promise was a promise, he reckoned.

But how far was he willing to go to uphold that vow?

Chapter 2

Sitting across from Stoney, Texanna had no trouble recalling what a handsome best man he'd made the day she married Sam. It had been the happiest day of her life—her husband and her good friend together.

Stoney and Sam had been inseparable in those days, and both men had come courting her. The two formed a friendly rivalry for her affection and wouldn't be outdone. Stoney had been the first man to kiss her and it would've been oh so easy to fall in love with him—except he was married to his job. There was nothing on this earth that would make him give up the Texas Rangers. Stoney had admitted he had no room in his heart for a wife and children.

Sam had been a different story, easily forsaking that dangerous life for her. So Sam Wilder had been the one she'd chosen. She'd grown to love him with her heart and soul.

But she'd always had a special, deep fondness for Stoney. Truth to tell she still did, although it wasn't wise to admit. Heated swirls rose up, turning her insides to mush.

Fondness might not be the correct name for what she felt. It'd be so easy to let go and start pretending.

The tall Texas Ranger presented an even more powerful figure now than he had back when they were courting. Hard muscle filled out his shirt and his shoulders had broadened. His square jaw and high cheekbones spoke of rugged determination. And he had a maturity that came with age and mental toughness.

His prickly standoffish attitude puzzled her though. For goodness sakes, he hadn't even wanted her to touch him. Surely the heated exchange they'd had after Sam quit his job wasn't the reason. But that had to be it. He'd evidently held the grudge for seven long years. She might as well get to the ugly truth.

"You're still angry with me. I can see it. You are."

"You had no right to do what you did," Stoney growled. "Wasn't your choice to decide. Sam loved his job. He was the kind of Ranger you find once in a coon's age."

Texanna fidgeted with the edge of her apron, searching for the right words. "Are you sure you're not confusing your desires with Sam's? You probably don't want to hear this, but I'll say it anyway. He never thought about the Texas Rangers the way you do. He didn't obsess over that job. I know he was happy here with me." She raised her eyes to meet his stormy stare. "And besides, do you honestly think I could've made him do anything he hadn't wanted to do? When that man dug in his heels, God and all his angels couldn't change his blessed mind."

"I know he didn't waste time in giving up his dream," Stoney argued.

"Dreams change," she said softly. "For all of us. Sam was no exception. He loved being a father to Josh and a husband to me. Can you just forgive the past and let go? Please?"

"I'll try. Won't make any promises though."

Texanna threw up her hands and got to her feet. "I swear! You're as stubborn as Sam was. Want more coffee?"

"Don't mind if I do."

When he looked at her with that steady gray stare, she suddenly got weak in the knees. She found herself wondering if his black-as-midnight hair was as soft as the last time she'd run her fingers through it so many years ago, when she was young and oh so foolish.

Memories long forgotten swarmed back. Things she hadn't thought of in a long while.

Texanna refilled Stoney's coffee cup. "Remember when we rode our horses to the top of the bluff overlooking the San Saba River just to watch the sunrise? You built a fire and we made coffee. We sat there talking until well after daybreak."

"About Sam, if I recall." His deep voice seemed to vibrate the very air.

"And you told me what a good husband Sam would make. You were right. I got the cream of the crop."

"Wasn't anyone better. Never thought I'd live to see Sam end up in the undertaking and barbering business though."

"The businesses belonged to my father. Sam took over when Papa couldn't take care of them anymore. Papa died soon after. It was like he found a replacement and could leave this world in peace. I'm glad Papa doesn't know about Marcus."

"You've had a passel of heartache." He took a sip of coffee. "Do you have any friends in this town you trust enough to talk to?"

"A few. Loretta Farris, who owns the boardinghouse. And Dusty Haws. You probably remember him. He used to be a Ranger too."

"Yep, I know Dusty. The old codger got an eye put out by a piece of lead and had to retire. He's as good a man as they come. Heard he was living in Devils Creek."

"Dusty tried to help me with Marcus, but he can't see all that well and he's coping with bad health." Texanna stepped to the sideboard and picked up a dish towel. "Soon as I get these dishes washed I'm opening up the barbershop for business." She gave him a pointed stare. "You could use some barbering."

"Yes, ma'am. I could at that." He rubbed the dark growth on his jaw that added a dangerous attraction, and Texanna's heart fluttered.

What was the matter with her? She couldn't care for anyone else. And it was for sure too soon to be thinking of kissing and romancing. What was the matter with her? Texanna plunged both arms into the dishwater and set to scrubbing egg off the plates.

Knowing when he'd been dismissed, Stoney grabbed his hat and went to check on his horse. He needed to pay the livery man for feeding and boarding Hondo.

The main street of Devils Creek was a tad on the icy side, the way folks stared when Stoney passed by. The town welcomed him about as much as a steer did a red-hot branding iron.

Well, he wouldn't be here any longer than he had to. Of course, he hadn't exactly figured out what to do about Texanna's problem. Maybe he could take her and Josh to Menardville with him and set her up there. That had possibilities.

Sunlight spilled through the door of the livery. Stoney strode to the stall he'd put Hondo in the previous night.

"Hey, boy." Stoney petted the dark withers. The faithful buckskin gelding snuffled against his shirt. "You can look all you want, but there isn't an apple in there. You're out of luck today, old boy."

A faint rustle came from behind. "Can I help ya, mister?"

Stoney turned. The long leather apron the tall bearded man wore suggested he was the owner of the livery. When the man stepped into the shaft of sunlight, Stoney noticed the cloudy white film over his left eye.

"Dusty Haws, you old sonofagun!"

The man squinted to see better and scratched his head. "I recognize that voice but can't rightly put a name to you."

"You'd better recognize me. Stoney Burke."

"Well, the hell you say! What brings ya to Devils Creek?"

"Business. Supposed to pick up a prisoner and deliver him to Menardville for trial. How's the world been treatin' you?"

"Cain't complain." Dusty cackled, showing his tooth-less gums. "Wouldn't do me a lick of good if I did. Don't reckon anyone'd want to hear it. You see Texanna yet?"

"Just came from there. She fed me breakfast. Told me about this LaRoach fellow after I broke up his little plan this morning. Thought I'd woke up in the middle of a range war or something. A god-awful noise." Stoney rubbed Hondo's nose when the horse poked his head curiously over the stall rail.

"I tried to stop Marcus. He knocked me out with the butt of his pistol. Left me with this to remember him by." Dusty pointed to the gash on his bald head. "I ain't much use against the likes of Marcus. Done got too durn old and stove up."

Stoney rustled up a grin. "Bet you could still give 'em hell if the occasion arose. Never took you for a quitter."

"Reckon not. Wisht I was as young as I used to be." A far-off look swept over his face. "Those were the days."

"I wondered what happened to you after you retired. Some said you vamoosed down Mexico way and got your-self hitched to a pretty senorita."

Dusty cackled again and slapped his thigh. "You always were a josher. Women are a whole mess of trouble. I'd rather wrestle a water moccasin." Suddenly the man turned somber. "I stuck pretty close to your friend, Sam Wilder. Reckon Texanna told you what happened."

"She did." Stoney was still trying to picture Sam lying dead in the barbershop with a straight razor in his hand instead of a Colt.

Dusty motioned to Hondo. "This feller your horse?"

Stoney nodded. "Hope you don't mind me making myself at home. Wasn't anyone about last night. I also made use of your loft. Needed a place to bed down."

"Glad you did. You can sleep there anytime."

Reaching into his pocket, Stoney brought out a couple of silver dollars and handed them to Dusty. "Here's enough to feed and put Hondo up for a few days. Another thing—are you keeping the prisoner's horse?"

"Yep. Let me know when you need 'im and I'll have 'im ready for you."

"Appreciate it, Dusty. I'm on my way to check in with the sheriff. I'll know more after I see him."

Stoney left the livery and sauntered toward the jail. He was approaching the Pig and Whistle Saloon, the only watering hole in town, when the batwing doors swung open and Marcus LaRoach swaggered out.

The man's glare could've singed the hide off the meanest feral hog. It didn't impress Stoney though. The pencil-thin mustache twitched when the scalawag's lips tightened. Eyes glittered beneath the narrow brim of his bowler. His swollen nose and black eye made him look almost comical. Stoney held back a grin that threatened to form.

LaRoach hooked his thumbs into a gun belt strapped around his waist and deliberately stepped into Stoney's path.

"I don't cotton much to Rangers who think they can ride into someone's town and take over. Neither does anyone else. You don't belong here."

"That so?"

"I own this town. I own Texanna Wilder and her snot-nosed brat. Did you know the boy steals? Whatcha think about that?"

Stoney clenched his fist to keep from striking the lying varmint. He'd like to stick a pin in the man and see how much hot air would spew out. LaRoach definitely had an elevated view of his own importance. "I wouldn't believe you if you said lemons are sour."

"I suppose you think you're man enough to stop me?"

He didn't waste his breath with a reply. Towering above the wiry man dressed in a gambler's finery, Stoney felt a muscle in his jaw bunch when he set his back teeth. "Step aside."

The beady eyes brimmed with hate. Hate made men do stupid things. Stoney kept his gaze trained on LaRoach's hands, ready at a second's notice to unleash his Colt from its holster.

Training and steady nerves gave him the edge. He'd met up with a passel of men just like LaRoach, who thought they could bully people into doing what they wanted.

He'd shown them the error of their ways. He could this one too, if it came to that.

Stoney stood his ground even though they'd drawn a crowd. The milling people would make the pissant even less inclined to back down. The man had already lost face once today.

Making sure his Colt was within easy reach, Stoney planted his feet. When he drew his pistol, he meant to use it. "A fellow might've thought you'd learned something this morning. How's the nose?"

A growl rumbled in LaRoach's throat. "I owe you."

"Then either come collecting or go home. I'm getting a little tired of standing here waitin'."

Shielded by the low brim of his hat, Stoney's narrowed gaze flicked to the edge of the crowd of gawkers. Texanna stood apart from the others. Anguish in her face and the chewing of her lip spoke of worry.

She'd lost her husband, her security, and life as she'd known it. Except for a blind-as-a-bat old Ranger, not one person in town had stood up for her when LaRoach had bound her and dragged her through the street.

Stoney had shown up and offered his help.

He couldn't take the sliver of hope from her that had brought a light to her eyes.

Whatever else she'd done, the pretty lady had spunk. She was a good mother to Josh and she didn't flinch from honest hard work. That counted for a lot. Maybe he'd been a mite too rough on her.

Sitting at her table over breakfast hadn't been all that difficult. In fact, it was downright pleasurable.

Maybe she was right about dreams changing.

Chapter 3

Stoney considered his options. He could shoot Marcus LaRoach and spare everyone a lot of grief. Or he could walk away. Shooting the little pissant was looking more promising by the minute.

All of a sudden a man wearing a sheriff's badge barreled his way through the throng of people. The man's deep, rumbling voice seemed to come from the tips of his toes. "Mr. LaRoach, you're making a god-awful spectacle of yourself. You shoot him and you'll have a mess of Texas Rangers breathing down our necks. You've never had a problem like you'll have if you rile them up."

"I don't pay you for advice, Sheriff. I know what I'm doing."

That seemed debatable. Stoney watched the exchange, curious to see if LaRoach would listen to reason.

The sheriff sported shocks of long white hair and a snowy mustache that parted for his mouth and dangled below his chin. He mumbled something under his breath that sounded a lot like "pompous ass" before he spoke aloud. "You pay me to keep the peace and that's what I'm trying to do here. Don't be stupid. This Ranger can take that hogleg away from you and stuff it down your gullet so fast your stomach'll think it's a tough hunk of meat. And he won't even hafta draw his Peacemaker to do it."

Grudgingly, LaRoach backed out of Stoney's way, but gave a parting shot. "You're a dead man, Ranger. Make no mistake about that."

Stoney squinted beneath the low brim of his hat and fished a toothpick from his pocket. He stuck it in his mouth, wallowed it around for a moment, and drawled, "Any time. You'll find me easy enough. I'll be waitin'."

The scoundrel collected tattered remnants of his pride and stomped back into the Pig and Whistle, swinging the batwing doors nearly off their hinges.

"Aw, don't pay him no mind. He's harmless." The sheriff took out a pouch of tobacco and some rolling papers from his shirt pocket. "I'm Bill Ezra."

"Ranger Stoney Burke."

"Reckon you've come to collect the notorious Newt Colfax."

"Was on my way to the jail when I got waylaid."

"Reckon we can take care of that now, if you've a mind. Just show me your papers and you can march Colfax to the hoosegow in Menardville."

Stoney cast a glance to where Texanna had stood, chewing her lip. She was gone. He wasn't surprised.

He swung a quick glance at the barbershop, but she hadn't opened it yet. Maybe she was writing down LaRoach's measurements over at the undertaker's. Or his. He let a wisp of a smile curve his lips before it vanished.

Or she could be building a coffin. At that thought everything stilled inside him.

Would she mean it for him or LaRoach?

Stoney could imagine what a hard life she'd had since Sam Wilder's death. If not for taking over the undertaking and barbering business, she and Josh probably would've starved.

But what a grueling business for a woman, being an undertaker. When it was the only one around though, gender didn't matter that much.

Fort McKavett, some twenty miles to the east of Devils Creek, had a morgue, but the military had abandoned the operation a month earlier and closed the fort. Stoney had hated seeing the military leave the area. Riffraff and scum would seize the opportunity and make the Texas Rangers' job of keeping a lid on the criminal element harder. The scourge of Scabtown, a settlement across the river from the fort, would spread like wildfire. Where there were lawless, there would always be a need for the Texas Rangers.

His motto was to take one problem at a time though. And right now he had his hands full with ne'er-do-wells in Devils Creek.

He tossed the toothpick aside and fell in step with Sheriff Ezra.

"Want a smoke?" The sheriff held out the tobacco and rolling papers.

"Nope. Appreciate the offer though."

While they walked, Ezra filled one of the thin papers with a row of tobacco and expertly rolled up a smoke. He propped the narrow cigarette in the corner of his mouth and struck a match on his pants leg. Stoney watched the whole procedure, glad he'd never taken up the habit. Couldn't see the good in anyone drawing smoke into his lungs when they worked perfectly well without it.

They had almost reached the jail when a small boy sprinted from an alley with at least a dozen men and women giving chase.

"Stop him! He's a thief," a man with muttonchops yelled, shaking his fist.

Stoney's heart sank when he recognized the child.

Josh Wilder.

As if Texanna needed more problems.

Bill Ezra's age didn't slow him down. The sheriff quickly intercepted the mob and stopped them before they caught the boy. "Goldarn it! Calm down. What's the trouble?"

Seizing the opportunity, Josh made a beeline for the shed that housed coffins and the black hearse. The frame structure sat adjacent to Wilder's Undertaking Emporium.

The white apron of Mr. Muttonchops flapped against his pant legs as he answered the sheriff's question. "It's that Wilder kid again. When are you going to do something about him?"

"Whatcha want me to do, string him up? He's just six years old. What did he take this time?"

"He stole my account list. I have no way of knowing who owes for what," Muttonchops exploded.

"And he swiped a letter that just arrived from my brother in California," said a heavyset woman. "Swiped it right out of my hand before I even had a chance to see what Leonard wrote."

Stoney didn't wait for Sheriff Ezra; he strode toward the undertaker's. This didn't seem like the same boy who'd perched on his knee and looked up at him with tears in his trusting eyes. It concerned him that Josh might've taken up a dangerous habit. If so, it needed to be nipped in the bud, and fast.

He prayed there had to be some logical explanation.

Stepping inside, Stoney gave his eyes a moment to adjust to the dimness. On first glance the shed appeared to be empty.

But he'd plainly seen Josh scooting inside.

Then he heard a faint scrape of wood coming from a coffin.

His stomach turned over. He balked at disturbing the confines of a coffin, whether it held an occupant or not. But he had to find the boy.

Stoney edged toward a newly finished pine box and

eased up the lid. Curled up in a ball, Josh looked up at him with eyes that appeared too large for his small face.

"What are you doing, little guy?"

Trembling, Josh answered, "Hiding."

He gently reached for the boy's arm. "Come on out. I won't let anyone hurt you."

"You promise?"

"Cross my heart."

Josh sniffled loudly. As he crawled out, he looked warily about, as though half expecting to see a lynch mob.

"Now, tell me—"

Texanna burst through the door, interrupting Stoney's interrogation. Her chest heaved as though she'd run full-out. "Heard the commotion and that Martin Truebill over at the mercantile was accusing Josh of taking some things. I have to protect him."

"I was just about to get down to the truth of the matter." Stoney guided her onto an overturned crate. "Get your breath."

Texanna sat down but hopped right up again. "They've accused him before for no good reason. They're trying to make him pay for what I'm doing. Marcus has to be behind this."

"Maybe, maybe not."

"Are you saying Marcus has suddenly become a saint?" Her back stiffened as hurt swam in her stormy gaze. "Or that my son's a thief?"

"Don't get your tail feathers in a wad. I'm saying we don't know the facts yet." He calmly turned to Josh. "All right, son, why were those people chasing you?"

Josh shrugged his thin shoulders. "I dunno."

"You know when you do something you're not supposed to, you need to come clean?"

The boy's bottom lip quivered. He nodded his head solemnly.

"Did you do anything wrong?"

"I—I don't think so."

"Were you in the mercantile?"

"J—just to get my marble that rolled in there."

Texanna tapped her foot. "See? He's innocent."

Stoney let out an exasperated huff. He shot her a black stare then he swung back to Josh. "Did you see a list of names and papers on the counter?"

Tears swam in Josh's big eyes. "No."

"What about that woman's letter? Did you snatch it out of her hand?"

"What letter?"

"She claims you grabbed a letter from her and ran."

Texanna put her arms around Josh and clutched him tightly to her breast. She didn't help matters any by coddling the boy. Stoney had a job to do here. Couldn't she see that he'd do everything he could to spare her and Josh?

Yet her mutinous glare told him she didn't apologize for bushwacking his questioning. "There's one way to prove he didn't do those things. Do you see them on him or inside that coffin?"

She had a point. If the kid had taken them, they should be where he'd hidden. While Stoney searched the coffin, Texanna felt in Josh's pockets and pulled out a rusted metal button, a white rock, and his green shooter marble.

Sheriff Ezra strode into the undertaker's shed. "I'll have to take the boy in, Mrs. Wilder."

Texanna gasped and held Josh tighter.

Stoney stepped in front of them and raised his hands. "Hold on. You're not taking him anywhere. I've questioned Josh and there's no sign of the list or the letter anywhere here. He didn't do it."

"Plenty of folks out there claim he did."

A muscle tightened in Stoney's jaw. "They're wrong."

"You'll vouch for that?"

His sharp nod left no room for doubt. "I will."

"A mess of people aren't gonna be too happy. They're out for blood." The breath of air that blew from the sheriff's mouth ruffled the white mustache. "I'll leave the boy in your care then since you're god-awful certain."

"I'll stake my life on it."

Sheriff Ezra started for the door and turned back. "I'll expect you at the jail to take care of our business."

A short while later, Stoney strolled into the stone jail.

The sheriff stood in front of a potbelly stove. He swung around to see who entered and motioned to the battered pot that had seen better days. "Want a cup of coffee?"

"That'd be mighty good."

Two of the cells were empty. In the third, Newt Colfax lounged against the metal bars. The outlaw's lip curled in a sneer. "You think you're tough enough to get me to Menardville, Ranger?"

Stoney took the cup Ezra handed him and strolled to the cell. "Oh, I'll get you there all right. I can't guarantee it'll be in one piece. Guess that'll depend on you. I'd go quiet-like if it were me. Save yourself a lot of grief."

"Well, you're not me, are you?" Colfax shot him a black stare and dropped onto his cot.

The seat behind the desk creaked when Ezra folded his tall frame into it. Stoney took a chair on the opposite side.

"I'll see your authority papers and the Ranger warrant for Colfax now," said the sheriff.

Stoney slid his coffee onto the desk and reached into the inside pocket of his vest.

It was empty. Not even a scrap of paper.

He patted his shirt pocket. Nothing there either.

"I don't know what happened to them. They were here when I left Menardville. You know I'm a Ranger though."

"I don't know any blooming thing." The chair protested when the sheriff leaned back and propped his feet on his desk. "You say you are, but that's only your word, just like it was your word that the Wilder kid didn't filch those things."

A hot flush rose. "And my word's not good enough?"

"Not this time. God and everybody could waltz in here and claim to be a Ranger. You could've stolen that badge. For all I know, you might be in cahoots with Colfax."

Stoney's jaw clenched. "I'm not."

"Until you produce those papers, Colfax ain't going anywhere."

Chapter 4

Something rotten was afoot. What were the odds for so many things to suddenly come up missing? Josh swept through his mind, but he quickly dismissed the boy. The boy was only six years old, for Pete's sake. Not only that, the boy hadn't had access to the documents, he didn't think. No, someone else had taken his official Ranger papers.

Let him catch the thief and it'd be hell to pay.

Meanwhile he had no choice but to wire Texas Ranger Company D in Menardville for replacements. His commander wasn't going to be happy. Leaving the jail, he made tracks for the telegraph office. They'd send new ones, but it'd take days for them to arrive. And no doubt he'd have to endure a good bit of ribbing over losing them.

Within several minutes, Stoney had that taken care of. Stepping out of the telegraph office, he looked across the street. The barber pole turned in the breeze.

Texanna had opened up.

He reckoned there was no time like the present.

Crossing the street, he told himself that a shave and haircut were the only things on his mind.

But he couldn't quite ignore his breath, which came just a little bit quicker the closer he drew to the shop.

Intent on lathering up a customer, she spared him a quick glance when the bell above the door jingled. "Have a seat. I'll be right with you, Ranger Burke."

Stoney took the chair closest to the door so he could catch what little breeze came through and also keep an eye out for trouble should it come calling. He untied the bandana from around his neck and wiped sweat off his brow. The July day had heated up and promised to be a scorcher.

His attention turned to Texanna.

Despite her shortcomings, there was no woman more desirable than Texanna Wilder.

It seemed odd for a woman to be involved up to her pretty little neck in a man's occupation. Stoney could tell the way her customer squirmed that her close proximity affected him. But when it was the only barbershop in town, men had little choice but to endure a woman's bosom inches from their faces. Not that many would complain, mind you. Their wives, surely, but never the men. It occurred to him that possibly that accounted for the reason no one had come to her aid this morning.

He admired the way Texanna had stepped right into Sam Wilder's shoes and taken the reins of two businesses into her hands.

That she appeared extremely capable came as no surprise. She'd always been a lady who grabbed the bull by the horns instead of standing around wringing her hands. He liked that about her, along with numerous other things.

In fact, their only disagreement had been over Sam.

As if sensing his thoughts, she glanced up and sent him a hesitant smile.

Though her high-necked dress kept everything prim and proper, she couldn't disguise her soft curves. In the worn calico with its row of lace and frayed hem, she was all woman.

And one he'd carried feelings for since he'd met her all those years ago.

But Sam had been the lucky fellow who'd caught her eye. It was always Sam.

Stoney watched her expertly sharpen the razor on a long leather strap and begin scraping away the man's stubble. He wondered what might've been, how different his life would've turned out if he'd told her how he felt about her years before. He'd once stolen a kiss before Sam wooed her away from him.

Seven years wasn't long enough to erase the sweet softness of Texanna's lips. Stoney closed his eyes for a moment to fully capture the remembrance of the taste of her.

But she wanted a husband who'd be home every night for supper. Stoney rarely spent more than two straight days in one place. He liked the freedom to go where his job took him.

Still, thoughts of having a wife and a couple of children to carry on the Burke name had been coming pretty regular of late, sometimes the depth of the fervent wishing catching him by surprise. He wouldn't deny that a family held certain benefits, especially for a loner like him. He kinda liked the idea of someone somewhere waiting for him to come home.

Again, her words came back to him. "Dreams change for all of us."

Maybe they did, for a fact. He wouldn't admit that to her though.

Using long, smooth strokes, it didn't take Texanna long to finish shaving her customer and then Stoney settled into the chair.

Her arm brushed his cheek when she put the threadbare barbering cape around his neck. Her nearness created warmth that he couldn't exactly blame on the July sun.

The fragrant scent of shaving soap and bay rum mingled in the stifling air.

"Glad you came in. Your hair can use a trim," she said.

"Can't recall the last time I was barbered." He gave her a wisp of a grin. "In my line of work such pleasures are few and far between."

She ran her fingers through the long locks. A flash of heat raced through his blood. Texanna's touch was soft and sensual, and made him think languid thoughts of long nights and feather beds. Of sated urges and the tangle of sheets underneath.

Ahhhhh, he'd been without a woman too long.

But this wasn't exactly what Sam had in mind when he had asked Stoney to take care of Texanna. He wrestled his thoughts back to the barbershop, frowning as the snip of scissors lopped off a handful of hair.

Texanna stilled. "What's wrong, Stoney? You did want it cut, didn't you?"

He glanced at himself in the mirror. "Yep. Why?"

"You frowned and looked ready to bolt from the chair."

"I was thinking about something, that's all." Searching for a safe subject far from beds and kissing, he told her about the missing papers.

"That's peculiar." Her silky voice put him in mind of a hot, sultry summer day. "When did you last see them?"

"When I left Menardville. I remember folding them up and putting them in my vest pocket. They never left my person."

"Could they have fallen out?"

"Don't see how."

Texanna held the scissors in midair. Her face was stricken. "You're not accusing Josh? Are you?"

The air suddenly chilled by a good thirty degrees. Her claws had come out. She seemed extraordinarily defensive.

Stoney mentally waved a white flag. "Have no reason

to accuse your son. Merely saying it beats me what happened to them, is all."

Apparently mollified, she resumed trimming his hair, her long slender fingers handling the comb and scissors with practiced ease. He'd noticed her hands that morning. They were calloused and rough and her nails jagged. Probably from making caskets, sawing boards, and hammering and the like.

"Maybe your papers fell out when you were in my home. I'll look after I finish here."

"Appreciate it." He hoped he was making something out of nothing and they'd turn up. A companionable silence, broken only by the snip of the scissors, filled the shop. It was as good a time as any to broach moving away. "Have you ever thought of packing up and leaving Devils Creek? Letting LaRoach have the businesses and be shed of him?"

She came around the chair to stare, as though he'd announced he was studying for the priesthood or contemplating robbing a bank. Worry darkened her gaze to a shade of deep sapphire.

"Where on earth would I go? How would I make a living? I wouldn't stand a chance in competition with male barbers and undertakers already established in other towns."

"I can take you to Menardville. Surely there are other things you can do. Seamstresses are always in demand. And if you don't want to do that, open up a laundry. The Rangers will keep you in business. Menardville's a bustling community."

The flash of fire that'd been in her eyes at the seamstress remark faded a bit. "This is my home, Josh's home. It's where I grew up. It's where I buried my husband, laid him to rest in the little church cemetery. I'll fight LaRoach and anyone else for the right to live here as I see fit."

"And what if that fight ends up killing you?" he

asked tightly. "What'll happen to Josh? You have to think of him."

"I do. Every second of the day. He needs roots, and those roots, are here. Marcus talks big, but I can handle him."

Yeah, it looked like she was doing a mighty fine job, trussed up and dragged through the street. Women could be stubborn as a corral full of donkeys. Would it take LaRoach seriously harming her before she saw reason?

Lord help the fool man if it came to that, because he'd just as soon give LaRoach a case of lead poisoning as not.

Texanna finished the haircut and picked up the duster to brush the hair from his shoulders and neck. "What is this about? I won't have you feeling obligated for my safety. And just because you and Sam were best friends won't wash."

Stoney reached and pulled her around to face him. He gently took her palms in his. "Look at your hands."

Sparks of fire sprang up again. "What of them?"

"They're in pitiful shape, all cut up and rough. This life isn't for a lady. You work way too hard. I care about you and Josh. You deserve an easier life."

She jerked her hands loose. "I got along before you came and I'll get along after you leave."

Wrapping his face with hot towels brought an end to the discussion. While moisture softened his bristles, he could hear her adding water to the hard cake of shaving soap and whipping it into a fine lather with the brush.

After a few minutes, she removed the towels and lathered up his face. Her breasts were at eye level and inches from touching his cheek.

Heat rose from his belly.

There should be a law against stubborn women barbers!

Chapter 5

Texanna tried to calm her heartbeat as she cautiously laid the sharp edge of the razor against Stoney's finely chiseled jaw.

There was a connection, something linking her to this steely eyed Ranger, that stood apart from Sam. Stoney suddenly rode back into her life on a day when she was at her lowest. He disturbed her thoughts, the very core of her being. He'd awakened all those old feelings she'd kept buried for so long and made her think of rainy music on a tin roof. Of the breathtaking beauty of a rainbow after a violent storm.

And hot passion.

Heaven help her! Yes, Stoney definitely made her think of passion.

She couldn't let him know how deeply he affected her, for the feelings he carried turned more toward the murdering side than the romantic. She prayed he might forgive her in time. But it didn't appear his feelings would alter soon.

Keep the strokes long and smooth, she told herself, *and quit thinking about music and passion.* She'd never forgive herself if she marred his handsome profile.

Her breath seemed caught somewhere in her chest.

Stoney had a rugged strength that Sam had lacked. Not that Sam was soft. Her husband just hadn't had the fierce determination it took to survive in the rough Texas town. He'd believed that no one would harm you if a fellow lived his life and minded his own business.

That philosophy cost him—cost them all—dearly.

The bell suddenly tinkled over the door. Loretta Farris, the stout boardinghouse owner, limped inside. "I see you're busy. I'll be quick. Come by my place after you leave here and pick up a loaf of fresh bread. I just took it out of the oven. Josh loves it, the little darling."

"I don't know what I've done to deserve a friend like you, Loretta. I'll be sure to stop by and get it."

When the woman left, Texanna turned to Stoney. "I'll have supper at five. Josh and I will expect you." She swished the razor in a bowl of water to rinse off the thick shaving soap.

"I can eat in the hotel dining room." His deep voice vibrated the still air and the little pocket of hope she desperately clung to. "Or the little café I noticed, Mattie's Cook Shack. Hate to put you to any trouble."

"I insist. Josh will be heartbroken if you don't come."

And the night would be long and dismal for her as well.

"In that case, I reckon I'd better show up. I'd hate to disappoint Josh. He's as fine a boy as I've seen. You've raised him well."

"Thank you. I'll admit, it's not been easy."

"Nothing worthwhile ever is. Josh is all boy."

"He needs a man's attention though. He looks up to you, Stoney. You're a good influence on him. I've tried to keep from coddling him. Don't want him to be sissified."

"Glad you brought that up. I've been meaning to talk to you. You're stifling the boy. Loosen the tether a little. For God's sake, give him room to breathe."

"Are you criticizing me?" she asked in clipped tones.

"I'm just saying you need to relax a bit and let Josh be a boy. Quit being so damned overprotective. He's gonna make mistakes, but that's okay. Life's about learning."

"I suppose you could do a better job?"

He let out a long-suffering sigh. "That's not what I'm saying at all. I'd hate to try to raise a young'un." There was a moment of silence before he added, "Maybe it'd be better to forget what I said."

Her chin jutted out. "I'll thank you to keep your horseback opinions to yourself and don't try to tell me how to do my job."

"Don't worry. I won't make that mistake twice."

"Fine."

Fuming, Texanna adjusted Stoney's head so she could shave the other side. Concentrating on her task, she didn't realize how near she was until her breast brushed his shoulder. An electrified sizzle went through her. She quickly moved back.

In the depths of Stoney's unnerving stare lurked amusement and a challenge.

For a second, she considered telling him it might be better if he ate at Mattie's Cook Shack after all. Except Josh would mope around all night. She wouldn't do that to her son.

The breath that had gotten lost somewhere inside her chest found its way out when she finally finished up and Stoney left.

She dropped the two bits he'd paid her into the till. She hadn't wanted to take his money, but he was a persistent man. In the end he'd simply pressed it into her palm and sauntered out the door in that easy, fluid way of his.

Texanna stood at the window watching his tall form stride down the street, his red bandana flapping in a sudden gust of wind. Too bad he was so opinionated. Not that he was wrong. She just didn't want him pointing out her mistakes. Truth was, she knew she coddled the boy, but she couldn't help it. He'd lost his father. She had to make up for that.

Any mother would.

Her attention turned back to the Ranger who'd awakened long-dead dreams. Stoney cut quite a breathtaking figure.

Supple leather britches clung to his long legs.

The black Stetson pulled low on his forehead added a certain degree of danger.

And the lethal Colt in the holster that rode low on his lean hip made him a man to reckon with.

Stoney Burke had galloped straight into her heart and turned her topsy-turvy. All without giving her a say in the matter. And worse, he didn't give it nary a second thought. When he'd finished his business here, he'd leave and not look back. She'd likely never see him again.

Darn his hide! He made her care. He gave her hope where none existed. Her breath hitched painfully in her chest. Part of her would ride out with him when he left.

If wanting him was a sin, she was doomed!

The multitude of lonely nights crossed her mind. With a man like Stoney beside her, she'd never awaken in a panic, drenched with sweat, aching to feel the tender touch of a hand.

Trembling, Texanna pressed against the window as though she could call the tall figure back. She stayed rooted to the spot until she pulled herself together. It'd do no good to fall apart. She had work to do. Over the next half hour, she swept the shop, washed her scissors and combs, and tidied up. She was just putting the straight razor away when the door opened.

Her heart sank when she saw Marcus. "I'm sorry, I'm closing for the day. I have a funeral to prepare for."

Marcus LaRoach paid her no heed. The popinjay was too busy admiring himself in the mirror. Evidently satisfied with his reflection, he settled himself in the barber chair and propped his feet on the metal footrest. "Didn't come for barbering. I saw the Ranger in here. Burke can't save you, Texanna. He'll move on, with good riddance, soon. Then I'll get my wishes."

Her chin lifted several degrees. "There's a big difference between wanting something and actually getting it. You'll have to kill me to get me to the preacher."

"Believe me, sugar, that can be arranged. Don't tempt me. My patience is wearing thin." Marcus rose and leaned close to the mirror, smoothing his hair. "Now, I've humored you long enough. I'm the legal owner of this barbershop and Wilder's Undertaking Emporium, and I'm taking control. Turn all the money over to me."

She clutched the till, her knuckles white. If Marcus took what money she had, what would they live on? How would she provide for Josh? "This barbershop belonged to my father. It's my money."

The pompous weasel yawned. "Not in the eyes of the law, sugar. You know I have the only will Sam ever wrote, and he left everything to me."

"One of these days I'll prove it's fake."

Marcus grabbed her wrist and twisted. She let out a sharp cry.

Before she could yank free, Stoney crashed through the door and had Marcus in a crushing grip. The Ranger slung him against the wall with such force the boards of the little barbershop rattled.

"I told you what would happen if you didn't leave Texanna alone. It wasn't an idle threat." Cold steel laced Stoney's soft words. He was a man who wore authority as easy as he wore the Colt not far from his fingertips.

Marcus struggled to speak, but with Stoney's arm across

his windpipe a squeak was all he could manage. "You can't interfere with the law. I was only trying to take what's legally mine."

"Steal it, you mean. You have no claim to Sam Wilder's property. Not his businesses and not his widow."

Stoney wasn't one to back down and neither was Marcus. But Texanna clung to the knowledge that Marcus had never run up against a tough man like her Texas Ranger.

When had she started thinking of him as hers?

Sheriff Ezra marched into the small shop, derailing her train of thought. "What's going on here?"

"Arrest this man." Marcus squeezed out the words through the narrow opening in his throat.

"Let him go, Burke. I can handle this," ordered Ezra.

"Like you handled the way he hog-tied Texanna this morning?" Stoney snorted, backing away from Marcus. "You did a fine job of upholding the law then. What makes you think you can now?"

"Just a cotton pickin' minute. You start slinging accusations and I'll lock you up—don't think I won't."

"You might need reinforcements to do it." A deadly glint filled Stoney's hardened gaze.

Marcus adjusted his dark satin vest. "I'm pressing charges against Burke for assault. Arrest him."

Sheriff Ezra hooked his thumbs on his belt and frowned, clearly not wanting to have to cross either man. "Mr. LaRoach, you might want to think about this."

"If I go to jail, LaRoach will occupy the cell next to mine," Stoney declared.

The sheriff turned to Texanna. "What do you have to add?"

"Marcus came here causing trouble and Burke stopped him. The one in the wrong is Marcus, as usual. I have his handprint on my wrist to prove it." Her stomach turned upside down when she met Stoney's gray stare.

A sudden breeze through the door scampered playfully through Ezra's long white mustache. "I'm giving you both a stern warning. But anymore trouble between you and I'll cart your rears to jail."

Marcus was bending the sheriff's ear when they left the barbershop, threatening to fire Ezra, as he did anyone who didn't kowtow to his whims.

Texanna turned to Stoney. "You seem to be my knight in shining armor today. Thank you."

A wry smile crinkled the corners of Stoney's eyes. "I'm just sorry LaRoach keeps bothering you. One of these days he'll not stop at twisting your arm. And I may not be here."

"Evidently he'd been eagle-eyeing this place. He saw you leave and never in a million years expected you to come back." Recalling Marcus's brutal nature brought new waves of anger.

"He hurt you." With tiny circles, Stoney caressed the dark welts that had formed on her wrist.

"Could be worse. It'll heal."

"You're shaking." Stoney pulled her into the circle of his powerful arms.

His gentle touch curled her toes. Stoney's strong heartbeat rose above the roar in her ears. Texanna closed her eyes and reveled in the special scent that was the Ranger's. He made her more alive than she had ever been.

God help her, she wanted him!

The longing was almost more than she could bear.

She could picture their life together and what she saw made the torture that much worse. She could get her heart broken in a thousand jagged little pieces if she wasn't careful.

It did no good wanting something she couldn't have.

He'd already made it abundantly clear the only thing he wanted to be married to was his job.

Chapter 6

"I don't rightly recall anyone spit-and-polishing a hearse before." Stoney dipped a rag in a bucket of soapy water and sloshed it onto the long rectangular window on the side of the conveyance.

He cast a glance at Texanna, who looked a mess—a beautiful, stubborn mess that he'd keep at arm's length.

Her hair had come undone from the knot at her neck and spilled in rich, golden waves down her back. The smudge of dirt on her cheek added an enticing touch. It required all his willpower to stay focused on the chore and off the row of tiny white buttons down the front of her dress.

Josh was helping wash the hearse, so even if Stoney had been inclined to pull Texanna into his arms and kiss her silly, he wouldn't. Not that he even wanted to do such a thing.

It'd be foolish to let himself entertain such a notion.

She's just a frightened kitten you got out of a tree, he reminded himself. Nothing more.

"Just because you've never seen funeral wagons washed doesn't mean people don't," she answered. "I've always cleaned mine up before pressing it into service. I want to make a person's last ride the most dignified I can. It's out of respect for the dead that I make the hearse gleam. They might not have gotten everything they deserved in life, so I want to give 'em what I can in death, to honor their sacrifices."

Grudgingly he admitted they weren't so different after all. He could sure relate to dedication. "You're very committed to your work. I like that."

A wrinkle marred Texanna's smooth forehead. "It's more than a job to me. It's a life-calling. It's why I'm scratching and clawing to hold on to it . . . and why I can't abandon it to become a seamstress. Or a laundress."

Stoney tried to ignore the jab, but in the end couldn't let it pass. "Nothing wrong with that kind of work—it's honest."

"It's not for me." Her tone warned that he was coming close to stepping into a pile of horse poo.

How come she could recognize her dedication but not his? Rangering was a life-calling of the highest order. They'd been around that crook in the road enough. No need to keep going over it. He changed the subject. "Will you need help in the morning? I can do any lifting."

"I'd appreciate that, Stoney. I generally hire some men to load and unload the coffin. Sometimes Dusty helps me. And I always have to hire someone to dig the grave."

He leaned against the shiny black wagon. "How about if I dig the hole for you? That'll make me feel better about eating all your food. I'll take Josh with me."

Josh threw down his soapy rag, his freckled face lighting up like a beacon. "Oh, boy! Can I, Mama?"

"Don't see why not." Her smile blinded Stoney.

Without being told, he knew the smile was a simple thank-you for paying attention to her son. As if that took any effort. He had grown very fond of the boy.

"Then it's settled." Stoney tossed his soapy rag into a

bucket. "I'll grab some shovels and we can get started. We should have time before supper."

"I'll finish up here. You two go on." Texanna shooed them.

He located a big shovel for him and a smaller one for Josh. Throwing them over a shoulder, he set out for the church. Josh had to take two steps to his one in order to keep up, but the boy was as happy as a frog in a mud puddle.

Stoney followed Texanna's directions to the Mayness family plot and sank the shovel into the ground. Josh did the same. Stoney gave the boy a side glance. He was proud of the way Josh dug in wholeheartedly, no matter what job he was called on to do. Josh definitely didn't shirk from work. Sam must be looking down and grinning up a storm at the way his son had turned out.

There was just a slight problem with things seeming to disappear when the boy was around. Could be coincidence. Or something far more serious. He didn't know which yet, but he intended to find out before he left Devils Creek.

After an hour, they stopped to rest and wet their whistles with the sweet well water Texanna had sent with them.

"My pa is buried right over there." Josh pointed. "You wanna see his grave?"

"I would."

Stoney ambled behind Josh as he led the way. His throat closed up when he saw the tombstone. Somehow, seeing Sam's name chiseled in a piece of granite made his death more final.

Josh sniffled. "I sure miss my pa."

He put his hand on the boy's shoulder. "Wish I could change things."

"Pa said he was gonna take me fishin' sometime, but he never got to. Sure wish he had've."

"I'm sure he had lots of things he probably wanted to do with you and teach you, but he never had the chance." His gaze caught on a small headstone next to Sam's that had a baby lamb on top. The name read *Jenny Wilder*. The date of death was a year before Sam died. She'd been six months old.

What the hell?

Shock jolted through him. He ran his fingers across the chiseled words, *Asleep in Jesus*. Texanna hadn't breathed a word about a daughter.

Josh knelt down to brush the cold granite. "That's my baby sister. I was gonna teach her how to shoot marbles."

Stoney's throat tightened. Life could sure rear up and kick you in the teeth sometimes. Seemed unfair that Josh should have to know that kind of sorrow at such a young age. Stoney draped his arm around the slender shoulders, not knowing what to say.

Pounding hooves and the clanging of rigging broke his train of thought. He glanced up. The stage pulled to a stop in front of the hotel. It was too soon yet to expect his replacement papers. Somehow, having to hang around for a few extra days wasn't the hardship he'd first thought it would be.

"Reckon we'd better quit lollygagging and get back to work, son. Your mama's gonna have supper ready before long."

They finished the grave and headed for home. Texanna wiped her hands on her apron when they opened the door to the upstairs living quarters. "Wash up. I have everything ready to set on the table."

Stoney pumped water into a basin and let Josh wash first. After supper Stoney intended to visit the local bathhouse. That was one luxury he afforded himself. And after digging graves, washing hearses, and fighting LaRoach, he sorely needed to immerse himself in a tub of cool water.

"Will you say grace, Stoney?" Texanna asked when they'd taken their seats.

He wasn't accustomed to blessing food, so it was short and to the point. It must've sufficed though, because Texanna's eyes glistened when she looked up. Josh grabbed a piece of fried chicken the minute the amens were said.

"Slow down, young man." Texanna passed a heaping bowl of mashed potatoes to Stoney.

He grinned and scooped out a big helping. "Josh worked up quite an appetite digging that hole. Besides, he's a growing boy with places to go and people to see."

"I gotta hurry, Mama. Matthew's uncle got a new horse and we're s'posed to help him name it."

"That can wait until you eat. I won't have you sick with a bellyache." She took the mashed potatoes from Stoney and put a spoonful on Josh's plate along with some green beans.

"I won't get sick, Mama." The boy took a big bite of his chicken leg and chewed fast.

"He'll be all right," Stoney said. "Give the boy some air."

They ate in silence that was broken only by the clink of forks on chipped china plates. Finally Josh asked to be excused, took his dishes to the washtub, and bounded down the stairs.

"Josh reminds me a lot of me," Stoney said. "My mother always claimed I was hollow inside. I shoveled it in like it was the last meal I was ever gonna get."

"How is your mother? I hope she's well."

"Was the last time I saw her."

"Does she still live outside of San Angelo on the family homestead?"

"She does, along with my brother and his wife. After Pa died, Joseph took over the farm. They look after Ma now. You've never seen a more ornery or feistier woman."

It still rankled that his father had come near to losing

everything they owned. Although he loved the man dearly, Stoney swore he'd not turn out like John Burke. His father had been lazy and undisciplined. Instead of working in the fields making a living, you could always find the man at a favorite fishing hole or in town playing checkers with his cronies. If not for Stoney and Joseph, their mother wouldn't have had a place to lay her head or a morsel to put in her mouth.

"Care for some more green beans?" Texanna asked. At his nod she handed them to him. "I'm glad your mother's in fine shape. She's a sweet lady. Always real nice to me. I commend your brother for taking care of her. I wish my parents were alive. I really miss them."

"That's why you need to think about pulling up stakes and moving where you don't have to watch your back."

Texanna laid down her fork. "We've been over this."

"That was before LaRoach gave you added grief today."

Sudden tears welled up in her beautiful blue eyes. She stared at the tablecloth, smoothing it with her hand. "There's something I haven't told you. Sam and I had a baby daughter almost two years ago. Her name was—"

"Jenny. Her name was Jenny." He noted her surprise when he supplied the name. "I saw the grave today when Josh showed me Sam's resting place."

"That's another reason why I can't leave. Jenny needs me to watch over her. She was so tiny. It's my fault she's dead."

"How can you say that? You're a loving mother."

"No." Texanna shook her head. "I knew she was sick. Sam begged me to let him take her to the doctor at Fort McKavett. It was in the dead of winter. I told him Jenny would recover if we just kept her out of the cold. My baby is dead and I'm to blame." Her voice became brittle. "I deserve everything I get."

Stoney scooted back his chair and walked around the

table. He lifted her into his arms. "Hush now. Don't ever say that. You don't deserve to live under this strain."

He smoothed back her hair. He had one other ace up his sleeve.

And tomorrow he'd use it.

Chapter 7

Early the next morning, Stoney marched out of the livery and into the telegraph office. "I need to wire Austin immediately."

The skinny clerk looked like he'd swallowed a peach pit, the way his Adam's apple bulged out in a round knot. The man shoved a tablet and pencil at him. "Write down your message and I'll send it right away."

Stoney scribbled a plea to Judge Alexander Goodnight. If anyone could help Texanna out of her mess, it'd be him. He'd known the judge for years and considered him a good friend and one of the sharpest minds in the business.

Surely there had to be a law against taking a widow's means of support. If not, then maybe at least Judge Goodnight could stall LaRoach's takeover and give Texanna more time to look for Sam's legal Last Will and Testament.

Stoney hated to think of other alternatives in the event Judge Goodnight couldn't offer any help.

In fact, the choices were pretty limited since Texanna refused to leave Devils Creek. Not that he didn't understand. He did now, and he knew she'd never leave her baby daughter, who lay asleep in Jesus, next to Sam.

Seemed the only other solution was to marry Texanna. But damn! Could he go that far to save her?

He swallowed the lump that seemed stuck in his craw. Marriage?

She'd ask him to give up rangering and chasing outlaws. That wasn't even negotiable. He'd cut off his arm before he gave up the job that had made him the man he was.

Paying the telegraph clerk, Stoney stepped onto the sidewalk and glanced up and down the street that was just coming alive.

The bathhouse where he'd cleaned up last evening sat silent and still. He'd paid them to launder his clothes, but it didn't appear they'd opened up yet.

Delicious smells came from Mattie's Cook Shack. Dusty had told him the food there was passable. Instead of heading that direction, he found his feet taking him to the living quarters above Wilder's Undertaking Emporium.

Texanna answered his knock. A blue spark twinkled in her eyes. "Come in. I have breakfast ready."

She seemed a little breathless. Maybe because she hurried too fast to the door. That had to be it. He took off his hat before he crossed the threshold.

"Hope I'm not being a bother."

"Good heavens, no. I was expecting you. You'd hurt my feelings if you ate anywhere else." She lightly touched his arm and an odd sense of contentment passed through him.

Her nearness kindled sleeping embers. Texanna was a beautiful, vibrant woman. His gaze lazily roamed over her curves when she turned toward the kitchen.

She'd make someone a wonderful wife. She really would.

Too bad he wasn't looking for one. It would never work.

Josh came running in and skidded to a stop in front of Stoney. "Hi, Ranger Burke."

Stoney ruffled the boy's sun-streaked blond hair. "I think it's about time you called me Stoney. Friends use their first names with each other."

Josh's grin stretched from ear to ear. "Sure, Stoney."

"Come and sit down, you two," Texanna called. "Cold eggs aren't very tasty."

Again she asked Stoney to say grace. While prayer made him wriggle uncomfortably, he thought of the woman they were burying in a few hours and her husband, who now lived alone. And of the man who was making Texanna's life pure hell.

Stoney bowed his head. "Bless this food and watch over us. Comfort, protect, and keep us from harm. Amen."

If the food tasted as good as it smelled, he'd be in trouble. The plate of hot biscuits, fresh eggs, and ham was all a man could ask for. He took a biscuit and slathered it with butter. It melted in his mouth. Yep, he was in trouble. He reached for another.

"I may have some news for you in a day or two," he told Texanna, filling her in on his telegram to Judge Goodnight.

Hope glimmered in her eyes. "I pray he can find something in the law that'll help me. I know that darn will is around here someplace. I just have to find it."

"Is there anything I can do to help?"

"I appreciate the offer, but I can't think of a thing."

"Are you right sure Sam even had a will?"

"Yes, I saw it with my own eyes."

"Then we'll just have to find it. Did he have a special place where he put his papers?"

"Sam was horribly unorganized. His mind was always somewhere else when he put things down. I can't tell you the number of times he misplaced his pipe, his barber

scissors, or his reading spectacles." She laughed. "Once
his glasses were on top of his head. He'd forgotten he put
them up there."

"I didn't know Sam wore glasses." That was hard to imagine. The man who'd ridden by his side hadn't needed them.

"His eyesight was never real good, but he didn't want
you or the other Rangers to know it. Said you'd lose faith
in his ability to shoot. After we got married I convinced
him it's better to see than to be blind, so he took to wearing glasses. He cussed the blamed things though."

Stoney grinned, remembering how frustrated Sam could
get. "That was my best friend for you." He turned his attention to Josh. "How well can you sit a horse?"

"My pa taught me to ride real good."

"We had to sell his horse though," Texanna explained.

"I thought I'd take my gelding out this afternoon for
some exercise and if you don't object, I'd like Josh to go
with me."

"The pair we have left are the ones I use to pull the
hearse. They're slow, and old as Methuselah."

"I'll rent him a mount from Dusty then."

"Can I, Mama? Please?"

"Yes, you can go. But you still have to do your chores
when you get back."

The funeral proceeded without a hitch. Stoney drove the
polished hearse with its black curtains tied back with a
bow and heavy fringed tassels. Texanna perched next to
him. She was quite a sight in her crisp mourning dress and
becoming hat.

The sun struck her golden hair, making the lustrous
strands shimmer. He swallowed hard at the sight, fighting
to keep his mind on the job at hand.

Elegant and proud, Texanna Wilder stirred his blood.

She was certainly a sight. He gave himself a mental shake. Best to keep his thoughts confined to prodding the two ancient horses. He'd seen more life in a pair of holey, worn-out long johns.

Stoney had borrowed Sam's funeral clothes. That they fit surprised him. He hadn't recalled Sam being so tall and muscular. But the dark britches and frock coat saved him from having to buy some ready-made clothes for a one-time wearing.

He'd put his foot down though at wearing the tall, black top hat. His black Stetson looked fine enough to him. And it was broke in just right.

Tugging the felt hat down low on his forehead, he aimed the plodding animals toward the cemetery. A dozen or so mourners marched behind, paying their respects to the woman who had departed the earth.

A few hours later, Stoney and Josh finished filling in the grave with dirt and turned toward home. Texanna had already driven the hearse back, so they walked.

He looked forward to exchanging the funeral garb for his leather britches and worn gray shirt. He'd feel more like himself. Dressing like the Grim Reaper tended to sour his stomach.

When Stoney neared the Pig and Whistle, Marcus LaRoach stepped out, flanked by some of his cronies.

The man's glittering eyes cut Stoney to shreds. "Texanna got you doin' her work for her, Ranger?"

Stoney didn't bother to reply, just kept walking like he hadn't heard a thing. Loose chickens in the street squawked angrily, disturbed when Stoney strode with dogged determination through a cluster of them. Beside him, Josh kept his head down and his back ramrod stiff. Stoney knew the youngster shook in his shoes even though he didn't want to show it. He laid a hand on the boy's shoulder to let Josh know he wasn't going to let anything happen to him.

"Hope you don't expect me to pay you anything for your trouble," Marcus called.

Still they kept walking.

It'd be a sad day when Stoney took money from Marcus for his trouble or otherwise.

"I see you got her snot-nosed brat with you," LaRoach taunted. "I hope the brat steals you blind."

Stoney's hands clenched. He itched to lay into the little pissant. But that would be playing his game. Stoney had no intention of falling into that kind of trap.

Marcus didn't have sense enough to end it there. The man loudly remarked to his followers, "Appears the Ranger ain't only stupid, he's deaf as a post too. Don't know what Texanna sees in him. Guess he makes a good babysitter though."

The piercing glare Stoney shot them silenced their laughter and had them backing up against the batwing doors of the saloon.

He'd run into men like these before. They were awful brave until confronted, then they tended to scatter like dandelion seeds in a stiff breeze.

Stoney couldn't afford to let down his guard though. The men who seemed the least threatening were often the most dangerous.

Once they were past the whiskey-swilling establishment, Josh eased the tense set of his small body.

"You ready to go for that ride, son?" Stoney asked.

"Yep. I'm worried about Mama though." Josh looked up at him with his forehead wrinkling in thought. "Do you think we oughta leave her? What if something happened?"

From under the brim of his hat, Stoney glanced at Wilder's Undertaking Emporium just ahead. "I've been thinking that maybe we should ask her to go with us. How about that?"

"I think we should." Josh's grin was big.

Twenty minutes later all three strolled to the livery. Stoney carried a picnic basket that was filled to the brim with thick slices of ham, potato salad, pickled okra, and fresh bread. Judging by the weight of it, they wouldn't go hungry.

Dusty Haws saddled a gentle mare for Texanna and a paint gelding for Josh.

Hondo pranced and high-stepped, obviously happy to be exercised. Outside the edge of town, Stoney urged the gelding into a gallop. Texanna and Josh were excellent riders and kept up with the pace he set.

A good hour later, they dismounted on the lush banks of the San Saba River and let the horses drink.

Then, under the branches of a huge live oak tree, they spread their lunch.

Texanna's blue eyes rivaled the wide expanse of the Texas sky when she gazed into his face. Whatever he was about to say vanished from his thoughts and his tongue stuck to the roof of his mouth.

Before he could lasso wayward thoughts, his attention focused on her rosy lips. They lured a man with promises of stolen kisses.

Dear Lord, help him remember all the reasons why he had to resist her!

Chapter 8

Stoney returned to Devils Creek with Texanna and Josh in the shank of the afternoon. He didn't know when he'd had a more satisfying day.

He'd spent a great deal of time watching Texanna and Josh. Neither must've indulged in anything remotely similar to fun in a very long while. He was glad he'd been the one to brighten their lives and remind Texanna that too much work would make her grow old before her time.

Realizing what he'd just concluded, he squirmed inside.

He'd done nothing but work ever since joining the Rangers.

He'd most likely look back one day and wish he'd taken time to sow more wild oats . . . and dream of a family.

They were standing inside the doorway of Texanna's home. Josh had run off to find his friend, anxious to relate every detail of his horse ride. The boy bubbled with excitement.

The clock ticked loudly in the quiet room.

Texanna rose on tiptoe and kissed Stoney's cheek. "Thank you. This has been an incredible afternoon. It's been ages since I've enjoyed myself like this. I had almost forgotten what it felt like not to be looking over my shoulder."

Fresh air and sunshine clung to her like a thistle claw to a horse's tail. He sucked in a quick breath. "It was my pleasure."

Her nearness had the pull of a magnet. Those lush pink lips, the gentle curve of her cheek, lowered his defenses.

He tugged her into his arms and swept his mouth across her slightly parted lips.

The heady taste of wild strawberries they'd found along the trail lingered on her tongue. He deepened the kiss, aching for more of her. And she returned his kiss with warm passion.

Heat spread from his belly to his lower region. He hadn't felt this kind of wanting before—for any woman.

When Stoney finally lifted his head, she stayed in the protective circle of his arms, laying her head on his chest.

"I'm sorry. I shouldn't have done that." Stoney's murmur teased the silky hair at her temple.

"No, please don't say you regret it. Not ever that."

"I can't offer you anything, Texanna," he said gently.

"I know. But it's enough. Just to have someone hold me again, give me affection, means far more than you know. It's been so long since I allowed myself to feel alive." She stepped back to stare up at him. "Let me have this moment."

"What can come of it? I'll be leaving in a few days."

A flash of panic crossed her gaze. "How soon?"

Stoney brushed back a golden strand of hair. "My replacement papers should arrive in two or three days."

Her hand trembled when she clutched his vest. "I don't want to think about you going. It's too soon."

"That's why I want you to seriously think about coming with me. I can't leave you behind, knowing the situation. If anything happened . . . I'd never forgive myself." The husky voice sounded like it belonged to someone else.

"I lay awake a good portion of last night pondering my

choices. I can't ask Josh to give up his friends and head for a new place. What would that do to him?"

"What will it do to him if you stay? Think about that."

"Believe me, I have. His welfare comes before my own."

He ran a finger along her delicate jawline. "It'll have to be your decision, pretty lady."

Texanna chewed her lip. "Have you ever considered doing something else besides law work? Have you thought about having a family and settling down?"

A rigid stillness tightened around him like bands of steel. He firmly set her away from him. "I'll never give up being a Texas Ranger. It's my life. They're my family."

His jaw clenched. How could she ask such a thing, knowing his anger when Sam gave up rangering? The idea was inconceivable. He collected his thoughts, his pride, and his hat. It was time to leave before he said something he'd regret.

Texanna sagged weakly into a chair after the door closed. She'd gone and ruined a beautiful moment.

She'd wanted the kiss as much as Stoney had.

For most of the day her eyes had never strayed far from his powerful figure, which loomed so tall over her and the Texas landscape. The impressive size of him took her breath away.

The heat of his muscular body had radiated between them when he'd held her in his arms.

In the little things he did, she knew he cared for her. Like the way his large hands gripped her waist and swung her effortlessly from the saddle, and the care he took to notice how she preferred her coffee.

But more than that, Stoney had a rugged strength about him.

He was the kind of man who'd run barefoot through the

fires of hell for those who touched his life, and keep on coming despite whatever odds he fought.

A knock on the door interrupted her thoughts. Texanna opened it and found Loretta Farris.

"I'm so glad to see you. I need someone to talk to." Texanna ushered her friend into the small parlor. "How about a nice cup of tea? I was about to make myself some."

"That'd sure hit the spot." The stout woman smoothed her graying hair and limped to the kitchen table. Loretta had broken her leg in three places when only a child and it'd left one leg shorter than the other. Texanna wasn't sure what kind of accident had left her crippled. She figured it wasn't important. The woman's friendship had been worth more than answers to prying questions.

Texanna put water on to boil and got down two cups. "How are things at the boardinghouse?"

"Never a dull moment. Mr. Applebee and Mr. Samuels had words over a game of checkers and they're not speaking, the crotchety fools. And Miss Pennybaker, the new schoolteacher, lost a favorite cameo brooch. She thinks Mr. Applebee has it because he's taken quite a shine to her." Loretta giggled. "The fun is guessing who gets their nose out of whack next."

"Sounds like a royal mess." Texanna sighed. "Almost as big a one as my life."

"Does your problem involve a certain Ranger?" she asked, her brown eyes twinkling.

"How did you know?"

"Can't miss the fact that he's been passing a lot of time with you and Josh."

"I suppose it's pretty obvious at that. He wants to take me and Josh with him when he leaves. Says it's the only way to keep us safe."

"Good for him. I think you should go."

"I can't just pack up and leave."

"Why not? It's the best thing for you. Girl, use your noggin for something more than to hang a hat on."

"It's complicated."

"Then uncomplicate things."

"I have businesses to run."

"Marcus is going to take it anyway and leave you with nothing, even if you escape the marrying noose."

"What about Sam's and Jenny's graves? And my parents'? I can't just leave them."

"Girl, those things are insignificant. They're in the past. You have your whole future ahead of you. And what good is it if you're dead too? You and Josh have your lives to live. Think about what would happen to that little boy if you ended up six feet under yourself. Who would take care of him and raise him to be a man?"

The teakettle whistled and Texanna went to take it off the fire. She added tea leaves to the china teapot and poured the hot water over them to let them steep.

"Stoney says the same thing." Texanna brought the teapot to the table and sat back down.

"He's right. You should listen to him."

"I knew him before I married Sam. Stoney gave me my first kiss." Texanna ran her fingers across the smooth oak of the kitchen table. "I'm attracted to him, Loretta. There's this thing between us that we can't deny." She gave Loretta a sideways glance. "He kissed me again, tonight, just before you came."

Loretta laughed. "And that's a problem?"

"I ruined everything. He left angry."

Texanna poured the tea and continued. "I asked the unthinkable. I made Sam give up being a Ranger, and Stoney thinks it cost him his life." Texanna threw up her hands. "I don't know why I had to ask Stoney to forsake his job and take another. I knew how he felt. It's a sore subject between us."

Loretta took a sip from her cup. "We all do crazy things. You can fix this . . . if you want to. All it takes is some gumption. Stoney Burke is a handsome piece of manhood."

"That he is." Her stomach fluttered when he was near and she became as giddy as a schoolgirl.

"Is he offering you marriage, girl?"

"No. Just friendship." He didn't trust her enough to marry her. Therein lay the problem. And thanks to her blunder he would never give her a chance to show him she could change.

One thing for sure, there would be no changing him.

If she wanted him she'd have to accept him the way he was.

Did she want a husband who lived in constant danger and was gone for weeks on end?

Yes. Oh yes, if the man was Stoney Burke.

Catching a cool breeze in the doorway of the livery, Stoney opened the telegram that had just arrived from Austin. It was from Judge Goodnight.

As he skimmed it, his heart sank. The judge couldn't help unless they could prove beyond a doubt that the document Marcus had was a fake. And the only way to prove that was to find the real one.

The telegram hadn't helped a bit. The judge's hands were tied.

What was Stoney going to do about Texanna's problem?

You could always marry her, whispered a voice in his head.

That would protect Texanna and Josh, but wouldn't save her businesses. Marcus LaRoach could still take those.

But marrying her, even in name only, she'd issue all

kinds of ultimatums. His jaw tightened. He'd never take to a bit like a docile horse. Not for any woman.

There had to be another way.

He'd promised Sam he'd watch out for Texanna and he meant to do his best, but he had limits that couldn't be stretched and lines that couldn't be crossed. She might as well realize that.

Though supper time was about an hour away, Stoney would take it at Mattie's Cook Shack rather than Texanna's. He had to put some space between them for both their sakes. And after he ate he'd visit the Pig and Whistle. Maybe he could rustle up a poker game with LaRoach and take some of the little pissant's money. The picture of the man's angry face enticed him.

He climbed to the loft with the freshly laundered clothes he'd collected from the bathhouse and laid them on top of his saddlebags.

Just then a volley of gunshots erupted in the street below.

Sam Hill!

Stoney took the ladder at a run.

Chapter 9

Stoney ran into the street with his Colt drawn. Smoke, gunshots, and holy hell came from the sheriff's office.

Jailbreak!

Dodging bullets, he zigzagged his way toward the commotion, returning fire. As best he could tell, three men were hunkered down behind a buckboard loaded with barrels. He'd heard Colfax had some brothers and each one was more rotten than the next. He guessed these to be none other than the infamous Colfax brothers. His day had taken a turn for the worse.

The gunmen were sending volleys of shots into the jail. When they spied Stoney, they turned the hail of hot lead on him. Using a horse trough as a shield, he crouched low. Then his heart froze.

In the middle of the street, a little girl curled up in a ball with her hands over her ears.

If he didn't do something she'd be killed.

Without wasting a minute, Stoney jammed his Colt back in the holster and dashed toward her. Bullets peppered the ground around his feet as he scooped her up in his arms and sprinted for cover inside Truebill's Mercantile. He carefully sat her down. Tears created paths through the grime on her face.

"Stay here." He smoothed her hair. "You'll be all right."

Mr. Muttonchops came from the back of the store. "You go on. I'll look after her."

Leaving the girl safe in the care of the mercantile owner, Stoney rushed back into the fray. They wouldn't break Newt Colfax out if he could help it. Not today.

He darted into an alley, circled around and came up from behind. All three men were focused on the jail. They'd let down their guard. He eased up next to the closest outlaw and put his Colt to the man's head.

"Put down your weapons if you want your brother to live," he ordered the other two.

When they hesitated, he added, "Doesn't make any difference to me what you choose. You're either going to be dead or locked up. Make it light on yourself."

Growling, the trio slowly dropped their pistols to the dirt and raised their hands.

"You all right, Sheriff?" Stoney called.

"They got me."

"We're coming in. Don't shoot."

Stoney marched the threesome inside. Sheriff Ezra lay on the floor in a pool of blood. The prisoner, Newt Colfax, had also been wounded. He slumped onto a thin mattress in his cell.

Lifting the brass key ring from the sheriff's desk, Stoney locked the three men in an empty cell, then knelt beside Ezra.

"Is there a doctor in this town?"

"Nope. Being the barber and all, Mrs. Wilder generally takes care of the doctoring too." Ezra grimaced in pain. Blood seeped from his shoulder and thigh.

At that moment several wide-eyed townsfolk burst through the door. "Did you get 'em?"

"Yep. Go round up Texanna Wilder and get her here as fast as you can. Sheriff Ezra's in a bad way. Haven't checked on Colfax yet, but he's not moving."

Someone scooted out the door to do his bidding.

One of the three men he'd just put in a cell growled and launched himself onto one of the others. "Damn you! Why'd you hafta go and shoot our brother? You don't have the sense God gave a tree stump."

"How do you figure it was me?" the second one asked. "Coulda been anybody, even you. Even the Ranger."

That brought on more scuffling. One of them slammed into the bars of the cell.

"Go ahead and kill each other. It'll save me the trouble of carting you to Menardville," Stoney bellowed.

While the outlaws were going at it, he lifted Bill Ezra and carried him into the only unoccupied cell. The sheriff groaned when Stoney gently stretched him out on the cot. He removed the old lawman's shirt to inspect the shoulder wound.

A bullet had created a gaping hole and was still lodged inside Ezra's shoulder. Next, Stoney slit the man's pants leg to assess the damage to the lawman's thigh. The piece of lead appeared to have splintered the bone. He'd seen his share of gunshot wounds and this was one of the worst.

Texanna's breath was ragged as she sprinted into the jail. She carried a medical bag of sorts.

"I was afraid you were the one who'd been shot." Her clear blue gaze swept him from head to toe as though to make certain before she turned her attention to the sheriff. "Thank God it wasn't. How bad is Ezra?"

"Took two bullets. Both are still inside. Haven't had time to give Colfax more than a glance. He's unconscious and bleeding. You start on Ezra and I'll check on the prisoner."

She took out a metal instrument that resembled a long

pair of tweezers from her bag. "I haven't had much experience with gunshots, but I'll do my best. The last time I tried, the bullet was in Sam. I couldn't save him." She trembled.

In her line of work, she probably didn't get too many patients who were still breathing. Seeing all the blood, remembering Sam, took a terrible toll on her.

Stoney took her hands in his. "It'll be all right. I'm here if you need me." His lips brushed her forehead.

She nodded and took a deep breath. Her skirts snapped around her ankles when she bent over the sheriff. The business part of her had taken hold. She'd be all right.

Stoney unlocked Newt Colfax's cell. He proceeded cautiously, afraid the cattle rustler and murderer was simply faking. The outlaw's breath was shallow. Stoney turned Newt's head and saw the bullet had entered just above his ear. The man had no other wounds. He dragged the big outlaw onto the narrow cot and had turned to get a basin of water when Texanna called to him.

He hurried to her side. "How is he?"

Texanna looked up. Stoney was glad to see relief in her eyes. "He'll make it. I need your help with his leg. We'll have to put a splint on it. But I need to set the bone first. What's the verdict with Colfax?"

"Head wound. Gonna be messy removing that bullet. Not sure he'll make it."

"There's some water in the pitcher. You can wash your hands and we'll get started. Looks like we have our work cut out for us before the day is done." Texanna turned to Bill Ezra. "Do you have any whiskey?"

"Top drawer of my desk."

She went to get the bottle while Stoney washed and dried his hands. She sterilized the tweezers, then offered the bottle to the sheriff along with a dose of laudanum. "You're going to need this. It's going to hurt."

"Reckon I can stomach the pain. Just do what you gotta do," Ezra said through gritted teeth.

Over the next few hours, Stoney and Texanna removed lead and bandaged wounds. She gave Ezra another dose of laudanum to take the edge off his misery and moved to her other patient. The outlaw was still unconscious, which was probably a blessing, considering the nature of his wound.

Texanna washed the blood from around the bullet hole. Carefully, she probed the wound until she found the piece of metal. Dropping it in a metal tray, she bandaged his head. There was nothing more they could do for Colfax.

Sheriff Ezra called Stoney to his side. "Until I'm able to be up and around I'm turning over the reins to you. I know you're more than able to keep the peace."

"Appreciate the vote of confidence. I'll do my best."

"Just don't put too much stock in anything Marcus LaRoach says. The big bag of wind likes to hear himself talk."

"I can manage LaRoach. You focus on getting well."

Texanna shot a glance toward the prisoners and leaned close to Stoney's ear. "We should move the sheriff out of here."

"I agree. Where does he live?"

"Marcus gave Ezra a small house behind the hotel when he made him sheriff. But I don't think he should be alone. Not safe in his condition."

"Where then?"

"Loretta Farris's place. She'll watch over him like a mother hen. I'll go ask her while you find something to carry Ezra on."

Stoney left Texanna at the boardinghouse and went to locate a litter and get Dusty Haws to help him. The only thing he could find to use was a coffin lid. He and Dusty carried it back to the jail. Texanna had already returned.

She reported that Loretta had wasted no time in volunteering her services.

"You have another think coming if you expect to load me onto a coffin lid," Sheriff Ezra declared. "Goldarn it, I ain't dead yet. Quit rushing things."

Stoney grinned and shook his head. "It's the best I could do under the circumstances. You'll just have to deal with it, you ungrateful old coot. This is the thanks I get for saving your ornery hide. Next time you can get your buddy LaRoach to do it. But there'd be a price involved, I'm thinking. Speaking of the varmint, where do you suppose he's hidin'?"

"Under a rock would be my guess," Dusty rumbled.

The old sheriff added, "Somewhere safe from gunfire."

Despite Ezra's grumbling, they managed to get him onto the make-do litter and carried him to the boardinghouse. Texanna followed on their heels to see that Ezra got settled to her satisfaction.

Stoney's heart soared with pride at the way Texanna and Loretta hovered over the old lawman, whose face had turned three shades of gray, seeing to his every need.

"Now, this is much better." Texanna handed a brown bottle of laudanum to Loretta. "Give him another dose of this every two hours. I'll be back tomorrow. Get some sleep," she ordered the lawman.

"Yes, ma'am." Ezra gave her a snappy salute.

"You did yourself proud, Texanna." Stoney offered his arm as they left Loretta's. "You're quite the doctor."

Texanna gave him a wan smile. "Just doing what I can for the people who depend on me. If I weren't here, there'd be no one to call. What about Newt Colfax?"

"He's fine where he is. I won't endanger your life. Besides, I'll sleep at the jail until Ezra mends."

"All the same, I'll check on him before I turn in for the night." She suddenly clasped a hand over her mouth. "You haven't had any supper. I had it ready to set on the table when everything broke loose."

"Reckon I could use a bite at that. Then I can make my rounds." He let his arm drop to her trim waist, wishing he could kiss her again. In the next instant he remembered her asking him if he'd ever thought of getting into another line of work and his stomach lurched. He considered going to bed hungry.

The final vestiges of daylight vanished as darkness drifted over Devils Creek. Her skirts swished against his leg as they walked to her home.

Texanna preceded him up the stairs, and when she reached the top she made a low cry.

"What's wrong?" Stoney tried to see around her.

She turned. Color had drained from her face, leaving it ashen. She clutched a rock with a note attached. "This was lying in front of the door." Fear clouded her blue eyes. "Josh! I left him here alone."

Chapter 10

Stoney picked up the note that fluttered from Texanna's hand. In heavy black print on a piece of parcel paper were the words I'M WATCHING YOU.

Texanna opened the door and ran inside. "Josh!"

The boy jerked the top he was spinning. It whirled and spun away under a table next to the settee. He jumped to his feet, clearly shaken by his mother's sudden entrance. He was poised to sprint for cover, the same way Stoney did when outlaws were trying to fill him full of holes.

Texanna ran and threw her arms around her son. "I thought something had happened to you." She smoothed his hair. "Thank God you're all right."

"I'm okay, Mama."

Stoney dropped the rock to the ground below and crossed the threshold. It didn't take a genius to figure out who wrote the warning. For two cents he'd go find the slimy skunk and settle up with him. LaRoach was nothing but a coward who hid in the shadows, just waiting to strike when a person least expected it. Stoney'd take a stroll over to the saloon when he left.

It wouldn't hurt to see what was going on.

Besides, he was in charge of keeping the peace now.

* * *

A short while later, Stoney followed the sound of the tinny piano and stepped into the dimly lit Pig and Whistle. His narrowed gaze swept the crowd and found LaRoach at a card table. It had no vacant seats.

In no particular hurry, Stoney ambled toward the bar.

"Beer, please," he told the bartender.

The aproned man slid a mug with an inch of foam on top in front of him.

Taking the thick mug, he wandered over to the card game and positioned himself across from LaRoach. A measure of satisfaction filled him when Marcus glanced up and turned a sick shade of gray. The man evidently found Stoney's hard stare a mite difficult to take when it was turned on him. Marcus swallowed and hunched over his poker hand.

After a long minute, Marcus slammed the cards down and got up so fast his chair clattered backward to the floor. "You got anything better to do than ruin a man's concentration, Ranger?"

The other men at the table got up slowly, one by one.

"If you didn't have a guilty conscience, it wouldn't bother you." Stoney pushed back his hat with a forefinger.

"Don't have nothing to feel guilty for."

"Don't you?" Stoney set his half-empty mug of beer down on the card table. He didn't know how this might play out and he wanted both hands free. "Don't suppose you know anything about a note that was left on Texanna Wilder's doorstep this evening."

"Why should I? Are you accusing me?"

Stoney let the corner of his mouth quirk up. "Not yet. When I do, I'll arrest you."

"Any time you think you're big enough, just come ahead."

"You're not the only one watching. If I catch you so

much as spitting on the sidewalk, you'll find yourself in a cell. And come near Texanna or Josh and you'll get what's coming to you so fast your head'll spin. That's a promise."

The man's hand inched toward the .45 he wore.

"I really hope you draw that gun." The warning was soft and low. "It'll be the last thing you ever do."

Marcus snatched up his bowler hat and marched out the door.

Stoney watched him leave, knowing he hadn't heard the last of LaRoach. He'd be waiting for the man to mess up. Meanwhile, it was time he learned the gambler's habits.

Texanna awoke the next morning with a feeling of overwhelming dread. She wasn't safe. Josh wasn't safe. Marcus intended to destroy them as surely as the sun was rising. And Stoney could only do so much until the man broke the law.

But she wasn't going to sit around idle, waiting for the next move.

No, it was time she did something.

Before that though, she had patients to attend to.

She got dressed and woke Josh. Stoney arrived as she was setting the table for breakfast. Heated swirls rose up at the sight of the tall, lean Ranger and made her knees wobble.

Still wet, his hair lay in dark waves. She remembered the day she barbered him and the silky texture of it.

It didn't take much imagination to picture him lying next to her with his arms holding her tight, the hard substance of his naked body pressed to hers, his mouth taking liberties.

Lord have mercy!

She shook herself sternly and reined in her thoughts.

At one time Stoney could've felt that way about her. But

it was too late now. She'd said the wrong thing. All the progress she'd made had been for naught.

Noting the haggard look that hung like a set of clothes that were a size too large, Stoney didn't appear to have gotten any more sleep than she did. She wondered what had kept him awake.

The prisoners' snores perhaps? Or was it worry?

"Sure could use a cup of coffee." He planted his black hat on a hook beside the door. "Smells mighty good."

"Come on in. It's ready and waiting."

When she handed him a cup of the dark brew, the lines at the corners of his eyes crinkled with his lopsided smile. Her breath caught on the lump in her throat.

The thoughts she'd just reined in sprang free.

Why had she let him get away so many years ago? He was tender, yet he had a dangerous toughness about him that could put the fear of God in the worst outlaw.

And it didn't come from the Colt hanging low on his hip.

No, his steely strength came from inside. It came from having a good heart, one that held a belief of right and wrong in no uncertain terms. Stoney Burke upheld not only the law, but his personal beliefs as well—despite the valleys, darkness, and sheer hell he had to go through to do it.

God help her. She was deeply and utterly in love with him.

She couldn't deny her racing heartbeat and the flutters in her stomach when he entered a room. She glanced at his broad shoulders that tapered to a narrow waist and thought of the impossible.

Maybe the caring he had for her could grow into love.

And maybe buffalo were just big cows.

Stoney slid his rugged form into a chair at the kitchen table. "Had a talk with LaRoach last evening after I left here. Can't say that I got through to him, but I will say I gave him some things to mull over in that pea brain of his."

"Marcus can be quite determined when he wants something."

"So can I." The words were hard as granite.

"I was thinking about me trying to reason with him. Maybe I can—"

"No! Stay away from him. I mean it, Texanna."

She bristled at the explosion. "I can't make things any worse."

"Things can get worse—a lot worse, believe me."

"I have to deal with him when you leave." She put her hands on her hips, prepared to go toe-to-toe with him. But she couldn't escape the stormy charcoal stare.

Combing his fingers through his hair, Stoney rose and covered the distance between them. "I couldn't live with myself if anything happened to you."

"Exactly how do you feel about me? Am I just Sam's widow and you feel responsible for my safety?" She captured her bottom lip between her teeth, afraid she already knew his answer. "Or is there something more?"

Her heart stilled as she braced herself for his reply.

He lowered his head, his breath ruffling the loose hair at her temples. "My dear, beautiful Texanna. I—"

"Hi, Stoney." Josh bounded into the kitchen.

They moved apart quickly and Texanna felt her face redden.

"Hey there, little man," Stoney answered in his easy way. "You're full of energy this morning. You have a big marble game planned?"

"Yes sir. An' me and Matthew might go watch his uncle build a corral."

"Josh, I'd rather you stuck close today."

The boy's face fell. She knew how he chafed for his freedom. Stoney was right. She wasn't being fair to Josh by insisting they stay in Devils Creek.

Stoney met her gaze. "Your mother's right, son. What

about me taking you boys fishing? We can go after I settle some business."

"Oh boy! Is that okay, Mama?"

Texanna smoothed the top of his head. "Just you mind what he says, okay?"

Josh and Stoney loaded up their plates with bacon, eggs, and biscuits. As they filled their stomachs, the talk turned to worms and hooks. Texanna sat quietly, watching her little boy who wanted so much to be a man, and the man who gave her son the moon and stars and everything between.

She burned with curiosity. What had Stoney been about to say?

Stoney made the rounds alongside Texanna to check on their patients, though he already knew Colfax's state of health. After all, he'd slept a few feet away from the wounded outlaw.

At the boardinghouse, the sheriff's weathered face lit up at the sight of the breakfast Texanna took him. "I swannee, ain't this something?"

"How do you feel today?" Texanna touched his forehead.

"Got a gnawing ache in my leg, but a bigger one in my gut. Reckon I'm mite near ready to wrestle a bear."

Stoney watched Texanna change the bandage and fuss over the man. She had the old lawman wrapped around her little finger. Ezra flirted shamelessly and Stoney knew he'd have stiff competition on his hands if the old geezer were a little younger.

Since when had he started looking at other men and considering them competition?

Since you kissed her, you fool.

Texanna had snuck past his defenses and he knew leaving would be difficult if not damn near impossible.

She'd asked him how he felt about her, and that wasn't easy to answer. He'd been relieved when Josh had spared him from having to reply.

Truth was, he hadn't sorted out his feelings about Texanna yet.

He only knew he liked kissing her and having her in his arms. And he knew it went far beyond simple responsibility for Sam's widow.

Oh yes, she was much more than that.

Chapter 11

It didn't take long to teach a couple of rambunctious youngsters how to bait a hook and drop it in the water.

Stoney couldn't recall the last time he sat on the banks of a river with a fishing pole in hand. It had been years since he'd last engaged in the pleasurable pastime and he'd missed it.

The San Saba River's sparkling blue water lapped gently along the shore. His soul was at peace here.

Nearby, Hondo and Josh's little paint, which they'd rented again from Dusty Haws, grazed on a patch of nut grass.

Josh and Matthew reminded him of his younger days before he and his brother realized that their father's ambition didn't extend to actual work. John Burke loved fishing and enjoyed teaching his sons how to do it. But if John had tried to show them how to earn a day's wage, the man wouldn't have known where to start. He'd sure had loafing down pat though.

Josh glanced at Stoney. The big grin on the boy's face stretched from ear to ear. "Reckon we'll have enough fish for Mama to cook for supper?"

"I'm betting we will." Stoney's heart warmed. Such a

simple thing like fishing made the boy so happy. Lord knew Josh hadn't had much of a chance to be young and carefree.

From what Stoney could see, playing marbles was the extent of Josh's fun.

Texanna kept her son's natural curiosity tamped down under her mother-henning. But Stoney had it in his power to teach Josh some of the games he'd grown up with. A sudden idea jolted him upright. He stuck the handle of his pole in the moist dirt and stood.

"Have either of you boys ever played mumblety-peg?"

They shrugged their shoulders and Josh replied, "Nope."

"Then it's time you learned."

"What's mumblety-peg?" Matthew asked.

"It's a game played with knives. Do either of you have a pocketknife?"

"Nope," Josh answered.

Why was he not surprised?

"We can use mine. Lay down those poles and come here." Stoney drew a circle in the dirt and opened up his knife. He showed Josh and Matthew how to throw the knife so that the blade stuck into the ground as near to the center of the circle as he could get it.

This version was a lot safer than the one where each player measured a win by sticking the knife into the ground as close to his opponent's foot as he could without stabbing him.

It was harmless fun, he told himself.

Stoney demonstrated his knife-throwing skills by showing them this dangerous version, telling them never to play that way. An hour later he was just about to get them back to some serious fishing when Matthew screamed.

"What's wrong?" Stoney's belly twisted at the sight of blood dripping from Matthew's hand.

"I—I cut myself."

Stoney quickly lifted the boy and sprinted to the water's edge so he could wash off the blood and determine the severity of the wound.

"It'll be okay," he said in an effort to comfort Matthew, who by this time was sobbing uncontrollably. Or maybe Stoney was only comforting himself. There was no escaping the guilt that sat on his shoulders like a rampaging bull.

Matthew's palm gaped open in a bloody mess.

Damn! There was no way on earth to keep this from Texanna. She'd raise holy hell and probably run him back to Menardville.

"Is he hurt bad, Ranger . . . I mean, Stoney?" The freckles stood out even more on Josh's colorless face.

"Your friend won't be shooting marbles for a while. He's in need of some stitches."

Texanna would never forgive him for letting the youngsters play with a knife. Never in a million years.

He could already picture her walleyed hissy fit.

Untying the bandana from around his neck, Stoney wrapped it tightly around Matthew's hand.

"Josh, can you grab our fishing poles while I get Matthew on Hondo?" He wouldn't risk the boy falling off a horse in the bargain. Matthew would ride with him.

The boy hustled to collect the gear and was back in a flash. Stoney helped him into the saddle of the little paint.

The rock in his stomach had turned into a boulder by the time they reached town. They pulled up in front of Wilder's Undertaking Emporium just as Texanna was coming out.

Josh climbed from the horse. "Mama, Matthew's hurt."

"What happened?" Concern etched her face.

"He got cut," Josh supplied before Stoney could tell her gentle-like.

Stoney threw his leg over the saddle horn and dismounted. He lifted Matthew down and carried him into the building.

He'd give anything not to have to answer Texanna's questions. Damn, he could see no way to skirt the truth.

She gently unwrapped the boy's hand and examined it. "I'll have to sew it up. Josh, run and tell Matthew's parents."

"Okay, Mama." The boy took off in a flurry.

Texanna turned to Stoney. He squirmed under her icy blue scrutiny. "I don't understand how Matthew cut himself. A fishhook wouldn't make a wound like this."

"The boy sorta cut himself trying to play mumblety-peg."

"What on earth! What were you doing while this was going on?"

Yep, she was mad as a horned toad all right. Stoney prayed for a lie, but none came to mind. "Now, Texanna, don't get all riled up. I was teaching them, all right?"

With her eyes riveted on Stoney, she addressed Josh's friend. "Matthew, where did you and Josh get knives?"

Matthew wiped his tears. "Ranger Burke."

When she focused all her attention on him, Stoney prayed for a hole to open up and swallow him. None did.

Her voice was tight. "You took knives to go fishing?"

She made it seem as if he'd deliberately set out to go against her wishes. And that he had a whole arsenal.

"It was one pocketknife and it belonged to me." He raised his chin a tad. "And I didn't take them there with the intention of teaching them to play with knives. I was only trying to show them how to be boys and do boy things. Seemed a good idea at the time. Never thought Matthew would get injured. If you weren't so all-fired bent on keeping Josh from growing into a man, I'd never have taught them the game."

"So this is my fault?"

The woman, who fought tooth and nail to hang on to the son she couldn't bear to lose, had plenty of reason to be upset.

If only she didn't struggle so hard to still her quivering lip. He could handle her anger. He knew how to deal with that. It was tears and sorrow that sucker-punched him in the gut.

"Of course not. I take full responsibility. Can we place blame later? See to Matthew's hand first. Then you can chew on my butt to your heart's content."

At last Texanna calmed down. She got her medicine bag and took out her needle. By then, Matthew's parents had arrived. Stoney explained what happened. Unlike Texanna, they understood it was simply an accident. Thank God for rational heads.

Leaving the group, Stoney collected the horses and walked them toward the livery.

"Stoney," Josh called, running behind him.

"What is it, son?"

"Your pocketknife. You forgot it." The boy skidded to a stop beside him and held out the weapon.

Stoney took it, his heart light. Josh could easily have kept quiet. The fact that the boy returned it without being asked said a lot for his character. He couldn't be responsible for all the missing things the town accused him of taking.

"Thanks. I forgot all about it in the excitement."

"Sure is a nice pocketknife." Josh's freckled face was wistful. "One of these days when I'm big I'm gonna have one just like it. Then I'll be safe."

The boy was clearly worried about his Uncle Marcus. What was the price for giving Josh some security? Stoney weighed a thought. "I'll tell you what . . . why don't you hold on to it for me for a few days?"

"Oh boy!"

"But you have to promise that you won't take it out of your pocket and flash it around. Remember what happened to Matthew."

"I promise."

"I'll hold you to that."

Texanna would hold Stoney's feet to the fire when she found out about it.

He'd have to tell her. She had a right to know.

Lord, he didn't relish the chore though.

Chapter 12

"Got a letter for you, Ranger," yelled the owner of the Western Stage Line as Stoney emerged from the livery two hours later, after unsaddling and rubbing down both animals.

He strolled toward the man. "Much obliged."

The envelope bore the seal of the Texas Rangers.

His replacement papers. For all the good it did to get them now. He couldn't leave, with Colfax at death's door. And if the man died, he wouldn't need them at all.

Funny how fast life switched horses on a man.

While he was contemplating that, a boy darted from Truebill's Mercantile with half of Devils Creek hot on his heels. The store owner lunged and tackled the boy, sending both to the ground.

"I've got you now, you little thief," stormed Muttonchops.

Stoney shoved through the angry circle that had formed around the two. "What in Sam Hill's going on here?"

"Why don't you ask him?" Truebill glared, his muttonchop sideburns outlining his face like a picture frame.

"Get off the boy and I will." Stoney gave the youngster

a hand. When he pulled him to his feet, his stomach plummeted.

Josh peered up with fear in his eyes.

"What did you do, son?"

The boy shrugged his small shoulders.

"Look in his pocket and you'll see," spouted a by-stander.

"Josh, show me what's in your pocket," Stoney asked in as gentle a way as he knew. No reason to frighten the boy any more than he already was.

Josh pulled out the pocketknife. Next came an envelope fluttering to the dirt. Stoney bent to pick it up.

The envelope was addressed to the mercantile owner, Martin Truebill. He turned it over and noticed the seal was still intact. Disappointment stabbed him. This didn't bode well for the boy to whom he'd entrusted his pocketknife.

"That's mine," said Truebill, stomping around in a circle. "It just arrived. I didn't even have time to open it. This is the last straw. I'm going over your head and wiring the circuit judge. It's time somebody did something with this kid."

"Give me a chance to take care of this."

Truebill glared. "Not on your life. You're awful cozy with Mrs. Wilder. You're not going to do what needs to be done with her son. The boy needs a firm hand. He either needs a father or a jail cell. Put him in there and throw away the key. We won't tolerate any more of his thievery. Lord knows Mrs. Wilder can't, or won't, handle the wild ragamuffin."

Josh kept his gaze fastened on his bare feet. Stoney heard a loud sniffle.

"I'm only asking for a day or two before you wire the judge. Seems only fair given the boy's tender years."

Martin Truebill was silent while he mulled it over. Then he nodded curtly. "One day, no more than that."

With disgruntled murmuring, the group dispersed. Stoney took Josh in tow and headed for the sheriff's office.

Texanna intercepted them halfway, worry turning her eyes a deep shade of purple. "What are you doing with Josh? You're not putting him in jail. I won't stand for it."

"I'm going to have a quiet talk with the boy, find out why he had Truebill's mail in his pocket. It's time to sort out this mess once and for all. Folks are ready to string Josh up and I've got to find a way to put a stop to it." He continued his trek, keeping a firm hand on Josh's arm.

"I'm coming with you." She fell into step.

"No, I need to talk to Josh without you telling him what to say."

She put her hands on her hips. "But I'm his mother."

"No one's disputing that. This is one time you can't smooth things over. This is the last button on Mabel's drawers." He stopped. The tears gathering in her eyes almost undid him. "Let me do my job. I'm not going to hurt the boy, but I am going to get at the truth. Now, go back to the barbershop and I'll talk to you after I'm done."

Thirty minutes later, he emerged from the jail with Josh. The frightened boy had admitted to taking the envelope as well as Stoney's missing Ranger documents and all the other papers the townsfolk had accused him of filching. Josh led him to the shed of the undertaking shop and dug up a metal box that was buried under some tools. Inside were all the things he'd taken, along with some of Texanna's recipes.

"Why did you take these, Josh?"

The young boy swiped his nose on his sleeve. "I was only trying to help. Mama said she's looking for some important papers, and I thought these might be it an' I had to keep 'em safe from Uncle Marcus. I didn't mean to hurt anyone. I promise." Josh's wide eyes brimmed with tears. "Are you gonna put me in jail and throw away the key?"

Stoney placed an arm around the trembling boy and drew him close. "No. But you're going to have to return these to their owners and say you're sorry. What you've done isn't helping your mother. You understand that you can't take things that aren't yours?"

Josh nodded, a strangled sob escaping.

"You won't have to face those people alone. I'll go with you." Stoney's heart ached for the little boy who felt such a strong responsibility toward his mother.

Josh definitely needed a father, no two ways about that.

The only clear resolution that would be acceptable to the townspeople and allow Texanna to keep Josh was a drastic step.

He'd have to marry her.

It was the only way to save Josh from being shipped off to some juvenile home.

Texanna glanced out the barbershop window to see Stoney marching toward her. His face was stern and unyielding.

What had Josh done?

He was just a scared, fatherless little boy.

She chewed on her bottom lip, her stomach churning.

Stoney's gray gaze met hers the minute he came through the door. "We have to talk."

Nodding mutely, she took a seat in the empty barber chair.

Quickly he told her what had happened. "The only way you can keep Josh and spare him the juvenile home is if you marry. The boy needs a father and I'm willing to take on that challenge and see that he walks the straight and narrow. On certain conditions, mind you."

"Are you asking me to marry you?" Her voice was quiet and still, but inside butterflies created sheer havoc.

His big hand swallowed her small one. "I am."

"For Josh's sake?" While she wanted to blurt out her acceptance, it hurt that he only offered his hand in order to spare Josh the town's wrath.

"That's one reason."

"It's not very romantic."

"You want romance or to save your son?" His jaw hardened.

"What's wrong with both? If you want to marry me, you'll have to do better than that, Stoney Burke. Otherwise you'll be no better a choice than Marcus LaRoach."

"You drive a hard bargain, Texanna."

Suddenly he lowered his mouth and swept it across hers. Tingles cavorted up her spine and buttery warmth spread through her body. And just when she thought he'd end the kiss, he pulled her tightly to his chest and ground his lips to hers.

Her hands stole around his neck, underneath the ends of his length of hair, and held on to keep from drowning with desire.

The kiss stole her breath, her thoughts, and her intentions. It was one that could make a woman forget her name and spin her world on its axis.

Her breath mingled with his and with it came raw need.

She loved this man and wanted him in a way she'd never wanted any other.

Stoney broke the kiss with tiny nibbles along her jawline. "What if I tell you that I've always desired you. You drove me crazy because it seemed you only had eyes for Sam."

Her heart soared. Stoney wanted her.

But that didn't mean he loved her.

Did it?

Texanna twisted in his arms. "Can you live here in Devils Creek?"

"Only if it's where you'll be."

"What about the Texas Rangers?"

The muscles beneath her fingers tensed. "It won't do for you to tell me to give up the Rangers. That's a deal breaker as far as I'm concerned. I'm a Texas Ranger and I'll always be one. Nothing gonna change that. Can you handle that, Texanna?"

"I want you to be happy. I have no objection to your choice of occupation as long as you don't object to mine."

Some things were instilled in a person's soul and there was no prying them out.

She'd take Stoney Burke just like he was. The man who loved her son as his own would always have her heart.

His uncommon strength had nothing to do with his ability for gunplay or his powerful, muscled body. It came from within.

"Then, you'll marry me?" he asked.

For a brief second she went over her dresses in her mind. She reckoned her Sunday dress would do just fine.

"Yes. I'd be honored to be your wife."

Chapter 13

Shades of gold, echoing the promise of happiness to come, arrived with dawn the following morning. It seemed a perfect day to throw in her lot with Stoney's and begin a new life.

Midmorning, Texanna readied for the ceremony. Her fingers shook so badly she had trouble fastening the buttons on her fitted bodice of sprigged muslin that brought out the cornflower blue of her eyes. She slipped her feet into her shoes and was peering at her reflection in the mirror when Josh found her.

"Mama, do I hafta wear this dumb bow tie?"

"It would look very nice, don't you think? And you'll only have to suffer with it for a little bit. Bring it here and I'll tie it for you."

He trudged to her, scuffing the toes of his boots on the floor. Texanna took the scrap of fabric and made short work of tying it, then she kissed the top of his head. "You're such a handsome young man. I'm so proud of you. Don't ever forget that." She picked up her white gloves. "Are you okay with me marrying Stoney?"

"Shoot, yeah! He's a lot nicer than Uncle Marcus."

She chuckled. "Yes, by far a better choice."

At least now she shouldn't have to worry about the man's unwanted attention anymore. Or be frightened and alone. This wedding would solve all that.

But far more important was that she'd spend the rest of her days loving the honorable man who could make her stomach do somersaults with a mere glance.

With jittery fingers, she set her hat on her head and anchored it with pins, giving herself one last look of approval in the mirror. Her fervent wish was to make Stoney proud, not only today but every day henceforth. She prayed he'd never regret marrying her.

If only she could believe he truly loved her.

She couldn't thank him enough for sparing Josh, but she needed to know he took this step for her.

Ushering Josh out the door, she headed for the church to meet Stoney. Just as she passed the Pig and Whistle, Marcus stepped out and into her path.

"Don't think you're rid of me, Texanna," he sneered. "I still own your businesses." The man inspected his fingernails. "I might even sell 'em if the price is right."

"Stoney might have a thing or two to say about that." She relished the way the color trickled from his face. "Now, pardon me, I have a wedding to get to."

Sweeping past the obnoxious man, she said a prayer that Marcus wouldn't cause them more grief. Then she prayed that she'd find Sam's Last Will and Testament. And soon! She meant to redouble her efforts.

But first she had a date with the preacher.

Stoney, dressed in a crisp white shirt that contrasted with his black vest and pants, stood waiting on the church steps. Quivers of excitement danced up her spine. The tall Ranger, whose muscular figure made her thoughts race ahead to steamy nights and wrinkled sheets, grinned in that sexy way that vowed he had certain things in mind for her.

A warm excited glow spread through her.

He offered her his elbow. "I was afraid you'd backed out."

She got tangled in the unspoken promises that lurked in his eyes, which at times looked gunmetal gray but today resembled hazy smoke. "Not a chance. I've dreamed of this moment for a long time."

Leaning close, he murmured in her ear. "Have I told you that you're the most desirable woman I've ever seen?"

"Not yet," she said, her heart skipping a beat.

"Then consider it done. You take my breath away, lady. And that's not all."

Tingles sashayed the length of her. Suddenly she knew she was doing the right thing. This man held her heart in the palm of his hand and treasured it as a rare find.

Not only today, but forever.

With friends looking on, they spoke their "I do's," promising to love and cherish each other.

Then came the kiss that sealed their vows.

Stoney took her upturned face between his big hands and lowered his head. His lips settled on hers as though he'd waited his whole life for this moment and didn't intend to be rushed.

The slow, sensual kiss created a fire that blazed from the tips of her toes to the top of her head. She couldn't wait to feel his body next to hers and to know he truly belonged to her in every way possible.

Stoney wasn't in the mood to twiddle his fingers until dark. After the ceremony and a small gathering at the boardinghouse for cake and lemonade, he arranged for Josh to spend the night there with Loretta Farris. Texanna seemed as anxious as he did to get back to her home. Their home now.

"It's still daylight. Everyone will know what we're doing!" Texanna stood fretting in the middle of the parlor. She removed her hat and laid it on a small table.

He put his arms around her and pulled her close, nuzzling her ear. "I should hope that everyone knows what a man and woman in love do. If not, they need to learn."

Breathing in her sweet fragrance, he hardened with desire.

His maddening, sensitive wife aroused every nerve ending.

He loved her more than he'd thought possible.

With great care, he unfastened the tiny row of buttons to expose the silky skin beneath. He kissed her shoulders, which had borne a heavy load for so long. He'd gladly take that burden now.

Scooping her up, he carried her to the bedroom and set her down.

The soft cotton chemise and drawers followed the dress and petticoats, floating to the floor in a puddle of ruffles and bows. It wasn't until he had her bare as a newborn babe that he permitted her to undress him.

At last they collapsed onto the bed in a heated rush.

"I've waited for this moment, never daring to dream I'd have you for a wife. You're so beautiful, so perfect." Stoney burrowed his face in the gentle swell of her breasts, laving them with his tongue.

A moan rose in her throat.

"Oh, Stoney," she murmured. "Don't stop."

"As if I could if I wanted." He leaned back. "A wild herd of horses couldn't hold me back. I intend to have my way with you, Mrs. Burke."

He left a trail of kisses down the slender column of her throat, across her breasts, and on to her taut belly.

"Your skin is soft and supple, your body ripe for the

taking." Stoney lifted the hard planes of his body atop her and slipped inside, relishing the tight flesh that gripped him.

A little while later, he rolled off and pulled her against him. A sheen of moisture coated both their bodies. Her long lashes hid the blue gaze he loved, which could flash fire or declare the depth of her love.

Stoney propped himself on an elbow and wrapped a finger around a silky strand of golden hair. "Now aren't you glad you didn't convince me to wait until dark?"

Texanna brushed his jaw with the tips of her fingers. "Extremely."

"You don't care that everyone knows what we're doing?"

"Not even a little bit."

"That's good, because I'm not done with you yet. I have a hunger for you that I suspect will take a lifetime to sate."

"You're scandalous," she said, grinning.

Daylight had faded into dark shadows when growling stomachs sent them to the kitchen. Texanna, clad only in her wrap that was belted at the waist, stirred the coals in the stove and added wood. She took some eggs from the larder, pausing to give her new husband an approving glance.

Her pulse raced at the sight. Stoney had hastily pulled on his britches but had left them unfastened. Fine dark hair trailed from his broad chest and disappeared into his britches as though beckoning her to follow.

He was a handsome, virile man, this Texas Ranger of hers. And she'd never get her fill of him.

While she scrambled the eggs, he sliced some bread and buttered it. Then, adding a fresh tomato, she divided the fare onto their plates.

Afterward in the darkness of the bedroom, they memorized each other's bodies, pleasuring each other until sleep overtook them.

* * *

A few days later Texanna returned from caring for Sheriff Ezra's and Newt Colfax's wounds, heartened that Colfax had regained consciousness at last. A customer politely waited for her at the undertaking emporium.

"I'm sorry to hear about your son's death, Mrs. Butterfield." Texanna pressed a handkerchief into the sobbing woman's hand. "John was a wonderful man, who I'll miss very much."

"I trust his remains with you. Can you see to his burial?"

"I'll be honored." Texanna crossed to the desk that had been Sam's. She took out a ledger and picked up a pen to record the date and name. It was important to keep good records of those she'd buried. When she went to shut the drawer, it hung partway open. Having no time to see about it, she'd wait until Mrs. Butterfield left to find out what prevented it from closing.

Mrs. Butterfield dried her eyes and looked up. "I forgot to congratulate you on your recent marriage. Please forgive me."

"There's nothing to forgive." Texanna put her arm around the woman's shoulders and hugged her. "You had your hands full seeing to your son and now coping with grief at his passing."

"I'm glad you found a good man to look after you."

"Thank you. Stoney and I are extremely happy."

The grieving mother left after making arrangements for Texanna to deliver a coffin to the Butterfield home for the wake. The funeral and burial would be the following day. Texanna turned back to the errant desk drawer.

She made several unsuccessful attempts to shut it, but to no avail. Something blocked it. Finally, pulling out the drawer, she discovered some crunched-up papers at the back between the drawer and the desk. She removed the wad.

Carrying them to the light, she straightened them out.

A sob caught in Texanna's throat.

It was Sam's will.

At long last, she found what she'd been searching high and low for.

She ran to the jail to show Stoney. "I found it!" she announced when she opened the door.

Standing by the potbellied stove with a coffeepot in his hand, Stoney turned. "That's wonderful, honey, but what exactly did you find?"

"Sam's will. I found it."

"Hallelujah." He put down the coffeepot and twirled her around.

"We'll put it in a safe place until the traveling judge comes through here."

"He should arrive tomorrow."

"The sooner the better. This'll put Marcus in his place once and for all." The relief in his eyes matched the lightness in her heart. Joy bubbled up. She rested her head on the hard planes of his chest, more content than she had a right to be.

"I can't imagine anything that'll give me greater satisfaction than doing that."

Texanna kissed him, regardless that the Colfax brothers looked on. "It feels so good to be rid of the shadow that's loomed over me."

"This calls for a celebration. How about supper in the hotel dining room tonight? You, Josh, and me."

She trailed her fingers along his cheek. "Have I told you how much I love you?"

He grinned. "Don't mind hearing it again. As many times as you care to say it."

Chapter 14

Stoney left the traveling judge the following afternoon and made a beeline for the Pig and Whistle. He found the slimy vermin nursing a mug of beer at a card table.

Keeping a wary eye out for trouble, Stoney ambled his way over.

Marcus glanced up. "Can I interest you in a game of chance, Burke?"

"Nope. Just thought you should know . . . the traveling judge ruled that the papers Texanna found yesterday are indeed the Last Will and Testament of Sam Wilder. It's legal. You don't have a claim on anything. This is the last time I'm going to tell you this. Harm her or bother Josh again, it'll be with great satisfaction that I end your miserable life. No more warnings. There won't be a rock or blade of grass you can hide under where I won't find you."

"Is that a threat?"

"Nope. It's a promise."

LaRoach wiped the beer foam from his thin mustache. "I could've had it all if you hadn't showed up."

"But I did, and that's that."

"Reckon you won this round, Ranger. You never know

who you'll find in your shadow. I'd watch my back if I were you."

Stoney's gun hand twitched. "I always do."

Along about dark, Texanna had supper on the table and yet Josh hadn't made it home. She went down onto the street and scanned its length. There was no sign of her son.

She saw Stoney coming out of the hotel with the prisoners' meal in hand and ran to catch him.

"Have you seen Josh?"

"No, darlin'. Not since morning."

"I can't seem to find him and I'm getting worried."

"Here, you take this tray to the jail and I'll go look for him. Just set it on my desk. Don't you get near those outlaws. I'll give it to them when I get around to it."

Unshed tears filled her eyes. She'd never felt so loved and cherished, not even when Sam was alive. That Stoney cared so deeply for her son that he'd drop everything to go to his aid brought a warm glow. She was a lucky woman who'd found a one-of-a-kind husband. He gently caressed her cheek.

"Darlin', I'm sure he'll turn up. I'll search all the places Josh likes to go. It's not like him to disappear."

Just then they spied Josh's best friend. Texanna stayed by Stoney's side as he approached him.

"Matthew, have you seen Josh?" Stoney asked.

The barefoot boy burrowed his toe in the dirt. "He said he was goin' home to supper. Ain't he there?"

"I'm afraid not," Texanna broke in. "Do you have any idea where else he'd go?"

"No, ma'am." Suddenly the boy looked down the street. Fear filled his face. "Fire!" he yelled.

Texanna whirled, her heart pounding. Wilder's Undertaking Emporium and her home were ablaze.

"Run and sound the alarm," Stoney told her. "I'll do what I can until help arrives."

Throwing the tray aside, she ran. By the time she pulled the alarm bell, flames licked out the windows and across the front. The fire's greedy appetite was gobbling up the structure. She grabbed a bucket, filled it from a nearby horse trough and stood shoulder to shoulder with Stoney as men and women alike raced to the scene.

Oh God, if Josh had returned in the short while she'd been gone . . . She couldn't stop the scream.

"Josh!"

Just then the upstairs living quarters crashed into the bottom floor. Sparks and flames intensified with a fury. The fire was like a hungry beast, devouring everything in its path. It had already spread to the newspaper office next door and didn't appear to be slowing down any.

She couldn't hold back the sobs any longer. They came hard and fast.

Stoney stopped his attack on the flames to comfort her. "Josh is a smart kid. If he was in there he'd have gotten out at the first sign of smoke." He kissed her forehead. "I'll find him as soon as I can. Don't worry."

A bucket line snaked from the well in the center of town. Every able-bodied man, woman, and child who could pass a bucket of water stood in the line, with Stoney manning the front.

Before they had extinguished the flames, half the town lay in smoldering ruins. Stoney had had to hurriedly remove the prisoners when the jail caught fire. He'd stashed them in a storeroom in the hotel, with Bill Ezra to guard them. Thank goodness Ezra was up, hobbling around a little, and had come to see the commotion.

The Pig and Whistle Saloon had also lost the battle.

But they'd saved Ezra's little house and Texanna's barbershop, along with the livery, boardinghouse, and mercantile.

Exhausted, Texanna stared at the devastation all around. Had she caused this? She went back in her mind. Maybe she'd left a skillet on the stove when she went out to look for Josh.

Dear Lord, how would she forgive herself if she was to blame?

Her stomach twisted in knots. Her son had vanished and she'd lost their home in one single blow.

Footsteps crunched on the pebbles as Stoney and Loretta Farris came alongside. "I found this tacked to the door of the barbershop." He handed her a piece of brown paper. He held up a lantern so she could read it.

"'I have your sniveling brat. By the time you put out the fire we'll be miles away. This could all have been avoided if your Ranger hadn't interfered. Now there's no hope for your son. Revenge is sweet.' It's signed Marcus."

Tears ran unheeded down her cheeks. She sagged in Stoney's arms. "Oh no! Not my little boy. Please, God, no."

Loretta spoke softly. "Texanna, come with me to the boardinghouse. I've got room for you."

"Darlin', I want you to go with Miss Loretta now." Stoney set her firmly on her feet.

"Where . . . what?"

"I'm going after Josh. I'll not come back until I have him. I promise." His voice was as hard and cold as steel.

"Be careful. I'd die if I lost you too."

Stoney hurried to the livery and saddled Hondo. Then he followed the tracks in front of the barbershop that led east out of town.

He'd find them. There wasn't a question of that.

But he just wasn't sure what would be waiting for him when he got there. Fear gripped him, that he'd be too late to save the boy. LaRoach was unstable, and those kinds of men were the most dangerous.

He nudged Hondo's sides with his heels. There was no time to lose.

When the trail veered slightly south, Stoney knew LaRoach was headed to the abandoned ruins of Fort Mc-Kavett. It'd be hard to locate him in the darkness that draped over the rocky terrain like a heavy wool blanket.

Picking his way through the inky night, he took care to avoid gopher holes. If the horse stepped in one it could spell lameness or a broken leg.

Setting the fire had bought Marcus extra time to get away. The man had calculated they'd work to save the town before coming to look for him and the boy. He'd been right.

LaRoach had gone too far this time.

Stoney's jaw hardened and his blood turned to ice. He'd show the man no mercy. This time he'd kill LaRoach on the spot if he hurt Josh in any way.

A glance at the moon said it was around midnight. Stoney didn't know how much time had passed since he'd ridden out of Devils Creek, but it seemed like hours before the jutting stone structures of the old fort came into view. The thin moon created ghostly shadows where soldiers once lived.

He paused to listen for sounds that might indicate a human presence. The saddle leather creaked when he eased to the ground.

At first only the sound of Hondo's gentle breathing broke the black stillness. Then Stoney froze.

A child's faint whimper came from somewhere in the eerie, vacant depths of the ruins. It had to be Josh, for Stoney couldn't feature any other child being in the vicinity.

The noise swirled in the slight breeze, taunting him. It seemed to come from everywhere and nowhere at once.

Leaving Hondo standing in a patch of nut grass, Stoney lifted his Colt from the holster and quietly crept toward the row of houses that had served as officers' quarters. He put his ear to the door of one. Nothing. The whimpering had stopped.

Stoney's gaze swept the length of the compound and back. He tried to put himself in LaRoach's mind. Where would he choose to hide? Up above or down below?

Snakes like LaRoach would always go underground.

From the frontier forts he'd seen, only the commanding officer's dwelling had a basement. He assumed this one to be the same. The one in front of him was a two-story affair and most imposing. It had to be the place.

He treaded lightly on the wooden porch, approached the door, and turned the knob.

As he'd feared, the door's squeak announced his presence.

Wasting no time getting inside, Stoney flattened against a wall and listened. Hurried footsteps on the basement stairs invaded the musty, spider-webbed house.

And the whimpers turned into loud, shuddering sobs.

"I know you're here, Burke," shouted LaRoach. "Ride back out or the boy dies."

"Can't do that," Stoney growled.

"Then you'll have his death on your conscience."

"Kill him and I'll save the hemp committee the effort. I'll leave your body for the buzzards."

"Might be a tall order, since you'll be the first one to die. I seem to be holding a full house in this poker game."

That remained to be seen. Stoney had one or two aces up his sleeve. "So far all you've done is kidnap the boy. Murder him and you'll buy yourself a trip to hell as fast as I can send you there."

Suddenly the pitch dark held a flicker of light. A candle, Stoney presumed.

LaRoach pushed Josh into view. They stood just inside the room at the head of the basement stairs. The man had a gun pressed to the boy's head. Beads of sweat rose at Stoney's temples. He'd save Josh or die trying. Fate couldn't ask Texanna to give up another child. It couldn't be that cruel.

Besides, Josh was his son now, and he took his new role of fatherhood very seriously.

"Son, are you all right?" Stoney asked quietly.

"I—I think so."

"I'll have you out of here in a minute and back home where you belong. Just think of your mother and Matthew and playing marbles."

"Okay."

"You think you're gonna waltz in here and I'm gonna give you what you want? Even a Texas Ranger ain't that stupid," LaRoach sneered.

"Let the boy go. I'm the one you want. Let him go and I'll lay down my Colt. Fair enough?"

LaRoach appeared to mull over the attractive offer.

Tears trickled down Josh's face. The boy was terrified. Stoney's heart went out to him. Then he remembered the pocketknife that Josh had. It might be the solution they needed. Of course, perfect timing would be crucial for the plan to succeed. And the boy would have to read between the lines.

That was a lot for one child who hadn't even had a chance to wear long pants yet.

"Josh, remember when we played mumblety-peg?"

The youngster swiped his nose with the back of his hand and nodded.

"Never saw anyone pick the game up so fast. You're a natural."

"Shut your yapping," LaRoach snapped.

"You've scared the boy half out of his mind. I'm just

trying to calm him down a bit," Stoney replied evenly, conscious of the weight of his Colt on his right hip. He noticed Josh's slight movement. The boy had stuck his hand in his pocket. Stoney prayed he was feeling for the knife. LaRoach hadn't appeared to notice. So far, so good.

"LaRoach, what'll it be? You're slower than molasses."

"You seem in an awful big hurry to die, Burke."

Josh withdrew his hand from his pocket, and if Stoney's guess was right, he had the knife.

Now to distract LaRoach.

"Just tired of waitin' for you to make up your mind, that's all." With an eye on the gambler, Stoney let his hand inch to the butt of his .45.

"Keep your hands where I can see 'em," LaRoach barked, waving his pistol toward Stoney. "Don't try anything."

The distraction worked. Josh managed to open the knife and LaRoach hadn't seen him do it.

Stoney forced air into his lungs. He prayed the youngster could do what he'd asked of him. He steeled himself for whatever came next.

In a lightning move, Josh slammed the knife down to the plank floor with all his might.

Chapter 15

LaRoach screamed in pain. The gun dropped to the floor with a clatter. The knife had gone through the man's boot and stuck into the area near the toes.

Josh quickly leaped to the side, out of the way.

Wasting no time, Stoney dove across the space, tackling LaRoach. The first blow knocked the man to his knees. The second one laid LaRoach out. Stoney retrieved the knife from the shoe leather and wiped it off.

"Is . . . is he dead?" Josh's face had turned ashen in the dim light.

"No. Are you all right?"

With that, Josh ran and threw his arms around Stoney's waist. "I was so scared."

Stoney ruffled the boy's hair and pulled him close. "You're safe now. He can't hurt you. You make a good partner, you know that? You knew exactly what I wanted you to do and you didn't bat an eye."

Josh looked up. His face was tearstained and streaked. "I'm gonna be a Texas Ranger like you when I get big."

"That would make me very proud, son." Stoney gave Josh one last squeeze. "Whaddya say let's go home?"

The words had barely left his mouth when he remembered

their home was a smoldering pile of rubble. That little fact had moved down the list of importance. What mattered most was that they were still breathing and would all be together, wherever that might be.

The first rays of dawn were painting the town a rosy hue when Texanna quietly ventured out onto the wide porch of the boardinghouse. She paced the length of the porch, too nervous to sit in one of the rocking chairs lined in a row.

She turned around when the door closed softly.

"Did you get any sleep at all?" Loretta asked.

"No. Did you?"

"Not a wink." Loretta limped over to Texanna and slipped her arms around her. "Everything's going to be all right. These old bones don't lie."

Feeling hopeful, Texanna smoothed back her hair and lifted her gaze. Two horses had emerged out of the dawn's mist at the end of Main Street. Her heart skipped a beat. "Loretta, look down the street. Do you reckon that's them?"

"Sure looks like it, honey."

Texanna lifted her skirts and took off running. When she drew closer she could see Stoney sitting tall in the saddle. Perched in front of him sat her son.

Saints be praised!

After she saw that they appeared to be no worse for wear, her gaze shifted to the second horse. Marcus's hands were bound and his glum expression, accented by a black eye and swollen lip, made her want to leap for joy.

"Mama!" Josh jumped from the saddle. "We caught him."

She grabbed her son in a hug, giving silent thanks to the good Lord for sparing his life. "I could squeeze you half to death, young man."

Still grinning, Texanna stared into Stoney's weary eyes. "What's this 'we' business our son is talking about?"

The saddle leather creaked when her rugged husband climbed from the buckskin.

Her heart swelled with pride. She leaned into his embrace and lifted her mouth eagerly for a kiss.

When Stoney's firm mouth swept over hers and stole her breath, she had no thoughts of anything except how good it felt to be in his arms where she belonged. If she lived to a hundred, she'd have passion and music every time he touched her.

When the kiss had satisfied some of her longings, Texanna sighed happily and asked again, "Now tell me about this 'we' business. Don't think you can ply me with kisses and I'll forget all about it."

A lopsided grin formed. "Yes, ma'am. I doubt things would've gone very well if not for Josh's quick thinking with a knife. He helped me corral this vermin. I'm really proud of him. He has the makings of a fine Texas Ranger."

Her chest lurched when she heard the knife mentioned. Sounded as if the knife saved Josh's life though. Still, she'd lay down the law again on knives first chance she got.

She planted her hands on her hips. "I declare, Stoney Burke. Isn't he a little young yet to be signing him up?"

"Nope, the Rangers like to get 'em early, especially when they have as much courage as Josh has. Don't tell me you're gonna be one of those mothers who keeps her son tied to her apron strings."

She wrinkled her nose. "Would you still want me?"

"My ornery, beautiful wife. I'll always want you, no matter what. My job is to keep untying those strings. And I take my job very seriously."

The gleam in his gray eyes let her know he wasn't talking strictly about Josh.

Delicious tingles swept up her spine as she looped her arm

in his. "We have a lot of work ahead of us, dear husband. When can we start rebuilding our home?"

Texanna sighed contentedly when he tucked her closer to him. His voice vibrated through her. "Reckon I'll start on it as soon as I get my prisoner locked up. But anywhere you are is home to me, darlin'. I know how you set great store by having four walls around you, and I'm going to make that happen. But as long as I have you, my life is complete."

One Woman
One Ranger

PHYLISS MIRANDA

To my beautiful daughters, Kathleen and Jennifer,
who have given me the room and encouragement
needed to follow my dreams.
I love you both for following your own dreams while
sharing mine; and for my eight precious grandchildren.
Mama

*In memory of Brandon Henriquez
July 12, 1990–July 3, 2009.
A young man who left footprints
on every heart he touched.
You are missed and loved.*

Chapter 1

Texas Panhandle
Summer 1881

Not only was he tired, hungry, and dirty, but technically, Hayden McGraw guessed, he was still on suspension from the Texas Rangers. The last thing he needed was to become involved in the quarrel that seemed to be brewing in Buffalo Springs, Texas. It wasn't any of his concern . . . yet.

Only an hour earlier, the lawman had ridden into town and straight down Main Street, which was lined with scant frame buildings crowded together in order to hold one another up. He had tied his gelding, Stewball, to the hitching post outside of Chip and Hell's, the first drinking establishment he came across.

The lawman now settled in at the bar, not sure which he wanted most: the shot of whiskey the bartender was sliding his way, or finding a place called Molly Lou's. It'd been one hell of a day, and from the looks of the crowd milling around the saloon, much like a herd of cattle spooked by blue lightning, it wasn't about to get better.

"Chip, fetch us some beer over here, pronto," yelled a guy in the corner.

"We'll all be hog-tied and saddled with a dozen young'uns, if you don't get on the ball," hailed a man whose forehead didn't stop until it reached the crown of his head.

"If you don't like my service, get your sorry butts across the creek and drink at Molly Lou's," the bartender fired back.

The mention of the other saloon piqued Hayden's interest.

"But it ain't free there," Baldy grumbled.

Another patron clanged his mug on the table. "But it's stronger."

"If you like rotgut." The slow drawl wafted through the thick air. "I'll drink free any day."

Hayden raised a questioning brow. Free-flowing beer was a sure sign that somebody wanted something mighty bad, attracting a big crowd, assuring a favorable outcome. But this time it seemed different.

He surveyed the patrons. An odd assortment of folks. Citizens who no doubt had never seen the inside of a den of iniquity. Others obviously hadn't seen outdoors for a while. The lawman took a deep breath and tried to remember whatever was eatin' on them wasn't his concern, unless he was invited in.

The bartender placed another glass of whiskey in front of him. "On the house."

Hayden pulled out a couple of coins. "Appreciate it, but I'll pay. Where is this Molly Lou's?" He laid two bits on the bar.

"Half a mile on the other side of the creek, where trouble lives."

"Town got a name?"

"Naw, it's just called Buffalo Wallow. Them type of renegades and gamblers aren't welcome in Buffalo Springs. Need to keep their kind together, so Sheriff Oldham will know where to find trouble when it comes a callin'."

"Thanks." Hayden slid another coin to the chatty bartender.

Hayden turned his back to the bar, resting his elbows on the edge, again surveying the crowd.

"Where's that dern Justice of the Peace anyways?" A boisterous voice boomed. "He called this meeting."

"Probably at Molly Lou's, showing off his new book of marriage licenses, trying to make the gamblers and dance-hall girls see the error of their ways," Mr. Baldy answered. "He says you've gotta get hitched if you're livin' without benefit of clergy—"

"What in the heck is that supposed to mean?" A woman, not so ladylike, spouted.

"Means everybody in Newman County has gotta get legit. No marriage license, no beddin'." Baldy's eyes narrowed, brows knitted together. "I'm jest quotin' the JP."

Hayden tilted back his Stetson a tad. So much for the purpose of free beer. It guaranteed success for the JP. Hayden had heard the rumors that when the first book of marriage licenses reached Newman County, the Justice of the Peace planned to make money by forcing every man and woman living together to comply with his interpretation of the law and record their marriage. He focused mainly on the cowboys, gamblers, and dance-hall girls, but nobody was exempt.

To Hayden, it didn't seem right to force any grown man or woman into matrimony just because they could now record their union. Glad he wasn't here to resolve the town's differences of opinion. On second thought, with the increasing numbers packing the sawdust floors of the saloon-turned-meeting-hall, his experience in mob control might come in handy. Where in the blue blazes was the sheriff? Nothing could be more important than keeping this crowd in check.

Baldy's roar drew Hayden's attention back to the discussion. "Goldarn it, the law is the law."

The majority of the folks nodded in agreement, just before they took long draws on their beers. "Yep, gotta do what a man's gotta do to make 'em legal," another voiced.

A chorus of "and women too" filled the air.

"Trouble. Trouble. Trouble," Chip muttered behind Hayden's back, just before the lawman heard something smack the batwing doors.

Looking up, he watched a tall woman push aside the swinging doors with both hands. The doors vibrated to and fro for half a dozen swings before stilling. It didn't take a second look to see that the woman—who was gussied up in some fandangle pink dress, all glossy and lookin' way too hot for the dog days of summer—was prepared to fight a prairie fire with spit and guts.

A blanket of silence spread over the crowd. He didn't know who the woman was, but obviously the town either respected her greatly or was scared as hell of her, but he figured he was about to find out.

The fiery woman made her way to the front of the crowd, accompanied by two other women. One woman stood about a head taller than their leader, and repeatedly bobbled her flaming red hair, covered with tiny curls that made Hayden think of screws dangling from a string. The other, frumpy, a tad shorter, and too old to still be a saloon girl, left no doubt by her stance why she was there.

Before any of the three women could speak, Baldy bellowed, "Patience Stevenson, you stay out of this. Ain't your problem. Take your girls and get back down to Buffalo Wallow where you all belong." Glasses clanked together. "Ain't nobody from your part of town belongs up here during broad daylight, Little Woman."

Openly aggravated, the woman outfitted in pink, now identified as Patience, leveled a stare over the crowd. "I'm not going anyplace. Ladies and"—leaving no doubt where she stood on the subject by the tone of her voice, she transferred her gaze directly at the table Baldy occupied before continuing—"and gentlemen, first off, I'm nobody's "little woman," and nobody can make me, my employees, or anyone in this county take out a marriage license unless they want to."

"And we don't wanna, either." The redhead plopped her hands on her hips. "And nobody is gonna make us leave this saloon—"

Patience broke in. "Women have rights, and we're nobody's *have to!* We don't *have to* do anything, just because a man tells us to do so."

Infectious bravado broke out throughout the saloon. Voices melded into a thunderous concerto of cheers and jeers. One couldn't distinguish a yea from a nay, a good natured slap on the back from a mincing chop to the jaw.

Over the roar, the incensed young woman pronounced, quite emphatically Hayden had to admit, that laws were meant to be followed, but only if they were interpreted correctly; otherwise, they were simply wrong and were meant to be challenged.

"Wanna 'nother whiskey?" the bartender asked.

Hayden nodded, never taking an eye off the crowd. He felt uncomfortable because the mob was swelling by numbers instead of dispersing. Generally in an explosive situation like this, cool reasoning would eventually prevail, and after the folks got tired of yammering the pros and cons they'd head home, usually in time for supper. But he didn't see that happening.

Scanning the crowd, Hayden tried to make sense out of

the comments. The arguments had now turned personal, beyond a spirited debate. He'd seen full-fledged riots less volatile. He might be forced into action after all.

Hayden had an uncanny way of watching everyone, yet no one. Part of his training. He was continually drawn back to the lady in pink. She seemed to have a rattler by its tail and didn't know whether to keep holdin' on or take a chance of letting it go and getting bitten.

No doubt Hayden's nastiest mood wouldn't hold a light to the best of the woman standing in front of the crowd with her arms folded across her chest, impatiently tapping her foot. And to think, somewhere her ma and pa were probably laughing their butts off at naming their daughter Patience. He'd observed her for less than ten minutes, and this woman was probably so impatient that she couldn't understand why tomorrow couldn't have come before yesterday.

Out of nowhere came a pathetic-looking man just a little over five feet tall, but he'd have to stop slouching to even reach that height. His face was pasty, with an odd-shaped mustache that didn't stop until it reached each of his ears. His deep-set, sullen black eyes told Hayden the middle-aged man was cantankerous as hell.

All heads turned toward the man as he fought his way through the crowd toward the three women, who were firmly planted facing the gathering.

Mr. Baldy bailed to his feet so fast that a mug of beer tipped over and crashed onto the floor. But he didn't seem to notice, as he engaged his mouth. "And Muley Mulinex, what in the hell are you doing here? You don't have a dog in this fight." Baldy sneered. "Oh yeah, you do." He furrowed his brow at Patience. "You oughta be ashamed of yourself for associating with such women."

"Her name's Ella," said Muley. "You know that nobody calls her Patience, and I gotta keep my job. She pays the bills since her pa headed for the hills, leaving us high and dry." He touched the Colt hung low on his hip. "Got any particular reason for wantin' to butt into my business?"

Baldy picked up another beer mug from the table, hurled it against the wall, and stumbled for the door.

Muley meandered toward the end of the bar. "Chip, I need a sarsaparilla, you hear!"

Hayden was too damn tired to deal with what was coming down. From the moment he hit town, all he wanted was a stiff drink or three and to find a bath house to clean up and get a shave. But first, he needed to find Molly Lou's. He'd hoped to pick up an envelope there containing his new Warrant of Authority, the only proof he had he was a Texas Ranger, and be out of town by break of day.

He tried not to think about the old, illegible warrant in his pocket. As much as Hayden disliked having to make a side trip to Buffalo Springs, he'd caused it himself. Some things weren't meant to swim—paper being one. But stopping here saved him a dreary hundred-mile round-trip to company headquarters and back to pick up a new warrant. Plus, the more space he put between him and his captain the better.

Before he could bed down for the night he had to take care of Stewball, about the ugliest horse in the world, but his name fit—patches of white over red, reminding Hayden of a bowl of chili topped with cornbread. He hoped the sorry-lookin' critter was still tied up outside the saloon. The sucker had a tendency to become impatient, work his reins loose, and make a beeline for the first place he found food.

Hayden ran his hand over his scraggly beard and realized that his gelding was better groomed than his grungy owner. Even a honyock of the worst sort would be ashamed of the lawman's shaggy appearance.

Once he got the warrant, he could get back to the only job he'd ever known: being a Texas Ranger. Until then, Hayden McGraw was a lawman with no authority. One thing for dern sure, he intended to steer clear of the pretty woman inaptly named Patience.

Chapter 2

Ella Stevenson tried unsuccessfully to put a stop to her foot tapping. It was a detestably bad habit that took over when she felt annoyed, which was most of the time. "Muley, you don't have to defend me."

"Not meant to offend, Miss Ella. Just taking my stand." His piercing stare punctuated his statement. Again he touched his Colt.

She wasn't sure how she'd gotten here, but intended to make certain someone spoke up for those who couldn't do so themselves. Ella turned and addressed the crowd. "Nobody at my place, Molly Lou's, is living in sin, and I do not hire people of questionable character." She shifted her weight, hoping to slow down her foot tapping. "I'd sure as hell make more money if I allowed soiled doves to operate in my establishment." She didn't even flinch at either her usage of the swear word or her reference to the oldest profession known to man.

"That's a matter of opinion," a woman lashed out, as she grabbed her umbrella and darted toward the door, as if breathing the same air would harm her. "I'm tired of waiting for the JP. He'll just have to call another meeting." She opened her umbrella at the same time as half a dozen cowhands tried to enter. Confused, they ducked and scattered.

A handful of patrons wandered out.

Ella moved to the table cleared by the exiting citizens, followed by her two friends, but never sat down. She watched as first one resident then another skedaddled. Those left behind were more interested in free beer and a spirited verbal exchange than the reason they had gathered in the first place. Had she gotten her point across?

Her gaze settled on the rugged man standing near Muley at the bar. Rugged was a nice word for him; unkempt and flat-out scraggly was more like it. She shuddered thinking about how he must smell, but then she'd always loved rawhide and puredee ol' cowboy. Rode hard and fast, maybe? His presence seemed to fill the room, exhibiting a classic, fearless lawman persona. She frowned and thought back to her childhood.

By the time she was ten, she could pick out a lawman, gambler, or a con man from the customers in her father's saloon. Maybe a game she played, but mostly because one or more of them usually wanted to have a heart-to-heart with her gambling–con artist father or arrest him.

"He's one fine-lookin' cowpoke, isn't he?" Audrey Jo's bobbing red curls emphasized her statement.

"I've seen plenty of men just as easy on the eyes." Dixie pushed back her graying black hair. "Had my share."

"What man?" Ella pulled her gaze away from the man at the bar. "Who are you referring to?"

"The cowboy at the bar. And, I don't mean Muley," Dixie added.

"Didn't notice." Ella nodded a thank-you to the bartender, who set glasses of tea in front of them.

Yeah, she didn't notice how tall the devilishly handsome stranger was beneath his grubby appearance. No way was she aware of his bulk, even betting he didn't have an ounce of fat on him. And she sure didn't want to recognize a smile trying not to form, or the dimples barely peeking over his heavy beard.

His eyes intrigued her. Eyes that seemed to capture everyone in the crowd, yet he stared directly at her, making her feel like he could see all the way to her soul. His eyes showed no age, but experience and lots of it.

A chill ran through her veins. Tarnation and damnation, she could bet a double eagle that he was a Texas Ranger . . . a despicable Texas Ranger.

As if cued, the piano player clanked out some tinny notes. With free beer at Chip's place, Molly Lou's would have few if any customers, so she saw no reason to leave a cool glass of tea behind. Besides, she could deal with the lawman later. She eased into a chair, and tried to focus on the musician's struggle to play. It might help to block out Dixie's and Audrey Jo's opinion of every woman in attendance, from the color of her dress to how much weight she had put on since having her last child.

Ella took a sip of tea. That's when she noticed the smudge of blood on her thumb. Dern it! She should have taken time to wash her hands more thoroughly. But when she found out about the meeting, the horse she was tending to had to wait . . . she needed to protect her employees, and ultimately her business. When she finished her beverage, she'd go back, check on the animal, and hopefully find his owner. Dang his hide, he'd been pretty select in what he chose to eat. If only she'd taken the freshly dug carrots inside, instead of leaving them on the porch behind the saloon. Guess there'd be no carrots this evening. One of her hard-and-fast rules: all of her workers had to eat supper. She knew a full stomach led to contentment. Good, honest employees were hard to come by in the rugged new frontier.

"Ladies, I don't like having to close up the saloon even

for an hour. It's hard to make ends meet without having the JP give away beer." She found herself keeping time to the music. "I gotta get back down there."

"I know," Dixie agreed. "I reckon I'll stick around and watch out for Muley. I've never seen him so riled. Seen schoolboys with a crush-on more self-assured then he normally is."

Audrey Jo piped up. "I saw a woman reach over and touch his mustache one time. He turned red, ducked his head, and went to the back room. I swear, I don't think I saw him for two hours."

"Do you think he's got a snootful today?" Dixie asked.

"Nope. Never seen him touch a drop, but that don't mean he isn't partakin' when he's not around us. You know it gets hot out there in that little cornfield he fools around in when he's not bartending. Maybe he's hiding a bottle out there."

Both chuckled.

As long as Ella had known them, the women had debated Muley's attributes—sometimes favorably, sometimes not. Although she didn't totally agree with their assessment, she had seen nothing to contradict them. After all, Dixie and Audrey Jo had worked together, running a saloon of some sort, ever since she could remember.

Ella thought back to earlier in the day when Muley had shuffled into Molly Lou's and announced, in his bland, factual way, that a Texas Ranger had been sent to enforce the JP's plans. Since she wasn't living with anyone, except her two bar maids and the bartender, who all had rooms over the saloon, she figured it best not to trouble trouble until it troubled her. But after being approached by Dixie and Audrey Jo about their concerns, she knew what was right was right, and the JP's demands were flat-ass wrong. She had to speak on behalf of those unwilling or not brave enough to protect themselves. Seems she'd always been bold enough for two people.

Some might see it as humiliating to march up to the sacred part of town and face the citizens in order to speak on another's behalf, but not Ella. As long as she could remember, she'd fought for what was right. She'd come this far, and nobody or nothing would stop her . . . especially a Texas Ranger. The man still stood at the bar drinking whiskey. A man who hadn't taken his eyes off her. A man who could rest assured he had a formidable opponent, if he decided to butt heads with her.

She glanced back up at the man, who seemed content drinking whiskey and watching her. Ella purposely lifted her chin and boldly met his gaze.

As much as she hated to admit it, his presence did something funny to her. She was strangely flattered by his attention, but she didn't need a distraction. She broke the stare.

It was bad enough that the hypocritical citizens of Buffalo Springs refused to associate with the group of folks who'd been forced across the creek to a section of town detestably referred to as Buffalo Wallow, but scrutinization by a Ranger was intolerable.

"How did Buffalo Wallow get its name?" she asked.

Dixie jumped onto the question. "Because folks decided that Shantytown was too good of a name, and since they felt everyone down there acted like buffalos wallowing around instead of upstanding citizens like them, the name stuck."

"We got the reputation for being rough, lawless, with too much six-gun justice," Audrey Jo added.

"I'd prefer to think of our folks as being self-reliant and spiritedly independent," Ella said. Although, in fairness, it had lived up to its name, and if there was a brawl it generally had roots in Buffalo Wallow.

Raising her gaze, she found the Ranger still watching her. For a moment she studied him intensely before lowering her head. Ella began tapping her finger against her glass, trying hard not to think about the man.

Although she'd always had respect for the notorious Texas Ranger outfits, they were the ones who had caused her the problems she was faced with. Particularly one Captain Arrington, who had been hell-bent on cleaning up Mobeetie. Her father had seen it coming. Trying to stay one step ahead of the law, he had pulled up stakes and left her and her mother to fend for themselves. He headed to lawless fresh territory.

A motley crew of con artists, gamblers, horse thieves, and fancy women followed.

Seemed Buffalo Wallow, a crossroads of renegades and cowboys, was a natural nesting place for them.

Until the urge to find her father overshadowed common sense, Ella had lived comfortably in Mobeetie, where she was happy running a highly respected millinery shop with her mother. Much different from her raising—one saloon after another.

There were advantages. Much to her mother's chagrin, by the age of ten Ella could spot a card cheat across the room, and could handle a gun as good as any man.

Before she celebrated her seventeenth birthday, her father had disappeared.

Only months later, her mother gave up trying to defend her husband. Brought on by the disgrace of secrets she was forced to keep, she gave up her will to live, shortly passing to the life hereafter.

Ella had picked up the pieces and continued to operate the businesses, but in the back of her mind she knew she had to locate her father, so her mother could rest in peace.

One day, Ella realized she had plenty of her father's daring blood and boldness in her veins, and struck out to find him.

To her disappointment she learned he had accomplished exactly what he had set out to do—stay ahead of the law. But once she located the last place he had owned and operated before he again disappeared, she was determined, come hell or high water, she would make a go of the run-down saloon, operating out of a makeshift combination wood building and tent, in a location she later learned was disreputable Buffalo Wallow.

Thus, she blamed all of this not on her father but on the Texas Ranger captain who decided to clean up Mobeetie. That certainly justified her not takin' kindly to the lawmen, although she had to confess not all of them were cut from the same cloth. She'd run across a few of the colorful body of fighting men who symbolized a spirit and sense of purpose when faced with some of the toughest and most desperate outlaws around. So far, that hadn't changed her opinion of the Texas Rangers in general.

The music stopped, and quiet grasped the air. The saloon darkened noticeably, as a giant of a man suddenly filled the doorway, blocking out the light of day.

"Patience Eleanor Stevenson, you're under arrest!"

Chapter 3

The biggest man Hayden believed he'd ever seen—and he'd seen his share of gigantic men—had to duck to get through the entrance to Chip and Hell's. His barrel chest extended around his hips, making his gut hang heavy over his gun belt. His badge clung vicariously to his vest. Physically it would have been impossible for him to draw a weapon.

His voice was as commanding as his stature. He sternly repeated, "Miss Stevenson, you're under arrest." He marched toward the three ladies, seized Ella by the arm and pulled her to her feet.

Hayden set his glass down with purpose and squared his shoulders. Ella had done nothing threatening to the three-hundred-pound ogre. No man should lay his hands on a woman . . . lawman or not.

Hayden was ready and willing to enter the fracas.

Time had run out.

Muley appeared at his side. "Leave it be, Ranger," he said. He took two steps, then turned back and added, "Redhead is Audrey Jo and the other one is Dixie. They're used to this sort of malarkey and will take care of her." He strolled out of the bar.

As if they'd heard Muley, the two women bound to their feet and surrounded Ella like mother hens protecting an injured chick. "Arrested, for what?" they asked simultaneously.

From a far corner, several of the cowhands who had just come in edged forward, creating a half circle around the women and the sheriff.

The table of poker players folded their cards. One crushed his cigar in a dish, and the other three slid their chairs back, prepared for a swift exit or to make sure their six-shooters could clear leather.

A dance-hall girl slipped off the lap of a patron and headed for the stairs. Chip continued to wipe down the bar, without taking his eyes off the ruckus brewing.

"Turn me loose." Ella tried hard to pull free.

"Can't ya hear, Sheriff?" Audrey Jo grabbed her friend's other arm. The lawman made a big show of tightening his grip, pulling Ella toward him.

"I can hear fine, girl," he bellowed. "Seems you're the one who doesn't know to speak only when you're spoken to."

The exchange ignited Ella, who began thrashing about, kicking the hem of her skirt and then at a chair leg, obviously trying to redirect her anger toward anything that wouldn't kick back.

Dixie began chanting, "Lordy, lordy, lordy."

Time stopped. Tension hung heavy in the air, sucking the breath out of sensibility.

"Please don't." Hayden's temperature rose, and he murmured softly, "Mother of mothers, don't do it."

He'd seen this scenario play out many times. Any lawman worth his salt oughta know better than to try to restrain a prisoner in such a way, even a 110-pound woman. He knew exactly what was fixin' to happen. Somebody was gonna get walloped, and hard—generally it'd be the person doing the holdin'.

Bad, very bad idea, Lady. Hayden shuddered.

Sure enough, Ella jerked her right arm out of Audrey Jo's grip. Spinning, she landed a blow with her fist against the sheriff's chin, which set the flab on his neck jiggling like a wattle on a stew-ready rooster.

The sheriff raised his left hand to defend himself in what McGraw realized was a natural instinct, but to some it would appear he was about to return the blow.

Hayden had never seen a man deliberately strike a woman in public, and couldn't stomach even the thought. Such men were scum, the lowest of humanity, nothing but a Burrowing Owl preying on a prairie dog in its hole.

A mortified expression curtained Ella's face. She stiffened her body and shrunk back in a defensive stance, as though protecting herself from a likely retaliatory blow. She covered her face with her free arm. This wasn't the first time she'd defended herself from physical cruelty . . . an animal cowering for protection.

Hayden's heart dropped to the pit of his stomach. His fist tightened, and he had to take a deep breath in order to curtail his own temper.

"That just added another charge—assaulting an officer of the law," Sheriff Oldham bellowed, fumbling for his handcuffs.

"I have a right to say what I want." Her voice trembled as she pulled herself up straight. "First Amendment to the Constitution . . . freedom of speech."

Hayden took a deep breath, expecting her to recite the Constitution word for word, probably including the punctuation.

"You've gotta learn to hobble your lips, Woman." Apparently giving up on finding his handcuffs, the sheriff proceeded to steer her toward the door. "It isn't your freedom of speech; it's your whole damn attitude that's gotcha in trouble."

"Let go of me." Ella's voice dropped so low that it could barely be heard above the mumbling crowd. "I'll go freely."

"Can't take that chance." His face flushed blood red, and he heaved his chest heavily. "I'm tempted to just hang you right here and now, Little Woman."

"For what?" Her voice was as unyielding as limestone. "I didn't deliberately hit you, and you know it."

Baldy rushed in, waving his pistol in the air and shouting, "For thievery! She stole a horse. A real ugly one."

One man yelled, "Hangin' offense, ugly or not—"

Another behind him broke in. "Don't need to wait for the circuit judge. I seen her do it."

One of the cowhands punched another. "Yep, we witnessed it. Dern sure did. Bold as can be."

A woman from the far corner yelped, "At least take a vote." She waved her handbag. "I vote to rid the town of one problem. Those in favor say yea."

A thunderous yea ensued. Noticeably the not-so-feminine scalawag didn't ask for a nay vote.

"Take it outside!" Chip rounded the counter, and began shooing the patrons out like he'd do a flock of mourning doves. "Free beer's over."

A man bellowed, "We'll get the rope."

Baldy yelled, "I have a horse."

Another directed, "The old cottonwood by Boot Hill."

"No, at the courthouse," the sheriff roared. "I want it lawful." He stepped between the crowd and Ella, who seemed dazed. "And damn quick too."

The vigilante lynchin' committee rushed out into the daylight.

Ella shot the sheriff a barbed look, then softened it as she caught Hayden's gaze. Heartfelt desperation and a plea for help flanked her face. Her eyes, as dark as sapphires, caught him off guard, sending a quake throughout his body.

It didn't take a book on laws to tell Hayden he had to step

up and take control, keeping the gathering from becoming a full-fledged riot. He could no longer consider himself a visitor in town; he was now the ranking lawman. It was obvious the sheriff was in over his head in vigilante justice, and his self-importance had surpassed common sense.

Enough was enough.

Hayden preferred to work with the sheriff, not toss around his authority. But he'd come across too many cocky lawmen like Sheriff Oldham, who got their jollies out of flaunting their power much like a mockingbird pestering a cat.

Sheriff Oldham firmly guided Ella toward the door, with Audrey Jo and Dixie right on her heels. The saloon quickly emptied into the street. The vigilantes obviously thrilled at the thought of breaking the summer heat with a hangin'.

Hayden broke through the crowd, just as Baldy tossed a rope over an ancient cottonwood.

"Stop!" Hayden yelled, as he drew up even with the sheriff. "If you can't control the mob, I will."

Sheriff Oldham handed the woman over to Baldy. Grinning like a possum eatin' a yellow jacket, he pulled Ella alongside him.

The sheriff turned to face Hayden, eye to eye. "I don't know who in the hell you think you are, but I'm the law in this neck of the woods. And I'll arrest you for interfering with me doing my job." He slipped a noose around Ella's neck.

"Hayden McGraw, Texas Ranger First Lieutenant." He glared at Baldy. "Put another sleazy hand on the lady, and you'll have me to contend with."

"Shows how new you are round these parts, Ranger. She ain't no lady." The sheriff spat tobacco juice in the dirt.

"Apparently you are no gentleman."

"And, you're *apparently* in cahoots with her."

Obviously the lines had been drawn between the Ranger

and the sheriff. Nothing new to either one. There seemed to be no gray area where law enforcement tangled. Either they got along to take care of the matter at hand or they detested one another. Generally the local sheriff set the tone for their relationship. Sheriff Oldham was definitely not extending his hand in welcome.

The crowd quieted considerably. Respectfully, most stepped back several feet. Some seemed interested in seeing what the lawmen would do, while others decided it was time to go about their day. The excitement of witnessing a hangin' had fizzled out. Nobody cared about a disagreement between two lawmen. One would win out, one wouldn't, but there'd be no hangin' today.

Hayden pulled his badge from his pocket. Sunrays danced off the silver.

"Anybody can have a blacksmith make one of them from a Mexican silver coin. Jest 'cause you have a badge doesn't make you a Ranger," Sheriff Oldham said.

Infuriated, Hayden's heart fumed at the insult. He remembered the exact moment the badge was pinned on him by his Ranger father, who had received it from Hayden's grandfather, a feared *los diablos Tejanos*—a "Texas Devil." An outfit of Rangers who rode courageously, straight into the arms of death, and were scared of nobody or nothing. He bristled at the sheriff's bad taste.

"That's a slap in the face to every Texas Ranger who ever lived," Hayden spat out.

"Then show me your Warrant of Authority."

Hayden McGraw had problems . . . big problems.

A beautiful woman with a noose around her neck, no proof he was a Texas Ranger, and a pompous ass of a sheriff with hangin' on his mind.

Chapter 4

It took every bit of self-control to keep Hayden from pistol whippin' the local lawman. The Ranger needed air. His father had taught him that in order to be the best, he had to be unhurried and courageous enough to take a fraction of a second longer to make sure he was accurate, as well as fast with a gun. This advice served to remind him that he must take the extra time necessary to let cool judgment, rather than hasty emotions, prevail. He set his jaw and took a deep breath. The hot, dusty air burned his lungs.

He glanced back at Ella, who was watching him intently. Strength and understanding, yet uncertainty, veiled her face. Genuine tenderness reflected in her eyes. He tried to give her a reassuring smile to let her know she'd be safe with him; but for some reason, he didn't think she'd see it that way.

Determined to do the job he'd signed up for—stand tall between society and its enemies—Hayden must make his position clear. "Sheriff, I am taking possession of the prisoner, and carrying her back to Mobeetie for trial."

"You're not going anywhere with *my* prisoner," the sheriff growled. "Get me a warrant or get out of town, unless you wanna end up in the hoosegow with her."

"I've got one waiting. All I need is twenty minutes to pick it up." Hayden prayed Molly Lou's wasn't any farther than half a mile away.

"Not good enough. Show it *now* or no prisoner."

Hayden McGraw had been tested many times, but this jackass had gone too far.

In long-legged strides, Ranger McGraw took the courthouse steps and pulled up near Ella. Turning to the crowd, he said, "Ladies and gentlemen, I'm a Texas Ranger, and I'm taking control of this situation." He pinned his silver badge on his jacket then pulled back his coat and rested his hand on his Peacemaker. "Go on home. Excitement's over. There'll be no hangin' today."

Sheriff Oldham puffed out his chest. His face flushed, turning blood red. "Go on, folks."

Hayden wasn't sure if the lawman was tuckered out from having to work for a change or relieved he could get his humongous heinie out of the sweltering sun.

A few citizens wandered off, shaking their heads. A fistful of nosey-butts lagged behind.

Obviously realizing he was up to his tin star in cow patties, Sheriff Oldham tossed out his final demand. "The only way I'd put her in your custody is if you're family."

"I am!" Hayden almost choked on the words.

The sheriff guffawed. "I still wanna see that warrant in no more than twenty minutes."

"It'll be here."

"Do tell." Sheriff Oldham smirked in a *gotcha* way. "And I reckon you don't even know her name."

He plastered on a possum-eatin' grin on his snout, apparently figuring he'd played his best card, not knowing Hayden had an ace in the hole.

A knack for remembering details to a flaw.

"Patience Eleanor Stevenson." He pushed his Stetson back with his thumb. "But I call her Puddin' Cake." He turned to Ella, and said, "Don't I, *wife?*"

If looks could kill, Ella's face would be on every wanted poster between the Canadian River and the Rio Grande. She set her chin in a stubborn line and glared at him, either in suspicion or surprise. Now why in the hell didn't she look all that pleased with his efforts? After all, he'd saved her from a neck stretchin'.

Baldy backed away when Hayden reached for Ella, pulling her to his side.

The Texas Ranger deliberately rested his hand on her hip, patting her lightly. Through the bustle, he knew she didn't feel his touch, but he figured the sheriff would see it as intimacy.

Hayden had to admit, she sure as hell felt good at his side. "Come on, Puddin' Cake, I rode long and hard to get here, and I'm ready for a hot meal and some husband time."

She shot him a half smile that could have turned sunshine into snow. And he'd been the one suspended for having a piss-poor attitude?

Redemption was imminent.

"I know I'm pretty ragged lookin', darlin', but I didn't take time to clean up 'cause you were always on my mind." He grinned.

Sheriff Oldham would have wanted to know their kinship sooner or later. Hayden didn't know the woman from Bass Outlaw, but now he'd claimed her as his wife. Had he done the right thing? Of course, there was still the possibility that in due time she'd face a hemp committee for horse thievery. But not if he could help it.

Ella looked at him in a questioning, almost fearful way.

Damn bad time for Hayden to notice her long, mahogany hair shining in the sunlight. It reminded him of a handsome bay; and just think, he'd been accused by some of not having a tender bone in his body. Maybe it was because he'd never known anything but rangering. He figured he'd been raised by the famous lawmen, because that's about all he ever remembered. His father, grandfather, and the Texas Rangers.

He didn't mean to, but he found himself lookin' her up and down before settling his gaze back on her face. Even her fiery, dark sapphire eyes added to his vision . . . black mane and tail.

Hell, if he thought the woman was prettier than a bay mare, surely he wasn't totally made of stone. A slow blaze ignited in his belly, just watching her.

As though reading his thoughts, her eyes flashed with fury.

The look left no question in his mind what he needed to do. Get to Molly Lou's, pick up his warrant, and present it to the sheriff. Then after he investigated the facts, he'd figure out what to do with the woman. That should take an hour, tops, then he could get cleaned up, and feed and water Stewball.

The marriage ruse would be over, and he could be on his way to headquarters.

A simple plan. Probably too simple.

A nondescript gentleman who Hayden had noticed hanging around for a while, stepped up on the courthouse porch and halted in front of Ella, Hayden, and the few folks who'd stayed, waitin' in the shade.

"Miss Stevenson—uh, Mrs. McGraw." He hesitated. "Uh, I'm Wilson Scott, Newman County JP. This won't take long. Reckon we gotta get the formalities out of the way." He opened a black ledger. "If you'll both sign here, then all I'll need is the fee, and your union will be duly recorded as required by law." He smiled meekly.

Mortification hit Ella's face, and she peered up at Hayden. He stiffened, knowing his expression wasn't any better.

"Can't this wait? The missus and I are tired and hungry. And I want to clear up the matter of the warrant."

"No, sir." The JP stood his ground.

"Nope, Ranger. This needs tending to . . . now!" Sheriff Oldham interjected.

"Gotcha fee right here." Dixie pulled a stringed bag from between her breasts and began counting out coins.

"Twenty minutes, Ranger, and the clock's tickin'," Sheriff Oldham reminded him.

Twenty minutes!

Reluctantly, Hayden signed his name to the ledger.

Ella folded her arms across her chest and tapped her foot, resisting the JP's demands. As if it were Hayden's fault, she furrowed her brow and sent him a *go to blue blazes* look, which scathed all the way to his toes and back again.

"It's them or me." Hayden nodded toward the sheriff and Baldy, who now held the noose.

Almost knocking the JP off the porch, she seized the ledger. In an exquisite script, Ella scrolled her name across the paper. She shared her frown with Dixie as she handed over the fee.

Dixie raised an eyebrow and shrugged her shoulders. "Should I let them hang you?"

Not waiting for a response, Dixie joined Audrey Jo and they strolled toward the bridge that crossed over the creek to Buffalo Wallow. They were nearly out of sight before Ella bound down the courthouse steps and began her march after them.

As much as Hayden would have preferred to ride, he couldn't take the chance of letting the spirited woman out of his sight even for a minute, so he followed her, presuming she would lead him to Molly Lou's sooner or later. At the moment, he'd put money on later.

* * *

Ella didn't want to look back at the sheriff or Baldy, but the overweight lawman was probably already passed out on a cot in his office, and the bossy bald guy was likely trying to find more trouble to stir up.

Struggling to capture her composure, she attempted to sort through things. What would make a total stranger, a Texas Ranger none-the-less, come to her rescue? As they walked along, a smidge of her anger evaporated, leaving more uncertainty than anything else. Her mind swirled with doubts, a mixture of hope and fear. Something was fishy and didn't sit well with her. But she had to make sure he knew what she thought. She'd never held her tongue in check, and didn't plan on starting now. She didn't need him, or any man for that matter, riding into town to rescue her.

Ella turned so quickly she almost ran into the man following her. "You're a flannelmouthed bushwhacker, Hayden McGraw." She stirred up dust as she kicked one pebble then another out of her way, before whirling around and heading down the middle of the street. She shot over her shoulder, "And one in need of a bath and shave too."

"And a good meal." He pulled up alongside her. "Puddin' Cake, you oughta be glad you're not hangin' from that damn cottonwood instead of being watered off at me." He walked faster, making her take two steps to his one. "I hope you weren't kiddin' about your place only being half a mile away," he stated.

"I don't know what you plan to find there."

"You hold some mail for certain folks, don't you?"

"You know we do, Ranger." She kicked another stone. "Talk to Muley—he knows who he's holding mail for." Another stone flew. "And, before you ask, I don't give a rusty rat's ass who it belongs to."

Storming ahead, she slowed when she neared her saloon. Piano music and laughter came from inside. She stopped in her tracks. Hell's bells and cockleshells, she'd forgotten all about the horse she'd been tending to before she struck out for the meeting in Buffalo Springs. Someone had tethered him to a post on the side of the saloon near the water trough.

"What in the hell!" Hayden came to such a sudden stop, dust whirled around his boots. He turned to her and roared, "You *are* a horse thief!"

After she summoned up all the courage she could, she plopped her hands on her hips. "I sure as hell am not."

"Tell me the truth!" A warning cloud settled across his brow. "What's my horse doing all the way down here . . . at your place? I'm in no mood to mess with you, either."

How dare him! She pressed her lips together, trying to corral her unruly feelings. She'd already figured one thing out about the surly man. His stubbornness made it impossible for him to consider another's viewpoint.

Determined to outwait his anger, if that was possible, she set her jaw and knitted her brows together.

"He didn't tether himself." Hayden quirked a questioning brow at her.

Double-dog damn him. As a matter of principle, she'd not tell him a thing. After all, it was his horse that had wandered onto her property and eaten her carrots. She didn't know the ugly critter belonged to the man. How would she know? The brand wasn't familiar to her. In truth, she'd simply forgotten about the gelding. A little thing like being hanged had occupied her mind.

Nope, not one blasted explanation to him until he changed his attitude toward her.

The look on his face and the star on his chest made her rethink her stance. He didn't appear to be a man who could be pushed and not fight back. "I found him. That is the truth! I've never, ever stolen so much as a pickle from the mercantile, much less an animal."

"If that's the best you can come up with, I'll turn you

back over to the local law, and you can fend for yourself, Little Woman."

She bristled at the curtness. He could call her all the cute, insincere names he wanted, but not refer to her as a "little woman."

Ella flexed her fist. They couldn't hang her twice, could they?

Just about the time she tossed the foolish impulse aside, the devil tempted her bad—real bad. She reared back and, with a crack that could probably be heard all the way to Mobeetie, whacked the lawman across his cheek. "I'd rather be hanged than to be a 'little woman' to a man . . . particularly a Texas Ranger."

"Ma'am, I'm fixin' to give you your druthers."

Chapter 5

As though she'd simply given Hayden a peck on the cheek, Ella straightened her back. Scared to look at him, she focused on the strange-lookin' horse nibbling on the grass in her yard.

Horse thief!

Hanging!

Ugly horse!

Realization slammed her between the eyes. She had been accused of stealing a Ranger's horse. Not only had she slapped the daylights out of Hayden, but now he had no reason to believe anything she said.

She gulped and tried to gather her wits. Slowly she turned to face the Ranger, who was within spittin' distance of the gelding.

Ella crossed her wrists in front of her, signaling defeat. That'd make it easier for him to handcuff her before carting her off to jail.

"Put your hands down," Hayden growled, and began checking on the gash in his horse's foreleg. "You're already in my custody."

"I, uh, I shouldn't have slapped you."

"No, you shouldn't have." A frown clouded his face as

he continued to examine the gelding. "I've been hit harder by a mesquite branch though."

"Can we start over?" She offered him her right hand in a friendly gesture. "Hi, I'm Patience Stevenson, but I prefer Ella."

Hayden wasn't about to accept her apology without plenty of grappling first. If he hadn't been so exasperated with the woman, he might have found her approach humorous. He didn't take kindly to the idea of "starting over." Not to mention, he wouldn't be around long enough to start anything over.

Then there was the issue of Ella being responsible for the kettle of fish she'd gotten herself into. Slapping the living tar out of him didn't help his attitude toward her an iota; although he had to admit he might, just might, have deserved it. She'd made her dislike for being called a "little woman" clear, and he'd chosen to ignore it.

Damn, the lady's sheer presence disturbed him in ways he'd almost forgotten existed. He didn't want to take the chance to feel the things in his heart that he'd tried so desperately to keep hidden for so long. A slow burn settled below his belt. He wouldn't give in to being human. He was a Ranger first and a man second.

Hayden looked up. Searching her face, he forced back a smile.

She stood with crossed arms, foot tapping.

"What happened to Stewball?" He realized he was being a tad short with her, but time wasn't on his side.

Hayden untied the bandana from his neck and used it to wipe off a layer of dirt and pieces of grass that had stuck to a light film of ointment. On closer inspection, the wound seemed minor. "You doctor him?" Hayden asked.

"Yes. I found him near my backdoor, eating carrots. The knife I used to dig them with was on the ground, so I figured he'd knocked it off and cut his leg." She patted the horse between his ears when he nudged her hand. "I fixed him up the best I knew how." She looked up and boldly met his gaze. Sincerity played in her eyes. "I didn't steal your horse, Ranger."

"I believe you." Hayden wiped his palms before stuffing the bandana in his pocket. "Who in their right mind would steal such a hammerhead?" His attempt at humor failed miserably, as did the smile he tried on. "Thank you for carin' for him." Extending his hand, he added, "I'm Hayden Charles McGraw."

She accepted the gesture meant as friendship. He still wasn't all that sure about the "starting over" idea. In his estimation, they had to begin and finish before starting over, but it felt good to hold her hand. It was strong, and not all soft like he'd expected. The woman was used to hard work. Something he admired.

For a wild, startling moment again she stirred things inside of him . . . feelings he'd just reminded himself didn't need awakening. He didn't want to let her hand go.

"Ranger McGraw." Dixie busted out the backdoor, waving an envelope. "This whatcha waitin' for?"

Hayden met the woman halfway. He accepted the parcel and impatiently tore it open.

Only a single sheet of paper.

His replacement Warrant of Authority. Nothing else.

Although it was a slim possibility, he thought maybe his captain had sent him his new assignment. Damn his hide. Surely enough time had passed to where he'd let Hayden back in his good graces.

"That's one fine-lookin' horse." Dixie stopped to admire Stewball. "Your gear's over by the shed." She pointed toward a wooden structure a hundred yards away beside the bank of a fast-running stream. Made of an odd assortment of materials, the building leaned precariously downhill.

"Thanks. Guess I'd best get this back to Sheriff Oldham."

He folded the paper, pleased that he hadn't called the ol' toad something profane. "No need to put unnecessary weight on Stewball's leg right now. Care if I leave him here until I get this warrant delivered?"

Ella nodded an okay.

"I'll be back directly." He headed up the road leading to Buffalo Springs. Suddenly he stopped and turned, catching Ella's eye. He tipped his hat and said, "Thanks again, Patience Eleanor Stevenson."

"Supper at seven," Ella said, barely loud enough for him to hear. "Don't expect carrots."

Whistling, the Ranger turned and walked away.

Chapter 6

Ella watched Hayden until he crossed the bridge. Her heart told her that he'd not be back for supper or anything else.

A few minutes later, after washing up and changing clothes, Ella stood in the middle of her tiny kitchen area off the saloon. She had piled her long tresses on top of her head and secured them with one of her mother's delicate wooden combs. At least her neck felt cool.

The laughter and merrymaking from the saloon bled through the thin walls. Generally that would make Ella smile, but not today.

A lot had happened in a short period of time. She picked up one of her mother's aprons hanging on a hook. She ran her fingers over the familiar flour-sack fabric, settling on a red embroidered heart on the yoke. She found herself caressing the motif and thinking about her mama. Sometimes she missed her incessant mothering. Ella thought back on how she had resisted her mother's sage advice, which sometimes resembled orders. She sure could use some maternal nurturing at the moment.

She pulled the apron on and tied it behind her, then sat down at the kitchen table.

Suddenly, tears welled up in her eyes. She put her face in her hands and let them flow. Something she never did.

Ella hated showing weakness of any sort, yet she'd let a good-lookin' man turn her head. There should be no shame in not being strong, but that wasn't what her mama taught her. Strength is character. Without it, she'd be nothing. Yet she had allowed herself to show emotions, be vulnerable and exposed, which equated to weakness. Ella had reacted without considering the consequences. Had she gone mad? Yes, showing her emotions was a weakness and it had never been acceptable . . . not yesterday, not today, and not tomorrow.

Taking a deep breath, she brushed away the tears and rose to her feet. Maybe she had simply responded humanly to an ugly situation.

Besides, it wasn't every day a woman could speak her mind to a mob at a snobby town-hall meeting, nearly be hanged, and get married to a confounded Texas Ranger.

But she wouldn't have to worry about the lawman much longer. After today he'd be gone. She saw it in his eyes. Every man she'd ever known had let her down, so why should she trust Hayden? What made her think he was any different? Yet there was something about him. A shared attraction. Something she couldn't quite put her finger on.

It was only mid-afternoon, too early to begin supper. Another chorus of hoots and loud laughter seeped through the cracks in the wall. Probably a joke or maybe a winning hand of poker. Hilarity was always plentiful in the saloon.

Unless there was a problem she wouldn't see Dixie or Audrey Jo until suppertime, when they'd each come eat a bite and then get back to serving drinks and smiles to customers.

Emotionally drained, yet with a business to take care of, Ella tried to clean out the fickle cobwebs in her mind, not to mention the visions of Hayden.

Tomorrow was supply day. The drummer, Willard Porter, would arrive shortly after dawn, so she didn't have the luxury to wait until later to gather her order. No time for daydreams.

Ella opened the pie safe and counted the bear claws. She needed to bake more before morning so she'd have enough to barter sufficient lard and flour for the next batch. She scanned the Mason jars lined up side by side and made a mental note. Twenty-four, all apple jelly. That would bring enough to pay for any fruit in season that Willard found between Mobeetie and Wagon Mound, New Mexico. She pulled a notebook from the top of the cabinet, and added paraffin, sugar, and cornmeal to her list.

Without the liquor order, mostly whiskey, which Muley and Dixie took care of, Ella might come out with enough extra money from the marmalades and pastries to put aside a little bit for something special for herself. Maybe a brand-spankin'-new dress. Her current wardrobe consisted of the pink one she'd just taken off and hung to air out, and the pitiful, faded calico on her back.

Ella sighed. Most likely there'd be no extra money by the time Willard and Muley bartered things out. There seemed to always be more on her "needs" list than she could keep up with by making jams and jellies and baking.

The day was running long, and the room was getting hotter by the minute. The smell of simmering beans hung in the air. She pulled an iron skillet off a nail beside the cupboard, and opened the cornmeal canister. Less than one cup. Then she recalled the last time she filled the can and thinking how quickly the cornmeal was vanishing. For all she knew, Muley might be putting it on the floor instead of sawdust.

Even less sugar in its container.

The door opened and Dixie fluttered in, carrying a napkin-lined basket.

"Is everything okay out there?" Ella put on a smile, and replaced the skillet. "What's that?"

"Sourdough biscuits. They're having a rip-snortin' good time. You're the talk of the town," Dixie said.

"Nearly being hanged gave the gossipmongers plenty of fodder, huh?"

"Nope. Lots of folks were makin' bets that your Texas Ranger wouldn't let you down. I think some even made money off him." She giggled. "Nope. None of that. It's how you stood up for other folks' rights that's got their gums aflappin'."

"I don't understand."

"The saloon is filled to the brim. We got more business than anybody else in town. They all said they want to buy beer from somebody who didn't mind setting the hypocrites of Buffalo Springs straight." Dixie set the basket down. "Don't fix supper tonight. Ladies brought in some chicken and dumplin's, even corn dodgers and two pans of apple brown betty to show their appreciation for standing up for them. Give me your word you won't tell anybody, but a couple of ol' biddies from Buffalo Springs brought food, and I think one was the sheriff's missus." Dixie wiped her hands on a tea towel. "It's about like a church social. Not that I've been to many. There's enough food for everyone, even the customers. Come see it for yourself."

That put a sweet-sour taste in Ella's mouth, and she forced a smile. "Thanks. Maybe after I finish my order."

Dixie walked to the sideboard and took out a cup. "They sure like that man of yours savin' your hide. Marrying you and all."

"He's *not* my man." Ella bit down hard on her lower lip. "Besides, he won't be coming back."

"What makes you think that?" Dixie said as she poured coffee.

"Oh, he'll come fetch his horse, but won't stay." Ella

forced a tiny smile, as she glanced out the little window over the sink. "He sure has a sweet disposition, doesn't he?"

"I presume you mean the horse, 'cause you sure as hell can't say Ranger McGraw's disposition is sweet." Dixie chuckled. "So what makes you so sure he won't return?"

"Just the way he walked away." Ella straightened her back, trying to hide her disappointment. "He's a Ranger. Doesn't stick long anywhere. It's in his blood. He lives and breathes rangering."

Dixie weighed her with a critical squint, making Ella wonder if she agreed or disagreed.

Out of habit, Ella touched the heart on her apron. "The man's not any good at saying hello, and worse at saying good-bye."

"He'll be back, girl." Dixie sat down at the table. "Besides, you all have to get the marriage deal straightened out."

Ice ran through Ella's veins. She hadn't thought about the fact that they were legally married. Kinda the opposite of what the law intended . . . to make those living without clergy legalized. She and Hayden were bound in matrimony by the laws of Texas, but not in the eyes of God.

"Got any idea how I go about getting out of this mess?" Ella felt unsettled. "Other than stealing Mr. Scott's book of records?"

"I don't rightfully know, except you gotta tell 'em why you are wantin' a divorce to undo it. Heard that down in Brazos County a wife told the judge that during their time together her husband had sold and squandered pert near all of her personal property. And, an Ezekiel Somebody-or-Other accused his wife of adultery. So I guess it doesn't really matter who says what. It's gettin' out of this pickle that counts."

"So I've got to confess to the world for an eternity that I married a Texas Ranger to keep from being hanged?"

Her stomach soured and she thought she was going to upchuck. "Where'd you get all your information anyway?"

"There was a lawyer-type gambler out there a while ago, who was givin' out advice for a free beer."

"Muley isn't giving beer away, is he?"

"Nope." Dixie squirmed. "I paid for it."

"That's twice today I've seen you squandering money."

"I just wanna help."

"So what advice, other than I have to tell everyone what happened, did he give?"

"It's not what he said, but what he didn't say that made me begin thinkin'."

Ella could tell by the way Dixie was fidgeting that she didn't necessarily know how to go about saying what she had on her mind.

"Okay, Dixie, quit beatin' the devil around the stump."

"Don't ask me how I know this, but if you don't . . ." Dixie obviously was having problems spitting out the words.

"Don't what?"

"You know." Again Dixie hesitated, turning her palms toward the ceiling, as if trying to push up—more like erect—something. She repeated, "You know."

Ella watched intently, not sure exactly what the older woman meant. "No. I don't know."

Dixie looked around, as though there were others in the room, and leaned close to the younger woman. Dropping her voice to nearly a whisper, she said, "You know. Whatever you do, don't do *it* with him."

"It?" Ella lowered her voice in the same manner.

"The thing you don't allow in the saloon," said Dixie.

"No cheating at cards?"

The blank look on Dixie's face said it all. *It* became abundantly clear. Ella felt downright stupid for not getting

Dixie's drift immediately, but the whole conversation wasn't exactly one she'd ever had before with anyone.

Trying to slough off some of the uneasiness, Ella joked. "Cussing?"

Dixie raised a questioning eyebrow. Pained, she said, "No! You know . . ."

"Oh, my gracious!" Ella cried, as though surprised.

"Yep, the thing soiled doves do."

"In other words, I gotta make sure we *do not* consummate our union."

Ella wasn't convinced the ol' dance-hall girl knew the gist of the two-dollar word, but had no doubt that "consummate" and "it" had the exact same meaning.

Dixie twitched her nose and smiled, probably happy that she had finally made some headway with her explanation. She stood. "Whether you recognize it or not, girl, from the way you look at that rascal of a man you don't want to accept as your husband, it might be harder than you might think to keep him out of your bed."

"It won't be hard 'cause he won't be back."

Chapter 7

About the time Hayden crossed the wobbly bridge separating Buffalo Springs from Buffalo Wallow he got his second wind, almost forgetting how tired and hungry he was.

It didn't take him long to get to the sheriff's office. He walked in and caught the local lawman sitting with his feet on his desk, leaning back, his hat covering his face. It took every ounce of resistance Hayden had not to give a little shove to Oldham's boots and send him off his perch head over teakettle. Hayden struggled with the temptation, but slammed the door shut to jar the ol' coot awake.

The chair almost tipped over backward as the sheriff struggled to sit up. "McGraw, been waitin' on you," he said, reaching out for the warrant.

Yeah, just like a boar hog waitin' on slop.

Oldham barely glanced over the paper and handed it back, obviously not going to make excuses for being asleep.

"Looks to be in order, but let me get one damn thing straight. You lied for Ella Stevenson. She wasn't your wife until the JP stepped in, but she is now. I'm figurin' the captain won't take too kindly to knowin' he has a renegade

Ranger out harassing good folks. Keeping the JP from doing his job." He took out a plug of tobacco and chewed off a piece. "Just remember, she's your responsibility now, and everybody will be keepin' an eye on you two." The sheriff's cheek rounded as he fiddled with the tobacco in his mouth. "Better make sure you and your prisoner, who is now legally your wife, are livin' together, like all the respectable married folks in this town. And if you touch a hair on the little woman—"

Hayden turned abruptly. "I can assure you my wife isn't anybody's little woman." Damn, even his tongue couldn't deny she was his wife.

Stalking out, Hayden only vaguely heard the sheriff's parting shot. "If I find out she wasn't your wife when you took her into custody, I'll see your cocky ass is suspended permanently."

The damn pigheaded sheriff had upped the ante.

Obviously Hayden was in somewhat better graces with his captain or he would not have sent the warrant. All well and good, but now wasn't the time to give his ranking officer a reason to suspend him again. He had no choice but to send word to his captain that he was detained in Buffalo Wallow.

He headed for the telegraph office. Hayden stuck around after sending his message and received a reply from headquarters about as quickly as he'd ever seen a telegram turn around and be decoded. It said simply, "Status quo." At least he knew where he stood with his captain.

Three hours later, Hayden felt almost human again. He'd eaten a thick, rare steak at the Buffalo Springs Hotel dining room, and had a much-needed shave and haircut. Amusement tickled his throat. Bet Miss Sassy-butt wouldn't even recognize him.

He'd been out of tobacco for days and needed some.

Although he rarely smoked, he felt naked without having the makin's in his saddlebags. Some habits die hard.

A few doors down from the hotel, he saw a sign: SONNY WATSON'S MERCANTILE. He entered and walked straight to the counter, coming face-to-face with the woman who had stalked out of the town-hall meeting waving her umbrella.

"What can I get you?" the woman said curtly, making it known that she held mixed feelings between whether to respect him as a Ranger or toss him out on his ear for being married to a troublemaker from the other side of the creek.

"Bull Durham, ma'am." He didn't bother to look at her further, choosing to survey the canned goods on the shelves behind the counter. "Make it two."

She shoved two muslin bags in front of him. "That'll be two bits. Need lights or papers?"

"No, ma'am." He paid double the going price for the tobacco, tipped his Stetson, and turned to walk away.

A middle-aged man wearing a visor and apron stepped beside the clerk. "Ranger McGraw, just got in something that wife of yours might like." He nodded dismissively to the woman, who walked toward a waiting customer.

"I'm Sonny Watson and that's my wife, Emma." The proprietor reached into a display case and pulled out a tray of women's accessories—a half dozen rings, hairclips, and earrings. "She might like this." He handed Hayden a hairclip. "Mother-of-pearl chips in it."

Hayden accepted the piece. His gut told him the owner was more interested in having his say than selling anything.

Sure enough, the proprietor began. "That woman of yours is a fine lady, nothin' like her pa. She doesn't deserve the treatment some dish out." He picked up a broach. "This one'd make her smile." Mr. Watson looked Hayden square in the eye. "Just don't forget that every brown cow with a white face isn't a Hereford. So make sure you know the difference. Nothin' looks the same when it's turned inside out."

A true Texan—tell it like it is and let the chips fall where they may.

"I'll take the hairclip," Hayden said.

Everyone seemed concerned for his new wife's welfare. New wife! Hellfire and brimstone, he'd already gotten used to calling her that, and he hadn't even kissed her yet.

Hayden paid the man. Tucking the tissue-wrapped bauble in his pocket, he thanked the owner and headed out the door.

No more than a minute later, Hayden saw the sign above Chip and Hell's. Just about the time he came abreast of the entry, Baldy barreled out, blocking Hayden's path. One of the swinging doors hit Hayden smack dab in his shoulder.

"Didn't think you had enough cojones to come back up into this part of town, but I got a word of advice for you." Baldy wobbled a little on his feet, his words even louder than usual. "Watch your back. I don't like Texas Rangers, and I sure as hell don't like you."

"You threatening me?" Hayden casually pulled back his coat and flexed his fingers over his Colt. He was itching to draw on the jackass. No doubt he'd get the first and only shot in if it came to that.

"Not a threat. A promise." Baldy stalked down the steps.

Hayden wasn't sure whose plow he wanted to clean first, the egotistical lawman's or his arrogant sidekick's.

Hayden watched the weasel halt next to a brightly colored drummer's wagon sitting outside the livery. He nodded to the tall, lanky, weather-beaten man who stopped his unloading, looked around, and followed the trouble-maker to the other side of the wagon, out of sight.

Instead of taking the bridge across the stream, Hayden figured he could cool off by walking the banks and enjoying the sunset. One thing about this part of the world, he never got tired of seeing the horizon blazing alive with orange, yellow, and crimson, a field of Indian paintbrush. Tonight was one of those times that a magnificent setting sun improved the whole day. He needed to be alone and think. Maybe he was gettin' soft. Maybe he didn't crave rangerin' like he once had. Maybe a pretty woman was the cause of the knot in his gut.

Once Hayden spied the cornfield that he'd noticed earlier, he knew he was nearing the backside of Molly Lou's. As he recollected, the field was only a few hundred yards from Ella's small garden. He cut through the tall stalks.

After walking down a few rows, he came across a roll of barbed wire and corn shucks stacked waist high. Dry, too dried out for them to have been shucked today. They could begin a prairie fire in the dangerously hot, dry weather.

Hayden found Stewball more than content, munching on an apple. He'd better get the gelding away from Ella's garden pretty damn quick or the dang thing would have a stomachache so bad that he'd be laid up for days recuperating.

Meandering over to the outer building where Dixie had indicated his gear had been stored, he smelled the distinct tang of sourdough starter. Strange place to store leavening for biscuits. Light slipped between the crooked slats, casting catawampus shadows on the dirt.

Hayden didn't even have to get any closer to the shack to recognize Baldy's boisterous voice, overriding another man's short, choppy words.

"Everybody knows Ella is gullible." Baldy laughed contemptuously. "She's as stubborn as a damn mule. Trusts too much. Always gotta do what's right, but it got her into a heap of dookey this time."

"Hell, that Ranger won't be around long enough to find out he was had. We've seen to it." The other man chipped out his words. "That was the easiest setup I've ever seen.

He jumped on her like a lovesick bull with his lady. Worked like a charm."

Baldy barked, "Willard, enough fiddle-farting around. We gotta get more water in here pronto, you hear?"

"Where the hell is Mullinex?"

"He's busy. Just do your job, and let me worry about mine," said Baldy. "If you don't quit your lollygagging around, you won't be gettin' outta here for Wagon Mound until it's siesta time tomorrow."

Hayden couldn't see the man called Willard, and didn't recognize the voice as any of those he'd heard that day.

Until the reference to Muley was made, Hayden felt pretty sure the men were saying that Ella had set him up to marry her, but suddenly the facts didn't fit together. What would she get out of marrying him? He had no money, looked like a bear awakening from a winter's hibernation the last time she saw him, and was just about as cranky as one too. Nothing to offer a wife.

So why would she and her friends hornswoggle him into marrying her?

He'd just seen Baldy in town less than an hour ago, and now he was in Ella's shed, having water toted in? Nothing made sense. Not the water. Not the sourdough starter, and certainly not Baldy and this man Willard.

Years of experience and ol' fashioned instinct told Hayden something was wrong. Very wrong. And they damn sure weren't taking baths in there either.

Hayden had originally intended to go and talk to Ella. Apologize for his bad attitude, try to make amends, and then decide how best to take care of the marriage fiasco. He figured it would be better to clear it up with a judge than to battle the Justice of the Peace to have it annulled. He'd certainly not get any backing from the sheriff. But now, after everything he'd seen and heard, he felt the need to stick around. Since he hadn't received an assignment from headquarters, he was free to do whatever was necessary to protect the new frontier and its citizens.

On the back side of the shed, a mule brayed. A second one answered. Hayden wanted to see what was back there besides the animals, but he wasn't familiar with the building and didn't want to chance making noise. He couldn't investigate . . . not in the dark . . . not tonight.

How did the two men and Ella fit together? What kind of scam were they running? She didn't seem the type to be a con artist, but it wasn't like she'd wear a hatband saying such. She had made no bones about not liking Texas Rangers, but why him in particular? Either he was as dumb as a stump or was smitten by the multifaceted woman.

Hayden now had an even stronger desire to talk to Ella, but there were too many warnings bouncing around in his head for it to be the right time.

Low light flickered in the kitchen area off Molly Lou's. Nope, now wasn't the time; she was probably asleep, if she wasn't tending to the saloon. He knew if he did find her awake, he wouldn't be able to resist touching her, even tuck her into bed. Hell, sleep in the same bed with her—but that couldn't happen. She'd messed with his heart and made him think of things he'd like to do with a woman. But not just any woman . . . Ella Stevenson—uh, McGraw—and she didn't even know it.

Slowly circling the building, he took stock of the storefronts lining the street. He'd been on many main streets, but most still had a few businesses on the outskirts. In Buffalo Wallow, their main street could be called Lone Street.

All of the buildings had been quickly erected and were of poor quality. He was glad he'd picked up cigarette fixin's at Watson's, as there was no general store in sight, just a downtrodden livery, one small café, and at least a dozen saloons. Some in wooden structures, several in tents, and others a combination. No rhyme or reason for the material used. Seemed whatever could be carted in was good enough to erect a saloon with.

Maybe Muley could shed some light on the mysterious goin's on. Hayden strolled into Molly Lou's like he'd been there a million times.

The older man was nowhere in sight.

Audrey Jo worked behind the bar, while Dixie fluttered around delivering the orders.

A thunder of laughter hailed from a table of poker players. A man in the shadows strummed a guitar and sang, his voice more out of tune than the musical instrument.

"What can I get you, Mr. McGraw?" Audrey Jo grinned and bobbled her curly red locks.

Placing a goodly amount of coins on the counter, he said, "Whatever this will buy." He tried to smile back, but his social graces were so lacking that he knew the ol' dance-hall girl recognized it for exactly what it was—as out of tune as the guitar picker.

"That much dinero will take you a long ways here." She reached beneath the counter and held an amber bottle up to him. "One bit gets you whiskey, two bits the good stuff. Name your poison."

He nodded toward the bottle Audrey Jo had in her hand.

The bartender set the liquor in front of him, along with a glass. "Just remember it was your choice." She gave him a motherly, yet slightly flirtatious smile. "You sure do clean up nicely."

Before he could thank her, Dixie rushed their way, spitting out an order, setting the redhead into action.

"Evening, Ranger." Dixie mopped perspiration from her forehead with the back of her hand. "Thought you'd be with, uh, your bride tonight."

The remark threw him a bit, but his curiosity overshadowed the truth. He needed to find out more about what was going on, and so far he'd pegged the seasoned barmaid as a gal to ride the river with. He sure as hell wanted her as a friend, because she'd be one hell of an enemy.

"I'm sure she's sound asleep," he offered.

"Oh, I see." Dixie winked.

Hayden shot her a coy smile before he threw back a slug of whiskey. The hot liquid burned all the way to his toenails and nearly blew his boots off. He'd drunk more than his share of firewater, but this was the strongest he'd ever had the displeasure to drink. Hayden ran his fist across his lips trying to rid himself of the awful taste, and shuddered. "What in the hell!"

Audrey Jo slid four shot glasses to Dixie, who ignored them, snatching up the whiskey bottle instead.

Dixie spoke directly to the redhead. "You gotta be careful. This isn't whiskey, but a concoction I fixed up to . . ." She looked over at Hayden with an apologetic smile of sorts. "A concoction I fixed up to clean with." Dixie secured the jug under her arm and placed all four drinks in her left palm. "Gotta be more careful, Audrey Jo. Give him another bottle—and his money's no good here." She sauntered off, shooting over her shoulder, "I've got his drinks covered."

"Sorry about that. I wasn't thinkin'." Audrey Jo cleared her throat and stepped to the back bar and placed another bottle before him. "Don't think it'll kill you, but if you gotta puke, go outside." She shoved the coins his way, and refilled his glass.

"Where's Muley tonight?" Hayden asked.

"Out."

Audrey Jo's short response told him what he wanted to know. Muley's whereabouts were none of his dadgum business.

Tentatively, Hayden tossed back the whiskey. Much

better. He was no expert on liquor, but knew it well enough to know that the first drink had been tarantula juice at its finest.

Hayden thanked her, turned away from the bar and surveyed the room. A table filled with mostly empty bowls was in the corner. Don't believe he'd ever seen food, other than a few pickled eggs, in a saloon.

As he'd expect in any bar this late in the evening, a motley crew of gamblers, gunslingers, and businessmen sat at tables in various degrees of inebriation.

A buffalo skull hung on the wall. The bison had some of the biggest horns Hayden believed he'd ever seen in all his born days.

Dixie came in his view but disappeared through a door he was pretty sure didn't lead to Ella's living quarters. He wasn't buying the excuse that he'd been served cleaning fluid for a second. What was going on? Too many odd happenings made his gut turn over.

Although it was late, the saloon had too much business for only two saloon girls to tend to.

So where was Muley?

Just being told he was out didn't satisfy Hayden in the least. He took his drink and ambled toward where Dixie had exited, just about the time she came back through. She wiped her hands on her skirt, and said, "Sorry for the mix-up."

"Answer a question and all's forgiven." He deliberately tried to woo her with a smile.

"Sure, Ranger."

"Was the envelope you gave me today the only one that has arrived here for me?"

"Only one I've ever seen with your name on it. Muley generally handles what shows up for you all, if you get my drift." She bit her lip.

He nodded in agreement, and lowered his voice, "Safe

place for a Ranger who doesn't want to be seen to light. How long have you all been here?"

"A year or so back. Ella's father put this shack together before he took off. She's only been in town a little while, still learning the ropes."

"Took off?"

"Like he did in Mobeetie, but we followed him here. Needed our jobs. Her pa had a real problem with con artists, gamblers, or lawmen." Dixie stopped and weighed her words carefully. "But, Ranger, he loves that girl."

"But he still left her on her own?"

"More times than any gal should bear. He'd be here if he could. Gotta get back to work." Dixie looked uncomfortably at Hayden. The first time he'd seen the woman not exude a sassy attitude. "And, Ranger, Ella takes care of her part of the business and we take care of this side. She doesn't have a hand in running the saloon." She headed in the direction of a table of impatient drinkers.

Hayden clenched his jaw. "So he loved her so much that he forgot where he left her." He said under his breath, "One hell of a father."

Dejected and feeling like a castoff himself, Hayden pulled in his horns and moseyed back to the bar.

Audrey Jo piped up, "I forgot to tell you that your room is up the stairs on the second floor."

"My room?"

"Yeah, gotta have a place to sleep, so I said you could have my room and I'll bunk with Ella."

"Don't wanna be a bother. I'm not much at sleeping in a bed. Spend most of my nights on the ground. I could go to the hotel or—"

"No!" Audrey Jo wiped a glass. "This is what we decided to do. We don't close up until everybody is outta here, but your room's upstairs. Last door on the . . ." She set the glass down and looked at one hand then the other. As though double-checking, she turned her right palm up, then her left, before continuing. "That's right. Last door on the, uh, right. Yes, sir. On the right." She went back on task.

Thanking her for the hospitality, Hayden finished his drink. He left all the coins on the bar and sauntered out.

The walk from the saloon to where his saddlebags were stored might give him enough time to figure out whether he needed to fish or cut bait. Right now his brain said to cut bait, but his heart said fish. Although he was more accustomed to having the ground for a mattress and the sky as his covers, a soft bed dadgum it sure sounded good.

Hayden stuck his hands in his pockets. His fingers touched the tissue paper wrapping the hair clip. Damn, he'd forgotten about the little gift, and he'd used up his allotment of restraint for the day. He couldn't see the spitfire tonight because he'd for sure pull her into his arms and never let her go.

From what Dixie said, Ella had had a man walk out on her too many times, and he sure as hell was treading a very thin line as to whether he'd be the next.

Hayden took in the cool evening air.

No way in hell he'd let that happen.

A lot of unanswered questions rattled around in his brain. Rangers weren't known to air their dirty laundry in public, reckoning a good man was in enough danger without rumors and half-assed truths gettin' in his way.

So, how in the hell did Sheriff Oldham know Hayden had been suspended?

Chapter 8

Ella sat on the steps of her back porch and stared at the moon. Hazy shades of blood red settled against an ebony backdrop of darkness.

Taking a sip of coffee, she welcomed the slight breeze cutting across the porch. One of the nice things about late summer, the unwavering heat of the day always surrendered into cool evenings.

A shadow crossed the yard, and she looked up to see Ranger McGraw ambling toward the shed. She drew in a breath. He was more alluring in the dark. Without his jacket, he looked even taller than she first thought. His gun belt hung low over tight fittin' pants hugging slim hips. He walked in a cocky, authoritative saunter. This man projected vigor and command that undeniably fascinated her.

He picked up his saddlebags and threw them over his broad shoulder. The muscles rippling taut beneath his boiled white shirt quickened her heart.

"Good evening, Hayden." She hoped he wouldn't draw on her first and ask questions later; although she could bet her last jar of jelly that he knew exactly where she sat. He hadn't survived this long as a lawman without a keen sense of awareness that would make a coyote jealous.

Hayden made a slow turn, taking a step in her direction. His dark Stetson shadowed his face, but she could see he was clean shaven and oh, so touchable.

He tipped his hat. "Evening, Little Lady."

A smile curled on Ella's lips, and she shook her head ever so slightly. No doubt he was testing her, and she wouldn't give him the pleasure of a reaction. For some reason, maybe it was the effects of the relaxing end of a ghastly day, being called a little lady by this man didn't seem patronizing. At least he hadn't called her Puddin' Cake!

"Lookin' for Stewball, I believe you called him?"

"Yes, ma'am. Guess he's wandered off again. Dang his hide."

"Don't blame him. Seems everybody took a shine to him and figured he needed something to eat." She set the cup on the ledge. "Hope you don't mind, but I carted him down the street to the livery so he could get some grain before he got all bloated up and ended up killing himself eatin' carrots." She hesitated, gathering her thoughts. "Anyway, I figured you didn't plan on riding out this late . . . even if you came back."

"Much obliged, ma'am. I appreciate you taking care of Stewball." His grin flashed briefly as he stepped her way. "Mind if I sit a spell?"

His voice seemed to catch on the wind and linger before it lit on her. Now she could get a good look at his face. She'd seen other men like him who always sported a dark shadow even when they'd just walked out of the barbershop. He was definitely one of the rugged ones who had been cast that lot in life. He'd never be called clean shaven.

"Sure. How about some coffee and fresh bear claws?" She picked up her cup. "They're still warm and the coffee's hot."

"The way to a man's heart." He extended his hand.

"May I?" He helped her to her feet and escorted her inside, as though they were going to a fancy tea parlor after the opera.

Ten minutes later, Hayden's Stetson hung on a nail next to Ella's bonnet. She sat across from him at the kitchen table, watching him wash down the last bite of a bear claw with coffee. He tore into his second pastry. She couldn't help but admire his total lack of shame for enjoying the food.

"Ma'am, if you don't mind me saying, if I could end every day eatin' more of these, I'd marry you."

Time stood still.

Sapphire blue eyes captured his piercing ebony ones, throwing them both off guard.

She raised a questioning eyebrow. "You mean, if I weren't already married?"

The humor in their words made her giggle, which turned into a full, out-and-out expression of amusement. He joined in with his deep, warm, and rich belly laugh.

It felt good to enjoy the company of a man who wasn't overbearing. Hayden McGraw made her feel more than good; he made her feel as a woman should. A husband with his wife, except for one hitch: he was only temporary. Kinda like an incarcerated spouse, kept at arm's length, with iron bars separating them.

Ella studied his face. A tad bruised with life, but caressed by lots of sunrays. A half-moon scar imbedded in the dark stubble along his jawline made her pause with thought. Very intriguing. She let her imagination run wild, visualizing a mean-to-the-bones hombre looking for a fight, coming at Hayden with the butt of a Colt .45. After taking a whoopin' from the lawman, the outlaw probably lay crumbled on the ground, sorry he chose her husband to fight.

Her husband!

Damn, her brains had turned to mush. Cornmeal mush. A huge bowl of nothing but saltless mush, with no sugar or butter to make it go down easier. Oh, but how easy Hayden would go down!

Her runaway mind was halted at full steam when Hayden's voice penetrated her thoughts. "What? I'm sorry, I, uh . . ." Ella stammered.

"I was just saying that we need to talk about where we go from here," he said.

"Go from here?"

"Sheriff Oldham made no bones that if we don't make an effort to present ourselves as married to the community, he'll take you back into custody."

"But, he arrested me as a horse thief, and it was your horse, so surely you're not pressing charges."

"Of course not, but the sheriff still has assault charges on the plate, and he's the one in control of them." He wiped the sugar off his lips with a napkin. "And, Ella, I can't do a thing about it, Ranger or not."

Her heart sank. She knew he was right, but how could they manage to appear married when they both knew it was a flimsy ruse? On the other hand, if she had a choice between playing Sheriff Oldham's game or being tossed in the pokey, she knew exactly which she'd prefer.

"I've really got us in a mess, haven't I?"

"Seems we're both in a jam, but we'll get it worked out." Hayden offered a strong, coy, sexy-as-heck smile. "Together."

A short time later, Ella sat astonished as Hayden drained the last coffee from the pot and set two cups on the table. She couldn't remember ever having a man wait on her. Do something without being asked.

He returned to his seat, and it was as though any barriers that had been between them melted away. They had talked nonstop, each throwing out on the table their thoughts about how to best handle the predicament they were in.

The one thing they both had no trouble agreeing on: they had to appear to be a happily married couple for the time being. Once Hayden's assignment arrived, he would leave town to take care of his rangering duties, things would die down, and they could file for an annulment with little or no fanfare.

Agreed upon.

But Ella had a stipulation that must be addressed. And, a very big one. She swallowed, as if that would make the words come out smoother. "I promise to be the perfect wife, but . . ." The words hung in her throat. "Hayden, there's one condition."

He nodded, as though reading her mind.

"You can't. I mean, we can't . . ."

"Oh hell, Ella. After all you're my wife, so surely you can say it." He ran his hand through his hair. "We can't share a bed, right?"

"Yes." She gulped.

"Okay," he said, as simply as if he were approving a sack of flour being added to a grocery order.

She wasn't sure whether to be insulted or appreciative.

"Not until you want me there." He looked into her eyes, all the way to her soul.

Ella saw a heart-rending promise in his gaze. She tried not to be affected by his declaration, or the images swirling around in her head, but found comfort in his words.

She cleared her throat. "It's just a matter of law, Hayden. Keeping things uncomplicated. If we don't, uh, consummate our marriage, we can get it annulled; otherwise, there'd be the embarrassment of a divorce and a lot of—"

"Messy explanations, I know." He smiled. "It's for the best, but there are some other things we need to clear the air about."

"Anything." She breathed a sigh of relief. After their talk about intimacy, anything would be better. "I asked you for a big concession, so it's only fair that you ask for one."

"I'll save my request for later. Right now I need some answers about the people working for you. How well do you know them?"

"Well enough . . ." She found herself impatiently tapping her foot. "Just what are you asking, Ranger McGraw?" His insinuation dug deep, and seemed to deflate the enjoyment she had been having with Hayden. She thought she'd made her support of her workers and friends clear at the town meeting.

"You know that Rangers get mail here—"

"Of course. It's something Muley and my father were doing before he disappeared—a long time before I got here. I've been too busy trying to make a go of the business to get involved."

"You couldn't be around and not know some of the particulars," Hayden said.

"All I know is that nobody in Buffalo Springs has the backbone to be seen down here, so mail isn't delivered. They don't want us up there, so every now and again a mail sack is left by somebody in the trunk of a downed cottonwood tree by the stream. I asked Muley why that site, and he said that was all I needed to know. He watches for mail and gives it only to the person who it is addressed to."

"That location was chosen so the rider can follow the stream and not leave any tracks." Hayden filled in the blanks.

"My father was always on the other side of the law, so I can't imagine how he would knowingly help out the Rangers," she said.

"You might never know, Ella."

"You asked about the girls and Muley." She changed the

subject, as she'd spoken her father's name more with Hayden than she had with anyone in a long time.

"If I'm gonna stick around, I need to know more about them."

"Audrey Jo and Dixie worked for my father in Mobeetie. Dixie's like a mother to me, and Audrey Jo is just herself. I can vouch for both of them." She found herself tapping her nail on the table, as though punctuating her statement. "Muley was here when I arrived. He worked for my father and the women said I should trust him. I've been around saloons all of my life, and Muley is more reserved and shy, probably the most nonconfrontational bartender I've ever seen. He works his shift, eats a bite without saying any more than is necessary. I think he'd eat unsalted potatoes before he'd ask for a shaker to be passed to him."

"He was pretty outspoken today."

"The most excited I've ever seen him."

"What does he do when he isn't working?" Hayden asked.

"I figure it's none of my business, as long as he doesn't cause any problems. I provide him with a room above the saloon, but I don't think he's ever spent a night up there. I do know that he works in that corn patch of his and fiddles around in the ol' shed. At first I thought he didn't hang around here much because he's uncomfortable sharing quarters with women, but then decided the girls drive him batty, so he prefers to sleep in the shed instead of having to listen to them. He's very private." She took a sip of coffee. "Hayden, I trust Audrey Jo and Dixie, so I trust him. As long as he takes care of the saloon, so I can handle making pastries, jellies, and jams for him to barter with Willard, the drummer, I don't care what he does. All I want is to be able to pay them, provide a roof over their heads, and food on the table. He makes that happen."

"And you have enough money left over for yourself?"

Her back stiffened. Her bank balance, or lack thereof, was none of his concern. Needing a diversion from his scrutiny, she stood and walked to the sink. She wanted so desperately not to show how impatient she was becoming, but felt pretty sure she had failed miserably.

Hayden must've recognized he'd stepped over the line, from questions he needed to know to those she certainly called personal, because he asked, "What do you know about this Willard guy?"

"He's the peddler and comes through regularly, making deliveries and picking up anything I have to barter." Ella wrung out the dishrag. "Some nights he camps down by the stream so he can get an early start for Wagon Mound. I've seen him coming out of the shed, so he sleeps in there sometimes."

"What about the big, mouthy, bald guy who accused you of stealing a horse?"

"Never seen him before today."

"He just showed up?"

"I haven't been here long. As you noticed, the two parts of town are sparsely populated. I've seen just about everyone."

Ella tried to think back on how the bald guy had acted when she saw him, but things were happening so fast she couldn't recall it all. She did remember one thing. "From the way Sheriff Oldham reacted to him, I figured he knew him. It didn't take long for me to learn that the sheriff doesn't take orders from anybody. He seemed to go along with what was going on."

"Noticed that myself. Then Baldy doesn't hang around down here? You sure you don't have any business with him?"

"I said . . . I've *never* seen him before." Ella rubbed

down the counter with a vengeance before throwing the dishrag back in the water.

What was going on? Ella wondered. Simple questions had turned sour, and now were interrogations. Maybe Hayden's barbed questioning had something to do with him rescuing her from being lynched?

He needed to level with her, and then she'd force his hand, one way or another.

"In order to make this arrangement work out, and I never want you to think for a minute that I don't, honesty is essential." She folded her arms across her chest and frowned. "You've been asking all the questions, so it's my turn."

"Fair enough." He leaned back in his chair and stretched his long legs out in front of him. "Ask away."

"I don't want to know about your business, but I do need to know if you're working on something in particular in Buffalo Wallow."

"No, ma'am. Buffalo Springs got between me and the road, so I stopped for a spell."

She knew he wasn't telling the truth because no man in his right mind would just happen upon this part of the new frontier some called no-man's-land. A beautiful area of the Panhandle, yet it wasn't on the way to anywhere. No one deliberately went out of their way to get here. Not to mention, a new warrant was conveniently waiting for him at her saloon.

"I'm supposed to believe that you just wandered into town?"

"Believe what you want, ma'am. I had some time off, went fishing in the foothills of the Rockies and got my Warrant of Authority wet." Hayden locked his fingers behind his head and leaned farther back in the chair, curiously eying Ella. "Wired my captain for a new one, and got word a replacement would be at Molly Lou's. I didn't just wander into town—I was on my way to pick up the warrant and made the mistake of stopping for a drink first."

"And that's the truth?" She squinted a little, making sure he knew she didn't completely believe him.

"All I wanted was to pick up the paper, wet my whistle, and fill my belly before gettin' back on the trail. If you don't mind me sayin' so, I sure as hell didn't expect to get a wife with my whiskey."

"And I wasn't expecting to snag a husband!" She untied her apron and hung it on the hook. "It's late. I know you're tired, and I've still got some bookwork to do. If Dixie didn't tell you, your room is upstairs on the—"

"Audrey Jo told me." He stood. "Ella, I'm gonna honor your request about not comin' to you for husbandly favors, but I have one condition of my own."

Ella turned back. "That's fair. What is it?"

"Since it's my wedding night, I figure you owe me at least a kiss . . . a real kiss." He disarmed her with his smile.

Without reservation, Ella moved toward him and slipped easily into his waiting arms. He lifted her chin with his finger and ran his thumb across her lower lip, making her heart flutter wildly in her breast. She had no difficulty responding to the pressure of his lips on hers. The air between them seemed to vibrate with awareness.

Shamelessly her body pressed against his, and she slid her arms around his neck. Tangling her fingers in his hair, she felt every inch of his body mold over hers. So powerful. So thrilling. So naughty.

Their bodies took pleasure in the intimate contact, savoring the sweetness of the moment.

Sanity be damned.

One kiss spun into another, and then another.

She was in the embrace of a man—not just any man, but a Texas Ranger.

As quickly as he had taken her in his arms, he released her. Holding Ella at arm's length, he said, "Thank you. I do have one more request, Patience Eleanor McGraw." He shot her a sinfully delicious smile. "But I'll save that for another night."

Chapter 9

Hayden leaned against the porch railing and listened to the cicadas nestled in mesquite bushes sing their deafening chorus. He fought a smile, thinking back on the look on Ella's face when he said he had one last request. She was too damn sexy for her own good. Now what was wrong with requesting that she keep a supply of bear claws on hand?

He felt her stare from the kitchen window. He thought about the kiss. He hadn't meant to ask for one, but it just seemed the thing to do. A special, first time kiss; but he knew without a doubt it wouldn't be the last. No sir, it wouldn't be the last. He wouldn't have to go to her bed; she'd come to his. He'd seen it in her eyes. Hell, he felt it in every luscious, promising kiss. He had never experienced a kiss that satisfying, but then about every woman he'd ever played footsies with he'd known for no more than three drinks.

But was he willing to open his heart to the possibility of getting hurt? Suddenly Hayden had an undeniable need to protect Ella . . . to hell with his heart.

He took out what was little more than a cigarette butt from his shirt pocket. Pretty banged up. He tossed it and pulled up a blade of grass, sticking the stem in his mouth. The slight sweetness and drop of moisture only added to his memory of Ella's soft and dewy lips.

That's when he thought about the hair clip. He'd save that for another day. She'd been pretty displeased and impatient with him until he tried to lighten the mood. He was upset with himself for drilling her like a suspect. But, hellfire and brimstone, he could've been raised by a pack of curried wolves for all he knew about women. He was civilized enough to get along with the fairer sex, but could quickly turn dangerously inept with them if one tried to comb him.

By damn, he'd learn. For once in his life, he had a reason.

First, he had to settle the uneasiness he had in his insides that made him feel Ella was in jeopardy. The first person he wanted to scrutinize was the most unlikely. The one who couldn't be accounted for at the moment.

Muley Mullinex.

Hayden reminded himself that it was his nature for everything to be black or white, nothing gray. Same with people. They were either stand-up folks or shady. They couldn't be both. So just where did Muley figure on Hayden's scale of people? There was just something about him that made Hayden think he was good but had a dark side. Experience with people told Hayden that.

After checking on Stewball at the stables, Hayden returned to the saloon and circled to the back, thinking he might take that long awaited smoke before hitting the hay.

The drummer's wagon, led by two mules, pulled to a stop beside the shed. The driver, who Hayden recognized as being the man he saw in town with the big, boisterous, bald guy, jumped down. He spat tobacco juice on the ground and went inside the rickety shack.

In short order he returned accompanied by Muley, of all

people, who stumbled along juggling an amber bottle of whiskey. He stopped and took a long draw like he was trying to suck the bottom out of the bottle, then bellowed, "You're a sorry sonofabitch, Willard Porter."

Hayden didn't know where Muley had been from the time Hayden saw him in town to now, but sure as hell knew what he'd been doing. Yet Ella indicated he was a shy, bashful man. Like most drunks, the more liquor the bigger the mouth. With Muley's small, almost mangy-looking stature, it wouldn't take much to dull his brain and engage his mouth.

Hayden slipped into the shadows just out of their sight, and with a little work he positioned himself so he could get a good view of what was going on.

While Muley perched himself on a tree stump and took another slug of alcohol, Willard unloaded bags of sugar, two at a time. A whole lot more than what Hayden imagined Ella would use in months of baking and jelly making. And storing it in the shed didn't make sense either.

"If'n I weren't feelin' so poorly, I'd help ya." Muley slurred his words.

"Don't make me haul off and kick your ass, Mullinex," Willard barked. "There ain't nothin' wrong with you a good lickin' won't take care of."

"Still sore, ain't ya?"

"Damn straight." Willard lugged two wooden crates from the back of the wagon. "Cain't trust any man who doesn't have any hair 'cause with no coverin' his brains get fried."

Unnoticed, Hayden continued watching as the peddler unloaded more wooden crates of what looked like amber whiskey bottles. On the next trip, Willard reappeared with more crates and carted them to the wagon. He worked up a sweat, even in the coolness of the night, while Muley continued to drink and make surly comments.

Hayden had more than one question, but the most paramount—why was Willard taking empties into the shed and returning with filled bottles?

Were they storing whiskey? If so, why?

Bootleggin'?

The lawman had heard rumors that there was suspicious activity involving whiskey bootleggin' coming out of Texas and into New Mexico, but so far the Rangers had not been brought in to investigate. Not yet, at least.

Hayden stood very quiet, just barely in earshot. Willard knew what he was doing, and seemed to ignore most of the drunk's mumbling.

"Got no ears, Willard?" Muley said.

"Hush up, you ol' fool. You'll wake the womenfolk," Willard said.

"Ain't them I'm worried 'bout. It's that . . ." Muley rambled on beneath his breath, then took another snort. "It's that one that's snoopin' around." Muley pulled to his feet and stood there for a few seconds getting his bearings. Wobbly legs carried him in Hayden's direction. "Gotta take a piss."

Hayden had to make a move or be discovered. It was too late for a retreat, so he released the top two buttons on the fly of his pants and pulled his shirttail out, before stepping from the shadows not far from Muley.

"Just finished myself." Hayden buttoned his pants.

Muley smelled worse than being downwind from a skunk eatin' cabbage. Hayden shuddered and tried not to breathe.

Not bothering to acknowledge the lawman, Muley was more intent on taking care of his business right in the middle of the yard than with Hayden's sudden appearance.

Hayden moseyed toward the drummer, not sure if it wouldn't be in his best interest to holler a call to camp. He took his chances and said, "Evening."

"Evenin'. You must be Miss Ella's better half."

"And you're Willard." Hayden wiped his hands on his pants. "Ella told me about you. I'd offer to shake, but you've got your arms loaded. Need some help?" He reached for the crate the drummer was clutching.

Willard stopped and didn't respond for the longest time. Finally he said, "Sure." He held tight to the box. "Mighty kind of you. If you'd take this whiskey to the saloon, I'd be much obliged." He frowned in the bartender's direction. "Ain't got much help from Muley. He's feelin' poorly tonight. Reason he cain't work."

"Be proud to help out." Hayden almost had to pull the crate from the drummer's hands. Bottles clanged against one another.

"Would ya pick up Miss Ella's jars of jelly from the kitchen on your way back, so we can load 'em?" Willard disappeared into the back of the wagon.

"Don't mind at all." Hayden meandered past Muley, who was wobble-leggin' it back to his stump and his bottle.

Once Muley was out of sight, Hayden picked up speed. As fast as a ferret fetchin' food, he deposited the liquor on the bar, grabbed the box of jelly and swiftly made his way to his original vantage point without disturbing hardly a blade of grass. He focused and waited until the peddler came out of the shed and crawled up into the bed of the wagon.

"You yellow-bellied, sap-sucking numskull." A big dose of anger etched Muley's words as he bound to his feet. "I can git rid of the bastard better then ya did." He pulled his pistol and waved it through the air, balanced with the liquor bottle in his other hand. "I'll make sure he don't stick around." He teetered. "Lettin' him help us was stupid. Didja hear me, you idiot?"

"Pot sure as hell callin' the kettle black." Willard spoke from the back of the wagon, but loud enough for Hayden to hear. "I gave him something to do, so we can get those damn crates of whiskey hidden. We don't need no Ranger nosin' into our business. Besides, didja see those Colts he's flauntin'?"

"Yeah. Yeah. Ya always have the answers." Muley took another swig. "So many answers that we'll all be bait for the gallows before we turn around twice."

"As soon as we get that woman's damn little bit of nothin' loaded, I'm movin' out tonight for Wagon Mound. Cain't wait till mornin'" Willard hopped to the ground. "Lay low, you drunken imbecile, and nobody will be the wiser. Sober up and get back to business tomorrow, you hear!"

"Don't need to boss me around." Muley took a drunken swing at Willard, who sidestepped him. The scrawny man plopped down on the tree stump. "I ain't no imbecile and ain't drunk."

"If you weren't so pathetic, I might feel sorry for you." Willard slapped at a cast-iron skillet hanging from the side of the wagon. "If you hadn't been crawling inside a bottle, we'd never have to have that bald sonofabitch involved." Willard moved to the front wheel, searching the ground as he walked.

"It ain't him bein' around, it's that addlebrained woman who served that doofus Ranger out of the wrong bottle." He swayed on the stump, almost falling off before he pulled himself upright.

"Rangers don't bother me. They're nothin' but a bunch of irregular hooligans."

"Might be irregular as hell in everything 'cept gettin' the job done," Muley countered.

Willard turned his back to the path leading to the kitchen, and said, "It ain't McGraw I'm worryin' about. I can take care of him. It's that gal." With one hand, he pulled the bartender to his feet by the front of his shirt. "You better make it right or I will." He shoved the man to his knees. "You drunken fool."

Hayden couldn't afford to eavesdrop any longer or the peddler might decide his bullying wasn't enough.

Stepping out of the shadows, Hayden panted as if he'd been hustling. "Hell, guys, I ended up takin' the long way to the bar." He took his bandana out of his pocket and wiped imaginary sweat from his brow. "Guess I'll learn the ins and outs sooner or later."

Willard took the box. "Much obliged." He turned to Muley, who was trying to steady himself back on his seat. "I'm headin' back to Buffalo Springs for the night, so I can set out at first light," the drummer said.

In the still of the night, with the sound of the running stream and cicadas trying to drown out one another in the background, Willard climbed aboard his peddler's wagon, snapped his whip, and moved the mules forward toward the bridge.

When Hayden looked back, Muley had disappeared into the darkness, probably ready to nurse one hell of a hangover, if Hayden had to put money on it.

Not being as trusting as Ella, Hayden would reserve judgment on Muley until he knew more.

Earlier Baldy had also mentioned Wagon Mound, apparently the final destination for the drummer. Although the run to the little town in New Mexico from Mobeetie was a killer, it made sense. Mobeetie was in the early stages of being targeted for a general cleanup by the Rangers. Eventually it would be all well and good for the citizens, as they would be rid of the rustlers, gunslingers, and gamblers who created havoc in their community. Just rumors of the pending cleanup were enough to already push the smarter outlaws farther down the trail, many settling in Buffalo Springs.

Wagon Mound, with its volcanic outcroppings and lava

palisades, was easily recognizable and had sprouted into existence because it was on the Santa Fe Trail. Now that a railroad was being built, supplies, lumber, and liquor were in demand, and traders could expect premium payment for their efforts.

The goings-on around Molly Lou's were questionable at best. Something very shady was happening.

Hopefully, Ella wasn't involved, but at the same time, how could Hayden be sure?

Who could he trust?

And the orders he had from his captain—"Status quo." A cryptic message warning him to stay fixed; keep his mouth shut, eyes open, and guns cocked.

Chapter 10

Hayden threw his saddlebags over his shoulder. Although his brain felt like a steam engine on a downhill curve, a good night's sleep was welcome. Even in a bed, something he was unaccustomed to. He glanced up at the kitchen window and there was only a flicker of light dancing on the walls. He figured Ella had finally gone to bed. Even for a frontier woman, she worked a long day.

Walking around to the front of the saloon, he entered. The room once lively and noisy was now silenced and gloomy, except for a narrow ribbon of light on the floor. A low-burning candle sat on a table near the stairs, giving off enough light to keep Hayden from falling over things.

Making his way through the shadows, he picked up the candle. Behind him, a noise alerted him to possible trouble, and he whirled back in the direction of the door. A tiny calico kitten scampered across the walk, likely back to its mother.

Tough Texas Ranger and tiny Texas kitten tangle. Hayden chuckled to himself at the thought. Exhaustion had made him skittish as hell. He headed to the stairs.

The twelve bottles of whiskey were still on the end of the bar where he'd left them earlier. Now he could take time to check them out. He lifted one from the wooden crate. Tennessee Old No. 7 Sour Mash, best you could buy, in a faintly tinted amethyst glass bottle with a smooth base—certainly not the rough, dark amber ones he'd seen the drummer and bartender take out of the shed.

Based on the number of patrons Hayden had seen since he'd arrived in town, a dozen bottles sure as hell wouldn't run a saloon for long. According to Ella, the drummer made irregular deliveries.

Guided by the candle drowning in its own wax, he climbed the stairs.

Muffled girly giggles came from the far door to the left of the stairwell.

He sure hated to have Audrey Jo uprooted just to give him a room. He was more accustomed to sleeping outdoors, but she had insisted.

Turning right, as Audrey Jo had instructed, he found his room; a typical woman's bedroom that reminded him of a flower garden. Floral wallpaper, frilly lace curtains over a window looking out into a stand of cottonwoods. Framed silhouette cutouts of a man and a woman hung above a blue and white bowl and pitcher.

A massive four-poster bed was tucked in the corner. He could hardly see the covers because it was not only so far away from the window that moonlight didn't cast its light on it, but the thingamajig was topped with a lace-draped canopy. It'd been awhile, but he'd seen something similar in a brothel down in San Antonio.

Although it was against his principles to sleep under the dadgum thing, it didn't take long for Hayden to undress all the way down to his underdrawers, settle his saddlebags out of sight, and crawl between the quilt and pretty, good-feelin' sheets. He allowed the candle to burn out.

Knowing Ella was safely settled in down the hall, and probably giggling with her friends about forcing him to sleep in such a frilly bedroom, made it easy for him to go to sleep.

Ella took a frustrated breath and climbed down from the ladder in the storage room next to the kitchen. She sat on the bottom rung. Wiping the perspiration from her forehead with her apron, she took another breath. She'd been working so long in the tiny room that she hadn't realized the lantern had burned so low. The dim lighting and flickering signaled the end of a very long, yet eventful day.

As much as she wished she could have been able to stand at the kitchen window longer and watch Hayden try to decide whether he wanted to light up a cigarette or not, and as much as she had enjoyed poring over his strapping physique, chores waited, so she had gone about her business.

For some reason her ledger book that she always kept on the top of the pie safe was missing. She'd checked high and low, even moving the cabinet as best she could to see if it'd gotten caught between the rough wooden back and the wall. It was nowhere to be found.

She really needed to enter the quantity of bear claws and pints of jelly that she'd given to the drummer to barter for some of their other needs. Without it, she couldn't be certain that all of the supplies had been ordered.

Finding the ledger would have to wait until tomorrow.

Ella had helped the ladies clean up the saloon as best they could, since Muley never showed up. If she wasn't so weary and hadn't been closeted in the storage room for so long, she might've gone out to the ol' shed to check on him. It wasn't uncommon for Muley to disappear for hours on end, but he'd never shirked his duties before. She had seen the peddler arrive earlier than usual, so maybe that had detained Muley. Or possibly he thought he'd worked hard enough for one day. Even Ranger McGraw's presence may have spooked him.

Regardless of the reason, she had a business to run and needed everyone to take care of their duties.

Ella picked up the lantern. Leaving the storage room, she walked through the vacant kitchen and out to the yard. Nothing but a late summer moon smiling high above, cicadas, and a lonely coyote howling in the distance. Stepping around the corner of the building, she couldn't see any light coming from the shack, so she presumed Muley had bedded down for the night.

But tomorrow Calvin Mullinex would get an earful from her.

She wasn't all that comfortable with Audrey Jo's moving out of her bedroom for a few days, but the saloon girl had volunteered to do so, in order for Hayden to have his privacy. Ella had finally agreed, but only if Audrey Jo would stay with her. So the agreement was reached. Hayden would take Audrey Jo's room and she'd bunk with Ella until other arrangements were made.

The saloon was totally dark and the candle wasn't at the foot of the stairs, so Ella presumed everyone had gone to bed, including her husband. Tarnation and damnation, she had to stop thinking of him as a husband, and certainly quit imagining what it'd be like to lie in his arms. It would not happen. It could not happen.

The staircase railing guided her to the landing, where she continued to her bedroom.

The last door on the right.

Hayden didn't think anything short of a dynamite blast could wake him, but rarely slept without being cognizant of his surroundings—a piece of sage advice handed down from his Ranger father. It had kept Hayden alive, so far.

The bedroom door's rusty hinges squeaking had roused him. He reached for one of his Colts from his holster hanging on the bedpost and lay quietly, keeping his gaze glued on the entrance.

Moonlight created a catawampus pattern across the floor. He saw a shadow only a split second before the outline of a woman appeared. Ella tiptoed into the room. He breathed a sigh of relief.

Apparently she couldn't see him. Since the room was Audrey Jo's, it perplexed him somewhat as to why Ella would barge in . . . unless it was for some nefarious reason. She'd made it clear that she wouldn't come to his bed. But then she could be picking up something for Audrey Jo. The little he knew about the woman suggested to him that she'd be uncomfortable coming to her own room with a man in bed, even if it were for something as necessary as a toothbrush.

Ella slowly, methodically, for what seemed like an eternity, unbuttoned her dress and pulled it over her head, setting Hayden's stomach aflame. She hung the calico dress on a hook and stood in front of the window, stretching like a cat. With the moonlit window as a backdrop, he could see every sleek line of her body through the thin fabric of her chemise.

Hayden wasn't sure how much longer he could avoid taking a deep breath. Even a stifled groan. He'd sure as hell got himself into a heap of trouble. If he called out, she'd probably shoot him. Worse yet, she'd wake the whole house and create a scene. She damn well knew which room he'd be sleeping in.

So why was she undressing right before his eyes?

A gentleman would do the right thing. Stay put, close his eyes, and not embarrass her. But when in the hell had he ever been all that gallant? As much as he wanted to close his eyes, the devil made him watch her every step.

Ella removed her chemise and laid it on the back of the chair, releasing full, luscious breasts. She turned her back to the bed and kicked off her unmentionables. He wasn't sure what the proper term was, but all he knew was they no longer covered milky, taut buttocks and legs that went all the way to her slim hips and tiny waist.

Fire shot through his body and settled below his waist, making him feel a powerful need for her in ways he'd never thought possible. He didn't want to pull her into the bed and make her his, he wanted her to come willingly to him.

Ella retrieved a gown from the top drawer of the dresser and slipped it over her head, not bothering to button it up, exposing the swells of her breasts. Taking careful pains, she washed her face.

He had to get his mind off the pretty lady sitting at the dressing table, and thought back to his conversations with Audrey Jo and Ella. It was clear Ella knew exactly which room he was in. Maybe she was just dressing here and then would go elsewhere to sleep. Chancy at best for her to change clothes in his presence. She had more willpower than he did, and frankly, he wasn't all that sure that it was very considerate of her to undress in front of him. Hell, being a man he didn't mind enjoying her overwhelming beauty and womanly charms.

Opening a bottle, she dabbed oil on her wrists, releasing the scent of lilacs. She took care in brushing her mahogany hair, kissed by the sun and caressed by moonlight.

Ella placed the brush on the dressing table, and opened the drawer. Searching quietly, she removed a piece of paper, scissors, and a tack, and then studied the blank sheet for the longest time. Swiftly, wielding the scissors through the paper, she twisted, turned, and cut away small pieces.

When satisfied, she brushed the discarded bits aside, and examined what she'd cut out. Walking to the wall, Ella tacked a silhouette on the wall beside the others.

To Hayden's surprise, the newest profile looked a lot like him. A whole lot like him.

She lightly kissed the outline, touching the cheeks.

Hayden lay still. Her nearness kindled a longing that he couldn't deny.

Ella walked to the side of the bed and sat down with her back to him. Appropriate for the room, she smelled of a Victorian flower garden, sweet and succulent, humming with memories. Not like the wanton women he'd shared pleasures with over the years, but a field of wildflowers on a spring day. The warmth of her flesh kindled the fire in his gut. It was all he could do not to touch her.

Closing his eyes, Hayden took in the heady scent of lilacs. She was near enough for him to smell the cinnamon and vanilla in her hair.

He had only one choice: remain silent until she fell asleep, then slip out and go to the stables for the night. Where he should have gone in the first place.

But if she were to roll over toward him, all bets were off. All deals were void, and he'd spend all night long touching and kissing her the way a husband should a wife.

She laid her head on the pillow, and with a muffled voice asked, "Are you asleep?" She squirmed a bit. Nestling down in the mattress, she whispered ever so softly, "I guess not. Good night."

Hayden wasn't sure if he'd ever figure out women. It wasn't but a few hours ago he had reluctantly agreed that, although they would hold themselves out as husband and wife, it would be only in public. She had been adamant that nothing physical would happen between them . . . yet she'd come to his bed. What had changed? Uneasiness at the lack of logical answers lingered in his mind. Instinctively he shifted his weight and moaned.

"So you are awake." Ella rolled over to face him.

"Darlin', not only am I awake, but ready," he whispered

in her ear. One thing for sure, Ella was just Southern enough to understand the meaning of darlin'.

Shrieking as though he'd pinched her, Ella jumped to her knees, and began flogging him with her pillow, all the while repeating, "You . . . you . . . you're a . . ."

All Hayden could do was hold his right arm up so she wouldn't strike him in the face. Just as Ella plopped him on the head for the umpteenth time, the pillow broke open, and feathers flew all around the room, landing on anything they came in contact with. Floating from the ceiling, the soft down landed in Ella's hair, on her gown, and the bed.

Hayden brushed the sonofaguns from his chest and arms, blowing one from his lips.

Ella chuckled in joy. Uncertain but amused gazes locked. Her eyes sparked with the love of combat. She offered up an infectious, teasing smile that made him want to match it. All of a sudden, they were roaring with laughter at the humor of the moment. They rolled on the bed in frolic, shooing feathers in all directions, seeing how high in the air they could blow them and how long it would take them to land.

The mattress shifted with the extra weight on one side, as they both dove for a wayward feather. Without warning, Hayden found himself covering Ella with his body, locking her in an inescapable embrace. He lifted his chest and looked into her face. He brushed a feather from her chin and kissed her, urging her to savor the taste of passion. She matched his every desire.

With a thunderous boom, the bedroom door burst open and Dixie rushed in, waving a derringer pistol about big enough to get herself killed with, and shrieked, "I've got you covered, Ella." She paused and frowned. "I guess I should have said—he's got you covered."

Although Hayden didn't think the barmaid would shoot, particularly since she had the dang thing aimed somewhere closer to the ceiling than his head, he wasn't about to show his weapon. "Dixie, I'm unarmed." He slowly rolled off Ella, lifting his hands above his head.

Ella nodded an okay to the woman, as she threw the quilt over Hayden.

"Jumpin' Jehoshaphat, girl! I told you not to do *it!*" Dixie stuffed the dinky pearl-handled pistol into her housecoat pocket and turned around twice like a banty rooster having a conniption fit. "You did it anyway. Didn't you?"

Chapter 11

Dancing with fire, the sun peeped over the horizon as Ella set a butter dish on the kitchen table. She'd gotten up long before daybreak and had already fixed biscuits, now baking in the oven.

By the time Ella and Hayden, with the help of Dixie and Audrey Jo, had cleaned up the feathers in her bedroom, it was closer to the time to get up than to go to bed, but they did get a few hours of sleep. It was torture being alone in the big four-poster bed with Hayden just down the hall. She could still feel his body pressed to hers. His hands setting her flesh on fire. His kisses. How her body responded to his, wanting him to touch her everywhere. But that dream was short-lived since Dixie had burst into the room, halting any possibilities of Ella becoming Hayden's wife in every way.

Ella couldn't shake the mystery of her missing ledger. When she had come to the kitchen and lit the kerosene lamp earlier, she found it on the table. She knew she hadn't overlooked the dang thing, as she'd searched everywhere imaginable. So where had the book been? Maybe Muley had brought it in and left it for her?

She heard Hayden walking across the porch before the

screen door opened and he sauntered in with a coffee mug in his hand.

"Good morning," he said, heading straight for the oven. "Smells good in here. Sleep well?"

"Yes, thank you for asking," she said. "And, you?" Before he had a chance to respond, she looked up at him. Hayden was absolutely magnificent with an adolescent sunrise peering over his shoulder. She swallowed hard. "You know you didn't have to move your stuff to Audrey Jo's bedroom, don't you?"

"Yes, ma'am, but I didn't think Dixie's heart could have held out much longer if I hadn't gone." He shot her a wicked, mesmerizing smile.

"I should have warned you when I realized Audrey Jo was the one who told you which room was yours." She placed a knife on the butter dish. "Sometimes she really doesn't know her left hand from her right."

"She sure as hell knew which was which when she was jammin' her fingers in my chest because I hadn't listened to her directions." He chuckled. "Frankly Ella, I don't believe for a minute she didn't know exactly which room she sent me to."

"You might be right." She smiled sheepishly. "When you were outside, did you see Muley anywhere around?"

"No. Hope you don't mind, but I fixed myself a cup of coffee."

"Of course not. You're welcome to anything I have." She wished she hadn't said it quite like that, especially when she saw his eyebrows shoot up mischievously. "You know what I mean."

"I sat on the porch and enjoyed the morning before I took care of Stewball." He refilled her coffee cup and handed it to her before he poured himself some.

"Thanks." She took a sip.

"You're welcome." He smiled, warm and rich. "Where are your two mother hens this morning?"

"The girls are still upstairs. I haven't heard hide nor hair from them since they left to go back to bed last night."

"Doesn't seem fair." He shook his head and leaned against the sink. "After all the plannin' and connivin' Audrey Jo did, that you and I ended up in separate beds alone and they shared a bedroom."

"That doesn't make sense, huh?" Ella set her cup on the table and laughed tentatively, trying not to face Hayden because she was afraid he could read her mind.

As much as she knew she needed to forget Hayden's broad shoulders and muscular chest covered with thick, curly hair, not to mention riveting dark eyes, she couldn't. His sensual yet needle-sharp stare left no question about his desires. But that was last night. Today he was confident and seemed to have made himself at home. Was that good or bad? She chewed on her bottom lip and found herself tapping her foot as she tried to sort through some of her thoughts.

"Ella, I know you're worried about Muley, but please don't. I saw him yesterday evening and I know you don't want to hear this because you think he's infallible, but he was pickled."

"Drunk?"

"As a skunk. I figured you probably don't care to know the particulars, but I'm bettin' he's laid up somewhere nursin' one wingdinger of a Texas-sized hangover."

"I've never seen him take a drink, but I guess it is plausible." She removed the biscuits from the oven and set them on top of the stove. "He was apparently here, because he left my ledger on the table sometime during the night."

"No, he didn't. I found it on the porch this morning and brought it inside."

"I appreciate you taking care of it."

How did the book get on the porch? She was sure she hadn't taken it out there, and nobody except Muley even knew where she kept it, or had any need of it.

"Why don't I go check around and see if I can find him?" Hayden suggested. "He bunks in the ol' shed, doesn't he?"

"Yes, and thanks. I really am beginning to worry. At first I was pretty angry that he didn't tell me he was going to be gone, but drinking will certainly keep a man from making sound decisions." She bit on her lip again. "Hayden, I think I'm more worried, now that you told me about his drinking."

Hayden held his arms open and she stepped into his embrace. She molded into him, and laid her head on his broad shoulder. He kissed the top of her head. She enjoyed the security of being held by him, and never wanted him to let her go, but she had to, if Hayden was to see what he could find out about Muley.

Ella broke their embrace, but not before giving him a light kiss on the cheek. "Don't be long. Breakfast is just about ready."

Giving her a reassuring smile, Hayden left to find Muley, juggling a hot biscuit from one hand to the other.

Ella barely had time to fill the sugar bowl, and hoped to heck Muley had ordered another bag of sugar from the drummer, although there wasn't a bag in the storage room. She wished she could see the front of the shed from the kitchen, but it faced the stream. When she finished with breakfast and the girls got the saloon opened for business, she'd go out there and see what she could find. By that time, Hayden would be finished with his search around the grounds. Maybe he was right in the first place and Muley was more irresponsible than she thought. If he was drunk, it made sense that he might've gone with the peddler to Wagon Mound.

Dixie flounced through the door with her hair twisted on top of her head, looking quite rested; particularly when Ella knew Audrey Jo snored like a sailor.

"Good morning." Dixie looked around. "Where's Audrey Jo? I've been lookin' everywhere for her. She isn't upstairs. She isn't anywhere."

"I don't know. You saw her last," Ella said.

"No, I didn't. She slept with you . . ." Dixie stopped and looked up at Ella somberly, as if she already knew the answer. "Didn't she?"

"No. She left a few minutes after you, saying something about coming downstairs for a drink and some fresh air." An uneasiness came over Ella. "When she didn't come back, I presumed she had decided to stay with you."

"Ella, she didn't sleep in my room." Fear etched her face. "Something is wrong. Very wrong. Do you think her staying out all night has something to do with Muley?"

"Hayden is out looking for him right now." Ella looked up at Dixie, who had tears bubbling in her eyes. "Let me see if Muley made any entries in the ledger. Maybe it'll tell us something."

Ella grabbed the book, almost dropping it in the process. An envelope fell to the ground . . . addressed to First Lt. Hayden C. McGraw. She and Dixie both stared at one another.

"Aren't you going to read it?" Dixie asked as Ella picked it up. "It's already been opened."

"No. It's addressed to Hayden."

"You've got to. It might have the answers to where Muley and Audrey Jo have gone," Dixie encouraged.

Slowly, Ella removed the single sheet of paper, covered in a man's handwriting. She read it out loud.

"Warrant of Authority sent under separate cover. Status

quo on investigation of Miss P.E.S's establishment and involvement with unlawful operations between Mobeetie, Texas, and Wagon Mound, New Mexico. Urgent. Consider armed and dangerous."

The signature began with "Captain," but the rest of the name was illegible.

Ella sank onto one of the kitchen chairs. "Miss P.E.S. has to mean Patience Eleanor Stevenson." Ella's chest felt tight and she didn't think she could breathe. Webs of confusion filled her thoughts. She looked up at Dixie. "He's been lying to me. Hayden told me he wasn't on a case, and only came to town to get his warrant." She would not cry, come hell or high water.

Dixie crossed the room and stood beside her and patted Ella's shoulder. "It's not true. There has to be something else going on."

"Read it yourself." With shaking hands, Ella pitched the letter on the table. "Hayden was willing to marry me to get what he needed to do his job." Her voice broke right along with her heart. "I'm nothing but a job to him . . . an assignment."

"There has to be another explanation," Dixie said, as if she really meant it.

"Open the damn screen!" Hayden's voice boomed from somewhere in the yard.

Both women rushed to the door, just as Hayden stepped on the porch carrying a limp woman covered with blood . . . Audrey Jo.

Dixie was already pouring hot water from the tea kettle into a bowl before Hayden made it to the other side of the kitchen.

"Take her upstairs." Ella opened the door and led him from the kitchen, through the small storage room, back into the saloon. She rushed ahead of him toward the stairs.

"Can't wait that long. She needs help now." He crossed

the saloon and laid the motionless woman on a long table near the stairwell.

"Here." Ella shoved rags in his hands, just as Dixie set the bowl on the small table where the candle usually was.

"What happened, Hayden?" Ella helped him remove Audrey Jo's dirty, blood-spattered blouse.

"I found her on the other side of the shed like this." He stepped back, allowing Ella and Dixie to take over.

"Dixie, go up to Buffalo Springs and get the doctor," Ella ordered.

"I can take care of her. Then if we need him, I'll go." Dixie began cleaning the worst wound with warm soapy water.

It became obvious to Ella that Dixie knew what she was doing as she tenderly and efficiently went about caring for their friend. She methodically tended to her until the crimson flow turned a brighter, cleaner shade of red, then stopped.

"Wash the dirt off her face—be careful of the bruises," she instructed Ella. "I've been nursing outlaws and animals ever since I was knee-high to a prairie dog."

Audrey Jo moaned as Hayden helped hold her shoulders in place while Dixie cleaned the wound on her upper arm and Ella washed the sand and blood from her face, finally laying a cloth across her forehead.

Dixie continued to clean the minor wounds and scratches, applying lanolin, as she talked. "She's pretty-well beaten up and exhausted, but I don't think it's anything that plenty of care and sleep won't heal."

Hayden set his chin in a stubborn line and drew his lips in thoughtfully. "The bastard didn't want her dead. He wanted to teach her a lesson." He clamped his mouth shut.

Audrey Jo nodded her head ever so slightly in agreement.

"Can you hear me, Audrey Jo?" Hayden spoke with tenderness, yet with authority. "Who did this to you?"

Her only response was to turn her head toward Hayden. Seemingly taking every ounce of her energy, she motioned for him to lean closer. His ear was almost touching her lips when she whispered her response, so quietly that only he could hear.

Hayden pulled up to his full height, took in a deep breath, and squared his shoulders. The muscles in his neck tightened. He touched his Colt. The big man's lip quivered as he stormed toward the door.

"I'll kill the son of a bitch."

Chapter 12

Hayden was about as angry as he ever recalled being, and he'd been pretty damn mad in his lifetime. It didn't take him long to reach the livery, saddle up Stewball, and prepare to head out to search for Audrey Jo's attacker.

Hayden led the gelding out into the morning sunshine.

"Hey, boy." He spoke to the horse as though he was a friend. In every way that counted, a man's horse was his best pal. A cowboy could tell him anything, truth or lie, and be guaranteed it wouldn't be repeated. "Sorry I've neglected you these last couple of days, but I've got filly troubles." He patted Stewball, secured his boot in the stirrup, and swung into the saddle. "Yep, a filly. Betcha've had your own troubles with fillies, haven't you, boy?"

The Ranger and his trusted companion headed out of Buffalo Wallow. His heart told him to circle back and tell Ella good-bye, but common sense dictated that there was no time to waste. If things worked out the way he thought they would, he'd be back in her kitchen before the biscuits got hard; and if they didn't, well, it wouldn't be the first time he ended up with hardtack and camp brew for breakfast.

As much as Hayden resisted, logic told him it was time to bring in Sheriff Oldham. Audrey Jo's assault was officially in the sheriff's jurisdiction, but unofficially it was utmost on Hayden's mind.

But before he tried to locate the local lawman, Hayden had to step back and view things with a critical, nonjudgmental eye. He couldn't lose sight of the fact that rangering was a team effort, not one person making his own rules and going off half-cocked. He needed to think things through, locking out his heart. He had to be fair and impartial, regardless of who might be involved. At this point, he couldn't rule out anybody.

Justice for Audrey Jo was his only concern. Somebody wanted to shut her up, not kill her. The man had a brand of cowardice laid on him that held no redemption. He didn't play by the rules and couldn't care less who he took down with him. But why? It wasn't just her assault that bothered Hayden; it was every tiny fragment of what was going on around Ella that felt like a jigsaw puzzle without even the border in place.

Hayden convinced himself quite easily not to seek out the sheriff right away. Instead, he'd do some footwork first. He reined Stewball toward the shack where the peddler's wagon was last seen. Although the drummer gave a cockamamie story about heading back to Buffalo Springs to spend the night, something didn't settle well in Hayden's gut.

Ella had told him that Willard bedded down near the stream when he wanted to get an early start the next day. So why had he suddenly decided to go back up to Buffalo Springs?

In the dry, hard soil it was easy to trail the fully-loaded wagon's path, leading away from Ella's property. Hayden followed along, as the tracks circled back toward the bank of the stream where the mule team had apparently halted just this side of the fallen cottonwood tree.

Hayden reined Stewball in and dismounted, carefully following the driver's boot tracks leading away from the wagon and eventually disappearing into the stream, where Willard Porter could have gone in any direction without leaving tracks.

Relentlessly, Hayden walked the banks, keeping his eye out for fresh tracks while his mind retraced what he knew as facts.

Although hunting down Audrey Jo's assailant was paramount, Hayden kept going back to the shed and how the activities surrounding it might fit into someone wanting her harmed.

What was important enough for Muley to spend all of his extra time in the cornfield or the shed; yet not important enough for him to stay off the rotgut?

Facts. Facts. Facts.

Water carted in from the stream instead of the well.

A building reeking of sourdough starter.

Excessive amounts of sugar hauled in.

The only logical answer—moonshine. Sugar added to the starter, with a handful or two of cornmeal tossed in for flavor, would be the makin's for corn whiskey mash. Mule-kick. Add the brown bottles and a hauler and it was the formula for a booming white-lightnin' business. And if Hayden had to venture a guess, the yeast smell was coming from barrels where the mash was fermenting. To the best of his recollection, it'd generally take somewhere around two days before the mixture would begin to furiously bubble. Eventually it would quit working and what was left was pretty close to the kick of a mule colt.

That's what Audrey Jo had served him by mistake. A poorly concocted corn whiskey, as Hayden's taste buds could attest to.

No doubt in some form or fashion every man he'd seen at the shed was involved in making moonshine and boot-leggin'. He'd bring them all down, but the one he wanted most was the man who had hurt Audrey Jo.

The spineless, lily-livered bastard better pray that Sheriff Oldham found him before Hayden did, because he'd show him no mercy.

Audrey Jo had whispered the name of her attacker to him, but experience told Hayden not to stay focused on only one suspect, regardless of how guilty they might seem. He had to take the time necessary to think things through before developing a strategy. He couldn't mark anyone off his list.

Muley Mullinex, the retiring, bashful bartender who had a dark side when bending his elbow with liquor. He had everything to lose if the illegal operation was exposed; especially the only family he knew.

Willard Porter, the drummer, who transported the white lightnin' to the railroaders in Wagon Mound, New Mexico. The operation made him a lot of money.

Boisterous Baldy, the loudmouth who seemed to be everywhere and involved in everything that caused havoc. The newcomer to town that nobody seemed to know anything about.

Not giving up, Hayden continued tracking along the banks as far as he thought feasible and returned to where Willard's wagon was last seen. He methodically checked for boot prints in the direction of Molly Lou's and finally came across some fresh ones coming out of the stream very near a downed cottonwood. Probably the mail drop, if he had to make a guess.

Sun reflected off something shiny near the tree trunk. Loose dirt covered most of the round metal, which Hayden dug out with his fingers.

A Texas Ranger badge . . . exactly like the one he wore.

The find numbed his senses, made him lose focus on everything except the badge he continued to stare at. It was a sign of a Ranger's honor. His judge and his jury. An emblem of proud tradition. The strength of an oak and the peace of an olive branch. Everything he stood for and fought for.

A Ranger would never leave his badge behind on purpose . . . unless it was intended as a signal or warning.

A burst of sunlight hit Hayden between his eyes. He dropped to his knees. The last thing he remembered before falling deep into the depths of unconsciousness.

Chapter 13

For the third night in a row, Ella had kissed Hayden's silhouette hanging on the wall good night and crawled in the big four-poster bed. Wrapped in her private cocoon of loneliness, her heart ached like an old wound on a rainy day.

Consumed with sharing the duties of caring for Audrey Jo with Dixie, during the day Ella mindlessly went about her business. Camouflaging the deep hurt she felt from Muley abandoning them, she vacillated between how much she cared for Hayden and the fact that, for reasons only he knew, he'd lied to her about coming to Buffalo Wallow. But somewhere deep in the caverns of her soul she knew it was for the right reasons.

The endless night had finally grayed into dawn.

A slice of sunrise broke through the window and woke Ella. She resisted the intrusion. Closing her eyes, she burrowed down beneath her mother's quilt.

Her thoughts wandered to Audrey Jo. Ella said a prayer that today would be better than yesterday and tomorrow would be better than today.

Ella's heart broke for the woman. Since her injury, she had sat for hours in lonely silence, withdrawn; allowing the misery of the night she was beaten to haunt her. Although her visual wounds were healing, her heart wasn't.

Confusion lingered around Audrey Jo. So far, all she could recall was helping clean up the feathers in Ella's room, and going downstairs for a drink of water. She remembered a calico kitten scurrying across the yard and her following it. She vaguely recalled being grabbed from behind and a man's big hand covering her mouth. She thought he was going to take advantage of her.

Ella realized Audrey Jo was more fragile mentally than physically, but continued to gingerly ask questions about who hurt her. She shamefully ducked her head when she said he'd said awful things about her. The strong, tall man said something about "you womenfolk are imbeciles" and referred to her as "a pathetic fool." Then her next recollection was being picked up and carried to Ella's kitchen.

Although the memories came back to Audrey Jo in tiny fragments, no matter how hard Ella tried, Audrey Jo couldn't remember telling Hayden the name of her assailant. It seemed to be blocked from her memory.

A soft knock at the door brought Ella back to the morning.

Hayden? Had he returned and they could straighten out the problem with the letter and his assignment? Although the envelope was addressed to him, the letter wasn't, so that gave him the benefit of the doubt. They'd work things out one way or another. Hayden had not lied to her. She felt it in her soul.

Barefooted, Ella crossed the room. To her delight, Audrey Jo's red curls bobbled as she asked if she and Dixie could come in. At the moment, Ella wasn't sure who she would have rather seen standing at the door—Audrey Jo or Hayden.

To hell with the rest of the day! One of Ella's prayers had been answered. The three women sat cross-legged in the middle of the four-poster bed and talked until their stomachs told them it was time to eat.

"Ella, you know what I'm hungry for?" Audrey Jo said, but didn't wait for an answer. "Bear claws and apple jelly. You still have some, don't you?"

"Not any fresh ones, but I have the jelly. Let's go downstairs and you can help me bake a new batch." Quickly Ella threw on her ol' worn-out print dress, combed her hair without bothering to put it up on her head, and ran down the stairs.

Her friend was back!

Dixie put on a pot of coffee while Ella warmed the pastries and Audrey Jo got out plates, cups, and forks. While they waited for the coffee, the three ladies talked some more.

As they sat around the table, Ella decided now was the time to approach a subject she'd been thinking about for a while.

"Since the saloon has been closed for several days now, and I really don't have any desire to reopen, why don't we turn it into a café?"

They excitedly agreed, immediately focusing on the menu.

"But nobody but you knows how to bake," Dixie pointed out.

"Well, there's no better time than the present to teach you all." Ella bound to her feet, grabbed her apron, and pulled it over her head. "Dixie, sift some flour. Audrey Jo, get eggs. I'll be right back with the sugar."

Ella knew there wasn't any sugar in the storage room, but since it'd been marked off her supply list in the ledger, she knew the drummer must've left some.

Picking up a bucket, she crossed the yard, hoping Muley just hadn't found time to bring the bag to the storeroom before he went off on his drinking binge. The only logical place where it'd be stored was the ol' shed.

Gray haze colored the northern sky, and the smell of smoldering brush hung in the air. Most likely someone carelessly burning trash had caught some grass on fire. A worrisome but not an uncommon occurrence.

As she neared the stream she saw Stewball, still fully saddled, grazing. Hayden *had* returned!

Her heart thumped with joy. Her husband had really come back. Another reason to make bear claws. She hurried toward the door to the shack. She could barely lift the heavy wooden bar that kept it secured. On the second try she made it and entered.

The inside was somewhat like she had imagined, yet in other ways totally not what she expected.

Light came through the cracks between the planks making up the outer walls. Two bunks lined the end of the room, with a storage chest sitting at the foot of each one.

Four barrels sat in a row along one wall. Across from it, where horse stalls once stood, wooden crates were stacked five high. A lot of crates. She didn't have to get any closer to recognize amber whiskey bottles filling each.

Her heart sunk to the bottom of her stomach. Something had been going on right beneath her nose, and it didn't look like it was on the up-and-up.

And the stench. It nearly made her gag. The odor was like yeast and something else she couldn't quite put her finger on. Familiar, but not pleasant.

A noise from somewhere near the stack of wooden crates drew her attention. A small kitten scampered out, on the tail of a field mouse.

Her heart settled back to a regular beat.

Another noise. More of a moan. Probably a hurt animal. Ella set the pail down, and took two steps.

A louder, more distinct groan could barely be heard.

Caring only about getting help for the creature, Ella rushed to the crates and began moving them, clearing enough room to let in light so she could see what was back there.

Ella shoved another stack of crates out of her way, tipping them over. Bottles rolled across the floor. Glass shattered; shards of glass embedded themselves in the dirt floor.

"Oh my God!" Ella screamed.

Chapter 14

In the far corner Ella caught sight of a man, gagged with his feet tied together. His bloody shirt clung to his chest. She rushed to him, dropped to her knees, and tore the gag from his mouth. "Hayden. Oh, my God!"

Hayden lifted his head, his piercing eyes shallow and full of pain. Barbed wire was wrapped around his body, tying him to the support post left over from an old horse stall. With hands tied behind him, he was covered like a mummy from his shoulders to his waist with strand after strand of metal. Through dry, blood-caked lips, he managed to whisper, "I knew you'd come, darlin' . . ."

"Don't move." She managed to get his legs untied. Not caring that the barbs pricked and cut her, she attempted to reach through the metal to free his hands. She couldn't. "You need help."

A mask of stone came to Hayden's face, and he tried to swallow. "Go. Get out of here." His eyes closed then he forced them back open. "I don't want you getting hurt."

"I'm not going anywhere until I know you're safe." Ella pulled to her feet and began a frantic search for anything she could use to free him.

In the corner she found a pail of water. Ella had never

thought it was a good thing that her dress was old and the material worn, until she began tearing strips off of her skirt and soaking them in the water.

Carrying the half-full pail, Ella rushed back to Hayden, kneeled, and began wiping blood from around his mouth and dry, crusty lips. He opened his eyes and accepted the wet cloth, sucking on it until there was little moisture left.

"How long have you been here?" She removed the rag and again saturated it with water.

"I—I'm not sure." He shut his eyes and turned his head from side to side, as if that would clear his mind. "Two, three days. Right after I"—he stopped and licked his lips—"after I found Audrey Jo."

"Three days." Ella put the dripping cloth in his mouth. "Hayden, please don't suck on this. Just hold it and keep your mouth moist. You'll get sick if you drink too much too fast. Plus, I don't even want to think about what else has been drinking out of the pail. I'm going for help."

The smell of smoke crept between the cracks and wafted in the air. The fire had to be closer than Ella first thought. She rushed to the door.

Without warning, suffocating out all light, the door slammed shut. The heavy bar thumped loudly when it was put in place.

Panic like nothing she'd ever known welled in her throat. Icy fear twisted around her heart. They were trapped.

"Open the door," Ella shouted and struck it with her fists, again and again. "Get help. Hayden's injured."

She stopped to listen. Thunderous pounding began as a hammer struck nail after nail, permanently closing off the exit. Someone was separating them from the world. Someone who had to know they were inside.

"Help! Help!" She continued beating and yelling. "Help!"

"Shut up, you imbecile," a man hissed. "You and that Ranger can go to hell." A loud, boisterous laugh drowned out another round of nails being driven into the wood. "That'll teach you both not to stick your nose in where it doesn't belong."

Their only way out was blocked. There wasn't even a window in the building. Nothing but wood and dirt. And gallons of fermenting alcohol.

Ella took a deep breath. The air thickened with smoke, but wasn't unbearable . . . not yet. She had to free Hayden, but with what?

Damn, it was a shed after all. There had to be some sort of tools around. She searched high and low. What would she do? How could she release Hayden without cutting the wires?

She pulled her skirt up and hurried to the storage boxes by the bunks. Tearing the lid open on the first one, she tossed clothes and other personal items on the dirt floor. She scratched the back of her hand unlocking the second. Tools. A hammer. A saw. Then she saw a pair of wire cutters.

When she reached Hayden and knelt he was more alert. Having a little bit of water and the will to live helped.

Hayden's eyes widened when he saw the wire cutters and he spat out the rag. "Do you think you're strong enough to use those?"

"Better than you." She took a deep breath. "No gloves, so this will have to do." Ella removed her mother's apron, tore it in half, and wrapped it around her right hand. Using the fingers on her other hand and her teeth, she secured it with the apron strings. It was a sad imitation of a glove, but she thought it might do the job. She'd just have to do the best she could with her other hand being so loosely wrapped.

She tried to cut through two strands of wire, but they

didn't budge. The cutters slipped from her grip. Blood seeped as the scratch on her arm deepened.

"Take one wire at a time," Hayden said. "They're twisted together."

Using two hands on the cutter, one strand came loose, then another. "Hayden, I know this hurts, but I have to pull the wire taut to get the cutters around it."

"I've been injured worse by big-ass tumbleweeds in a blue norther." He attempted a smile, but he winced in pain. Closing his eyes, he said, "My money's on you, darlin'."

Ella's hair fell forward and into her eyes. She pushed it back over her ear and continued pressing hard on the shears. Her hand felt numb, but nothing could hurt her worse than seeing the man she loved in pain.

"Can you reach in my shirt pocket?" Hayden said.

"Now's no time to be cute."

"I bought something I thought you might like the day we got married, but never got around to giving it to you." He gave her a smile of almost embarrassment. "Get it out. It'll hold your hair out of your face."

She focused on the strands binding his chest nearest his pocket; finally she could reach in. She drew out a tissue paper–wrapped hair clip. Perfect. "I could kiss you for this." She pulled her hair back. Even with fabric-bound palms, she was able to secure it behind her head.

Ella knew Hayden realized they were trapped, but she didn't say anything. Maybe if they didn't talk about it, it wasn't true. One thing was certain, if he kept talking, it might take his mind off of how much he must be suffering. He'd gritted his teeth and squished his eyes closed, but she knew he wasn't shutting down the pain.

"Who did this?" She bore down on a piece of wire.

"I don't know. He hit me from behind." He stopped and caught his breath. "The next thing I knew I was in here.

Whoever did this wanted to slow me down. He isn't a killer or I'd be dead."

"And, so would Audrey Jo."

Hayden nodded. "I've done a lot of thinkin' the last few days. I don't remember much about my mother. She died when I was little, but I remember her telling me that a kiss would make the hurt go away." He clenched his jaw. "Ella, would you make the hurt go away?"

Ella kissed him tenderly. Brushing away some dirt from his chin, her lips grazed his again. She smiled tentatively before returning to work. "One strand at a time. Right?"

Keep him talking.

Keep his mind off the hurt.

Keep him safe.

"How'd you get that half-moon scar on your chin?"

"As much as I'd like to say an outlaw whipped my ass, I have to tell the truth. I got it about the fourth time Dad warned me that if I didn't steer clear of the backside of a mule, it'd kick the hell out of me. Dad was right."

Ella smiled. "Not exactly how I had imagined it." She couldn't resist a smile.

"The fire is getting closer, isn't it?" He grimaced as another wire sprang back, gashing his arm.

"You can smell it too?"

She continued laboriously working. The makeshift gloves hampered her progress, but without the wrapping she knew she'd not have made it this far.

Ella so badly wanted to bring up the subject of why he had lied to her about being on assignment. All the pieces had fallen together when she saw the barrels and smelled the fermenting whiskey. The bottles cinched it for her. She'd confront him later. They might even have a knock-down-drag-out, but right now her only concern was freeing the man she loved.

Just keep him talking, she reminded herself. It didn't

make any difference, just keep his mind busy. Block out the facts. The fire had to be inching closer. Audrey Jo and Dixie had no idea where Ella had gone. Hayden was in pain.

She snipped away.

"Hold on. I think I can pull out a couple of pieces about ten or twelve inches long. This'll hurt. Whoever did this not only wrapped it around you but made extra twists, so I can't just cut a few pieces and release the wire in between." She closed her eyes and bore down on the cutters.

The strand sprang loose. Blood surfaced on her arm and the wayward metal snagged on Hayden's shirt. But she had released a big piece of wire from around his chest. She could now reach behind and cut off the ropes securing his hands.

Hayden cautiously pulled his hands in front of him and rubbed his wrists. "Thanks. Give me the cutters. Once I get my circulation back, I think I can maneuver enough to cut some within my reach." He tried to turn the cutters upside down, but they slipped out of his hand and hit the ground.

Ella handed them back to him. "You never answered my question about the real reason you came to town. That warrant could have been picked up in a dozen more convenient places."

"The truth. If you haven't noticed, I don't have the best attitude in the world. Captain thought I was too surly and not particularly a team player. Figured I'd gotten too comfortable as a Ranger; impatient and enjoyed quick-triggered justice more than he thought I should. A throwback to the old Texas Rangers, like my dad and grandfather. Ended up that the captain ordered me to take time off and think things over. When he realized I thought he was just bluffing, he suspended me for a month and suggested I go fishing, which I did."

Gritting his teeth, Hayden came down on the cutters with a vengeance. Wire separated. "Until the last couple of days, I didn't see a damn thing wrong with how I viewed things.

I was being honest when I told you that I happened into town. But what I didn't mention was that I expected to have a new assignment when I got here." Blood squirted. "I didn't."

"Hayden, please don't continue playing me for a fool." She looked at him. "Your assignment instructions were in my ledger. The one you found on the porch the other morning." Every fiber in her body warned her that he was telling the truth, but logic countered it. "The envelope was already opened and I read it."

"What'd they say?" His stare drilled into her, and he tightly clenched his mouth. "If you don't mind sharing."

"Stay status quo on something to do with unlawful operations at Molly Lou's."

"Did it specifically say Molly Lou's?" His words were curt.

"Not by name. Called it P.E.S.'s establishment. It also mentioned Mobeetie and Wagon Mound."

"Anything else you can remember?" The tone of his words only accentuated the annoyance she felt with herself for reading the letter in the first place.

"Consider armed and dangerous."

The words struck Hayden's heart like an arrow. He stiffened. With the facts he'd sorted out since he'd been tied up, the picture was becoming clear to him.

"Ella, you didn't do anything wrong by reading the letter." Hayden chose his words carefully. "I'd've done the same thing. It was deliberately put in there for one of us to find. Probably me. I saw it sticking out of the book, and just shoved it back in."

"I didn't know about anything unlawfully operating out of Molly Lou's," she said in a broken whisper. "Not until I walked through the door a few minutes ago. I promise."

"I believe you. Who else uses the ledger?" A barb

scratched his bloody hand, but another piece of metal snapped.

"Only Muley. I keep the supply list in the back."

"Then he was definitely the one who left it on the porch, knowing I'd find it. Something happened that night he didn't figure on. Maybe going off with the drummer wasn't part of the plan. Ella, I think he's been protecting you." Hayden continued to cut away. "He wasn't near as drunk as he wanted Willard to think. He left me clues."

"Clues?" She cleared away the length of barbed wire, placing it in a stack beside Hayden.

"He said something that I've heard many a Ranger say. When Willard called the Rangers a bunch of irregular hooligans, Muley responded, 'might be irregular as hell in everything 'cept gettin' the job done.' I heard that all of my life." He had to stop and take a breath. "Ella, Muley's too old now, but he was a Ranger back in his younger days."

Ella coughed and tried not to inhale.

Hayden continued. "Something else. The guy I call Baldy knows something too. But I'm not sure which side of the law he's on. All I know is, Muley let him in on the bootleggin'. And one thing is for sure—Willard damn sure didn't like it a bit."

"The smoke is getting worse. I'm tying this around your face." She dipped his bandana in water and tied it from behind. At least it'd keep some of the smoke out of his lungs.

Ella followed suit, using a strip off her skirt.

The room was now filling with smoke at an alarming rate. Stifling, burning their nostrils and throats.

Suddenly, from somewhere outside, voices mingled with the sound of metal snapping. Hayden couldn't tell for sure how many, but there were several people throwing orders around.

"Help's arrived, Ella. Shout as loud as you can and beat

the hell out of the door. Do it like your life depends on it."
A wire snapped. "It does."

Like a madwoman, Ella ran to the entrance and began
banging and screaming at the top of her lungs.

"Keep up the good work, darlin'." Hayden coughed. "If
the fire gets near those kegs, it won't take much for them
to blow us to hell and back. The cornfield is probably on fire
and nobody will be able to put it out. Scream, Ella, scream."

Between shouts, Ella coughed. No doubt her lungs and
eyes burned as much, if not more, than his.

"If you can get yourself out, go," Hayden insisted.

"I still can't get the door open, and unless Dixie figures
out where I was headed, nobody knows we're in here." She
gave the door a firm wallop. Then another. "And I'm not
going anywhere without you."

More pounding.

"Hayden!" Ella cried, as flames licked at the dry planks
near the bunks.

A familiar voice hailed from outside. "Get water from
the stream and empty all the buckets on the path between
the cornfield and the shed," Sheriff Oldham's voice
boomed. "Bucket brigade."

"On the count of three." Baldy's distinct words dwarfed
the sheriff's orders. "One. Two. Three." Bodies hitting the
door shook the walls of the old building.

Ella looked back at Hayden. "If anybody can break
down the damn thing, it'd be those two lugs."

Someone shouted something in the distance, but
Hayden couldn't make out the words.

Baldy yelled, "To hell with the saloon. Protect this
shed."

Ella rushed back to Hayden and dropped to her knees.

"Begin pulling the wire out," Hayden choked out.

"I'll try, but it's gonna leave a whole lot of cuts and
punctures, Hayden."

"Just do it, Little Woman!" He fired back, knowing if anything would make her mad enough to forget how much it'd hurt, those words would certainly do that. He conjured up his best smile. "And, Ella, just in case they don't make it in time . . . I've figured out something else sitting here . . . I love you." He clenched his teeth.

"And I'm damn sure going to get you out of here because I want you to have to repeat that in front of the world." Ella took a deep breath. "Before I do this, I love you too."

Ella closed her eyes and pulled with all she had in her.

Hayden thought he was about to pass out, but he sure as hell wasn't about to give Sheriff Oldham and Baldy the satisfaction of finding him that poorly.

"One. Two. Three." The sheriff and Baldy counted in unison.

It sounded like a boulder hit the door. It barely budged, but the walls shook like a cyclone had hit them.

"Again . . ." Three times.

On the fourth try, the door buckled and sunshine rushed in, causing Hayden and Ella to blink until their eyes adjusted to the sudden brightness.

Sheriff Oldham and Baldy came charging in with their sidearms drawn like they'd come across a bank robbery.

In the distance, flames caterwauled toward the sky, gobbling up the cornfield on the way.

"Guess you came to finish me off?" Hayden roared. "I'm probably not worth the bullet it'd take."

"Damn it, McGraw," Sheriff Oldham thundered, and holstered his Colt. "You're givin' yourself too much credit, you egotistical, arrogant snipe."

"There's nobody in here but us," Hayden stated.

The sheriff motioned for Baldy to put away his weapon.

"Get us outta here, you sonofabitch!" With Ella's help, Hayden ripped away the severed wire tangled around his legs, as though it were nothing but hemp webbing. "You hit me from behind and hauled me in here, you bastard." Hayden tried to wiggle out of the wire. "It had to be you. You're the only one big enough to carry me." Hayden spat his words directly at Baldy.

"It doesn't take big, you honyock. It takes strong," Baldy charged back.

"Let's get them out of here and then you two can have a cuss fight, duel, or what in the hell you want," Sheriff Oldham ordered, stomping out the opening where the door once stood.

Flames lapped at the path between the cornfield and the shed, racing against time, hungry. Sated only by the taste of dried wood.

"Run!" Baldy ordered. "Run like hell!"

Knowing her dress would slow her down, Hayden grabbed Ella into his arms and ran for the saloon.

As if orchestrated, just yards from reaching the porch, Baldy, Sheriff Oldham, Hayden, and Ella fell to their knees and rolled to safety. A deafening explosion rocked the prairie. Cinders plummeted to the sky and flames engulfed the shed. Another angry outburst followed. A third and a fourth, until all the barrels were consumed.

Folks came from out of nowhere hauling buckets of water to put out the fire. Dixie and Audrey Jo broke through the throng of people and grabbed Ella. "We didn't know where you were. I promise, girl." Dixie hugged her again.

"You get those wounds some attention," Sheriff Oldham ordered as he picked up a pail. "I've got a lot of questions for you, Ranger."

"I have some of my own. Beginning with, where in the hell is Calvin Mullinex?" Hayden shouted over the noise.

Sheriff Oldham turned, and with a tone in his voice as serious as any Hayden had ever heard coming from a lawman, he asked, "You don't know?"

Epilogue

One year later

Sipping a glass of milk, Ella sat at her regular table in the Three Sisters Café. She tapped a swollen foot. For the first time that she could ever recall, she rested and let others do the work. From the day she told them she was expecting, everyone had been pretty protective of her. Especially her husband.

She smiled, thinking back over the last year.

The shed had been replaced with a barn and horse stalls where Stewball shared his time with Ella's filly, Puddin' Cake. A garden was now lush and green where the cornfield had once stood, leaving a majestic view of the stream and prairie from the new window added to the enlarged kitchen.

Audrey Jo and Dixie had both become quite the bakers. So what had started out as a way to keep Ella busy and out of Muley's hair so he could help crack the bootleggin' operation had ended up making money, lots of money, for the three women who shared and shared alike in the ownership of the newest café in town, the Three Sisters.

Hayden placed a CLOSED sign in the window, after

Emma Watson and Mrs. Oldham left, clutching their weekly orders of bear claws to their chests, as though they were gold. They'd both wished Ella good luck and gave Hayden a "we know how she got that way" look.

Hayden laid his hand on Ella's shoulder, lightly rubbing her neck. "Tired?"

"Tired and happy, Hayden."

The couple watched the corner table where twice a day Sheriff Oldham, Baldy, and Muley drank coffee and spun war tales with little or no ring of truth to them. Some had been so far-fetched that no doubt someday reality would become legend.

Muley still complained about how long it took Sheriff Oldham and Baldy to get him out of the hoosegow in Wagon Mound, where he was arrested along with Willard Porter—after he had gone back to Buffalo Wallow and trapped Ella and Hayden in the shed and then returned to Wagon Mound—by the U.S. Marshal for bootleggin'. One story started at a week, but now it was somewhere around a month, because Muley had had to walk all the way back to Buffalo Wallow.

The only fact that stayed consistent: Willard Porter was locked up for assault and kidnapping a Texas Ranger.

Then add attempted murder and bootleggin' to Willard's charges and they'd thrown away the key to his cell. Seems the government didn't give a hoot about a little moonshine being made, as long as it didn't leave the premises. But they didn't take kindly to the drummer profiting from and taking advantage of the railroad workers over in New Mexico.

Muley's only atrocity, besides taking the steps he thought best to keep his promise to Ella's father that she'd be safe, was trying to make some money to keep her business afloat. Cookin' up a batch of homebrew every now and again for the customers seemed a good idea. The rough and tough patrons of Molly Lou's knew the difference. They didn't give a damn if the saloon carried the good stuff or not, because the homemade brew was cheaper and stouter. That's what put Muley and Willard at odds in the first place. The more profit Muley made from the saloon, the less bartering needed.

There had always been a difference of opinion on how Ella's ledger had gotten on the porch.

Hayden knew exactly how it'd played out. Willard thought Muley was too drunk to remember the peddler hitting Hayden and taking him to the shed. That gave Muley, before Hayden was attacked, time to plant the two clues—the ledger and the badge—before Willard changed his mind and decided he'd better haul Muley, drunk or not, with him to New Mexico. Hayden had seen the truth in his eyes when he returned the retired Ranger's badge to him.

There are just parts of a Texas Ranger's character that another Ranger would recognize without question. A tough-as-nails Texas makeup, with guts and skills that allowed them to stand alone between society and its enemies with a spirit of independence and a bond shared only by a courageous and bold outfit of men known as Texas Rangers.

The part of the story everyone agreed upon: if Hayden hadn't got his Warrant of Authority wet and stopped in Buffalo Wallow to pick up his replacement, the plan to bust Willard Porter would have run smoothly.

The scheme was simple. Thanks to the first book of marriage records coming to town, Sheriff Oldham knew if they held a town meeting, Ella would be the first to show up and voice her opinion against the law, creating havoc. Sheriff Oldham would detain her for a while for inciting a riot, and that'd give Muley and the town's new undercover deputy enough time to blow Willard's operation sky-high. Well, it blew sky-high, but not exactly as they had intended.

There was no contingency plan for a little ruckus turning into a riot and requiring one Ranger to defend one woman's honor.

"Ella, you'll see him again. Your father will be back." Hayden noticed the faraway look in his wife's face when she went to the place in her heart that held her memories. "You know he will."

"I know. I know." Ella patted Hayden's hand still resting on her shoulder. "He can't afford to leave tracks and won't put us in jeopardy." She rested her other hand on her stomach.

"When it comes—"

Hayden hardly got the words out of his mouth before Ella broke in.

"We aren't having an 'it,' Hayden. It's a boy. I can feel it, and he'll grow up to be a fearless Texas Ranger just like his father, his grandfathers, and his great-grandfather."

"I think you need some rest, darlin'." Hayden took her hand and helped her to her feet. "You're going loco on me."

Halfway up the stairs, she turned and looked back at their friends sitting around the café rehashing the day.

Ella and Hayden looked at one another and exchanged knowing smiles.

Night after night, they lay in the big four-poster bed and heard Muley slewfootin' it down the hall to Dixie's bedroom.

And Audrey Jo joined Deputy Harry Jackson, who most folks knew better by his nickname, Baldy, every evening for supper and a stroll.

The gamblers and the gossipers.

The quaint and the inquisitive.

The renegades and the righteous.

It only took the love of one woman and one Ranger to bring a town together.

The Perfect Match

DeWanna Pace

*To my sister, Teresa Rose,
and to my niece, Dortha Hall.*

*To life's battles, win or lose.
All worth the effort when it's
love you're fighting for . . .*

Chapter 1

In His Corner

El Paso
February 1896

The alkali dust of the desert sandstorm swirling along the streets of El Paso, Texas, forced Thomas Longbow to pull his Stetson low, further sheltering his eyes. Walls of dirt hundreds of feet high masked the Franklin Mountains, which formed the eastern edge of the border town. The dusty cloud blotted out the sun and made it more difficult to follow his assignment. Even the weather seemed to conspire against him in getting the job done quickly and moving on.

A glance at the adobe and brick businesses that lined the plaza revealed that most of the citizens who had swollen the city to more than three times its size the past month were smart enough to stay indoors and out of the pelting sting of Chihuahuan dirt. A few strangers hurried past, not bothering to look his way and, for the moment, were apparently not trailing Maher along with him. The sports enthusiasts who had tracked the prizefighter from the moment Pete Maher stepped out of his door each morning to train until he called it a day had been nothing but pure aggravation for Thomas. Though Thomas had wanted to simply mix in with the crowd of fight fans, he had been tempted to show his star a time or two just to cull the herd.

Making sure Maher and his opponent, Bob Fitzsimmons, didn't find a secret location in which to fight was taking a hell of a lot longer than anyone thought it would. Personally, he hoped the two would just battle it out on a sandbar in the middle of the Rio Grande. That would satisfy all the bickering between Texas, New Mexico, and Mexico about whose territory the prizefight couldn't be held on.

Trouble was, every sports fan, newspaperman, and gambler from New York to Juarez was betting that the fight between the two heavyweights would take place, and they were ticked as hell that the authorities had called in the Texas Rangers to stop the fistic carnival from happening. For the first time in Ranger history, the entire force of what some called "the wrath of God" had been called to El Paso to enforce Governor Culberson's and President Cleveland's legislation against prizefighting in the territories. As far as Thomas was concerned, there was one Ranger too many in the mix. He could think of a dozen other legitimate squabbles along the border that needed taking care of.

Just as Maher turned the corner, dirt blasted Thomas's eyes. He yanked up the red bandana he wore around his neck and wiped away the grit, swearing as he wondered what kind of business had brought Maher out on such a miserable day. The boxer wasn't dressed in his running regalia; instead he looked like he was on some secret mission, dressed in a low-slung hat and yellow slicker that covered him from head to foot. He'd taken the Silver City Special in from Las Cruces, New Mexico, where he had his training quarters, leaving his manager behind. Thomas hoped like sin that this sudden need of Maher's to investigate the streets of El Paso would lead to some inkling about the fight's planned location. The sooner the Rangers found out where it would be held, the faster Thomas would be done with this slow drip of an assignment.

Impatience lengthened his stride as he hurried to catch up to his quarry.

In Her Corner

The bell jangled, announcing a customer had entered the shop. Laney O'Grady set down the mallet she'd been pounding to stamp the cowhide and dusted her hands upon her apron. She walked through the curtain that separated her workroom from the display room and offered the newcomer a smile. "How can I help you?"

The tall man took off his hat, dusted it on his thigh, then offered a quick apology. "Sorry for the mess, lass."

When she caught sight of his eyes, Laney almost gasped. Only good manners kept her from asking what in the world had happened to him. One was swollen shut, the other deeply red and matted.

He didn't flinch at her appraisal; instead he moved closer to the counter that separated them. "Can you keep a secret?"

She wasn't sure what she'd expected the customer to say, but his question caught her off guard. All of a sudden she was very much aware that she was alone and that he was a man of broad shoulders and extremely powerful-looking hands. "What do you mean?"

"The question's simple, lass. You know who I am, I presume, and I need to know if you can keep a secret."

Laney stared more intently and realized, with a start,

she did know him. Or rather, of him. Standing before her was the Irishman whose picture had been in every paper from Chicago to the local editions and had all of El Paso buzzing. Pete Maher, the fighter. No wonder his eyes were so bad. She'd read in the *El Paso Herald* just yesterday that the fight between him and the other boxer would be delayed because of Maher's eye infection. Everyone thought it was simply a ruse urged on by the Dallas promoter, Dan Stuart, to allow time to find a location for the fight and ultimately outwit the Texas Rangers. No one really believed Maher was suffering. "I'm sorry to hear about your problem."

"You still haven't answered my question."

Laney thought she saw someone's shadow stop at the shop door, halt, then move past. Poor man. Maher must be constantly followed. Ever since he and Bob Fitzsimmons hit town, the two fighters had suffered an entourage of hundreds. Everyone wanted to ride the wake of fame following the two heavyweights. Even on a day like this he apparently couldn't shake his shadows.

"I've kept a secret or two in my time," she answered truthfully, sensing maybe the man just needed something from someone who didn't want something back from him.

"Good." He held both fists up on the counter. "I need you to measure my hands and make me a new pair of boxing gloves. The deal is, though, you can't let anyone know how you're going to design them."

Laney motioned to the leather wares displayed in the room. "I'm a saddle maker, Mr. Maher. Sometimes I make a pair of boots or chaps, but I've never made boxing gloves before."

The challenge of making them appealed to her, but she had to be honest with the man about her lack of expertise in the area.

"I'll pay whatever your fee is, plus a bonus of a thousand dollars, if you can have them done in a week. That's how long the doc says I need to rest these eyes."

A thousand-dollar bonus. Money that would have taken her years to save. Money that would be hers alone and didn't have to go back into the shop. An answer to her prayers. Laney couldn't believe that luck had just blown in with the wind and landed on her counter. Still, she didn't know a thing about making boxing gloves. She wasn't even sure what they looked like. Using gloves to fight was something new in Texas. The few fights she'd ever witnessed were always bare knuckled. "All I can promise is to do my best."

"That's why I'm here. I was told you're the best leather-goods maker in the Southwest. I've written the specifics on this . . ." He pulled a piece of paper from his pocket, on which he'd provided a sketch of gloves, instructions on the material to be used, and several symbols. One of the designs was a shamrock with a silver harp inside it. "My good luck charm. I'm superstitious about it. Won't fight unless I got it on each glove seven times."

A frown furrowed his brow and made his dark mustache bracket the grim line of his mouth. "My trainer left the baggage that held my gloves in Dallas. No telling where they'll end up. The press gets wind of it and they'll have a field day. I want them replaced before anyone knows they're missing."

"I'll get my tape." Laney excused herself long enough to grab her measuring tape and writing ledger from the workroom. She quickly measured Maher from wrist to fingertip and wrote down the figures. She started to check the other hand, but Maher waved her off.

"They're a perfect match. Not an inch of difference in either," he announced proudly. "And one swings as good as the other."

The shop door opened, jangling the bell. Maher slipped his hands away from the counter and pulled his slicker closer around him. He started to turn away, but Laney stopped him. "I'll need to know when you intend to—"

Maher didn't let her finish. "Ten o'clock tomorrow. We'll talk more then. I'm due at the Gem Saloon. I can count on you not to say a word?"

"Not a word. Ten o'clock tomorrow then."

The boxer put his hat back on, tipped it in a polite, silent good-bye, then started to pass the newcomer entering the shop. The tall, ruggedly handsome customer directed his steel gray gaze at Mr. Maher, giving Laney the distinct impression that he was gauging the boxer in some odd way.

He turned for a moment and watched Mr. Maher go, then swung around abruptly and asked, "Just what have you promised not to say?"

Chapter 2

Backed in a Corner

"I beg your pardon, sir." The woman's pert chin lifted and her eyes flashed like sunlight glinting off an amber chandelier. "That's none of your business."

Of all the people he suspected might be working with the boxers and promoters to secure a fighting arena, a woman saddle maker was the last person Thomas thought would be involved. But from what he'd heard of that last bit of conversation with Maher, she certainly knew something that was meant to be kept secret. He could pull his badge and end any question of his right to answers, but something in the set of her shoulders and determined expression gave him pause and made him wonder if maybe he was too quick to underestimate her.

"Guess I've got a curious bone that's hard to shake." He offered her an apology, an act rare to his nature. Not that he was never wrong. He just preferred the justice that went with being right. Made life easier on him and everyone he had to arrest.

"I suppose you reporters have to be a bit nosy to do

your job well," she said, her eyes softening to a warm shade of golden honey.

A reporter? So, she thought he was one of the bloodhounds chasing Maher for a scoop. He didn't know her well enough to tell if she was teasing or just easy on forgiveness. Thomas found himself holding his breath for a moment before he realized what had made him do so. Her hair looked like the cinnamon brown of a male lion's thick mane, flowing in long waves past the almond-shaped, amber-colored eyes, high cheekbones, and full lips that gave her an exotically regal air. Her figure was slightly fuller than the current fad of petiteness seen in other cities, but he liked what he saw. She seemed solid and sturdy, well grounded on her feet. She wouldn't blow away with the first high wind of trouble, he'd bet. Thomas was no stranger to beauty, but hers was stunning. What was she doing walled up in a saddle shop?

Let her think what she would for now. Maybe she would be more willing to talk if she thought he was a newshound and might bring publicity to her business. Thomas didn't have the luxury of hoping she wouldn't be that sort. Time wouldn't keep him here any longer than necessary. Still, he hoped she wasn't someone whose confidence could be bought easily.

"Nosy—huh?" He liked a good challenge. Changing her mind appealed to him. "I prefer to think of it as keeping aware of things around me . . . of people."

She didn't blush at the husky tone his voice deliberately took on, and that appealed to him even more. She was no shrinking violet and not easily swayed. His last stint with the Ranger detachment north of Ysleta had left him no time for courting a woman worth her salt. The few times he'd taken release in the cantinas that offered such for the flip of a coin, he rode away with no readiness to return. Suddenly he found himself wondering if he would be as quick to leave her bed.

Thomas liked what he was feeling. The sudden rush of blood in his veins, the hint of adventure stirring in his mind, the thrill of sensing something he'd never done before. Whoever this O'Grady's Saddle Shop and Leather Goods woman was, she called to him like a seductive siren from some beckoning shore. The possibility that this assignment might take long enough for him to find out more about her might just be the one thing that made it worth tolerating this frustrating delay.

Maher had said he was headed to the Gem Saloon, the assigned gathering place in El Paso for journalists to interview the fighting community. Now that he gave it a second thought, Thomas remembered talk of the possibility of Rector's Kinetoscope Company being there this morning to meet with the boxers to discuss film rights to the bout. Edison's new camera was all the talk, and would allow the fight to be viewed in nickelodeons all over the world.

The most respected Ranger of all, Captain Bill McDonald from Amarillo, had been assigned to patrol the Gem Saloon. Maher wouldn't be able to flick a finger at a gnat, much less make secret arrangements, under the near-mythical captain's eagle eye. Nothing would happen under McDonald's watch. Thomas could take a minute or two to investigate this woman's involvement and to satisfy a little of his curiosity about her and why Maher had taken her into his confidence.

"You know who that man was, I take it?" Thomas waited to see if she would lie.

"He's my customer."

She was loyal, if not forthright, Thomas decided. "Is he buying a saddle?"

"I'm sorry. I'm not at liberty to discuss my customers' arrangements, sir." She placed her writing ledger on the counter as if to take an order, glanced down, then abruptly flipped the page.

Thomas instinctively knew something about Maher was on that paper. A location? He'd have to get a look. He moved closer to the counter.

She slipped the ledger into her apron pocket. "How can I help you, Mr.—?"

"Longbow. Thomas Longbow." He was going to tip his hat as he would to any woman, but instead the strong urge to touch her compelled him to offer his hand for a shake. "And yours?"

She hesitated for just a moment then abruptly stretched her palm across the counter, nodding toward the storefront window. "O'Grady. Killaney O'Grady."

He took her hand in his and felt the warm, calloused strength of her slender fingers. She was a woman who worked with her hands and relied on no servants to pamper her. "Miss or missus?" he asked.

"Widowed." Her chin lifted higher.

"Is that how you came to work in the family shop?"

"You are an inquisitive sort." Her hand pulled away and returned to her side.

"Goes with the job." This time no apology was given.

"I run the place. I make the saddles. You'll get a good buy for a fair cost. That's all that should matter to you, Mr. Longbow."

She didn't say she owned the place. She said "run" it. So, there was another O'Grady of some sort involved. A father or brother-in-law? Why weren't they here doing a man's work instead of making her do it? "How long does it take to make a new saddle?"

Relief eased the corners of her mouth and he realized she'd been tense. He hadn't meant to put her ill at ease and the fact that he had, made Thomas get down to the real business at hand. He needed some reason to return tomorrow and see what transpired between her and Maher and to see what was written in that ledger. Ordering something would provide him with a reason to return . . . on several occasions, if necessary. A saddle seemed the logical answer.

She pointed to a handsome example of her work that rested on a sawhorse made for display. "If you want one for show like that one, it'll take about forty hours. That style takes a lot of fancy stamping and shivving. But if you want one intended to last and to get a lot of good use from, it'll take sixty-five hours to build."

"Sixty-five hours!" He wanted to spend a little time with her, but everything about this damned assignment seemed to be demanding more time than it took to ride across Texas. "Something that takes that long to make better last a lifetime," he announced.

"Something worth having *should* last a lifetime, Mr. Longbow."

"Thomas," he insisted. "If I'm going to invest sixty-five hours with you . . . er . . . in your shop, then we ought to be on a first-name basis."

"All right then. Thomas it is." She offered her hand once again to seal the deal. "My friends call me Laney."

"Laney," he repeated, holding her hand. He liked the way the name suited her, and the sound of it on his lips. He could imagine whispering it in the heated rush of passion, and that simple imagining made him want her now—not someday, but now.

Clear your head, Longbow, he told himself, *before you make a fool of yourself.* "Okay, so when would you like to measure my horse for a fitting?"

"That won't be necessary." She grabbed a measuring tape from inside the apron tied around the becoming flare of her hips and moved from behind the counter. "I noticed you were on foot."

"Won't be necessary?" Thomas glanced at the door and back at her. "How did you know I was afoot?"

She laughed. "I didn't hear hooves on your approach

and I glanced past my customer when he walked by you as he went out the door. There's no horse tied to the hitching post."

The woman was observant. Admiration begrudgingly mixed with the mounting suspicion she stirred in him, as Thomas wondered if that was the reason she might be part of the mix in the boxer's game.

"Now would you care to step into my workroom to take off your pants, or would you prefer that I measure you with them on?" she asked, her eyes twinkling with challenge.

"Measure what?"

She extended the tape several inches and said, "Hmmm . . . that looks about the right size."

Thomas glanced down at where she was looking then back up at her. A full-blown grin stretched across her lips.

"I have to either measure the horse's cantle or your . . . shall we say . . . pant seam, if I'm to get the right fit for the saddle."

Thomas did what he had never done in all twenty-nine years of his life. He blushed. And, for the first time in his life, he wondered if he'd met a woman who might be too much for him to handle.

For a man accustomed to barreling inside places with no holds barred, the Ranger was in a hurry to back out of this woman's door. "You can measure my horse tomorrow."

Thomas rushed away from Laney O'Grady's saddle shop, certain a howl of feminine laughter now blended with the wind.

Chapter 3

Thrown Punch

Laney rode up in front of the tall brick building and halted near the Vendome Hotel's entrance. She leaned her bicycle next to the wall, wishing for the dozenth time that the business would allot curb space for bicycle enthusiasts as well. One would think, with it being 1896, the venue would allow hitching places for horse and bicycle alike. At least there was no worry that anyone would steal her mode of transportation. Few in these parts were ready to embrace the new contraptions yet.

Straightening her skirt over her bloomers, she gathered her confidence to enter the metropolitan meeting place for captains of industry, moneyed moguls, and high-hatted women. A quick glance back at the vast and raw desert that stretched south of the twin cities of El Paso and Juarez gave her strength. She might work in a city and behind a counter, but somewhere deep within her still ran a touch of the untamed Irish and Spanish blood that mixed in her veins. Both factions had known their share of tribulations and had fought fearlessly for the right to live and own property. But hers was the right best fought for, and she knew it. The right to love what was hers.

Dannell O'Grady, be forewarned, she thought, setting her shoulders with determination. *Thanks to a boxer and a nosy journalist, I'm finally ready to have my say.* She took a deep breath, garnering her strength of purpose, and suddenly felt like her ancestor warriors. Today she meant to get her stepson back.

Laney walked inside the busy lobby and headed straight to the hotel desk. She received more than one look of admiration as she passed the well-dressed men who lined the lobby. As well she should. She'd taken extra time to look her very best. She wanted Dannell, and everyone else who cared to look, to know that she was quite capable of caring well for both her and the boy. But fancying herself up for any other reason was the last thing she desired at the moment. Men were too much trouble, and she hadn't yet met one worth trusting.

"Please ring Mr. O'Grady's room and tell him his sister-in-law would like to see him," she told the clerk.

The clerk did as instructed, then after a few moments his forehead creased with apology. "Afraid he's not answering, ma'am. I believe I saw him leave earlier, but he usually returns around six for his evening meal. Would you like to leave him a message?"

"No, thank you." She opened the saffron-colored fan laced about her wrist and cooled herself. The matching yellow tea gown she wore was made of cool linen, but it offered little comfort when the temperature outside could melt an iron rail on one of the train tracks. These hotels might offer the finest luxuries, but the person who invented a way to stave off this ungodly heat would rule the world. "I'll just wait over there for him," she informed the clerk.

She motioned to a rosewood davenport that offered a

view of the front entryway as well as the dining room. Laney refused to let another day go by without Dannell knowing she had the means to have her way. "Please let him know that I'm here when he checks in with you."

Laney took a seat and began to study the room and its furnishings, focusing a particular interest in a series of designs on a small tapestry hung over the fireplace that took up a huge portion of one wall. She knew she wasn't like many women who oohed and aahed over every fabric and lace, but she did look for unique patterns and designs. They made her leather goods unusual, one of a kind. Buyers had come from as far away as England for her saddles. She'd deliberately set out to make her wares different than anyone else's, so she could ask the better price. The extra effort had helped her squirrel away her share of the profit in order to be able to afford to adopt her stepson.

It had taken two years, two long years of working into the wee hours of the night, of saving every peso, of putting up with Dannell's taunts that she would never see the day when she could afford to get any judge to sign over her stepson into her care. Not when the boy's very own uncle could give the boy everything she couldn't. *Everything,* she'd told him, *but the most important thing. A mother's love.*

It had broken her heart when Marc had died and she'd learned that she would not get custody of her beloved stepson. Dannell hadn't wanted his nephew. He wanted the yearly stipend left in Marc's will to take care of Gideon until he became of age and took over Marc's half of the shop.

The law had been clear on the issue. She was not Gideon's true blood. Dannell was and, unless she could find the means to legally adopt Gideon and prove Dannell unfit, she had no chance of keeping the boy.

But a visit with Judge Townsend gave her hope. He was

aware of some of Dannell's less-than-upstanding dealings, and had told Laney that if she could find a way to establish herself in business and pay the legal fees of adoption she stood a chance at winning her stepson away from his wealthy uncle—that Dannell's alcoholic ways would finally come face-to-face with justice. Well, Dannell would learn tonight that in one week she would have that money, and everyone from here to Liverpool could attest to the quality of her workmanship and ability to earn her way.

The shop had meant everything to Marc and so it meant everything to Gideon. Though she owned the other half, she put all the profits away in a fund for Gideon and allowed herself only a worker's pay. She'd lived in the back room of the shop, scrimping and saving, focusing on nothing else but the day she could save him from the clutches of an unloving uncle.

Laney blinked, moisture threatening to well in her eyes. She glanced away, unwilling for anyone to see her cry. She hadn't let herself do so these past two years. She wouldn't do it now in a hotel full of strangers. Willing the tears away, she focused on a group of resolute-looking men sitting at a table in the dining room. To her surprise, she realized one of them was the journalist who had ordered the saddle this morning.

Most of the men were dressed in white hats and buckskin breeches. Long revolvers rested against each man's thigh. A handful held ferocious-looking Winchesters. Texas Rangers. Everyone knew they'd been called to El Paso. No one else could look as formidable. What was Thomas Longbow doing in their midst? Getting an interview?

Curious, Laney moved to the other side of the davenport, trying to catch a hint of their conversation. She hid behind her fan, pretending the need for further air. Thomas didn't have any pen and paper with him that she could see.

His memory for detail must be really good not to need the benefit of written reminders.

"Two of us?" demanded Thomas, his eyes hardening to gunmetal gray. He reached inside his frock coat and tossed a badge on the table in front of the fiercest-looking of the men. "If my arrests don't speak for themselves, I don't need that and you don't need me."

"You've done every job I asked of you, Longbow," the leader said, grabbing the silver star and flipping it back to Thomas. Thomas caught it and returned the badge to its hidden pocket. "I just consider it a better idea for you to follow that saddle-maker lead and let Sawyer stick to the boxer while he's training in Las Cruces. That would leave you time to check out the O'Grady woman and track Maher whenever he's in town here. I know you're a damn miracle man, but even you can't be spending three hours on a train, going to and from, and track the woman too, if she proves to be the lead we've been looking for concerning the fight location."

"Guess I'm getting cagey with all this dallying," Thomas growled.

"Hey, I'll gladly swap with ya. I hear she's a real looker," teased the taller of the men. "That knuckle-jabber trains from dawn to dusk and frankly"—he patted his belly—"I've already lost more hide than I had to shed. You'd think he had some kind of steam engine driving him."

"She does make a man look twice," Thomas admitted, as if he wasn't really listening.

Laney had steam of her own building inside her. So, coal-haired, gray-eyed, steel-jawed Mr. Thomas Longbow was also a Texas Ranger, was he? Made her think he was a journalist out to get a story, had he? Well, she'd give him a story or two to tell when he showed up at her shop tomorrow, you just wait and see.

Bolting to her feet, it took everything she had in her not

to march into that dining room and tell the man just what she thought of him. He *had* been nosy on purpose, following that poor Mr. Maher when he was clearly in a state of physical discomfort. And he'd dared to try to worm out of her the poor man's reason for visiting her shop. She'd seen the way he had tried to get a look at her ledger. He thought she was in some kind of conspiracy with the man over the fight location. And he had the gall to besmirch her good name—with the Texas Rangers, of all people. Right when she was about to go up against her brother-in-law to battle for Gideon!

Lost in her anger, Laney didn't hear Dannell O'Grady enter the hotel until he was nearly at the door to the dining room. With his top hat and silver-handled cane, he reminded her of a fancy-dressed pied piper leading a pack of society rats. When he removed his hat, his thinning red hair stayed plastered on his head, with a split down the middle that would have made Moses proud. His face might once have been considered handsome, but his complexion was now ruddy with the apparent effects of the liquor that made him weave more than walk toward her. He must be deep into his cups today.

"There you are," he bellowed in a voice that could have been heard on Utah Street. "I saw that two-wheeled freak-seat out there leaning up against the wall. I knew you must be here. What is it you need, woman? You know Gideon is back east."

Laney directed her anger where it should really belong. "Sent away despite both his and my wishes, if I remember distinctly." Let his companions think what they would. She didn't care one feather if they thought her inappropriate for her anger at her brother-in-law's spitefulness. "If you'll excuse us, gentlemen, I won't keep him long, I assure you. My talk will be brief and to the point."

To her surprise, Dannell bid his friends farewell and

said he would join them at their table in a few minutes. He offered her his arm, but Laney refused to take it, knowing that it was merely for show. Instead, she walked slightly ahead of him to a table close to the Rangers. If Dannell became too belligerent with the news she meant to give him, he would think twice before making a scene.

Once they'd taken their seats, Laney called the waiter and ordered two cups of coffee.

"I'll have brandy," Dannell insisted, but Laney shook her head.

"The gentleman will have coffee here. If he wants his brandy, he'll have to drink it at the table where he plans to eat." She checked to make sure the Rangers were watching and listening. True to their reputation, they missed nothing.

She expected Dannell to storm off, but he remained seated. An uncomfortable silence ensued while they waited for the waiter to return with the coffee. Finally, when they'd been served, Laney took the papers out of her gown pocket and carefully slid them across the table to him.

"What's this?" he asked, unfolding the document.

"My petition for adoption of Gideon. It will be filed in Judge Townsend's office one week from today."

He chuckled and didn't even bother to read the first page, tossing it back to her. "So, you finally raised the money. Good for you."

She'd expected a lot of things from him, but certainly not a backhanded compliment. "I'll expect Gideon home at the end of the semester."

He took a sip of his coffee and deliberately locked his gaze with hers. "The money was only part of your problem, Killaney. You still have to prove yourself more fit than I to take care of the boy."

The threat in his voice warned that she should proceed

with caution, but with victory in sight she dared to throw her final punch. She slid the papers back to him. "Maybe you should take a closer look at those. You'll find the last page particularly interesting."

Dannell turned immediately to the last page. His ruddy face turned white, his alcohol-laced breath exiting in great fuming puffs. His hand shot out and grabbed her wrist. "You paid them to sign this, you witch!"

"You wish I did," Laney countered, struggling to break free of his hold. "Every one of them signed the petition willingly. You can't swindle your friends and expect them to stay character witnesses for you. Even you aren't that important. Now let go of me."

"I told you I'd marry you and then the boy would be yours again." His fingers dug into her wrists. "But you think yourself too high and mighty."

"For the likes of you, I do, Dannell O'Grady. You don't deserve your brother's name or his son." She tried to jerk her arm away from him, but he held on too tightly. "I said let go. *Now*," she insisted more loudly.

"You hard of hearing, mister?" warned a deep baritone voice she recognized from this morning. "Is this man hurting you, Mrs. O'Grady?"

Though Thomas Longbow's concern was aimed at her, his fierce expression never left its true target. The Ranger looked like he was carved from the face of Mount Franklin itself. "The lady said let go."

Dannell did as he was told and rose. "I don't know who your friend is, Killaney, but we'll discuss this another time."

He left without another word, turning briefly to look at her before joining his table of friends. She hadn't realized just how much her brother-in-law's threat affected her. Laney took a sip of coffee to settle the nervous trembling of her hands. Oh, she had been prepared to show him she wasn't afraid of him, that he wouldn't sway her from her purpose. But something in the look Dannell gave her before he joined his friends sent a shiver of fear down her spine.

"Th—thank you, Mr. Longbow. *Thomas,*" Laney said, trying to block out Dannell's threat and instead focus on her helpful customer. "Do you reporters often rescue damsels in distress?" she teased, playing the game that he had initiated between them. Teasing somehow made the fear fade faster.

Thomas's forefinger rose to his brow as if he were tipping his hat to her. "Yeah, even when she picks a fight in public that she thinks she can handle on her own." A grin flashed startlingly white against the sun-soaked hue of his skin. "Now, if you'll excuse me, ma'am, I've got a horse to fetch before morning. I'd advise you to be more careful around drunks."

Chapter 4

The Main Attraction

The day was already heating up to be a scorcher and it was barely midmorning. February in El Paso could give Satan a sunburn. Not having to worry about the train ride from Las Cruces to follow Maher back to El Paso, Thomas had gladly retrieved the black stallion from the livery stable and took a long morning ride. He missed the old days of galloping rides and of justice meted out swiftly. Today, it was all about riding the rails to get from one place to the other and catching cattle rustlers. Hell, the legislature would probably have them start using those new-fangled bicycles for transportation in order to cut the budget for horse feed.

As a cadet fresh from West Point, Thomas had headed back home to join the Texas Rangers, after fulfilling his military obligation, believing in the code they lived by and their role in the protection of his state. Seven years he'd lived and breathed the spartan existence, not resting his boots under any particular bed, riding where the wind and a criminal led him, living by the code to see wrong things made right. The adventure of it had always called to him and he loved the sound of its voice.

Maybe that's why this assignment pestered him so much. He felt no sense of anticipation that he was going to learn something new, help someone who needed him, right some terrible wrong. True, stopping a fight of some sort was what he did best. It seemed there was always somebody taking on somebody else. But trying to stop a fight from taking place when everyone in Texas other than the politicians wanted it, didn't appeal to Thomas's sense of wrong made right.

Last night when he'd come to Laney's defense, he'd almost wished her coffee guest would have dared to defy him. Thomas was aching for something more rough-and-tumble than his current assignment. He didn't go out looking for trouble, yet neither did he shy away from it. Putting the man in his place might have been just the thing to ease some of this cagey tension that had filled Thomas the past three weeks in El Paso.

"Well, Justice"—Thomas reined the stallion toward town—"are you about ready to get yourself measured by the feistiest gal this side of the border?" The Ranger chuckled at how she'd dared to insinuate that she was going to measure *him,* for pistol's sake. He had thought she joked at the time, but after hearing some of her conversation with that wrist bender last night, Thomas didn't doubt for one moment now that she had meant to do just what she said. Laney O'Grady wasn't a woman who shied easily, and he wasn't the sort who would have been measured without showing just exactly how attracted he was to her.

The prospect of having her hands on him added heat to his speculations and, unconsciously, he nudged Justice to speed up his gait. When he reached the saddle shop,

Thomas tied his mount to the hitching post and asked a passing stranger for the time.

The gentleman opened his pocket watch. "Five minutes until ten, sir."

Thomas thanked the man. Just on time, he thought. He knew Maher to be a particularly punctual man when it came to appointments, so Thomas had enough time to establish himself in the shop without looking like he had deliberately scheduled to be there in conjunction with Maher's visit.

The bell jangled as he entered the shop. To his surprise, the smell of cinnamon permeated the air and Laney was there waiting for him across the counter. His stomach grumbled and he didn't know if it was from the delicious aroma wafting from the cloth-lined basket sitting on the counter, or whether his hunger had been stirred by the morning freshness of Laney's beauty.

"Good morning, Thomas. I thought that would be you. Right on time, I see."

"Oh?" Thomas raked his memory. "I don't recall saying I'd be here at any particular time."

"True, but Mr. Maher did, and he's due any moment." Laney smiled sweetly. "I had a feeling you'd come in about the same time."

Clever girl. She knew she had him. *Well, round one goes to you,* he thought. "Never miss an opportunity for a story, I always say."

"I'm glad you're here a little early. I wanted to say a personal thank-you." She lifted the basket and held it out to him. "Cinnamon rolls. I hope you're hungry."

For more than you think. Thomas opened the cloth and reached for one of the rolls, so fresh that the icing was still melting down the swirls of cinnamon. "I haven't had one of these since . . ." He couldn't finish. As the taste of the roll hit his lips, Thomas's eyes closed and he thought he had died and gone to heaven. Sweetness blended with buttery heat, sliding down his tongue and stirring a long-denied sweet tooth. Campsite food rarely allowed time for baking pastries. "My God, woman," he said in appreciation, "you're one hell of a cook."

Opening his eyes proved Thomas's undoing. In that instant, he noticed her tongue licking a drip of icing on her own lips and it sent blood racing through his veins like Justice gone wild on locoweed. He quickly stuffed another roll in his mouth to avoid just reaching over and licking it off of her himself.

"I'm glad you like them," she said, putting him through further misery as she licked a couple of her fingers. "I'm too messy with them myself. I get them all over me, as you can see." She held up her forefinger and then stuck it in her mouth and sucked slowly. When she finished, she sighed. "I have to keep my fingers clean so that I don't stain my leatherwork."

Thomas was a betting man. Every instinct told him that she'd licked that last finger on purpose. *Thank* him? Yeah, right. The woman was toying with him. *So, round two goes to you too.*

He pushed the basket back toward her. "Two's plenty for me."

She placed the basket under the counter. "You can have the rest when you leave, if you like. I'll go wash my hands and be right back. I think I hear Mr. Maher coming now."

Thomas had been so caught up in his heated thoughts that he'd assumed the thundering beat he heard was lust speeding up his heartbeat. Now that he really listened, he could tell it was the tramp of hundreds keeping pace along the wooden sidewalk. Maher wasn't alone today.

Laney soon returned with the writing ledger Thomas

had seen yesterday. She laid it on the counter and opened it, noticed he was watching her, then quickly closed it.

"I know you arrived first this morning," she began, "but since you knew his appointment was exactly at ten and I wouldn't really have time to discuss your saddle at the moment, I hope you won't mind waiting until I'm finished with Mr. Maher."

He couldn't argue. It was only fair. Besides, Maher might distract her long enough for Thomas to get a chance at the ledger. "Go right ahead. I'll wait. I'll just look around at your goods."

The boxer entered, followed by a short, portly man and an older man Thomas recognized as Dan Stuart himself, the fight promoter. The portly man waved away the remainder of the crowd, insisting that no one else follow them in. He didn't appear to be much of a bodyguard, Thomas decided, but then as the owner of two of the world's deadliest fists, Maher could defend himself.

"A good morning to you, lass," the boxer greeted her, tightening the belt around his training robe. "Do forgive me for showing up in my running clothes. I'd have doffed my hat to you, if I'd had it with me."

"No need to apologize, Mr. Maher. A man works in the clothes of his trade." Laney stepped around the counter and offered her hand.

One brow arched over his barely opened eye. "See there, Stuart, what did I tell you? She's the one. Not one of those faint and fawners. She looks a man right in the eye, she does, and full of spit and vinegar I'd be guessing."

You'd be guessing right, Thomas conceded to the man's insight. Now why was that so all-fired important to the boxer? Thomas stepped closer to the showy saddle on the sawhorse, drawing him nearer to the ledger.

"This big galoot is Dan Stuart, lass, the brassiest promoter what ever latched his moniker to the fight arena."

Thomas smelled more than cinnamon in the air. These three were up to something. He just hoped she wasn't in on it. The thought of arresting her appealed to him even less than before he ate the rolls.

The elderly man tipped his hat. "Ma'am."

"And this squat body is my trainer—"

"Don't take too long, Pete," the trainer interrupted before Maher could complete his introduction. "Cool down too much and you'll lose that last mile of workout. You'll have to add another before lunch."

Maher's mustache lifted above a broad grin. "Can't have that, can we, Stuart? A man's gotta eat."

The boxer's eating habits were near-legendary. He was known to consume two whole chickens, a round of four or five vegetables, a loaf of bread, and two apple pies in one sitting.

Thomas noticed a heaping pile of unshaped leather on her work table. She must have been in the middle of something when he'd interrupted her this morning.

The older man nodded. "And we need to be checking with Fitz about that other matter we discussed."

Thomas had inched forward just enough to reach the ledger when Stuart's words stopped him in his tracks. He glanced up and saw a look of knowing pass between the promoter and the boxer. Fitzsimmons? Other matter? Something was going down about the location. He felt it. Sensed that Laney somehow held the key.

"How's my order coming along, lass?" Maher asked. "Any trouble with what we discussed?"

Laney looked up and realized where Thomas stood. "Thomas, if you'll excuse us a moment and please step back around the counter, I'll show Mr. Maher what I've done."

She grabbed the ledger and put it in her apron, just as she'd put Thomas in his place. "No problem," he said, reluctantly taking a seat out front that had been provided for waiting customers.

Even Stuart and the trainer remained on this side of the counter.

Maher's and Laney's backs were now turned away from Thomas and he could only guess at what they were looking at. Suddenly one of the unshaped pieces of leather was flung over Laney's shoulder.

"Does that suit you?" she asked. "Meet with your specifications?"

Now, why didn't I look under that pile? Thomas berated himself. *Leave no stone unturned.* This delay was making him lazy. The woman was distracting him.

A moment passed before Maher's head bobbed. "It's exactly what we'll be needing, lass. Couldn't be better. You've a fine eye."

"I looked everywhere yesterday and spotted exactly what I thought you were wanting. It won't take nearly as much arranging as I assumed it might. I have a lot of sources I can use."

She's almost confessing her part in it!

"Can you complete the task by the end of the week, is what I need to know," Dan Stuart interjected. "A lot rides on it."

"Maybe sooner," Laney said, the piece of leather disappearing from her shoulder before both she and Maher turned around. She motioned for the boxer to lead the way around the counter. "It's not going to take anywhere near as long as I thought it might."

"Good." Stuart exhaled a long breath. "Pete's eyes are getting better by the day. Sooner is better on all accounts."

Maher glanced at Thomas and paused. "Don't I know you?"

Thomas stood, guessing that the game was up. Maher was no man's fool.

"He's a reporter. He wants to interview you."

"Stop by the Vendome at lunchtime. I grant interviews while I eat. You know their restaurant?"

"He knows," Laney answered for him.

Maher bid Laney good-bye and said he'd return tomorrow about the same time.

When the men had gone, Thomas stood. "Well, I guess I should thank you for setting that up for me."

Laney pulled the ledger from her pocket and set it on the counter. "You're welcome, *Ranger*."

Chapter 5

Sizing Up the Opponent

"How long have you known?" Thomas didn't even attempt to deny the charge. What surprised him was that she had elected not to confront him with the truth in front of the others. Stuart and Maher both would have been hot in their handlebars if they'd known he was a Ranger and they'd been discussing anything in front of him. He'd felt certain Maher had recognized him and had been ready to call him on it.

"Since last night at the Vendome." She motioned toward the door. "Are you ready to get down to business?"

Never were truer words spoken. "I am. Just what gave me away?" he asked, opening the door for her. She passed in front of him, making Thomas aware that the top of her head came to the tip of his nose. Strange, but he could have sworn she met him eye to eye every time he had looked at her previously. Laney O'Grady had that kind of effect on a man, he decided.

"You gave yourself away when you came to my defense so readily with my brother-in-law. You looked like the archangel Michael himself, ready to tear Dannell's soul out of him. That, with the fact that you sat with all those other men who were obviously some of the Texas Rangers we all know are in town, and the fact that you didn't have any writing material with you, I just put two and two together. What I haven't figured out yet is why you told me you were a reporter."

Her brother-in-law? That explained more clearly some of the conversation Thomas had overheard between them.

Laney strode over to the horse and began examining his old saddle. "Hmm . . . Good. It clears the withers. There's free movement of the shoulders and it's the proper shape and length for its back." She rocked it back and forth. "There's good weight distribution." Her amber eyes finally focused on Thomas. "Which means a proper-fitting saddle that really doesn't need to be replaced. So what's your true story, Ranger Longbow?"

"In the first place, I never said I was a reporter. You gave me the role."

Laney looked thoughtful. "I guess I did. And everything you said could have been associated with either job. So, you're apparently trained with words. Are you as good with explanations?"

He saw no further need to keep the truth from her and was suddenly glad he could be aboveboard about his visits. "I tailed Maher into your shop, suspected you were in cahoots with him about wherever they're going to move the fight, and ordered the saddle so I had a reason to be there whenever Maher was. As you obviously heard last night at the restaurant, I was assigned to tail you."

Anger clouded Laney's face. "I don't appreciate you misleading me, Mr. Longbow. I could have taken another order yesterday, but didn't because I assumed I could count on the income I would make from your saddle."

Her eyes closed for a moment, and he could tell from

her expression that she was willing herself not to lose her temper.

"I've already chosen the tree horn and started some of the drying and shaping of the bull hide for your piece." Exasperation filled her tone, despite her effort to remain calm.

She never said she was innocent of his suspicions about her, Thomas noted, but her argument with her brother-in-law was apparently foremost in her mind. "Is this about the money for the adoption?"

If a look could cut a man down to size, hers was as sharp as an axe. She headed back inside. Thomas reached out to gently stop her. "Wait, Laney. I couldn't help overhearing your conversation with this Dannell character, just like you couldn't help connecting me with the Rangers. So we're square. And don't worry, I ordered that saddle. I mean to pay for it." He could feel her resistance slowly ease beneath his fingertips. "Come measure my horse. He deserves something new."

Finally, after a long moment of decision making, she moved toward the bicycle tethered at the hitching post alongside Justice. "Turn my sign around on the door so everyone will know the shop is closed for a while. We're going to take a ride."

Thomas turned the OPEN sign to CLOSED and mounted. He watched as she straddled the strange-looking bicycle, revealing a lacy edge of those bloomers he'd heard were the new rage for women.

He hadn't much taken a position on them before, but if they afforded him a sight of such pretty calves and ankles, then he was all for them.

"Where are we headed?" he asked, noticing the flex and lift of her long legs as she rode. He couldn't help but wonder how far they might wrap around his own legs, if she lay beneath him. *Get your mind where it should be,* he told himself, urging Justice into a slow trot just to see if she could keep up with him. She did.

The woman had stamina. A dozen delightful ways to test just how much, pumped hotly through his veins.

"Nowhere particular. The fit of the saddle doesn't just depend on measurements or even the horse," she informed him as she rode. "It's also about you. The better you use your own body control and feel to let the animal know what you want, the easier the ride. I wanted to see your balance, the way you move with him, how you cue him." She eyed Thomas from hat to boot. "You sit with your shoulders, hips, and heels aligned. That makes a balanced riding position. That's why you've had a lot less wear on your animal and the saddle. All that makes a difference in how I'll build your new one. About the only thing you could use to improve what you already have is a little talcum powder."

"Talcum powder?" Thomas tried to determine just where her eyes were focused when she said that. He almost didn't see a groundhog mound in the path, and had to steer Justice away before he crippled the poor beast.

Laney swerved for a moment, then regained her position alongside the horse. She nodded at the front of the saddle, grinning. "Your fenders. The straps attached to the saddle tree. They're squeaking. Just sprinkle some powder on them and you won't squeak when you ride."

Thomas had noticed the squeak before, but it had never bothered him until now. With her eyes trained on the saddle as he rode, he became increasingly aware of how sensual the movement of riding was when someone else was looking at where he sat. Especially someone he'd wanted to kiss since the first time he laid eyes on her. "What do you say we head back in? I've got other business to attend to." *Like trying to get your eyes off my squeak before I embarrass myself.*

"Fine by me," she said. "I've got to get back to work

anyway. I've got lots to do between now and—" She looked like someone who had caught a particularly wily mouse. "I mean, I'm expecting an important visitor in about thirty minutes. So I best be getting back."

"Fitzsimmons or Maher?" Thomas asked. "Dan Stuart?"

She quit pedaling and he reined to a halt.

"As a matter of fact, it's a judge. Judge Townsend, to be exact." The arch of one brow lifted higher. "Care to ask him whether I'm a reliable citizen?"

"Tell me what this is all about, Laney, and maybe I won't be so mistrustful."

"It's about nothing. Mr. Maher ordered something from me, just like you did." She stared Thomas squarely in the eyes. "I'm just not at liberty to say what."

Damned but if she didn't look taller than she was again. "I'm not talking about you and Maher. I want to know about you and your conversation with your brother-in-law. I think I got most of it, but don't leave anything out."

To his surprise, she told him. He figured she might tell him what he could do with his nosiness. He hadn't missed much of the conversation last night, but the part that he had missed made him madder than hell at Dannell O'Grady and even more convinced that she had reason to be in cahoots with the boxers.

A woman wanting to get back a child whom she loved would definitely resort to any measure.

And he knew beyond a shadow of a doubt that he was going to help her get the boy.

Trouble was, he hoped she just didn't step over any boundary that would force him to have to arrest her before they found a way to rectify the issue and put Dannell O'Grady in his place . . .

Or before Thomas had a chance to kiss her.

Chapter 6

The Better Man

The ride back took longer than Laney had planned. The cross path was blocked by fun-making members of the McGinty Club, a group of lawyers, bankers, and other businessmen who had struck up a rousing march from the waterworks and were headed up El Paso Street, the city's main thoroughfare. They drove a buckboard adorned with signs that read BARBEQUED BURRO MEAT AND ICE WATER, items that would be for sale for the upcoming boxing match. Laney half expected to see Judge Townsend and Dannell among them. Both were active in the club and took great pleasure in having their turns at firing off the cannon on top of McGinty Hill to announce upcoming civic festivities.

"Looks like the town's gearing up for trouble tonight." Thomas motioned toward two of the officials who were sitting atop a hay bale inside the wagon, trying to pour whiskey into two glasses. "It's not even noon and they've already started celebrating."

"The fight won't happen tonight," Laney announced,

shaking her head at the men's foolishness. "They'll be wishing they had saved that for another time."

"You seem sure of that."

Thomas's eyes focused intently on her now, and Laney realized too late that she had disclosed information that she shouldn't have. He was too sharp not to pick up on her mistake. She thought fast. "I mean . . . well, you saw Mr. Maher's eyes yourself. He couldn't possibly fight tonight."

"Tell me what you know about the fight, Laney."

"I told you I can't tell—"

"You said you couldn't tell me about what Maher ordered." The eyes of a man intent on his mission stared at her, waiting. "We're talking about two different things."

Grateful that the revelers had finally passed, Laney pressed down on the pedals and deliberately rode ahead of the Ranger so she didn't have to meet his gaze. "I don't know anything other than what's been in the paper," she said over her shoulder. "Surely nothing to inspire all this suspicion."

"You didn't grow up here, did you?" he asked, catching up with her.

Thomas changed the subject so abruptly she wondered where this line of questioning was leading. Her mind raced to think of reasons the truth might work against her, but it didn't come up with any. So she answered him forthrightly. "My mother visited Kentucky. She met my father there and they married. He worked as a horse breeder for the O'Grady family and I grew up on their place. So I guess you'd say I'm from the East, but my heart is here in Texas."

The Ranger took a moment before continuing. "So you fell in love with one of the brothers, I take it. The wrong one, in Dannell O'Grady's opinion, from what I heard last night."

He'd heard more than she'd wanted him to. She had

meant merely to have the Rangers rescue her if Dannell got out of line. "I married his older brother, Marc."

"Is that what brought you to El Paso?"

That and a dozen other reasons, she remembered. "He was ill and needed a drier climate."

"His brother came with you?"

Laney pedaled harder, making Thomas urge the horse into a trot to keep up. "Not in the beginning. We had some wonderful years together." *Two miserable years since.* "He showed up at Marc's funeral to offer me marriage. I refused. He always assumed I would marry him instead of Marc because Marc was so much older than I, but Dannell never stood a chance. It didn't matter that Marc had already been married once. He was the better man. Dannell never accepted that I preferred someone else over him, even if it was his own brother. When I refused to marry him after Marc's death, he convinced a judge that he was the proper guardian for Gideon."

She didn't say how Dannell had gone about defaming her to the judge. That was too much hurt to deal with anymore. Frustration and anger caused bile to rise in Laney's stomach, but she willed it away. She would not let Dannell make her feel threatened anymore. She had the means to win Gideon and that's where her mind needed to focus now. The future, not the past.

"I'm sorry for your loss, Laney. If there's anything I can do to help you with the boy, just call on me."

Sincerity filled his tone. She liked that about him. One of the *many* things she had begun to find appealing about Thomas Longbow. Though she was exasperated by his persistence, she also respected that same determination. She could understand the need to follow something through. She'd been forced to be careful and calculating in her efforts to regain custody of Gideon since her husband's death. She'd let nothing sway her from her goal—not lack of money, not hard work, not a man who refused to keep his hands to himself. To ask Thomas to do less in a job that he had been assigned to do would have made him less of a Ranger. His persistence might aggravate her, but she couldn't fault him for being the man that he was.

"Just don't get in the way of what I need to do," she said quietly, her legs pedaling to punctuate her determination. "It's been a long, hard road to get him back." The first year had been the hardest, growing accustomed to not hearing Marc's and Gideon's playful banter in the shop as they all worked together to make it a success. Marc had been so proud to set up shop and pass down his saddle-making skills to his son. Gideon was more than a worshipful son, eager to show his incredible eye for detail and handiwork. As much as Marc had taught her his skills, Gideon promised to far outshine Laney.

"Marc was my best friend," she whispered. How could a total stranger understand what she felt? Yet Thomas didn't seem such a stranger anymore, and the need to tell someone just what Marc had meant to her bubbled over. "Living with the grief of losing a man like Marc has been nothing but hell on earth. He wasn't afraid to let me grow. I didn't just have to be his wife, a pretty thing on a man's arm."

She couldn't stop herself. The grief kept coming, pouring out of her in a rush of emotion that had lain dormant too long. "But do you know what it's like, losing a child you've come to love as your own? It's almost more than I can bear some nights. I lie awake listening for Gideon. The sound of his prayers as he said them before he went to bed. The gentle 'thank you' when I finished tucking him in. The sigh of relief when I told him that I would sit with him until the thunder and lightning rumbled away. All of that and a thousand memories more have haunted my nights."

Tears brimmed in her eyes. "I finally understand how

much Marc must have felt when he lost Sarah to childbirth. Only I lost *two* people I cared for."

Though Marc had never given Laney his true heart, she'd been happy to spend her life with such a good man. Their affection for each other had been growing and promised to one day become more, if she had been patient enough. But death was an impatient mistress and had taken him before they'd had a chance to become more than two people who had married to give each other companionship and to raise Gideon with two parents.

Laney braked and took her hand off the handlebar for a moment to wipe her eyes. Thomas reached out and grabbed the bicycle to steady it, forcing her to stop pedaling. She sensed his eyes focused on her but she couldn't meet his gaze, knowing she would lose her composure altogether if she stared into the intense gray depths. Instead, she focused her attention on his nice strong hand circling the handlebar. Always curious about people's hands, she held a particular interest in the way certain professionals required different shapes and lengths of fingers to handle a task adeptly. Now that she'd seen Pete Maher's boxing fists, Laney was even more aware of the strength of Thomas Longbow's solid grip. A grip that might have possibly killed a man before, for all she knew. A Ranger's firm, trustworthy hold.

"I'm going to be late," she whispered, gently nudging him and taking command of the bicycle.

She was surprised when he let go and said, "I'll meet you at the shop."

He reined his horse away and rode ahead.

Laney wished she could just veer and take the day off, but she couldn't. Judge Townsend would be there any moment to get the papers started, and she couldn't afford the day away from the leather. If Thomas was good as his word about really paying for the saddle, then it would take every bit of her time to get the saddle and boxing gloves done on time. She wished now that she hadn't told him how long it would take to complete the saddle, but he had seemed so insistent about having it done quickly. She suspected his rush had everything to do with when he felt the fight would occur.

When she arrived at the shop, Thomas stood at the hitching post waiting for her. He had already tethered his mount, and extended a hand to help her off the bicycle. He remained quiet for a moment, but his eyes softened in compassion as he said, "Thank you for sharing your story with me, Laney. I know that had to be hard for you. I thought you might want some time alone for those last few streets."

His thoughtfulness touched her heart as surely as his hand gathered hers to help her off the bicycle. Her stomach tightened as the warmth of his touch enveloped her. Looking into those intriguing gray eyes filled with compassion and understanding, it hit Laney with a force so stunning that she felt herself lean into him.

She knew now why she'd opened up to Thomas.

She could fall in love with him.

Like she had hoped to do with Marc.

Chapter 7

Getting In the Licks

Their gazes locked. Thomas gently urged her inside the shop, not bothering to close the door behind them. His gaze lowered to her mouth, lingered, then raised to rest on her again. He smiled and carried her hand upward, brushing her knuckles with his lips. "Laney, I'm going to kiss you."

Her pulse hammered. Trying to ignore it, she failed. "I know."

"You're so beautiful," he whispered, running his thumb over the pulse at her wrist.

To her dismay, it beat faster and even more erratically than the moment before, and she found herself impatient for the taste of him. "Thomas." She whispered his name in a heated rush.

He cupped her face in his hands and looked deeply into her eyes; then, ever so exquisitely, he lowered his lips to hers.

His lips were more skilled than his hands—firm, yet soft and warm. He took his time, gently urging her to yield to his masterful manipulation of her senses. She sighed as he tantalized her to open her mouth and allow him to deepen the kiss with a gentle sweep of his tongue. She gave in to the sensations swirling like warm eddies in her bloodstream, igniting heat in their wake. It was only a kiss. An impossible kiss that somehow answered every unasked question she had about passion . . . until now. Until Thomas.

Reason whispered for her to stop, that she was heading into trouble, that she hadn't thought things out clearly. But for once, she wanted nothing more than to be impulsive, to enjoy what she felt and not question it to death. Laney wrapped her arms around his neck and kissed him back, meeting his tongue with hers in a hungry lick and parry that made her eager for more. A torrent of heat hotter than a windstorm over the desert flared between them, setting his skin ablaze beneath her fingertips, radiating through the cloth of his shirt. His lips blazed a trail of kisses down her neck, making her gasp with the sheer want of him. She moaned as the sound of her name exited his lips in a rush of heat at the valley where her throat ended. Her fingers curled into the soft, silky black hair at the nape of his neck, urging him closer still. Longing for more, every nerve ending in her body tingled with anticipation.

The iron band of his arm pulled her closer, as if he couldn't get enough of the feel of her. She sensed his desperation to have no clothes between them, for she felt it too. Laney arched toward him, pressing her breasts against him, wanting more, afraid she would never know the true depth of the glorious feelings his touch had ignited within her. All reason insisted that she hold back, to withstand the sensual onslaught of his lips, but something other than good sense gave a strangled moan within her and she gave herself completely to his kiss, their tongues equal contenders in a tantalizing tangle.

Someone cleared his throat. Laney blinked away the haze that had enveloped her, suddenly aware once more of her surroundings. It took her a moment to realize that the masculine sound had not come from Thomas, rather from Judge Townsend, who stood in the doorway. To complete her dismay, Dannell was with him!

The heartbeat that had been thundering in her pulse felt as if it raced to sink into her feet. She pushed away from the wall of Thomas's chest, trying to straighten her hair, wipe the kiss off her lips, and find some reasonable explanation for her actions.

What am I doing? What must they be thinking? Dannell would use this public display against her to prove her unfit, and she could blame no one but herself. Yet she'd never known such desire as when Thomas had touched her. Not even with Marc. She'd never dreamed that a single touch could set her soul on fire as if it were a match struck aflame. She'd thrown caution to the wind, wanting nothing more than to make mad, sweet love to Thomas right there in her shop, and with no conscious thought as to who might come in. She'd known the Ranger little more than twenty-four hours and wanted to rip his clothes off.

If she couldn't get her feelings under control, what would they be doing by the time she finished the saddle?

"This won't happen again," she insisted aloud, not sure if she was trying to reassure the men, Thomas, or herself.

"It was only a kiss." Amusement filled Thomas's tone. "Don't look so devastated."

"It looked a good deal more than that." Dannell's red handlebar mustache puffed as he spoke, a slow flush of anger creeping up his neck to match his ruddy cheeks. "Did it to you, Judge Townsend?"

"We'll wait for you out here, Mrs. O'Grady"—the judge graciously did not take her brother-in-law's bait—"while you say your *good-byes* to your friend."

For once, her brother-in-law was right. That had been a lot more than a kiss to Laney. How could she have responded to Thomas so wantonly? "Thank you, Judge. I won't keep you waiting."

"Remember, we're busy men." Dannell gave her a warning look, then took a step backward when Thomas moved closer to him. "Don't take too long."

"She'll take as long as she needs." Thomas shot him a deadly glare that sent a shiver down Laney's spine. Dannell nearly stumbled over his fancy cane as he backed out of the door.

"I thought so." Thomas laughed. "A man like that's all jaw and no jugular."

He strolled back to Laney, and when she realized he was going to kiss her again, she stepped backward, throwing up her hands to ward him away. But Thomas would have none of it. He grabbed her hands, pulled her to him and wrapped them around his waist, kissing her quick and hard.

He finally let her go, but his gaze remained locked with hers. "Whatever hold that man thinks he still has on you, Laney, we'll handle . . . together. Just like we're going to handle whatever this is that's stirring up between you and me. You're attracted to me"—he traced a finger down her cheek and tapped her upper lip—"and I'm sure as hell attracted to you." His voice became whisper soft. "That brother-in-law of yours can bank on one thing . . . nothing will stop me from seeing where it's going to lead us."

She sucked in a deep breath as he left her arms, moved outside, and mounted his horse. As he rode away, the sight of him sitting powerfully and masterfully in his saddle thrilled her. Sleek, hard muscles, well-accustomed to handling whatever came their way, formed the man who had laid claim to her senses. She closed her eyes and swore to herself, knowing that the voice that had whispered to tread cautiously around the Ranger ever since she met him, now lay in the silent ashes of her will.

Thomas Longbow wasn't a man who made promises lightly and she was a woman who had yearned to know a man's burn.

Chapter 8

Come Out Fighting

Laney dreaded facing Dannell, knowing he would be waiting to attack her like a cougar cornering a field mouse. Oh, he would keep his hands to himself in front of Judge Townsend, but he would verbally criticize what he'd just seen. He never missed an opportunity to make her look bad, mistakenly believing it made him look better. Not that she needed any help putting her reputation in question this morning. She'd done that well enough herself.

That kiss. That wonderful, glorious kiss. Why couldn't she get it and Thomas Longbow out of her mind? Why had she forgotten the time? Now she'd made a fool of herself in front of the judge and Dannell, of all people.

Her lips still tasted of Thomas. Warm, salty-sweet, masculine. A rush of heated thoughts threatened to redden her cheeks as Laney pretended to be in deep concentration when the two men entered the shop. She quickly excused herself to give her cheeks time to quit blushing. "I need to jot down some details concerning my last order before I forget them."

"I dare say you made fast friends with that stranger."

Disdain filled Dannell's tone. "I don't recall seeing him with you before yesterday."

"I make friends easier than some people," she said, scribbling down the mental measurements she'd taken into account for Thomas's saddle before she forgot them. *And we know who one of those "some people" are, don't we, Dannell,* she thought, hoping he recalled the list of names on the last page of the papers she'd shown him. Did he really want to play word games?

Laney hoped this new explanation would sit well with the judge and make Dannell think twice about saying any more. "Besides, if you'll remember, I needed to thank the man for rescuing me last night."

She glared at her brother-in-law, silently daring him to give her reason to tell the judge what had happened at the Vendome dining room.

Dannell's brow furrowed, his eyes taking on a hard glint. "I should think a handshake would have been sufficient."

Judge Townsend rose from the seat he'd taken on the bench and moved over to the counter, doffing his hat and offering a gentlemanly smile. "I don't know that I wouldn't have asked the same, if I were a younger man."

Laney smiled up at him. "I appreciate your understanding, Your Honor. And I'm sure Mrs. Townsend thinks you're just the right age for her."

They shared a laugh.

Laney had hoped she could count on the judge's good sense. Of all the litigators she had talked to regarding her desire to win custody of Gideon, Judge Townsend had been the one who had given her most hope. She was about to put her dreams in his hands and she hoped she could trust him to see through Dannell's manipulations.

"How can I be of help to you, my dear?" The judge took out his pocket watch and checked the time. "I agreed to stop by for a few minutes, but even that has been cut short, I'm afraid. Your brother-in-law informs me that I'm needed at the McGinty Club. It seems William Barclay Masterson is arriving from Denver and is to be the chosen referee for tonight's fight."

"Bat Masterson?" she asked, recognizing the name of the lawman who helped to settle Kansas.

"The same. I have the dubious honor of telling Mr. Masterson that his actions go against the peace and dignity of the great state of Texas, and that he will not be able to take that role upon himself. Tonight or any other night, for that matter."

"I don't know, Judge." Dannell shook his head. "The great citizens of El Paso are ready to flex their muscles too. Those two fighters are idolized by every wide-eyed boy, gambler, and sports fan on both sides of the border. Even the ladies are putting their forty cents down for a ticket. Not to mention the governor's own wife, Sally, isn't opposed to the contest. She says her husband was elected to carry out the will of the people, and we people have the right to what we want. How are you going to stop the inevitable?"

"Don't mistake me. I want the fight as well as any man. It's big business for the stores."

Dannell rocked back on his heels. "I know it's been good money for my businesses on Utah Street."

Your bawdy houses, you mean. Laney shot him a look of disgust. Why wasn't anyone up in arms about *that* kind of entertainment in town?

"The city has swollen to about twenty thousand people," the judge continued. "That makes for filled-up rooms and lodging houses. But there's more to this than making a simoleon. I'm hoping you all will have the good sense not to take on the Rangers. They've been ordered to shoot to kill first and arrest afterwards."

Laney couldn't hide her shock. "Surely not. There will be women and children among the spectators."

"Ask any one of them yourself," Dannell complained. "You seem to know one or two of them, it seems."

She would ask the one she knew. She couldn't imagine Thomas Longbow harming a child . . . but then, she didn't really know him at all.

So at least Dannell knew that Thomas was a Ranger. Maybe he wouldn't be so quick to cause her problems if he thought she and Thomas were something more than acquaintances. No—Laney shook her head—she wouldn't use Thomas like that. She'd fight her own battles.

"Mr. Longbow is the only one I know personally, and it's thanks to him that I can finally do this." She reached into the cabinet below the counter and pulled out a strongbox. "The reason I asked you to stop by, Your Honor, is that I have those papers we discussed, and some money up front to begin the process."

Judge Townsend scanned the paper, focusing on the last page. He shot a glance at Dannell then back to Laney. "I assume the two of you have discussed this together."

"We tried," Laney informed him, "but we didn't have much success with the talk."

Dannell cleared his throat as if something were caught in it, then said, "I thought we could discuss this further on the way to the McGinty Club. I believe my sister-in-law has taken liberties with some of the names on that list, and we should go talk to them together to see if there have been any . . . shall we say, *favors* offered for supporting her cause."

"How dare you accuse me of such things." Laney looked around for something to throw at him, but decided giving in to her rage would just prove her unable to handle this like an adult. "I believe if His Honor took a good look into your background, he'd discover whose favor you've been courting on Utah Street."

"I hope your sister-in-law is not correct in her accusation." Judge Townsend's face took on a stern expression. "You know what I've told you in the past regarding that matter. We're trying to put an end to the tenderloin district, and if I find out you're in any way involved with all of that, I will invoke your brother's will sooner. All she has to do is prove herself as a fit provider for her and the boy. These signatures suggest a very strong case not only against you, but for her right to custody."

Tears raced from her heart to well in her eyes, but Laney willed them back. She wouldn't let Dannell see her cry. No matter that these were tears of triumph. She hadn't won yet. She still had to finish the gloves and saddle. "Thank you, Judge Townsend. I was hoping that's what you'd say. I'll have the rest of the money to you in a matter of days. I just have two more orders to fill before I have it all."

If looks could burn, Dannell's fiery glare would have set her aflame.

"Then I'll take this with me, Mrs. O'Grady." The judge put the papers and deposit money inside a pocket of his frock coat. "I'll read over your petition more carefully this evening. Hopefully, I can get this Masterson situation under control and won't have to be dealing with a fight on my hands tonight."

"I can almost guarantee you won't," Laney said, knowing that Pete Maher would never agree to the battle until he had his lucky gloves. She needed the rest of the evening to finish them, maybe part of tomorrow morning.

"Sounds like you know something," the judge teased. "If you do, keep it to yourself. The less I know, the less likely I'll have you arrested."

"She doesn't know any more than anyone else," Dannell muttered, whining like a boy who'd been bested. "I'll bet she doesn't even know they've got a boxcar, filled with a circus tent and lumber, located where it can be attached to any rail line leading out of here. It's going to be used to build the arena." He raised his eyes to Laney and smiled smugly. "I'll bet even your Ranger doesn't know that Fitz has ordered it to be moved tonight."

"Tonight?" Laney asked. "Are you sure Mr. Fitzsimmons said tonight?"

"I heard him and Dan Stuart himself talking about it at Pete Young's pool hall." Haughtiness filled his features as he relayed information the judge apparently had not been aware of. "Fitz said that his wife and new baby would have to go back to the training quarters in Juarez tonight because he would be taking care of some business down at the rail yard. They talked a great deal about the car with the tent and the lumber being moved. They just didn't say where."

If moving the railcar meant the fight would happen tonight, she had to convince Mr. Maher to stop it. The gloves weren't ready. If he was forced to fight with another pair, she wouldn't get the bonus. She wouldn't have enough money to finish paying the custody-trial expenses.

She had to find where the boxer had gone for the day. "You wouldn't have any idea where I can find Pete Maher at the moment, would you?"

Judge Townsend nodded. "As a matter of fact, I do. He's meeting some reporters at Mrs. Darrow's shooting gallery. You'll find him there." He winked at her. "Despite what your relative thinks, I do keep track of the players in the game. I just don't know how long he'll be there."

Just so he's there long enough for me to catch him in time, Laney prayed, glad when the pair said they had to be on their way.

Chapter 9

Fancy Footwork

After lunch, Thomas was ready for Maher to head back to Las Cruces, but it looked as if the boxer had plans to spend all day in El Paso. For someone nursing sore eyes, Maher was getting around just fine. Thomas had wanted to go back to the shop and see how Laney had fared with her appointment with the judge, and find out why Dannell had tagged along, but he'd been instructed to keep a particular watch on Maher today.

Something was definitely on the stir. General Mabry had called a handful of Rangers to the rail yards to keep an eye on a boxcar that held the circus tent and lumber that was to be used to build the boxing arena. Word among the reporters tailing Maher was that the car could take track the moment any decision was made to move the fight somewhere outside of El Paso. With five trunk lines feeding the border town, the battle could be sent in any direction. Posting guards around the clock seemed the wisest and most logical move to make.

Thomas's assignment now seemed the lesser of those being dealt to others of his corps, and normally he would have minded being left out of the hub of action, but playing nursemaid to a railcar held no appeal at the moment. At least following Maher provided a bit of unusual entertainment and kept boredom at bay.

The Irish boxer seemed intent upon focusing his mending eyes and trying his very famous hands at hitting one of the targets in the two-million-dollar automatic shooting gallery, the only one of its kind in the entire world. Thomas stretched out his long legs in the booth and watched as a crowd of men placed bets as to how many targets the boxer would hit without missing. Considering his limited vision, the bets abounded. Thomas thought of it as a game for starched-collar men. Trying to make a musical maid beat a kettle drum, plug a trumpeter so he'd blow a bugle call, or catch an Italian spaghetti maker in the breadbasket seemed a lazy man's attempt at earning bragging rights.

He could think of a better way to spend his afternoon. Like kissing a cinnamon-haired beauty until she melted into sweet surrender. Laney had tasted like pure adventure taken human form, and he couldn't wait to see where that took them. He'd wanted to sweep her up into his arms, take her in and lock the shop door, and spend the afternoon showering her with bone-melting kisses. And he would have. She had wanted him to. He had tasted it in her kiss, felt it in the way she'd not shied away from stoking the fire that had burned between them. But that brother-in-law of hers had shown up. The man was getting to be a burr in Thomas's boot.

If Maher would ever call it a day, Thomas planned to pay Mr. Dannell O'Grady a visit and see what his problem was.

"Hey, there's a lion loose!" someone yelled, running in from the street. "And a nanny goat is chasing him. Somebody call the constable."

A dozen men ran to the door, reporters readying their Kodaks for a picture of the newsworthy excitement.

Thomas jumped up from the booth and shouldered his way through the crowd, but the reporters wouldn't get out of the way. "Move," he ordered, drawing his revolver to raise it and fire a warning shot, if necessary.

"No need to waste good gunpowder, lad," Maher called from behind him. "You'll have to square off with Fitz if you shoot his sparring partner. That two-hundred-pound puss is Nero, his pet. Bob will be following, you can bet on it."

"That goat must be Princess," the reporter in front of Thomas quickly informed everyone. "Baby Bob Jr.'s milk supply. Wonder what Nero did to butt horns with her?"

"Hey, Maher, you're right as daylight. Here comes Fitz. He's running like a steam engine," said another onlooker. "And there's two fellas chasing him."

Rangers, Thomas knew without seeing. The two assigned to follow Fitzsimmons. He put his gun away, backing off to let them do their job. They didn't need three heroes chasing a lion on the loose.

"He's going to try to tackle the beast. Get out of my way so I can get a picture," one of the reporters marveled, jockeying into position for a better shot. "My readers won't believe this."

Other reporters jotted down facts as fast as they could on anything they could get their hands on.

Maher laughed at the men standing in awe at the doorway and window of the gallery. He squinted and took a perfectly aimed shot at the metal trumpeter. "It's the goat he better take down for the count first. Remember, you said that Princess was chasing Nero."

A ferocious roar rent the air, echoing in unison with the trumpeter's bugle. One of the onlookers turned around and sputtered, "How'd you know that, Pete? That goat just butted ol' Nero in his hindsight. That big kitty is one mad puss."

"That's what I said, lads." Maher's eyes twinkled with challenge. "Ruby Bob Fitzsimmons doesn't know how to deal with us old goats just yet."

Everybody laughed, including Thomas.

The crowd watched the scene play out in the streets, calling back the details of the unusual battle between lion and goat. A mighty paw swung, a goat dodged and butted the cat in the side. Nero let out another mighty roar.

All of a sudden one of the men in the crowd started yelling, "Look out, lady! Go the other way!"

Like a giant wave rushing away from shore, the crowd was on the move, a hundred men sweeping out of the gallery door, taking Thomas with it.

"She can't hear us," a reporter yelled. "She's got her head down against the wind, pedaling for all she's worth."

"He'll tear her limb from limb." Panic filled another man's tone. "He tore Fitz's bicycle in two back in December, remember? Chewed it in half, he did."

Thomas's heartbeat thundered in his veins as every sense went into danger alert. A woman. On a bicycle. An enraged male African lion ready to mangle. *Please God, please don't let it be her. Don't let it be Laney.*

He shoved his way into the street, running as hard as he could, drawing his weapon and straining his eyes to catch sight of the woman.

Apparently God was busy and wasn't listening.

"Laney, for God's sake, look up!" Thomas yelled, taking deadly aim at the lion. *Put one scratch on her and I'll cut you up and serve you to that damned goat for dinner,* he vowed silently. "There's a lion in the street!"

She glanced up and froze, her body jerking forward as she stopped pedaling. He feared she might go over the handlebars. The lion caught sight of the bike and leapt. The goat took off down a side street. Thomas started to squeeze the trigger when Bob Fitzsimmons's back suddenly came into view.

Thomas's finger jerked away, trembling at what he'd almost done. Fitzsimmons tackled Nero and took him down. The two Rangers who'd been giving chase had to stop abruptly. They lost their footing and went head over boot.

Thomas's hand shook as he realized that if he had fired the shot, the bullet would have hit Laney, not the downed lion. He ran as fast as he could toward her, calling her name, telling her everything would be all right.

She seemed in a daze, white knuckles clutching the handlebars, her normally rosy cheeks now ashen.

He finally reached her, shoving aside the two Rangers who had regained their footing and were trying to get her to move to a safer place. "Stand back, everyone," he ordered, authority ringing in his voice. "She knows me. She'll listen to me."

The crowd who had finally caught up with him gave him no argument, keeping a respectable distance.

"Laney, it's me, Thomas," he said gently, touching her death grip on the handlebar, trying to make it ease. "You're safe now."

A visible shudder traveled from the top of her head to her shoes as her eyes blinked and finally focused on him. "Thomas?"

He took her hand and gently tugged, urging her to move off of the bicycle.

"I need to tell Maher that I'm not done with the gloves," she whispered. "He can't fight tonight. He's got to stall the fight."

"I'll tell him," he assured her, knowing she was not really hearing him, but sensing that she needed some kind of reassurance.

Relief eased her features for a fragmented moment, then her body shuddered once more and crumpled into his arms.

Chapter 10

The Gloves Come Off

Someone was watching her. Laney sensed it even as she fought to open her eyes. Her lashes parted, only to blink rapidly at the sight before her. A vaulted ceiling of some kind. Pleated patterns of light on the wall. The strange odor of cigar smoke and something musky and male.

"Laney. Laney, you've got to wake up, love," she heard a familiar voice say, yet she couldn't place to whom it belonged. She blinked again, trying to stir her memory. Hoping to remember who loved her.

"She's coming around," someone announced.

"Get her some water," someone else suggested. Men, she decided from the deep tones that echoed in her ears. I'm in the company of men.

"Help her sit up." A feminine voice took charge. "And all of you back away. You'll scare her to death."

Several voices blended now, making her aware that many people were with her. It was then Laney realized that she was lying on something hard. Her fingertips reached out to test the edges of her bed and discovered that it was not very wide and somehow elevated. She was inside a building somewhere, of that she was almost certain. But hadn't she been outside, pedaling her way up . . . ?

"A lion!" she gasped, jerking to a sitting position. She started swinging, defending herself against the lion she believed was charging her. "There's a lion in the street, watch—"

"Whoa there, feisty." An arm swept her sideways, pulling her into a broad, comforting wall of flesh. "You're safe, Laney. It's all right. The lion's been caught."

"Thomas?" She recognized him now, her fists uncurling and her fingers racing to grab hold of him. Relief coursed through her as the quiet strength of his voice offered reassurance and calmed the uncertainty of not knowing for sure where she was and how she had reached safety.

"I'm here, Laney. I won't leave you."

"Tell us what you thought when you saw that beast charging you," a man asked, a sudden flash from a camera sending a puff of smoke into the air.

A hundred voices seemed to mingle at once, volleying question after question in Laney's face. Reporters, crowding in to get the details. She was in a room full of reporters ready for an outrageous headline. "Get away from me." She glared at them, wanting to do nothing but bury her head into the protective wall of Thomas's chest, but refusing to allow the newshounds to swoop down upon her. Still, she could understand their curiosity. Who would have believed such a thing could happen, and in El Paso, Texas, of all places!

"You heard the lady. Get out . . . now!" ordered Thomas, the muscles beneath Laney's fingertips hardening into granite. Though he stood like a warrior now, ready for the fight, he held her securely. "Wait outside."

"Let me down." Laney pushed Thomas's hand away and swung her legs around to get off the table that had become her makeshift bed. She was in some kind of parlor. A man's gaming parlor. A quick glance at the lettering on the front windows revealed it was a shooting gallery. There was only one such place in El Paso. The lady's voice she heard must have been Mrs. Darrow's.

"You have no say in keeping us from getting our story," argued the reporter who had taken the picture. "You just want an exclusive."

Others mumbled their agreement.

Thomas's hand dipped into a pocket inside his vest and tossed something on the table. "I have all the say I want."

"He's a Ranger," said the echo over the gallery as Laney caught sight of the silver star that lay there for all to see.

"A Ranger?" Pete Maher's voice moved through the crowd. "Let me see."

The crowd parted and allowed the boxer to come face-to-face with Thomas. Laney's heart quickened as she realized that Mr. Maher might not be pleased to discover that a Ranger had been following him all this time. Would he wonder why she hadn't told him of Thomas's true identity?

It was then that memory struck her, full-blown. She had told Thomas why she was pedaling so hard. She had whispered why she needed to find Mr. Maher. Now Thomas knew about the gloves.

"So you're the one." Pete eyed Thomas from head to foot. "I heard two of you boyos were assigned to shadow me. I figured out your Las Cruces man from day one, but you I wasn't sure about until today." His gaze swept to Laney. "Is the lass in cahoots with you?"

The gloves. Laney's stomach churned and she found it difficult to concentrate. Now he would never buy them. She wouldn't get the bonus money. Gideon might be lost to her forever. Suddenly she felt more vulnerable than the moment before, when she'd faced the wall of reporters.

"I told you vultures to get out." Thomas's voice thundered off the gallery walls. Several reporters didn't need any further argument from him and rushed outside. For those who dawdled, Thomas rested his hand on his gun and finished his warning. "The lady and Mr. Maher have business to discuss. I insist that the rest of you let them do that alone."

The remainder of the crowd did as the Ranger ordered, but a few brave souls pressed their noses up against the windowpanes to peer in. Mrs. Darrow brought in a pitcher and water glasses and set them on the table, then hurried back into the room that must have served as some kind of kitchen.

Thomas poured a glass of water for Laney and handed it to her, then held out a chair for her to sit in. When she took her seat and drank from the glass, she watched both men over its rim.

"Water?" Thomas asked, pouring a glass for Maher.

The boxer accepted it and drank it in a matter of gulps, then wiped his mouth with his sleeve. "Thanks. Now that we've got the pleasantries over with, lad, I'd like an answer to my question. Is she part of your scheme?"

Thomas shook his head. "Mrs. O'Grady is only guilty of whatever the two of you've designed together."

The boxer didn't look convinced. "Then why did she let me think you were a reporter instead of letting me know your real profession?"

Thomas told the truth. "Because that's what I led her to believe. I believe you pugilists call it a feint."

Maher smiled, relieving the tension that Laney could almost taste in the air between the two men. "Well, you're good at it, lad. Fooled me, you did, and I'm not an easy taker." His gaze swept over Laney appreciatively. "She's one worth protecting, from the look of her. My gloves would come off, too, for someone like her. You're a lucky man."

Laney realized what the boxer was saying. Thomas

had put his job on the line. He'd revealed himself to all concerned and now everything he did from here on in during his stay in El Paso would be met with caution from others. His job would be much harder because of her. No more easy discussions around him, thinking he was just a curious reporter ready to encourage the fight to take place so he could entertain his readers. They all now knew that he would stop the fight by any means possible.

He had not hesitated to protect her, despite the cost to himself personally. She needed to repay him somehow for that extraordinary act of kindness. But how? What could a man like Thomas Longbow possibly need?

The two men started quietly discussing Laney making the gloves for Maher. Unfortunately, Laney was still too out of it to understand what they were saying, and others in the gallery could hear them addressing the pros and cons of having the fight. Laney thought of all the things she'd learned about Thomas since meeting him. There really wasn't much about the Ranger that hinted at something he might need or want, other than the clear message that he wanted to make more of the kiss they'd shared.

Laney couldn't allow her thoughts to linger there or the men would surely think she'd taken on the vapors again. She forced herself to concentrate on other aspects of Thomas and what she knew of him. The one thing that seemed to consume the Ranger was his role in making sure the fight did not take place, and the delay that meant keeping him in El Paso. Well, despite what he thought, she didn't really know when the battle would occur, only that Maher planned for it to happen. Otherwise, the boxer wouldn't be going to so much trouble in getting a new pair of gloves.

The one thing Laney did know for certain was that the fight couldn't take place tonight. She wasn't finished with the gloves and she needed one more night to complete them. Maybe that's all she could give Thomas—one more fight-free night.

"Mr. Maher." She interrupted the men's discussion. "I was headed here to let you know that your order won't be finished before tomorrow." She eyed Thomas cautiously to see if he would divulge what she had whispered to him in a state of mindless fear. "I had heard that you might need that order tonight, but I'm afraid there's no way it can be completed by then."

Thomas remained silent, and Laney could only thank him silently for not speaking up to ask more. For whatever reason, he was continuing to protect her from losing the order.

Peter Maher frowned, making Laney finally aware that his eyes were better than when she'd seen them earlier that morning. Had the rumors been true? Was the boxcar Dannell had mentioned being put into position for a rendezvous tonight? Had Mr. Maher been ready to meet Fitz? How would he react to this delay?

The boxer's gaze swept from Laney to Thomas then back again, as if he were eyeing future opponents and gauging their abilities. "In the morning it will be, then, lass," he agreed. "I'll check and see how it's coming, say around seven o'clock." One of his fists pounded into the open palm of his other hand, offering a resounding *thwack* that echoed over the parlor. "That sound too early for you, Ranger?"

"You're not going to make it easy for me, are you?" Thomas laughed, though his eyes were sharp with intent.

Laney watched as Pete Maher reached over and grabbed the silver badge off the table, flipped it to Thomas, and said, "Easy's for lesser men. And it wouldn't be me I'd spend my time following, Ranger." He stopped at the door before opening it to the horde of reporters who waited outside. "I'd not let that pretty little scrapper out of my sight, if I were you. Even if she isn't any good at lying."

At the sound of swishing skirts in the room just beyond the front gallery, Laney's head turned. Mrs. Darrow. She'd forgotten about the gallery owner. She must have overheard everything. No telling who would now learn about the situation. And worst of all, Mrs. Darrow and Dannell were friends.

"*Seven*'s perfect," Pete Maher stressed.

She realized that he'd deliberately chosen tomorrow's time for more reason than to pester Thomas. He was reminding her that it was all right if someone had discovered what he'd ordered. He just wanted to make sure the exact design of seven shamrocks was kept secret.

Chapter 11

Sidestepping

The Chinese inhabitants of El Paso were in full throttle celebrating their New Year, the Year of the Monkey, and weaving their parade through downtown. The "Celestials," as the local paper called them, were not the only ones causing distraction for the sleepless Texas Rangers.

Under the alert noses of the Ranger force stationed at the rail head, Dan Stuart and his associates had still managed to move out enough lumber and men to build not one, but two dummy boxing rings as decoys. No one could find the railcars containing the tent, lumber, and movie equipment.

Thomas had barely seen Laney back to the shop when General Mabry called a meeting with him and the other men assigned to Maher and Fitzsimmons. The Vendome looked more like a command center now than a hotel. One look at General Mabry's fierce expression when Thomas entered the dining room would have warned off any man with a shred of sense about him. Thomas didn't envy whoever had caused Mabry's sour mood.

"I've called you in to let you know there's word out that

the fight's going down tonight. One of the cars has been moved north of Juarez near the New Mexico line, and the other, three-and-a-half miles downriver in Mexico. Some local men say it's to take place between those two stone monuments that are about six miles apart and mark the border between Texas and Mexico. Stuart's thinking about moving the markers so the confluence of the three territories can meet smack dab in the center."

"I can just hear the papers now." One of the Rangers grinned. "Maher rushed Fitzsimmons in New Mexico, but Fitz dodged away and dashed into Texas." His grin instantly faded at the glare issuing from his superior officer.

"Stuart's playing a shell game with us," Mabry continued. "Now you see it, now you don't. He's been shifting the cars around on various sidings, shuffling them in among others, always one step ahead of us when we think we have them cornered." His voice thundered with anger. "Just when we're sure we have the right car, we open it and there isn't any gear to be found."

"I'm certain the fight's not happening tonight, General." Thomas spoke up, wishing he didn't have to bring Laney into the conversation but knowing duty required it.

"You know something we don't?" General Mabry's attention leveled on Thomas.

Thomas nodded. "That lead you have me investigating is making Maher a pair of boxing gloves. I can't say for certain, but I believe he won't agree to the fight without them. And I know for a fact that she's not done with them."

"The man has one pair of gloves?"

Thomas shook his head. "No, I've seen him spar with others, but something about the ones she's making for him is forcing Maher to wait before he takes on Fitzsimmons."

"I hope you're right, Longbow, but we've got to be

prepared in the event you're wrong. Do you know when she's supposed to be done with them?"

"In the morning." Thomas knew Laney would never forgive him for what he'd just done. "About seven."

"Then we've got what we want from her. I'm taking you off this business with the woman after she hands him those gloves, and I want you focusing all your attention on Maher. I don't want him making a single move that you and Ted here can't confirm." He gave the same instructions to the two Rangers shadowing Fitzsimmons, then told all four men to report back by midnight unless they were knee-deep in canvas and camera equipment.

Thomas reluctantly left the meeting and found where Pete Maher was having supper. By the time he reported in to General Mabry at midnight, followed the boxer wherever he intended to spend the night, and tracked him to the meeting with Laney at seven, he was in for a very short night.

Maher took a good while to eat, giving Thomas plenty of time to think about being pulled away from his investigation of Laney. Tomorrow would be the last time he'd see her. The last time he'd get a chance to see if she was all right and . . . and . . . well, to let her know she'd come to mean something to him.

But what? What could she mean to a man like him? A man with no roots. A man who wouldn't know the first thing about helping raise a child she so obviously wanted. A man whose one true strength was always being able to leave everything behind and ride on to the next adventure without any second thoughts. Maybe General Mabry had done him a big favor by ordering him away from Laney. Maybe he wasn't meant to have a woman like her in his life.

Twilight deepened to night and the sound of firecrackers brought Thomas out of his gloomy thoughts. Colorful flares lit the streets and dancing Chinese dragons made out of vibrant cloth wove their way in front of the windows. Interested in the revelry, the boxer left the remainder of his meal and strode to the door to watch with all the other on-lookers.

Thomas moved near Maher so he wouldn't disappear into the crowd. To his surprise, he noticed Dannell O'Grady marching along with the group of photographers who were part of the team of filmmakers who had brought the new Kinetoscope. What was he doing with them? The man always seemed to show up in the oddest places. Something didn't sit well with Thomas about O'Grady's presence among the photographers, but he couldn't leave Maher to find out more. He had a strong suspicion that he might have been investigating the wrong O'Grady all this time. He'd bet odds that the brother-in-law knew when the fight would occur.

Dannell noticed Maher watching the procession and waved his cane at the boxer. "Hey, Pete, come and go to the depot with us. Fitz is boarding one of the trains. Want to be there to help us see him off?"

A near riot ensued as people caught wind of Dannell's words and speculated at their hidden meaning. Maher vanished into the crowd, with Thomas in hot pursuit. People flocked from every side street, joining the parade. Dancing cloth dragons caused a maze of confusion, making it difficult to get anywhere fast. In a matter of minutes, a thousand people had joined the throng moving toward the depot platform where Fitz and Maher were supposed to meet up with each other. Half-a-dozen Rangers tried to control the gathering crowd. Dannell shoved his way onto the train, while others tried to board even as the conductor yelled, "All aboard!"

The train began to chug away before Maher could reach it, but the boxer suddenly halted in his tracks and started laughing uproariously. Thomas thought the man had lost his mind until he noticed what had caught Maher's humor. As the train pulled out, the notorious lion-taming opponent hopped off and waved to the departing Pullman. The rumor had all been a ruse!

The people who had tried so hard to make the train but couldn't, muttered under their breaths as Fitzsimmons strolled up to Maher and shook his hand. "Ever feel like the mouse that just made the cat chase his tail?" he asked, roaring with laughter. He gave his competitor a wink. "Proves my point, doesn't it. There's still plenty who want to see this thing come off. Don't let Stuart talk you down on your fee." He punched Maher good-naturedly on the shoulder. "We're still worth all this wait."

For two men whose goal was to beat the kingdom come out of each other, the pair of boxers seemed bosom buddies on the issue of keeping the rumor mill active and turning. Thomas considered Maher above such antics but, he supposed, with all this current controversy over his profession, the man had to keep things stirred up or lose the battle against the politicians.

Thankfully, Maher called it a night just before Thomas was due for his meeting with General Mabry, and Thomas was able to show up on time.

"Where's Sawyer?" General Mabry asked when Thomas and the men who were tracking Fitzsimmons arrived.

"Last time I saw him, he was on the Silver City Special," Thomas informed him. "Maher gave him the slip. Sawyer thought Maher was heading in to Las Cruces."

General Mabry was not pleased, and Thomas was glad he wouldn't be in Sawyer's boots when the man checked in with the general.

"I'm calling in Fitzsimmons and Maher in the morning after that meeting with the glove maker," the general informed them. "They're gonna know we'll board all trains at all hazards and keep a'coming. I'm tired of being laughed at. By them and everyone else who's got a hand in all this side play. I'll revoke those orders to fire high, gentlemen, if there is any more counterplay against us. I have the authority from the president himself to shoot the principals first, and fire on anyone trying to help second. Make that clear to everyone. And Longbow . . ."

"Yes, General?"

"That includes glove makers."

Chapter 12

Hitting Below the Belt

"Laney?"

Laney shifted in her work chair and laid down the glove she'd been working on. She stretched tired shoulders and yawned, exhausted from more than eight hours of working without a break. But she was almost done. All the padding had been stitched in. Seven lucky shamrocks on the right, six on the left. Just one more to go.

Uncertain that someone had actually called her name, she stood and moved into the front room of the shop. It had to be at least two-thirty in the morning. Maybe she'd only imagined the voice on the wind. Besides, who could possibly be paying a call at this time of morning. And for that matter, why?

"Laney, open up." The whisper came again, this time more adamant. Caution flared within and warned her to be careful about opening her door. No telling how many others now knew she was making Mr. Maher's gloves. She edged back the curtain to the front window and looked out.

Dannell. Standing there in his business clothes and cane. She expected him to be less sturdy on his feet, and in his usual alcoholic stupor by now. That alone should have been enough to make her go back to work and leave him standing there. But the light from the gas streetlamps revealed a strangely sober, panic-stricken face. She didn't trust him paying such an untimely call, but the fear that something might be wrong with Gideon overruled caution.

Her fingers trembled as she grabbed the key to the shop from her apron pocket and struggled to unlock the door. "Is it Gideon?" she asked, dreading to hear his reply, yet knowing that in past troubles Gideon had always counted on her to come to his aid, not his uncle.

Dannell pushed his way inside, not giving her time to stand aside. She stumbled backward, but he reached out and grabbed her wrist to keep her from falling.

"You've got to come with me," he demanded. "There's trouble."

Laney didn't ask any questions and didn't take time to lock the door. She allowed him to pull her outside to the waiting hansom, knowing he had no knack for manners when he could not handle a situation well. At least he had the presence of mind to come get her so she could handle whatever was happening.

A million thoughts raced through her mind as she took a seat beside him. Was Gideon hurt? Was he ill? If so, how could they get to him in time? She finally found her voice. "Is it Gideon? Is he all right?"

"I told him we'd call him back."

Dannell patted her hand to offer comfort, but she quickly jerked it away. They both might share affection for Marc's son, but she didn't trust Dannell enough to accept his show of reassurance.

"Then he's not . . . He's alive and talking?" The worst of her fears were eased now. A broken arm, a bruised ego, trouble with a headmaster at school, or anything else Gideon suffered she knew she could endure, but the possibility of losing him like she had lost Marc was almost unthinkable.

"Alive? Of course, my dear." Dannell tapped the roof of the hansom with his cane. "To the Vendome Hotel, driver."

When he saw the look of surprise cross Laney's face, Dannell explained, "I would have told you immediately if the boy had been killed. He's just in a little trouble and I'm afraid it's something I have no time to deal with. You and your work with Maher have made a lot of trouble for me that you can't even imagine, Killaney. I told Gideon that I would get you and the two of you could work his trouble out over the phone."

Anger welled inside Laney, making her wonder whether this phone conversation was meant to help Gideon or get her to Dannell's hotel room. "And the phone I'm to use is in your room, I suppose?" she asked suspiciously.

"Where else at this time of morning, my dear?" Dannell sounded as if she had lost her only sense. "We wouldn't want to make family improprieties public knowledge, would we?"

He'd never thought twice about any of his own improprieties. Whatever a twelve-year-old boy might have done could hardly be considered reputation killing. "I'll make the call to Gideon in the lobby," she insisted, knowing full well if Dannell managed to get her alone in his room, he would try to take advantage of her. "I know for a fact there's a phone by the dining hall. If anyone cares to listen in, I'll give them an earful when I'm finished talking with Gideon."

She couldn't hide her disgust, now that she knew Gideon was not in any real danger. "I've got customers who are going to be plenty upset if I'm not back in time to complete their orders this morning."

Dannell smiled. "You mean Pete Maher's gloves, don't

you? Not done with them—eh? Excellent. That's even better than I hoped."

"What do those gloves have to do with you?" she asked, deciding he must have learned about them from Mrs. Darrow.

Laney realized that she had left the door to the shop unlocked. Anyone could steal the gloves and no one would be the wiser for it. Did Dannell know about the bonus as well? Did he know that without it, she had no chance of getting custody of Gideon?

"Let's just say I used some of my friends' money to place a few bets. Bets that need Fitzsimmons to win the bout."

"You've embezzled your customers' money, haven't you?" Her disgust deepened. He was playing several games. Gideon was just one of them.

"They'll never know. I'll win it back. Having you with me assures that. Maher won't box without those gloves, and we both know it." Dannell raised his cane and tapped again. "To the depot. I've changed my mind."

Laney reached for the door to the hansom, but the cane flashed out and struck her hand sharply. She jerked it back, facing the man whom she'd grown to disapprove of immensely over the years. "Where are you taking me?"

Dannell chuckled softly and kept his cane ready to strike. "That depends entirely on you, Killaney. We can do this my way or your way. I think you might prefer it my way, if you ever want to see the boy again. And if you really must know, there are a couple of boxcars that I've helped to keep mighty secret. No one will find you there."

She'd been duped. No, she'd allowed herself to be fooled. Tired from trying to get the boxing gloves done, she hadn't listened to her good sense about not opening the door to Dannell. She hadn't even waited to see if his panic-stricken face was brought about by concern for Gideon. She just assumed it was. She had not been careful and it might now cost her a price she prayed she wouldn't have to pay. "This isn't about Gideon or the money, is it?"

Dannell laughed bitterly. "I always said you were too smart for your good looks, girl. Maybe it's all about why you refused to marry me and take *me* to your bed instead of my brother."

"I told you why years ago, but you wouldn't listen. I'll have no man who can't be a true father to Gideon. You made it clear you don't really want him as your own. You just want whatever having him as your ward provides for you. If that wasn't reason enough, you've made it very clear I would only be one of many women in your life. No woman wants a man who is unwilling to love a child or commit himself to her alone."

"And you think that Ranger of yours will give up his lifestyle for living your dull, simple life? You think he wants to raise a boy who's not his?"

"Thomas has nothing to do with this. With me or Gideon."

"That's where you're wrong, Killaney. The man loves you. I see it and you know it. And I'm going to see that he never has you. That he never has that boy's trust fund. He'll never want you after I'm through with you."

"You leave him out of this," she demanded, taking her elbow and jabbing him in the side. "You keep Gideon's trust fund, for all I care. It's never been an issue for me. I'll never touch a penny of it for myself anyway. It's Marc's gift to his son, not to me or to you." She wanted to spit in his face. "And I'll die before I make this easy for you."

He thwacked her legs with the cane. Pain shot through her thighs and she began to fight him with everything she had, gouging and scratching with her fingernails, pulling what little hair he had left, biting where her teeth met flesh. The carriage rocked back and forth as he retaliated, landing a fist to her face and kicking her with his boots.

Laney did the only thing she could think of, using his own weapon against him. She grabbed the cane and shoved it backward, hitting him below his belt. A great puff of air escaped his throat, ending in a startled gasp of pain. For a single moment, Dannell let go of her and that was all she needed. She threw herself against the door, jerking the handle with both hands and throwing her body out of the speeding hansom.

"Driver, stop!" came Dannell's angry bellow.

Laney tumbled for several feet across the roadway, shoulder over hip, ending in a thud against a wooden sidewalk. "Help!" she screamed, but it came out only as a squeak between swollen lips that tasted of blood. Struggling to her feet, she realized both Dannell and the driver were running toward her. The driver was in on the scheme!

"Help, somebody!" she screamed again, finding her footing and breaking into a crippled run. Her head was spinning, her body ached. She had no idea where she was. She only knew that she hurt in a dozen places.

Steady footsteps chased after her.

Into the night she ran, hoping for some sign of human kindness that would stop these men from catching her, or worse. Where was one of those mighty Rangers who always seemed to be everywhere except when she needed them?

A light shone just ahead like a beacon of safety, if she could just reach it. Only a few steps more. Three houses away. Two. "Help!" she yelled, mustering every ounce of breath left within her. She thought she saw a shadow move in the lit window. *Open the door,* she willed the shadow to hear her. *Open it now!* "Help me, someone, please!"

Something hard, cold, and excruciatingly painful crashed into her head, sending her downward, into a darkness deeper than the night that cloaked her attackers.

Chapter 13

Going the Distance

Seven o'clock couldn't come too soon for Thomas. He was so eager to have a few minutes with Laney that he almost missed seeing Pete Maher leave his hotel room to head to the appointment. Fortunately, the boxer had had an equally short night, so he dispensed with the five-mile run he normally took to get his training in for the morning and just ran the distance from the hotel to the saddle shop. Thomas supposed he was just as eager to see how the gloves had turned out.

As Thomas ran, keeping pace behind the boxer, he let his thoughts stray to those that had kept him awake for the few hours he should have been sleeping. General Mabry's orders last night meant that he wouldn't be able to see Laney again until this business with the fight was over. Sure, he would have to settle up for the saddle, but that wouldn't take but a few minutes. And what if the trail of the fight took him away from El Paso before she finished the saddle? As far as he could see, she hadn't spent all that much time on the saddle, focusing more on Pete Maher's gloves.

But it wasn't the thought of an incomplete saddle that was bothering Thomas. Instead, it was the reality that he would not be spending time with Laney that made him want to curse all those times he'd wished to be done with these frustrating delays. He'd had to ask himself why she had come to mean so much to him in such a short amount of time. He'd always found it easy to be alone, to let duty keep him occupied and interested. But now that the general had assigned him other duties, Thomas knew he would never feel the same contentment he found in fulfilling any duty that was assigned to him. Without a doubt, Laney had somehow become the adventure he wanted more than any other.

By the time they reached the saddle shop, Thomas was good and winded. He considered himself a fit man, full of health and enough stamina to do a good day of whatever was required of a Ranger. But keeping up with an athlete of Pete Maher's caliber was no easy doings.

"You still with me, Ranger?" Maher asked, stopping in front of the saddle shop. "Not too fast for you, am I, lad?"

Thomas wiped his forehead with his sleeve. "I can go the distance, Pete. Count on that, friend."

Maher laughed and opened the door, letting the overhead bell announce their arrival. "I have no doubt that you have, Ranger, long before you ever started tracking me."

Following the boxer inside, Thomas was surprised to see no lamp lit in the front area. A glance at the workroom just to the right of the front counter revealed that one shone behind the curtain that separated the two spaces. He waited a moment, expecting Laney to appear from her workstation. No one came.

"Laney?" he called. "It's Thomas Longbow. Mr. Maher's here for his gloves and I'm with him."

Still no answer.

Something didn't feel right. The two men exchanged glances.

"She knew I was coming," the boxer insisted.

"She should be here. Her bicycle is outside at the post." Thomas stepped around the counter and into the work area, noticing the gloves lying on the table, the lamp on. He moved through the kitchen and small area she used for a bedroom and bath. The bed had not been slept in. "She's not here anywhere. I don't like this."

Maher picked up the gloves and examined them closely. "Wherever she is, she left them unfinished."

"You're sure of that?" Thomas realized that she'd left the writing ledger open on the table next to the gloves. She would never have left that out for anyone to see. She'd protected it from his eyes too many times. He stepped over to examine the ledger, then ultimately chose not to. She'd show him when she meant for him to see it. Something was wrong and his instinct for trouble kicked into high gallop.

"I'm sure. The design is incomplete." Maher pointed to the wrist of one glove. "This one's only got six."

"She must have been interrupted before she was finished." Thomas started calculating what or who might have urged her away from something that meant so much to her to complete. Only one foul name came to mind—Dannell O'Grady.

"Mr. Maher, I need you to tell me everything you and Mrs. O'Grady have discussed about your gloves. Leave nothing out," Thomas insisted. "It might mean the difference in her life or death. Whatever secret it is she's kept for you, I give you my word as a man and a Ranger that I won't reveal the details to anyone else."

Pete Maher showed Thomas the gloves and told him about the symbols and the bonus he said he'd pay her. "That's all it is, lad. Just some good-luck charms that I've been superstitious about for my whole career. Seven on each, I win. Fourteen's my lucky number. You can understand that, can't you, man?"

No, he couldn't. And he wished he hadn't made such a big fuss over disbelieving that Laney had no role in staging the upcoming fight. All because of a man's superstitious nonsense. And all because she needed money to get her stepson back. Well, not only did he need to possibly save her life—now he needed to apologize to her too. For not believing in her. For mistrusting her.

"I need you to do something for me, Mr. Maher." Thomas handed the gloves back to Maher. "Take these and don't let anyone talk you out of them for any reason. A lot of people were in the gallery when we talked about her making your gloves. Someone may have kidnapped her so you'd pay some kind of ransom money or something so she could finish them for you. I haven't figured out yet why they didn't just take the gloves, but maybe they thought she could just make another pair."

"Take away the fighter, there's no fight," the boxer commented.

That was it. Take away the glove maker and there would be no gloves. "If everyone believes you've already got the gloves, then they'll have no reason to hold her. Make a big show of them, will you? All over town. To every reporter within eyesight."

"Where are you going?" Maher asked as Thomas headed for the front door.

Thomas thought about how much explaining there would have to be to General Mabry and decided the man would just have to do the listening this time instead of the talking. "I'm going to disobey some orders."

Chapter 14

Sucker Punched

Word spread quickly. From the bordellos along Utah Street to the wooden barracks housing the soldiers out at Fort Bliss, word was carried by men in serapes and sombreros, businessmen in derbies and suits, journalists with ink-stained fingers—all spread the news that Peter Maher was ready to fight and sporting a new pair of gloves he was ready to break in. The fight was on.

The steady stream of people who had grown tired of waiting for it to happen and had pulled up stakes came to a sudden halt, just as Bob Fitzsimmons had predicted the night before. Fight fans filled the depot to the brim all afternoon, in anticipation of the promoter's next move.

Thomas spent the entire day searching for Dannell O'Grady, but the man was nowhere to be found. Thomas had checked back at the saddle shop twice and Laney had not returned, so he knew his concern for her safety was real. She would have insisted upon seeing Maher by now if she'd been able to.

The streets were full of people, so spotting her among the crowd proved almost impossible. The boxers were holding court at the Lindell Hotel, where the press corps milled around a display that showcased the pen the president had used to sign the anti-prize bill into effect. She would have attempted to meet with Maher there, if not at her shop.

Thomas's mood was foul, his temper edgy at best. The Ranger's earlier surveillance of O'Grady revealed that the man had broken his usual schedule and not appeared anywhere Thomas had expected to find him. Deep in his gut Thomas knew that Laney's brother-in-law had knowledge of her whereabouts. Everything inside him said that if he could just get his hands on the man, he would find Laney.

Not knowing where else to look, Thomas decided to check the Vendome Hotel one more time. It was almost five. The clerk said Dannell usually checked in for his mail before going up to change into evening attire. Hopefully, the man's penchant for looking dapper would provide just the stroke of luck Thomas needed at the moment.

His frustration mounted as it took precious minutes to work his way through the crowd and into the hotel. Stopping at the lobby desk, he glanced at the mail slot for O'Grady's room and noticed it was empty. A good sign, he hoped.

"Has Dannell O'Grady checked in?"

The clerk seemed evasive, shaking his head but avoiding Thomas's direct gaze. "N—no, sir. I don't believe he has. Would you care to leave a message?"

"I'll take the message to him myself." Thomas didn't wait for the elevator to return to the lobby and instead took the stairs leading to the upper floor.

"But wait, sir. You can't—"

"I'm tired of waiting." Thomas didn't care who heard him. Let anyone get in his way and they'd see just how tired he was of feeling so helpless. Doing something was all he knew, and right now that meant finding where the hell O'Grady was.

When he finally reached O'Grady's room, he stopped and

pressed an ear against the wooden door panel, listening for sounds of someone inside. At first, he heard only the ticking of a clock at the end of the hallway.

A phone rang. A voice whispering. The slightest swish of something sliding open. A window? The clerk had warned O'Grady!

Instinct and anger propelled Thomas to rear back and kick the man's door in. A splintering of wood ripped the door from its hinges and sent it crashing to the floor. A woman screamed somewhere down the hall as Thomas barreled into the room and rushed to the window just in time to catch the culprit by his collar. "You're not going anywhere, you son of a cur." Thomas jerked O'Grady backward into the room, preventing his escape.

Dannell landed on his back, curling into a fetal position, blocking his face with both hands and whining, "Don't hit me. I'm a cripple. Please, don't hit me."

"Get up," Thomas ordered, looking down at the pathetic excuse for a man. Five long pink scratches furrowed his left cheek and huge hunks of his hair were missing in spots that had not been bald when he first met the man. O'Grady looked like he'd tangled with a wildcat. Laney? He'd fought with Laney?

Rage filled Thomas so completely that he grabbed the blackguard by his fancy lapels and jerked him to his feet. He wanted to knock his teeth down his throat, but he resisted the urge, knowing it would just delay the man's ability to tell him what he needed to know. "Tell me what you've done with her," Thomas demanded, locking eyes with Dannell, "and you better hope to God that when I find her she doesn't have a scratch on her or I swear you are a dead man."

"She's fine. Perfectly fine," Dannell insisted, his eyelashes batting, a sure sign to Thomas that the man couldn't look him straight in the eye and was lying about something. "I'll tell you where she is, just let me go. Don't hit me, please."

Thomas couldn't stomach the sight of the man and wanted nothing more than to lay him out unconscious for days, but if he beat him senseless now he'd never get the truth out of him. He had to get to Laney. See how hurt she was. From the looks of Dannell, she put up a pretty good fight.

Thomas slowly uncurled his fists but remained close enough so the weasel of a man wouldn't run. "Why didn't you leave through the front door? You heard I was looking for you. I left enough messages all over town."

"I—I thought you'd be upset because I *do* know where she went, and she told me not to tell you."

Laney would never confide in the man. Of that Thomas had no doubt, but he'd play O'Grady's game. "Why'd she tell *you?*"

"She thought you'd think she was guilty of what you suspected all along about her." Dannell began to straighten his collar and tidy his suit, taking Thomas's easier tone as less reason to fear. "She really didn't know where the fight would be held until just this morning, I swear."

The man should have been more afraid. When Thomas got quiet, he was far more deadly. "So where's she gone that she doesn't want me to know?"

"She's in one of the cars headed for Langtry. It's a little depot about 389 miles from here. Judge Roy Bean's jurisdiction."

"Why would she get on the train?" *Why before the gloves were finished?* Thomas wondered.

"That's where the fight's taking place tonight. Maher was supposed to pick up the gloves at her shop and take them with him. She and the boxer are going to meet up in Langtry to finish them. Maher wanted her on the train before he got on to make sure she didn't get lost in the crowd. With everybody vying for seats, there wasn't any guarantee she could get one."

Thomas thought through this morning's scene with

Maher at the shop. He hadn't seemed all that displeased that the gloves had one more symbol to go. Had that all been a ruse because the boxer had known he was meeting up with Laney anyway? Had he agreed to show the gloves around town just to keep Thomas offtrack and unaware of their scheme? His gut instinct told him that Dannell was lying, but finding Laney might depend on something the man revealed in the lie.

"How did she find out which car to get on?"

"Dan Stuart's keeping close tabs with the telegrapher and the telegrapher owes me money. He told me and I told her which one."

Thomas put all the facts together and something still didn't quite fit. There was still the issue of the scratches on the weasel's face and his missing clumps of hair. "How'd you get so scraped up? Fall out a few windows today?"

Dannell shook his head. "I got in the way of Nero's and Fitz's punching bag. His cat thought I was the bag."

The man did seem to travel with Fitzsimmons's entourage. He was capable of such a foolhardy act. One last question would tell Thomas all he really needed to know. "Did Laney leave her shop willingly this morning?"

Thomas could read a lie in a man's tone, in the look he gave him, in the way he held his body.

"Willing and adamant about going," Dannell answered.

O'Grady wasn't lying, but neither was he telling the complete truth. "You're coming with me," Thomas ordered, handing the man his cane and pushing him toward the gaping wound that was once a doorway. "Watch your step. You're going to need a new door."

"Where are we going?" Dannell asked, making his way precariously over the wooden panel.

"To a boxing match."

Chapter 15

To the Finish

Dannell O'Grady had not lied about one thing. It seemed everyone in town now knew that the fight was taking place tonight and that the train fare for a round trip would be twelve dollars. It was as if a gun had been fired to start the race to Langtry. Everyone and their considerable kin seemed to have bought tickets and now stood in droves on the platform, waiting to board. The Rangers had their hands full just trying to stop the countless pickpockets from relieving travelers of their wallets while they waited.

With the rush of passengers, Thomas had four Pullmans, two tourist sleepers, a dining car, and several day coaches to search for signs of Laney in. He could only hope that she had not taken a seat on an earlier train carrying the fight and film paraphernalia to the site. If so, she was already in Langtry.

Thomas had left Dannell with Ted Sawyer in the car that had originally been furnished for the Rangers to ride free by Dan Stuart himself. He told Sawyer not to let Dannell out of his sight and to make sure the man didn't get off the train. If he tried, then Sawyer should wound him enough to stop his flight. Though he had not been tied up, Dannell had seemed respectably subdued and compliant.

Thomas checked the day coaches first. Laney was nowhere to be found. Next on the list was Maher's tourist sleeping car. Each boxer had been assigned one of the two sleeping quarters so they could ride in comfort and be rested before the fight. It made sense that his car would be the most likely place for her to make the trip. He wanted to be done with the search of the two sleeping cars while the boxers were granting interviews in the dining car with several reporters and dignitaries.

Thomas hoped he was wrong about where he might find her. Though it was 1896, an unmarried lady spending time alone with a gentleman in his private quarters still wasn't considered proper conduct. Not that Thomas gave a damn what anyone else thought, but Laney was trying to gain custody of that boy. She hadn't thought this all through clearly enough. If she meant to impress Judge Townsend, Thomas hoped Townsend didn't catch wind of this possible mistake in her judgment. He had to find her and get her out of Maher's car before anyone discovered she was there.

You just want her to be your lady, his heart whispered, realizing he cared more than he wanted to admit. *You don't want her spending time with Maher. You don't want her to be in on any part of this fight game with him and the others. You love her, you want her, and you won't be happy until she's yours.*

"Where are you?" he whispered as he opened the door to Maher's car, his frustration growing by the moment. Whatever Laney's role in this, whatever her reasons, he just needed to have a look at her and reassure himself that she was okay. That Dannell O'Grady hadn't lied to him about how he got those wounds.

He half expected to find one of Maher's men there to

bar the way, but Thomas found no one to prevent him from entering. A quick inspection of the sleeping parlor and the water closet that provided a bathing tub and space to hang his fight gear gave no sign of Laney's having been there. With both relief and disappointment, Thomas moved on to Bob Fitzsimmons's car.

When he opened the door, he was met with a loud, disgruntled roar.

Nero! He'd forgotten the lion, and that Fitzsimmons traveled nowhere without his sparring partner. Thomas froze in the doorway, not daring to move. His heart beat thunderclaps in his throat. He waited to be tackled by a crushing force or shredded by massive claws. Nothing happened.

"Laney," he dared. "Are you in there?"

"M—momas?" a voice came, weak, unsure, muffled.

A thousand lions could not have kept him from her. Thomas barreled past the door, prepared to tackle the African beast. But the animal was caged in a corner and none too happy that he couldn't wrestle this new trespasser arriving in his master's quarters. He roared again, sounding his discontent. Next to the cage, with her hands tied behind her back and her mouth gagged, lay Laney. She looked up at him with pleading eyes. Her face was a mass of bruises, her clothing torn.

Thomas swore vengeance on Dannell, rushing to Laney and pulling a knife from his boot to cut the cord from around her hands. She reached up to pull at the gag, but he gently pushed her hands away. "I'll get it, love," he said gently. "Just be still a minute more."

She sat up, her hands rushing to encircle his waist and her face pressing into his chest. As he hurried to unknot her gag, Thomas could feel the dampness of her cheeks and realized she'd been crying or frightened. Rage deeper than the Rio Grande roared through his veins as surely as if it had taken Nero's voice. Dannell O'Grady had sealed his fate.

"Laney, Laney," Thomas whispered, trying to find some reasonable thought to anchor him. "You'll be all right. I won't let him get away with this. I'll kill the—"

"No," Laney sobbed as the gag came off. She clutched Thomas tighter. "He only slapped me around and I gave as much as I got. He's not worth the effort. Just stay with me, Thomas. Hold me. Don't ever let me go."

"I won't, Laney," he whispered, willing everything within him to calm down enough to keep his word. "I'll hold you as long as you want me to."

"Forever, love." Laney pulled his head down to offer her lips to him. "Just hold me."

He gathered her to him and kissed her ever so gently, careful not to hurt her lovely lips any more than they already were. The kiss was filled with tender, silent promises to love her for the eternity she had just requested. Long moments later, he gave a heartfelt groan and grumbled, "You know I want to make love to you, don't you?"

She smiled and sighed. "Me, too, but we can't. Not here. Not now. We're not alone."

Thomas knew she meant more than Nero. There was a train full of people who would have something to say if the pair of them was found in the throes of passion. "The first thing you and I are going to work on when we're married is better timing and location." He laughed, raining gentle kisses over her cheeks, the tip of her nose, and down her neck.

Her laugh was soft and seductive.

Thomas's tantalizing trail returned to her lips, but he halted there and looked deeply into her eyes. "Know this, Laney. You're the one thing I'll wait on forever. You just tell me when."

Chapter 16

The Perfect Match

The train was behind schedule when it pulled into Sanderson, Texas, for a brief meal stop. Fitzsimmons and some of the El Paso civic leaders occupied the dining car, but the cook there could not serve the thousands of fight fans on board. Pete Maher decided to forego the meal for once, and instead chose to get a run in and stretch his legs. A battle royal ensued among hungry passengers racing to the few restaurants in town.

"Let's see if we can get something here," Thomas suggested, steering Laney toward one of the restaurants that seemed less crowded than the others. "You've got to be hungry."

She nodded, grateful that he had not insisted upon going straight to Dannell and confronting him. She wanted nothing more than to curb the rumble in her stomach and get an opportunity to see how bad she must look. "I haven't had anything since that cinnamon roll yesterday."

"Hold tight, they're all pushing." He guided her through the horde of people to a table occupied by three men who wore Ranger badges. When one of them glanced up from his meal and saw Laney approaching, she could tell that she must look a frightful mess. Sympathy washed over his face as he stood and grabbed his plate. "Y'all sit here. I'm done."

"Thank you, Ranger." Laney smiled and accepted the seat. "Do I look *that* bad?" she whispered.

"Don't worry about it." Thomas shook his head and allowed another woman seeking a seat to take the unoccupied chair. He pressed a kiss on the top of Laney's head. "I'm going to see if they have a biscuit or some hardtack we can take with us. There isn't enough time to order a plate. It won't get here before the train whistle." He patted her shoulder. "I'll see if someone's got a brush I can buy off them."

When he walked away, Laney glanced around the room and realized that she didn't need to worry about her state of grooming. Everyone was in such a rush to eat they had no time to concern themselves with anyone else.

"Hey, Chinaman, get the lead out of your boots," complained a dapper-looking gentleman sitting at the next table with a group of men.

The Chinese waiter continued to slowly place the bowls of soup in front of each customer.

The complainer stood, grabbed a table caster and started to get the waiter's attention by conking him on the head. One of the Rangers sitting next to Laney checked the gentleman's arm in mid-swing. "Don't hit that man," he requested, maintaining his iron grip.

The complainer stared at the tough Ranger and said, "Maybe you'd like to take it up."

"I done took it up," the Ranger replied calmly.

The two men faced each other, and a hush fell over the crowded room. This was not the sort of fight anyone had planned to see and spectators might get hurt. Laney prepared to dive under the table.

"Well, Bat Masterson, you old cuss," Thomas announced, making his way back to Laney's table. "I see you've met Ranger McDonald here from Amarillo. Saved me the effort of introducing the two of you."

"*Bill* McDonald?" Masterson stared at the man whose grip remained on his arm. Everyone knew that the fiercest Ranger of all could pick cherries with a rifle. No one wanted to get into gunplay with him.

Bat smiled. "Any man's a friend of Longbow's, he's a friend of mine."

"Then I'd take it kindly if you let that man finish serving his soup."

Bat relaxed and set down the caster. "Soup's getting cold anyway."

When Masterson and McDonald both took their chairs again, the roomful of people seemed to exhale all at once.

Laney was proud of Thomas and how he'd handled the situation with an expertise that must have come from long years as a Ranger. He was a man who knew how to handle other men and how to calm a fight. There were a million things more she wanted to know about him and the thought of discovering all there was that made up such a man seemed a thrilling prospect.

But just as quickly as that thought came, another dampened it. What about her own life would excite him? How would a man like Thomas find contentment being tied to one place and a woman with a child who was not his? They hadn't talked of Gideon other than her need to regain custody of the boy. Could Thomas accept him as his own? Did he want other children?

This rush of love she felt for the Ranger had come so quick that she hadn't thought out everything else their lives together would involve. She didn't even know if he would remain a Ranger or if he would be willing to make a home in El Paso with her and Gideon.

They needed to talk things out. Make sure that each of them was ready for the changes that would come for both of them. To find a way to perfectly match what each wanted and needed, without hurting the other's dream.

"You're looking mighty serious." Thomas offered her a towel that had been tied to form a makeshift basket. "Hungry?"

"Can we eat on the train?" she asked, wanting to get somewhere alone with him. Suddenly the room of people seemed to be closing in on her.

"Sure. Let's go." He scooted back her chair and took her hand, leading her out of the restaurant. "The whistle ought to sound any minute now anyway. We'll beat the rush. Where would you like to ride?"

"I don't have a ticket," she reminded him, knowing the worry in her voice stemmed from more than whether she would be thrown off the train.

"We'll travel in the car Stuart provided for the Texas Rangers. I'll pay your fare if anyone has an issue with it. Better yet, I'll make your brother-in-law pay for it. It would serve him right."

The mention of Dannell O'Grady seemed to conjure him up in her line of sight. "Isn't that him there?" she asked, pointing.

Thomas spun to see where she meant. Sure enough, the woman-beater was stepping out of Pete Maher's tourist car. "I told Sawyer to watch him and not let him leave the train!" Thomas grabbed Laney's hand and hurried her to a car farther down the train. He reached into his pocket and handed her a hairbrush. "Will you take this and the food and wait for me in there?" he asked, helping her up the two steps that allowed her to board. "You'll find the Rangers and maybe Judge Townsend inside. Just tell them you're with me and I'll explain later. They'll let you ride."

"What are you going to do?" She looked down the

tracks. "Promise me you won't do anything to him. He's not worth it."

Thomas reached up and gave her a swift kiss. "You're right, he's not. But you are."

"Where do you think you're going?" Thomas grabbed Dannell O'Grady by the back of his coat and swung him around. "I told you to stay put."

"Your Ranger friend had to follow Maher. I got hungry. I wasn't sure when I would get something to eat next." Fear etched the man's face, making him unable to keep his jowls from trembling.

Thomas needed to have a talk with Sawyer, but the Ranger was following General Mabry's instructions about keeping track of the boxer's whereabouts. Guess he couldn't put up too much of an argument. "Does Maher know you were in his car?"

"Ask him yourself. I wasn't doing anything under-handed. He invited me there himself."

"I will." Thomas took him by the scruff of the neck and jerked him up the steps that led to Maher's car. The train whistle sounded and the conductor yelled, "All aboard!"

Dannell O'Grady started sputtering. "There's no need to be so brutal."

"Mister, don't give me a reason," Thomas warned. "It's only by the good grace of your sister-in-law that I'm not beating you to within an inch of your worthless hide. I promised her I wouldn't, but I'm kind of new to this kind-ness thing. So don't test me."

"My sister-in-law?" he squeaked. "Y—you've found her?"

"Knock on the door, you weasel," Thomas ordered and pushed O'Grady forward. "I found her and I'm thinking of making you kitty food at the moment. Big-kitty food."

Pete Maher answered the door. "Mr. O'Grady? Did you forget something?" He glanced at Thomas and said, "Ranger Longbow, I see you're acquainted with Mrs. O'Grady's brother-in-law."

Thomas pushed Dannell past as Maher stepped aside and allowed them in. "Sit, and don't make another move, O'Grady."

Dannell took a seat on one of the chairs near a table beside Maher's sleeping bunk and grumbled, "See there, I told you that I was here with his knowledge."

"I was just in the Rangers' car when I mentioned that I was looking for you." Puzzlement filled Pete's face. "I wanted to see if I could give you Mrs. O'Grady's money. But this chap here said that he was her brother-in-law and he would be glad to see that she got it. I didn't have it on me because I'd been running, and I didn't think he was foolish enough to test my good faith. So I had him follow me here to get the cash. He just left here with it."

"Now, I—I was really going to give it to her." Dannell started sinking in his seat at both men's threatening expressions.

"The money for the gloves?" Thomas asked, and received Maher's nod. He grabbed Dannell and demanded, "Where the hell is it, you boot scum? Every damn dollar of that custody money better be on you."

Dannell fumbled inside his frock coat and handed Thomas the money. "Here it is. All of it. I haven't spent any of it."

Thomas thrust the cash at Maher. "Take that back and don't give it to anyone else but Laney. This man would cheat her out of her boy, so he'd damn sure cheat her out of that." Glancing around, Thomas asked, "You got anything made of twine or cord, a rope of any kind? I'm tying him up till we get to Langtry. Then I'll let Judge Townsend deal with him, or maybe let Roy Bean deal with him. See how much justice he gets then."

"I've got just the thing." Maher stepped into his water closet and produced a jump rope he used for training. "That ought to do. Where are you going to tie him?"

"Let's talk to Fitzsimmons. I've got just the place. Maybe he won't go around telling lies about lions after this."

"No, please," Dannell begged, struggling as Thomas tied his arms and legs securely. "Not *there!*"

Chapter 17

Undisputed Champion

"Is everything okay?" asked Laney as Thomas entered the Rangers' railcar and took a seat beside her. "Where's Dannell?"

"Let's just say he's tied up for the moment." Thomas wrapped an arm around her and eyed her closely. "How are you?"

The Rangers had been kind to her, giving her a bench of her own and allowing her to groom herself while they had their backs to her. "I'm fine now," she assured him. She opened the towel and offered him a biscuit. "I saved this for you. I couldn't eat much."

He lightly traced her lips with his thumb. "I wanted to kill the man for doing this to you."

She clawed the air with her fingers. "He'll think twice before he ever does it again, I assure you."

Thomas smiled, his eyes taking in the defiant lift of her chin. She was a scrapper and he loved her for it. "You definitely made your point, but you should never have had to experience that. No woman should."

"You're a good man, aren't you, Thomas?"

Her eyes were asking more than her words, and he wasn't quite sure how to answer her. "I try to be. Sometimes I fail. I guess all men fall short in some ways."

"Could you . . . I mean . . . would you . . . do you think yourself capable of being a father? Of living with me and making a home?"

Since he'd met her he'd wanted that. He'd thought of little cinnamon-haired, amber-eyed girls bouncing on his knees. Of a rowdy boy or two to teach all he knew of horses and justice and wrong made right. The adventure of being a husband, a father, a lover, all those things called to him like a lost trail that needed searching. But she was asking about Gideon. Could he love another man's son?

The answer came as swift and as sure as any decision he'd ever been called upon to make, knowing it was the right thing to do. It seemed one more adventure to test his mettle as a man. "I'd be proud to call Gideon my son, Laney. If you love him, I don't see how I won't. At least, I'll give everything within me to love him as any boy should be loved."

"Oh, Thomas, that's what I hoped you'd say." She didn't care that they'd promised to be more discreet where they kissed. She had to kiss him now, more than ever before. And she did.

After a few moments, someone cleared his throat. "Is she why you disobeyed my orders, Longbow?"

Thomas looked up. "Yes, General Mabry."

"Then by all means, son. Continue on."

Judge Roy Bean met the train personally, but before anyone could ask about where the boxing ring had been set up, General Mabry had all the Texas Rangers assembled, guns at the ready. Other U.S. marshals joined them, clearly outnumbering Bean, who thought himself the only law in this butt-end of Texas wasteland. General Mabry ordered Thomas to go with the judge and take a look at this ringside that supposedly did not violate Texas law.

"I'll be glad to accommodate you boys." Judge Bean waved at his Jersey Lilly Saloon. "Why don't you let the good folks get some liquid refreshment while they wait for us? Only a dollar a bottle and the finest mescal this side of the Rio."

General Mabry gave the okay and the passengers disembarked for what they hoped would be a quick quenching of their thirst.

"May I go with you, Thomas?" Laney asked, preferring to remain in his company. Though she felt safe with the Rangers, if trouble started she wanted to be with the one Ranger she trusted best.

Judge Bean shook his head. "Little lady, you can come if you like, but the ring is at the bottom of a two-hundred-foot bluff. Then you got to cross a bridge out to the island."

"An island, you say." General Mabry's expression remained stern. "Then it's not in Texas?"

"It's 'tween here and the state of Coahuila, Mexico, closer to the Mex side of things if you care to measure. It'll take them *rurales* in Juarez a couple of good days to get here fast enough to stop the fight. No, General, it ain't going down in Texas. I'm upholding the law."

"We'll wait and see. Longbow, verify the judge's story."

"You wait here for me," Thomas told Laney. "I'll be back as quick as I can."

It didn't take Thomas long to check out the fight site, and Judge Bean was true to his word. Reassured now that no one would be shot for civil disobedience, the well-lubricated crowd hit the trail down the rocky path that led to the beach. Two hundred feet below the canyon's rim, a pontoon bridge led to a topless tent that surrounded the arena. The battleground had been built on a sandy flat in a big bend of the Rio Grande, and true to Judge Bean's word, it lay closer to the Mexican shore.

The sky had turned overcast and drizzly, too dark for the Kinetoscope camera, so the photographers could not film. General Mabry decided that since no Texas statutes were being broken, the Rangers would take position on the canyon rim and watch things from there. Laney joined them, sitting on the cliff beside Thomas.

It took a few moments for everyone to get seated and the introduction of the boxers to be made. Laney looked on with pride at the gloves Pete wore, feeling that she had somehow played a small role in the history that was about to be made. She was glad now that he had asked her to hand stitch the last shamrock onto his glove when the train had made its last stop before arriving in Langtry. She wasn't sure the thread could hold up under the brutality of blows, but she'd done the best she could do without her stamping tools.

The two boxers went to their corners. Fitz wore blue trunks with a sash made of the triple American patriotic colors. Maher's black trunks reached to his knees and were held up with a belt that honored his Irish homeland. The referee—who, oddly enough, was not Bat Masterson after all—signaled the contenders to meet in the center and shake hands. They did. A whistle blew. Someone yelled, "Time!" and a gong echoed over the cliffside.

Fitz swung two quick punches—a left, then a right. The boxers met in a clinch. Before the referee could order the men to make a clean break, Maher landed a right on Fitzsimmons's cheek.

"Foul!" cried Fitz, echoed by the spectators.

"If you do that again," the referee warned Maher, "I'll call the fight against you."

"Let it go," Fitz said, bouncing back and forth on each

foot, jabbing the air to show off his striking range. "I'll lick him anyway."

Both men went at each other again, swinging, hitting, missing, swinging again. Maher tried to close in, leading with his left. Fitz stepped aside and lashed out with his powerful right arm, his glove landing solidly on Maher's chin.

Maher twisted halfway around, then came crashing down.

"One." He tried to get up.

"Two. Three." Fitzsimmons returned to his corner.

"Four. Five." The countdown continued.

". . . *Ten!* You're out!"

Laney couldn't hide her astonishment. "All that delay for a fight that didn't last two minutes. It doesn't seem worth all the fuss."

Thomas wrapped an arm around her and pulled her close. "Oh, I don't know. I can think of one delay worth the trouble."

Laney smiled at the undisputed champion of her heart. "You talking about your saddle?"

"That too," he whispered, "but sixty-five hours isn't going to be nearly enough time to get this right. I figure it's gonna take a lifetime."

Books by Bestselling Author
Fern Michaels